"Sweeps Rich Boyer into the front ranks of those whose territory is crime fiction's number one locale in America—the New England murder belt."

John McAleer
Edgar Award—winning biographer of Rex Stout

"A sure winner ... Clips along like a sailboat running before the wind."

Mystery News

"Rick Boyer writes with verve. Freshness in both plot and place keep you hanging on for the violent and ironic conclusion."

The San Diego Union

Also by Rick Boyer
Published by Ivy Books:

THE DAISY DUCKS
MOSCOW METAL
PENNY FERRY*

*Forthcoming

BILLINGSGATE SHOAL

Rick Boyer

IVY BOOKS • NEW YORK

Ivy Books
Published by Ballantine Books
Copyright © 1982 by Richard L. Boyer

Library of Congress Catalog Card Number: 81-7259

ISBN 0-8041-0551-0

First published by Houghton Mifflin Company. Reprinted by permission of Houghton Mifflin Company.

Manufactured in the United States of America

First Ballantine Books Edition: January 1990

For my parents,
Betty and Paul Boyer,
and for Tiny

Author's Note

The places in this book are real; the people aren't.

The author wishes to thank those who helped in the various stages of the manuscript's development: Captain Leo Jordan and his staff of the United States Coast Guard; Detective Lieutenant Jack Dwyer of the Massachusetts State Police; Dana Booth, D.M.D.; David Savageau, friend and advisor; and the numerous fishermen I spoke with on the docks of New England. Any errors or inconsistencies, deliberate or accidental, are mine.

I owe special thanks to Elaine for keeping the faith, and the greatest gratitude of all to my training wheels: Larry Kessenich and Bill Tapply.

BILLINGSGATE
SHOAL

Loomings

CALL ME DOC.

I'm Charles Adams, a doctor who lives with his wife, Mary, and two almost-grown sons in Concord, Massachusetts. I'm an oral surgeon, a cross between a doctor and a dentist, who performs tooth extractions and general and cosmetic surgery of the lower face and jaw.

My most interesting recent operation was quick, spontaneous, and without benefit of surgeon's tools or anesthetic. I cut a human head in two, right down the middle. Deliberately. The operation was a success because the patient died.

Listen: I didn't ask for any of it. If anyone had told me that all the pain and killing would begin with my sneaking a look at a stranded fishing boat I would have called them nuts. It sure looked innocent enough. It was just sitting out there on the sand flats. It looked like a Winslow Homer watercolor . . .

1

Two and a half miles directly offshore from our cottage in Eastham, Massachusetts, on Cape Cod, lies Billingsgate Shoal. It appears on nautical charts in a color between that of either land or sea. This is because Billingsgate is a sunken island and is visible only briefly, in all its soggy splendor, twice a day at tide's farthest ebb.

The body of water that surrounds the island in this corner of Cape Cod Bay is called Billingsgate Sound, and stretches around the sunken island from Eastham on the south to the entrance of Wellfleet Harbor on the north. The sound is a bank rich in mollusks, especially the large marine clam called *quahog*, which is excellent in chowder, and the small, delicate, and tasty bay scallop (not to be confused with its larger cousin the sea scallop). Besides the proper conditions to promote the growth of these mollusks, Billingsgate Sound also has a large number of spider crabs, which dine almost exclusively on starfish. Since the starfish is the primary predator of the mollusks, one can see, by following the steps of this rude syllogism, that there must be fewer starfish here and (ergo) more mollusks. This is so.

At high water the small bay trawlers, dozens of them, can be seen in the distance, crawling across the water hauling their big metal chain-link drags on the ocean floor behind them. Sometimes the wind shifts, bringing with it the faint

growl and whine of their diesels. Another constant sound is
the hoot of the groaner buoy at the foot of Billingsgate. It
goes hoooo-*ooooot*! every fifteen seconds, round the clock,
and is saying *keep away . . .*

To the south, on the horizon in a direct line between our
cottage and the village of West Brewster, lies the wreck of
the *James Longstreet*. It was wrecked there deliberately
by the United States government. This old Liberty Ship from
the Second World War was towed in and sunk in the shallow
water to be used as a target for the navy and air force. Planes
dive at it, pelting the ancient concrete hulk with cannon and
rocket fire. It is said that the *Longstreet* is "a bunch of holes
held together by their rims." It's an apt description. The
derelict ship sits immobile, ruined, on the horizon.

Our cottage is situated on a bluff overlooking Billingsgate
Sound. At low tide it is a place of frightening vastness, haunt-
ing noises, and optical tricks. No trees. Low sand hills. Miles
and miles of marsh grass and water weed. And most desolate
of all are the endless sand flats that grow for miles in the
slow wake of the receding tides. These are absolutely flat
and barren. People walk out on these vast stretches of damp
sand. Some carry odd-shaped bent garden forks—these to
dig out the quahogs, razor clams, and bay scallops. You could
live off these flats with no problem whatsoever; the only thing
not provided is the chilled chablis.

But most of the people aren't diggers—they're beach-
combers, people on vacation who wander out to see what
there is to find. From a mile away they look like moving
specks. Tall, dark, slow-moving lines are adults. Short specks
that dawdle, or run on winking legs, are children. Sometimes
you can see low specks that travel with incredible speed, and
leap into the air. The faint barking tells you they are dogs.
Occasionally the wind will bring the sound of laughter, or a
mother calling a child, from miles away. And it is weird,
even unsettling, to hear the voices and laughter clearly, coming from these tiny dots that move slowly to and fro on the
shimmering sand far, far away.

It is quiet when the tide is out. Gone is the crump and hiss
of breaking waves. The gulls don't shriek overhead; they are

out on the flats, waddling around officiously pausing, pecking, squabbling, and gobbling up the tiny hermit crabs—no
bigger than garden spiders—that scamper in the shallow tide
pools.

"Looming" is what Melville called it, an optical phenom-
enon caused by thermal inversions in the atmosphere. These
thermal inversions have the effect of layering the air, and
these layers, like the elements of a lens, cause light waves to
bend, allowing objects beyond the horizon to seem to be
visible. The object floats high over the horizon upside down
and shimmers ghostlike in the dancing air currents. It happens a lot in our corner of the bay.

The far-off sounds, the wrecked ship, the ghostly and desolate flats—all of these add to the general feeling of the place.
And if a vacation is a change, then Sunken Meadow Beach
overlooking Billingsgate Sound is a vacation indeed from the
pine forests, hills, and thick meadows of Concord.

One morning in late summer I got up just a bit too early.
Three hours too early. It was getting to be a habit. I couldn't
sleep. Moe Abramson, my colleague, said it was only a midlife reshuffling of values and not to worry. He gave me pills
to help my depression and insomnia. Mary said it was because I'm an idealist and dreamer, and wanted everything to
be perfect. She gave me loving and scolding to help my depression and insomnia.

Gee, I had lots of help.

It wasn't working.

Every night for three weeks I had risen between three and
four A.M. Not rested. I had awakened exhausted and irritable. The month-long vacation was supposed to cure all this.

It didn't. It seemed to intensify it. Mary, my short-suffering
wife, wasn't about to put up with much more of my Welt-
schmerz.

"Shape up or take a hike, pal," was her comment.

Who could blame her?

So there I was at five A.M., out on the deck of our cottage
gazing off over Cape Cod Bay. The tide was out; I was looking mostly at the immense expanse of tidal flats. It was so
early all things were dim and blurry. Most of what I looked

at was full of the fuzzy little specks of nighttime vision. I
was still half asleep. Or was I asleep—finally—and dreaming
this? No, I was awake. I'd almost forgotten what sleep felt
like. I sat and propped my feet up on the railing and stared
at the vast gray emptiness before me. I waited an hour. I
could either take a downer and return to the sack or have
coffee and make it another early day. I decided on the coffee.
When it was perking I heard the bedroom door open and
Mary came out in her robe. She comes to coffee like a buz-
zard to a bloated carcass. She can see and smell it—*sense
it*—a mile away.

She sat down next to me with her mug and drew the robe
tight around her. In the semidarkness she looked very dark,
like a black woman. When a Calabrian spends three weeks
on the beach the results are awesome.

"Again, huh?"

"Uh-huh."

There was a slow sigh.

"How far did you run yesterday?"

"Seven miles."

"And you took two sauna baths. You had a split of wine
with a big dinner. And you can't sleep?"

"I think the running makes you sleep less. You sleep
harder or something. But that's not it. Basically, toots, I don't
want to be who I am."

She absorbed this minor detail in silence.

"You what?"

"I don't want to be Dr. Charles Adams, tooth-puller."

"I'm so worried about you lately, Charlie. We thought the
month down here would help you, but I think it's made things
worse."

"I think you're right. And now I'm beginning to see what
the problem really is."

"What?" She looked at me, searching for a ray of hope.

"Boredom. It's what you've been saying, Mary: we've got
it. We've *done* it. So what do we do now? I think what set
this whole depression off was a line I read in John Berryman's
Dream Songs."

"Who? What? Never heard of him."

"John Berryman was an alcoholic poet who ended his life by doing a swan dive off a bridge at the University of Minnesota and blasting himself to pieces on the rocks a hundred feet below."

"Oh *that* John Berryman. Christ, no wonder you're depressed."

"No. His death was the good part. The "funsies" at the end. It's the words he wrote, a line from *Dream Songs* that's got me down. It's got me down because it's so damn true."

"And the line is?"

" 'Life, friends, is boring. We must not say so.' "

Another silence.

"That's it?"

"Yep."

"Well, Charlie, I think you should go and see Moe Abramson on a regular basis."

"Nah. I already asked him about therapy and he said I don't need it. But I'll tell you, this vacation has done me no good and I don't want to return to my practice. I don't seem to want to do anything, including sleep. It's all boring, Mary. BORING!"

She snuggled her fanny down on my lap and put her arms around my neck. Thank God for her at least—

"What about Betsy Kelly?"

I luxuriated in the thought of Betsy Kelly (which is not her real name). If I want anything on my tombstone (and I suppose I'm bound to have one—another discouraging thought), it's the fact that I performed a four-hour operation on a girl that changed her appearance, personality, and her whole life. Betsy Kelly was born, poor thing, with a prognathic jaw so pronounced it made her look like a cross between a bulldog and Tyrannosaurus rex. Needless to say, she wasn't pretty. But four hours under the knife, bone saw, chisel, and mallet had made her emerge looking not only normal, but almost pretty. Her parents cried and wrung my hands for three hours. That wasn't pulling teeth.

"If all my patients were Betsy Kellys I'd be the happiest person on earth."

"But you're not."

"No. I'm dissatisfied and bored."

"Look: you can't keep being a dropout, Charlie. You left medicine after two years—"

"When Peter died."

"When Peter died. Then you settled on dentistry."

"That was *really* boring—"

"Fine. Then you compromised on oral surgery, a profession that combined medicine, surgery, and dentistry. You're good at it. You've provided for us well with it, you—What are you staring at?"

"There's something out on Billingsgate. A dark blob. See it?"

"Uh huh. But what I'm driving at is, that's two dropouts in your life, Charlie. You can't do it again. You're almost fifty. Especially when you're so good—"

"It looks small from here. But of course it's over two miles away. It's not a tent or trailer. It's gotta be a boat—"

"I think Moe can have you squared away in no time. And I think you should read *Passages*. It explains a lot about these midlife crises."

"Yeah. It's a boat. Aground out there on the sand."

"You know Moe really thinks you're *very* talented—"

"But why did they run her aground? Maybe they just want to get her hull up out of the water to work on it—"

"Maybe just a couple of talks with Moe . . . maybe he could make a few concrete suggestions."

I left the deck and retrieved my aluminum camera case from the inner depths of our bedroom closet. I keep it hidden there under piles of dirty clothes in hopes that thieves, if any, will overlook it. I took out the Canon F-1, a 500-millimeter lens, and grabbed my tripod. I returned to the sundeck and rigged up the equipment. What I now had, besides a camera, was a telescope of sorts. Viewing through the camera I could get a close look at the boat wedged up against the toe of Billingsgate Shoal.

"Will you see Moe or not?" Mary demanded, taking little interest in the proceedings.

"Sure I'll see Moe. I always see Moe; his office is two doors down from mine, remember? Except that if I let him even think for a second it's professional the Shylock will take me for every cent we've got."

She sat back down in the chair.

"I'm assuming," she said with a deep frown, "that's meant in irony."

"Of course. The dope gives away more than he earns, and he earns plenty, believe me. The jerk doesn't even buy himself a house. Do you know that that Airstream he lives in was built in 1957? Can you believe it? One of New England's finest shrinks living in a beat-up old trailer in Walden Breezes Park? But you know what they say about psychiatrists: they're all nuts—"

It was low tide; the sand flats were extended to their maximum length. Billingsgate was barely visible as a low patch of tan on the horizon. I aimed the huge lens at the distant speck on the tan patch. Long lenses, even on a heavy tripod, exaggerate camera motion and cause the viewed image to shake and dance about. I draped a sand-filled sock over the end of the lens to reduce this tendency and brought the long tube into focus. I peered through the eyepiece and made the necessary adjustments. The wavy blob of green became clear and crisp. I viewed the trawler as if I were a few hundred yards away instead of on the deck of our beach cottage over two miles away. The conditions could hardly have been better. There was low cloud cover. A sky of stratocumulus clouds rolled away endlessly into the distance, like an inverted ocean. The light shone through these clouds with various stages of intensity, giving the sky a metallic, galvanized look like crumpled lead foil or hammered zinc.

But as is often the case with this kind of sky cover (which usually means nasty weather coming), the level visibility was superb, causing objects on the horizontal plane to appear clearer, closer than they ordinarily would. I don't know why this is so, but it is. I could now see the stranded vessel with amazing clarity.

Naturally, I assumed the grounding had been unintentional. Had she lost power in the ebbing tide and been stranded? Was her skipper foolishly trawling near Billingsgate as the tide fell and ran her aground? Either one did not seem plausible; the weather had not been bad and all the local skippers knew about Billingsgate and the tricky Wellfleet channel in general. Didn't he have a chart?

Two men were walking around the boat. They looked calm. Of course they were in no danger. They could even have *walked* to Wellfleet via Jeremy Point and Great Island in less than an hour if they wished. A third man appeared on deck. He was lugging at something heavy. Soon afterward he threw something over the side: a sledgehammer. One of the men on the sand picked it up and swung it low underhanded at the boat's hull. I could hear the rhythmic deep booming from across the sand flats. It sounded like a muted timpani when the wind was right. Clearly they were making some kind of repair to the hull, however crude.

Perhaps they had grounded the boat deliberately by anchoring her over the shoal in high water, then letting the ebbing tide strand her. This would be less expensive than having the vessel hauled out on a donkey. It would be the sensible, thrifty thing to do (in true Yankee fashion), *if* the repair was minor.

I was losing interest in the whole project when I noticed one of the men return to the deck and enter the wheelhouse, only to reemerge immediately with binoculars. He stationed himself behind the bows and swept the glasses to and fro. Since the early morning sun was directly behind me, I could see its reflection off the lenses as they swept by me. Now why were they doing that? Perhaps they were in difficulty after all and needed help. I stood up on the picnic table and waved my arms slowly, as a sign I'd seen them. But in all likelihood I was invisible—hidden in the rising sun as a fighter pilot is hidden when he dives out of the sun at the enemy plane below.

It grew warmer gradually. We sat on the deck and chatted and sipped coffee and watched the green boat on the sand. The faint sheen of distant water puddles that were growing ever larger told us the tide was beginning to ooze back in. Whatever those guys out there were doing, they'd better hurry; they didn't have a lot of time left. It was now after eight o'clock.

"Should we call the Coast Guard?" she asked.

"I'll try to get their attention."

"From here? You'll look smaller than a gnat to them—"

I dragged the big beach umbrella up onto the deck and opened it. Its panels alternated blue and yellow. Mary sat at the camera-telescope and sipped coffee while I got back up on the picnic table and waved the huge contraption back and forth like a semaphore.

"Well? Any reaction?"

She said no, but to keep trying. Our cottage, fatuously named *The Breakers* after the elegant Newport mansion, sits atop a solitary steep bluff. It is the highest cottage around. Therefore, perched as I was atop the table on the deck, I was above the horizon. After twenty seconds of signaling, Mary said the man in the bow had apparently seen me.

"He's calling the other guys, Charlie. The other men are climbing up on the deck to have a look too. Keep waving."

So I did.

"Now they're kind of scurrying around. One guy's raising his hands up and down. I think they're *arguing*, Charlie."

I dropped the umbrella and had a look. The deck was deserted. I said I was going to call the Coast Guard, but Mary suggested we wait because they had made no attempt to signal us back. I sat a while and watched the boat. There seemed to be no sense of alarm aboard her. Just the same, I phoned the Nauset station and said there was a stranded fishing vessel perched on the southernmost tip of Billingsgate Shoal, and that there was no apparent danger.

"Is the vessel damaged?"

"Can't see from this distance. But they're pounding on the hull with a hammer."

"Could be a repair; we've got nothing on the distress frequency."

"The same thought occurred to me. Just thought I'd report."

"Thank you. Your name, sir?"

"Dr. Charles Adams, North Eastham."

Not long after I'd hung up, the phone rang.

"Who could that be?" asked Mary.

"The only person I know who would have the bad taste to call this early is Moe," I said.

I picked up the phone.

"Hi, it's Moe."

"Figured."

"Just thought I'd phone to see how you're getting along, Doc."

"Not so good."

"Still can't sleep?"

"Nope. Think I need to be shrunk, Moe?"

"No. You're definitely not psychotic and I don't think you're neurotic either. You're just a bit . . . uh . . . off the track is all."

"Off the track? What's that?"

"I see it a lot in our age group. Career doubts. Life doubts. Excessive self-analysis. Self-pity. Self-doubt. Self-obsession."

"My symptoms exactly."

"Well listen: get outside yourself. Submerge yourself in other things. Believe me, it's the best medicine. It's also the one common theme in the advice given by all the great and wise people who have ever lived."

"And you, I presume, are one of those great people?"

"No. Still learning. But passing gon their advice. Listen: the more you try to make yourself happy the more miserable you'll be. To save yourself you must throw yourself away. What about your hobbies and interests? You like music. Get into some new types. You said you like Bruckner and Vaughan Williams. How about Elgar, Sibelius, Dvořák, Mahler?"

"Yeah I see what you mean. I could really get into it—"

"And more important, Doc, *out* of yourself!"

"OK."

"And you can work out some chess problems so I won't always beat you so badly. It's embarrassing gI tell you."

"Uh, right."

"And how about photography? You're a great photographer you know. Devote the next several weeks to being *really* great. Another Ansel Adams, who knows?"

"Exactly."

"Take pictures everywhere, and forget about yourself. Nothing makes people more miserable than worrying about themselves. Nothing gives them more peace than finding ga cause, or a devotion, *outside* themselves. Remember Tolstoi said that; you gave me the book—"

"Ah yes. *The Kingdom of God Is Within You.* By the way, I want it back."

"No such luck. I'm keeping git."

"Moe, take a hint. Lay off the hard g's. Say 'it,' not 'git.' It sounds much more high class."

"Class? I should talk to you about class? Maybe I should talk to a penguin about life in the Sahara—"

"Do you know what a royal pain in the fanny you are?"

"You're no balm to the derrière yourself pal. Look: keep taking the Librium. Keep running, too, even though the medication may slow you down a bit. And be sure to take that lovely creature you're lucky enough to be married to into the sack as often as possible."

"Thanks, Moe," came a female voice.

"Mary! What are you doing gon the extension?"

"Doing *on*, not doing *gon*, Moe," I said.

"Thanks again, Moe," said Mary, and hung up.

"By the way Doc, you owe me some money."

"What? All you did was recommend Librium. Big deal. I could've done that myself."

"Yes, but not with my expertise and finesse."

"OK. How much?"

"Four hundred?"

"What!"

"Listen, Doc, the Sea Scouts of Beverly need a boat. Now I bought one for them for two grand and I'm a little short. In fact I'm out. I thought you could help out a little, OK? Also, Mr. Empty Pockets, I happen to know you bought yourself a boat this spring. Twenty-something feet. Sleeps four . . . auxiliary engine . . ."

"So?"

"So? So give the kids a break, huh?"

"I can't stand it."

"I'm not asking for you to stand it; I'm asking gyou to *send* it. I, uh, sort of promised the bank you would. Now listen: you'll never be anything but a half-assed chess player if you quit hanging garound me, so *give*. And take pictures. And take the medication. And take Mary. Good-bye!"

He rang off.

"That son of a bitch."

"Charlie, you love him and you know it. A lot of times he's the only thing that gives you hope in the human race. I'll get the checkbook."

Mary and I had breakfast and got ready to go sailing. As we left *The Breakers* at nine-thirty I took a last peek at the boat. The tide was rising; water was now lapping at her. Two men were walking knee deep in it looking down at the hull, which I could not see because of the angle at which she lay. The men stopped walking. One pointed upward. I heard the drone of the engine. Through the binoculars I could see the twin-engine plane bank steeply, beginning a tight circle. On the fuselage was the red slash that identifies all Coast Guard vehicles. I went back to the scope. The crew seemed to be excited. Then they *did* want help . . . no, they were arguing; Mary was right. No, they seemed to be deciding—

Then it began. I knew it would. Through the powerful magnification of the long lens, which compressed thousands of yards of space into what seemed less than 100 yards, the ground began to tremble. The sand flats began—ever so slightly—to shimmer and wave. Monstrous ghost puddles appeared on the nearby dry sand. Water where there was none. Then the figures, and the boat itself, began to wave and dance. Soon the men would be mere blobs of color: grotesque wriggling reflections in fun-house mirrors. *Heat.* The early morning heat was doing that.

As faint as it must have been in the early morning, the heat from the warm sand was sending up thermal currents—like the air over a hot wood stove—that jiggled and danced. That was it. I had been granted this brief chance to spy on these men and their boat, but no more.

"You coming? C'mon honey, I want to be back early. Remember Jack's coming."

To hell with it. Help was there if they needed it. We got into the car and headed up Route 6 to Wellfleet, the next town north of Eastham. Our boat, *Ella Hatton*, was moored in a slip in the harbor there.

We parked in the big lot and walked over to the *Hatton*'s slip. She rode motionless on the quiet water, as broad as a sunflower seed. She is a sloop-rigged catboat, twenty-two feet long and over twelve feet wide. Her hull is like a tapered pie-pan. Our slip was nestled amongst those reserved for the smaller pleasure boats. The other side of the harbor, which was once the center of America's clam and scallop trade, is reserved for big commercial vessels, mostly draggers. These big, blocky boats have high steep bows to fend off the chops and troughs that develop in the North Atlantic. The freeboard is low aft: the gunwales taper smoothly down to the stern. This low freeboard (or low height of the hull above the waterline) is to facilitate the easy dumping of the iron dredges that are dragged all over the bottom of Cape Cod Bay, slurping up those bay scallops and clams. These boats are heavy-timbered and beamy, with big diesel engines to push them through the steep swells while hauling heavy trawls. The average coastal or bay trawler is between forty and sixty feet long. They are mostly deck, with a small wheelhouse usually located forward. Behind this, standing toward the middle of the wide-open afterdeck where the crew works, is the diesel engine and its stack. The short mast is here too, with the radar on top and gafflike arms and A-frames attached to it. These are the tackle that lift and lower the drags, and get their power also from the diesel.

We saw one fisherman preparing to go out. He wore a flannel shirt, bill-fisherman's canvas hat with big visor, and the huge rubber overalls that are the primary stamp of the New England fisherman. A sticker stuck to his wheelhouse bulkhead read:

BUSINESS IS SO GOOD I COULD PUKE

I shot a picture of him and the sticker. He looked up in confusion that bordered on suspicion. People don't like having their pictures taken by strangers. I shouted I was an amateur feature-story photographer for the *Globe*. He brightened and waved. His diesel was grinding away. A big cable-wound drum near the stack was turning slowly. He nodded at us, smiling, and cast off. His boat eased away from the pier and whined softly through the harbor.

And as he left, trailing a wispy, almost invisible plume of oily smoke, we could see another trawler heading around the breakwater. She was green, and the right size too.

We watched the boat circle the point and come chuffing and grinding into the inner harbor where we were preparing to depart. There was an aura of desperation about her as she rolled in the faint current.

She was riding low. She paused on the far side of the harbor and dropped her hawser. Quick as a wink a dory came scooting around from her far side with a man hunched over in the stern, steering the little outboard. The dory zinged along, whining through the outer raft of moored sailboats, and snaked its way up to the harbormaster's dock. The man steering had scarcely finished throwing a hitch around a piling before he left the small boat and was sprinting up the ramp to the office. The green boat, which was without doubt the same one stranded on my doorstep an hour earlier, swayed lazily around her anchor cable. But I noticed her crew had dropped another hook off her stern, so that she kept her bow toward us. A boat of almost any size is impenetrable head-on. Her engines were still working, and fast. The whine was audible even from where we stood, and the plume of smoke shot straight up from her stack. I nudged Mary.

"See why the engine's working overtime?"

I pointed to the thick stream of water gushing from the boat's bilge pipe. It came squirting out in thick, ropy geysers. Had it been red it would have resembled a severed artery.

"What's that, the cooler?" she asked.

"No." I pointed to another stream of water, this one a straight hard jet of clean spray. That was the outlet for the sea water that had just run around her engines, cooling them.

No, this rust-colored water coming in torrents was bilge water. And there was a lot of it. Almost before my eyes the boat seemed to rise higher in the water.

"They're pumping her out. Did you see how low she rode as she came in? I'd say she was close to sinking. No wonder he was in a hurry."

"Who? The man in the little boat?"

"Yep. Well they've made it in all right. I bet the motion of the boat through the water was what intensified the leak. Now that she's in still water they can keep her up until she's repaired properly."

Allan Hart was ambling up the dock, clad in his scuba suit. A big strapping kid we'd known since he was six. It was Allan Hart who finally gave Jack (then called Jackie) the courage to put his head underwater and do the dead man's float. The two had been inseparable ever since: the Mutt and Jeff of our summers on Cape Cod.

"Hey Allan!" shouted Mary, waving her arm up high.

He was wearing a wetsuit top and carrying a big stainless steel tank under his arm. Across his wide shoulders were strung a yellow weight belt and a huge pair of swim fins. He grinned at us and hurried along. Allan was a native Cape Codder who lived with his mother, a widow, in Eastham. He was strong; those tanks, regulators, and weight belts weigh considerable. I know because I've tried to heft them. And yet Allan was moseying along the dock with all his gear tucked away under his arm and on his shoulder as if he didn't even notice it. In his right hand he carried a long shiny object. Spear gun. I saw the reddish-tan pieces of surgical latex tubing bounce and flip around with each step he took. Those were the elastic ropes that drove the barbed spear through fish.

"How ya doing?" he asked as he set his gear on the gray boards above us. He looked down approvingly at the catboat. I snapped two pictures of him.

"See you're goin' out. Is Jack back yet? Tell him to stop by—"

"Why don't you stop by? He's due up here around four or five. C'mon over to the cottage then and—"

"Thanks, Mrs. Adams, but I've got a date for dinner in Chatham."

"Well stop by anyway on your way down for a beer. Jack would be glad to see you, I'm sure."

"Good. OK I'll do that. And if I get lucky today I'll bring some fish for you."

He sat on the pier, his legs dangling over the side. He strapped on the tank and regulator and slipped the weight belt around his waist. I saw the yellow-painted steel rectangular weights spaced evenly around the nylon webbing of the belt. There were a lot of them. There was a biggish knife with a cork handle in a red plastic sheath strapped to his right calf. Staring out at the green trawler, he put on a rubber hood that was bright gold, and had USN on it in big letters.

"You join the navy, Allan?"

"Naw. I just borrowed this from a friend. If you can keep your head and chest warm you can stay down a long time. That water out around the outer breakwater is deep and cold, but that's where the big tautog hang out. Hey she looks mighty low."

We all turned and looked back at the boat.

"Why don't you swim out there and see what you can see?" I asked. "Take a peek at her hull. Bet you see a gash somewhere."

He put on the big flippers. They made a sound—*squidge, squidge*—as he slipped them over this feet.

"OK. It's right on my way over to the breakwater anyway."

We mentioned seeing the boat stranded out on Billingsgate, which seemed to increase his curiosity still more. Then I noticed he also carried a small flashlight, encased in black hard rubber, which he tested, then fastened to his belt. The face mask was resting up on top of his head as he inserted the mouthpiece, then spat it out.

"Guess I'm ready."

The *Ella Hatton*'s little diesel was grinding away nicely under the cockpit hatch. Mary had removed the sail cover from the long boom and stowed it beneath the seat. The lunch basket was tucked into the corner of the galley counter, right near the sink. We were ready too.

"Wonder why she's out in the middle of the harbor anyway?" mused Allan. "As low as she's riding you'd think she'd wanta come right up to the big pier."

"Hey how's your mom been, Allan?" Mary asked.

"She's been pretty good. She still hasn't got a boyfriend or anything yet, but you know, something'll turn up."

"Well we'll have to ask her over some evening," I said.

Mary grabbed the heavy lines that Allan flipped down to her; I put the engine into gear and we purred slowly out of the slip.

"See you at around five, Allan. Get us a fish!" yelled Mary.

He waved back, replaced the mouthpiece, drew down the mask, and pushed himself forward off the dock with his arms, turning around in midair, and fell backward into the sea. He entered the harbor water softly, quietly, for such a big guy. He surfaced again, doing a slow lazy flip-flop with his fins. As we began to thread the *Hatton* through the maze of moored boats toward the harbor mouth we saw a last flutter of brightness just under the water's surface, a quick glimmer of shiny tank and yellow diving hood. Then there was a little flip of motion, and he was gone, heading out to the green boat, which was riding much higher in the water now.

Still, the boat's half-submerged look intrigued me. It wasn't a sight you saw every day. I clacked away at it with my camera. The motor drive advanced the film quickly with a loud *whirrm* in between clacks of the mirror. A man appeared on her foredeck, looking anxiously at the tiny harbormaster's shack. He had a faint beard and wore a canvas jacket. I snapped more pictures. The man didn't notice me; he was too busy gesticulating to the two figures talking near the shack. One was Bill Larson, the harbormaster. The other was the fellow who'd just run ashore in the little dinghy. As we neared the harbor mouth we passed the boat's quarter at about thirty yards' distance. I could read her name and port on her transom: *Penelope*, Boston. I was snapping a final shot when the man turned and looked in our direction. When he saw me I saw the hint of a snarl start to form on his lips. But as if he thought better of it, he turned and disappeared into the wheelhouse. No doubt this had not been one of his best mornings. Still I felt the prick of curiosity, and spun off my 50-millimeter lens in exchange for a 135 and snapped a few more photos of *Penelope*, whoever she was, before we got out around the breakwater.

After three hours on Cape Cod Bay we headed back. Mary was at the helm, holding the teak wheel that sits at the end of the big round cockpit. *Ella Hatton* was close-hauled and heeled over slightly, churning her way up the outer channel into the harbor. Two sportfishermen roared by us. The men stood over the transoms laughing and drinking beer. No doubt they had been out since before dawn hunting bluefish and striped bass. I stared enviously at the big boats, with their flying bridges and long outrigger poles. The tall towers swayed far and wide as the boats rolled in the swells, their big engines growling and sputtering.

A big boat was rolling out of Wellfleet toward us. She tipped and plunged in the wake of the two sportfishermen. It was our friend the *Penelope*; she was hustling too. We passed each other off Jeremy Point. The big green dragger chuffed by us with nobody visible except a dim shape in the wheelhouse. Evidently the repair was satisfactory; she was riding high and quick. Seconds later her skipper opened her engines up; the dark smoke shot up out of the stack like Old Faithful and the engine's whine increased to a thunderous roar. She shook a tailfeather south around Billingsgate Shoal (now invisible but still treacherous), where she'd been stranded hours earlier, and headed off due west, toward Plymouth, with remarkable felicity.

"Geez, honey, look at her go," I murmured.

Mary turned to see the long sloping plume fast disappearing in the distant haze. We dropped sail a few minutes later, stowing the jib down the forehatch and fastening the main and its gaff along the boom with shock cords. We motored in the rest of the way and gently glided *Hatton* back into her berth. The sun had been making good progress all morning, and now was halfway out. We left the harbor and hurried back to the domicile where Mary promptly changed into her swimsuit and flopped down on the deck, swatting at greenheads. I went running.

I left the cottage and began my run along Sunken Meadow Road. I ran up to the main road, then along it until I came to the old windmill (Eastham's landmark), and then back. It was slightly over six miles, and during the last part I was setting a pretty good clip. I staggered into *The Breakers* and paced around until I cooled off, flicking on the sauna bath. I grabbed my bucket and digging fork, and an old-fashioned tin salt shaker, and strolled out onto the flats. The tide was ebbing; by 5:30 it would be out. Already though, the long tan flats stretched away for hundreds of yards. I was looking for razor clams. Half a mile from the beach, I began to see tiny ovoid depressions in the damp sand. Sprinkling salt from the shaker on these, I watched the long, rectangular creatures squirt up out of these depressions, exposing half of their delicate shells to the air. Sometimes they dove down the other way, into the sand about a foot. Then I'd pry them out with the fork. They were six to eight inches long and shaped like a folded barber's razor. In forty minutes I had filled my bucket, and started back to the cottage. I stopped at a tide pool and filled the bucket to overflowing with brine, then padded back to the beach.

Our cottage was a bluish gray rectangle on the bluff top. The American flag hung limp on the mast. I squinted and could see the three metal cups of my anemometer slowly turning. The dull, cold gray of the weathered cedar shakes belied the coziness of *The Breakers*. The smallish rooms with low, beamed ceilings. The library corner of the living room, where you could sit for hours, *days*, under the brass student lamp with the green glass shade and listen to the surf crash, or the thunder roll. The kitchen with its skylights, wineracks, copper pots, and smells of coffee, roasting meat, sizzling fish, clam chowder. I liked hunting my own food out on the flats. There was something elemental, even prehistoric, about the act. Like sex, it was something that came to me unfiltered by modern civilization. It was animal. I was a hunter-gatherer. The damp sand felt good under my bare feet. I climbed up the bone-colored wooden steps and placed the bucket of clams in the shade on the deck. I would cook them up in butter in a big iron pot, then add the clam liquor, potatoes, onions, cracked pepper, celery, milk and perhaps some leftover corn and little pieces of cooked bacon. I drooled at the thought.

I went into the sauna. The temperature was 190 degrees. Perfect. I baked in there three times, coming out only long enough to shower under cold water each time. Finally I showered for good. I felt so laid back I couldn't have gotten it up even if I were naked in the sack with all three of Charlie's Angels.

No, wait. I take that back.

I made the chowder. Soon the big iron pot was simmering away and I tended to it as I sipped a Gosser beer.

"Isn't that Jack, Charlie?" shouted Mary from the bathroom. The cream colored Toyota Land Cruiser swept into the gravel driveway, and number one son climbed out. On his back bumper is a sticker that reads: STOP THE WHALE KILLERS! BOYCOTT JAPANESE GOODS!

Now you don't stop to think about this until you realize that the sticker is affixed to none other than a Toyota, for Chrissake, and that we've been guilty of laying nine grand on the "killers." Not to worry though, *not to worry*: there's another sticker on the other side, saying: IF I'D KNOWN ABOUT THE WHALES, I WOULDN'T HAVE BOUGHT THIS CAR!

Oh, well, the kid's heart is in the right place.

Number two son, Tony, was working a summer job as a grounds keeper at a resort in Franconia Notch, N.H. He called a few times to say the job was crummy, it didn't pay well, and was hard work, but that he was having "a great time, especially at night," which meant, I suppose, that he was mostly getting laid. But then, what are summer jobs for? Jack was doing graduate work in biology at the oceanographic center at Woods Hole, and so was at *The Breakers* fairly regularly.

He sauntered in, snagging a beer from the refrigerator. He stirred and tasted the chowder, nodding his head and grunting. I walked with him back out onto the deck, and scanned

Billingsgate with the marine glasses. It stood on the horizon, a dark streak surrounded by red shiny water. We had a drink and watched the sun and listened to the gulls. We waited for Allan, then gave up on him.

"Probably forgot," said Jack, thrusting a big paw into the nut dish that sat in the middle of the picnic table. "He's got a new girlfriend down in Chatham."

"Yes, I remember him saying he had a dinner date," said Mary.

"Have you heard from Tony? How is number-two son?" I asked.

He looked up quickly and stared at me level for an instant with his turquoise eyes. He took after the Adams side of the family—the Nordic side. Tony looked like his mother: with deep olive skin and coal black eyes—eyes so dark you could never see the pupils. Jack was blond, and wore a bright yellow beard to match his hair. He had medium skin and pale blue-gray eyes. Both boy-men are enormously handsome. But then what would you expect their daddy to say?

"Huh? Why do you want to know?"

"Because he usually writes us or calls regularly," said Mary, "and he hasn't been lately. Well?"

He shrugged and munched more nuts, swigged at the mug of beer in his left hand. He looked out over the sand flats and ocean.

"Dunno . . ."

"Jack, I know you pretty well," I said. "Sure there's nothing you—"

"Nope. Let's eat. I'll call Allan first thing tomorrow."

We ate on the deck: the chowder accompanied by asparagus in lemon and butter, fresh sugar-and-butter corn on the cob and chablis. Of course afterward I realized that the quarter-pound of butter that had made everything so delicious had probably more than undone the afternoon's running. Oh, to hell with it. I did a little writing after that, working on a paper to be presented at the next meeting of the New England Oral Surgeons. Its working title was "The Use of Epoxy Hardeners and Porcelain-Resin Compounds in the Cosmetic Capping of Peg-Lateral Incisors.'' It was as exciting as cold oatmeal.

I went in and nestled up against Mary's warm, soft flank, and slept. As I dozed off I heard the sound of the tide easing back in: slow cadence of *crump* and *hiss*, and wind blowing through the dune grass.

2

TIME: 5:45A.M. LOW CEILING. WIND: NORTH-NORTHEAST, 12 knots and freshening. Barometer: 29.8 and falling. Temperature: 68°. Sky: leaden and darkening.

It did not look promising. The scattered rows of stratocumulus clouds of the previous day that had almost cleared had regrouped into an ominous thick gray goop. The barometer and wind gauges also foretold unpleasant weather. The wind was turning eastward by the minute, and an east wind almost always is "an ill wind that blows no good."

Over after-breakfast coffee Mary and I decided to flee the Cape and head back to the main domicile in Concord for the day. There were assorted bits of house husbandry that needed taking care of, and Mary had a batch of pots and ceramic sculpture that needed glazing and firing. So we went. I mowed the lawn, collected mail and magazines, and developed the film I'd shot over the past two weeks. I didn't make prints; just left the celluloid strips hanging in the dust-free dryer until I had more time. Mary busied herself in her workshop annex. She does this thing called rock salt glazing which takes immense heat and long periods in the kiln. We built specially constructed kilns for the process in the backyard, beehive-shaped domes that draw their heat from bottled gas. When the temperature reaches some astronomical figure, and certain clay cones inside the structures bend and dissolve, Mary throws in handfuls of coarse kosher rock salt, which promptly vaporize and affix themselves, in the form of a slick finish, to the pots on the racks above. It is an ancient glazing process, she tells me, but produces pots and vases with a finish that is distinctive, simple, and very handsome.

After lunch we headed back and picked up our three dogs who had just been dipped to prevent ticks, which are common on the Cape. They attack Angel and Flack, the two wire-haired dachshunds, especially, since they are low-slung and furry. Danny, the yellow Lab, is more immune. Anyway we gathered them in the car, all smelling like new telephone poles, and headed for the cottage.

Call it intuition, a hunch, or clairvoyance. Whatever it is, I sensed it as we swung into the driveway at half past three. Something wasn't right.

Sure enough, Jack was pacing the deck when we showed up. He didn't wave as usual. Instead he waved his arm backward, motioning us to hurry. He met us in the front hallway.

"Allan Hart's dead," he said. "He drowned in the harbor."

I was hearing him but I wasn't; his voice was coming to me from far, far away, as if he were speaking into one end of the Alaskan pipeline up in Barrow and I was sticking my head in the other end down in the Lower Forty-Eight. I remember looking at the lampshade and thinking how nicely they'd rendered the nautical chart on it, and that I had some tobacco ash still left in my pewter ashtray. I realized everything but what was actually told me. Like a time-delay fuse, my mind had stopped momentarily to absorb the jolt. Then Jack handed me a paper.

Then I was looking at the article—at the picture of Allan. But I wasn't at the cottage when I found myself reading it; I was half a mile down the beach. My three dogs were staring up at me, concerned. They whined and wagged their tails slowly, tentatively, as if in fear of rebuke.

I shooed them away and walked, read, walked again, sometimes slapping the paper against my thigh. The gulls were low, diving and wheeling about. The dogs scampered after them, barking. It was all a dream. I returned to the wooden stairs, and suddenly was up them, all thirty-nine of them, without doing it.

Then the two of them were sitting in the living room staring at me.

Mary's crying brought me back to the real world for good. I sat next to her on the couch and we read the article together, over and over again. But no matter how many times we read it, it stayed the same.

3

EVENING QUIET AT WELLFLEET HARBOR. I SAT STARING AT the water. It swished and riffled languidly along the break-water's edge. It glimmered in the soft, gold-gray light of dusk, of late mellow sunlight through clouds. The light played on the water in streaks of brightness. It was like a Monet painting.

I heard a car door slam far behind me, then the quick footsteps of a woman approaching.

"Thought I'd find you here," said Mary.

I said nothing.

"You ready to come home?"

"Remember what I told Allan just before he went in? I told him to swim out to the boat."

"So? They found his body way out in the channel near Lieutenant's Island."

"The tide could have carried him out there. I think maybe if I hadn't told him to—"

"Stop it, Charlie. Stop it now. There's no way of knowing exactly how Allen died. Scuba divers get killed pretty frequently I think."

"Not in a shallow harbor they don't. Jack says Allan did a lot of deep diving. That's when a diver gets into trouble. A big strong kid like that just doesn't die hunting fish in Well-fleet Harbor."

She sat down next to me on the old stone quay. We watched the boats sway slowly around on their mooring cables. Mary said she'd been unable to find Sarah Hart at her home even though she'd driven by several times. We decided she was with her doctor or close friend.

"It's almost dark, Charlie."

"I just can't help thinking that if I hadn't asked him to swim out there—"

"Dammit, Charlie, *stop it*! You'll drive yourself crazy. Why don't you find the boat's owner and talk to him? He probably never laid eyes on Allan."

"That's what I'm thinking; that's what makes me feel so bad about it. Here's Allan swimming around underneath the boat and the guy probably started the propeller. Remember how fast that engine was revving, pumping out all that water? Well if the screw started suddenly the propwash could've sucked Allan right into it—"

"Good Christ—"

"And one of the blades could have nicked him on the head—remember the article did say there was evidence of a head injury—knocked him cold and his mouthpiece slipped out. There was a lot of air left in the tank."

She tugged at my elbow and led me back to the cars.

"I don't see Bill Larson in his shack. Tomorrow morning I'm coming back here and get the name of the boat's owner. I think if I just get a chance to phone him I'll feel better. Maybe they saw Allan swim out past the boat, in which case I'll feel a little better. Not much, but a little."

After dinner we located the funeral director who told us that Sarah Hart was temporarily in her doctor's care. Her husband had died eight years previous and Allan had been her only child. Good God. I tossed and turned far into the night, thinking about the boy swimming out to the big green boat. I knew it would never leave me alone until I laid to rest at least a little of the guilt that gnawed at me.

On my way to the harbor next day, weary and edgy from almost no sleep, I stopped by the Eastham police station and talked to the desk sergeant. The story was exactly as the papers had reported it. A lobsterman had seen the body in the shallows off Lieutenant's Island in early evening. The body wasn't floating because of the heavy gear and weight belt. There was a deep bruise on the head that had no doubt resulted in unconsciousness, and eventual drowning. I asked the sergeant if the diving hood had been torn, and the nature and extent of the head injuries. He replied that he didn't know; he wasn't that familiar with the details.

"Can you tell me if there are any theories as to how the injury occurred?" I asked.

"I'm not sure, but I think the assumption is that he hit his head while diving, maybe on the breakwater."

"People in scuba gear don't dive into the water headfirst. They fall backward into it to avoid damaging their equipment. Besides, I saw Allan enter the water."

He told me to leave my name and number and a certain Lieutenant Disbrow would be in touch with me. I thanked him and proceeded on to the harbor. I headed over to Bill Larson's little shack. He's the official harbormaster of Wellfleet and also operates a small emporium selling marine paints, hemp and nylon lines, caulking compound, basic marine hardware in brass, aluminum, bronze, and the like. I asked him who owned the green dragger that had pulled in two days previous.

"Didn't think to get his name, Doc. I was about to head out to her in my skiff to see what the trouble was but they beat me to it—came right up here in a little boat and asked me where the nearest weld shop was."

"Yeah I saw it. What happened to her?"

"Said an old seam had worked loose between a coupla plates. She'd been shipping water since she left Boston so they thought they'd better stop and have her sewed up. Seems to me they didn't stop any too soon either."

"Did you know they were out on Billingsgate at dawn?"

"Hmmmp! Well whaddayuh know—"

"Where was the repair made? I'd like to get the owner's name if possible."

"Right over there. Reliable. See it?"

"Oh yeah. Did they say anything else, like having seen a guy in scuba gear?"

"Oh you mean the Hart boy? Too bad, eh? Nope. Didn't say anything about that."

He worked at an eye splice with his big wooden fid.

"I'm sure they got the owner's name because they did the repair."

I entered the barnlike structure from the street side and looked into the gloomy cavernous interior. Straight ahead of me was a set of railroad tracks that led down into the water. Winched halfway up this track was a big cradle, empty.

"Help you sompin?" asked the bearded old man at the workbench. He was busy fitting a new head gasket to a long marine engine that stood near the bench, hung in a frame made of giant I-beams. I counted six huge holes in the block. A straight six, and each of the cylinders seemed big enough to hold a bowling ball. That's what gave the draggers their spunk. I described the boat that had visited them.

"Oh yeah. Gash in the starboard side just forward of the beam. Bout as big as a cigar box, only longer."

It didn't sound like a weld seam working loose. But I decided to keep this tidbit to myself.

"Was it high up, or toward the keel?"

"Pretty high up. Just below the waterline. Wish you could talk to Sonny. He's not here now though. Sonny did the job, less than forty-five minutes."

"That seems mighty quick for a weld job that big. Sonny musta run a good bead."

The old man nodded triumphantly.

"Yup! Good bead all right. *Real* good bead."

He reached around behind the bench and pulled out what looked like a giant Fourth of July sparkler.

"Uses these certanium production rods. Best welding electrode made. He can run a bead three yards long without a rod freezing. He had a good teacher. *Me.* I'm Sonny's daddy, mister. Who in hell are you?"

I explained that I was an interested bystander.

"You seem to know welding, mister. Ever done it?"

I answered that I once worked a summer in Peoria as a welder at the Caterpillar Company. I said that welding was one of the very last Skilled Occupations. That a good welder was worth his weight in gold ingots. This seemed to please the old man, who grew talkative.

"But what was odd, mister, was this: that boat was pretty tore up, but her skipper didn't want nothing but a fix-it job. You know, enough to get her back home. All Sonny did was slap a sheet of quarter-inch plate over that hole, then run his bead around the edge. Slick as a wink, you know? We charged him ninety-nine dollars and ninety-five cents, you see?"

"No I don't see."

"Well by the law any damage to a vessel over a hundred dollars must be reported to the Coast Guard. It's just like a car accident. Well, a lot of skippers don't want the hassle, so we just charge ninety-nine ninety-five."

"That's a nice cheap fee."

"Well sure," he cackled, "but the hauling charge makes up for that. You see we charge a fee for hauling the vessel out so we can work on her. Hauling fee is a hundred bucks. But that's like a tow truck: ain't got anything to do with the *damage*, you see?"

"Ah, *now* I see . . ."

"But strange thing was, mister, this boat dint want no decent job. Just what we call a jury-rig—like I said, enough to get back home on."

"Which was Boston?"

"Don't know."

"Well it said Boston under her name."

"What was her name?"

"Penelope."

"So you know her name and port, so why'd ya ask, mister?"

"I'd like to get the owner's name. Call him. You know that kid who drowned? Well I want to know if anybody on the boat saw him; I think he might have gotten swept up in the propwash. Can I have his name? Would you mind?"

"Don't have it."

"Well didn't you fill out a work order?"

"Naw. The guy showed us his money and we went to work. What makes you think the boy got in trouble with her?"

"I'm not sure. I just want to check. I want to reassure myself he *didn't* get in trouble under her."

He spat a thin stream of dark brown juice over the engine block. He cocked his head slightly with an amused look. Then he shook his head just a tad.

"Mister, I don't know much about you, but I'll say this on a hunch: you *overthink* things. Right? Am I right? Now when you take a leak, do you think about your kidneys working? Yeah, I bet you *do*. I *don't*, mister. That's the difference. This is a hard business. Somebody comes to you, you take them on. You don't have *time* to think. You've gotta make the buck. *Savey-voose*?"

"I understand, I just want to know one more thing. Did they say what caused the damage?"

"Yeah. Said they hit something."

"Well *what*?"

"Now there you go overthinkin' again, mister. It wasn't my business. Why don't *you* ask him?"

"Good idea. How?"

"You got the boat's name and her home port. Go to the Coast Guard and look up the registry. But he never said his name. I didn't ask either. He paid cash and left. Nice new bills . . . could've been ironed they were so crisp."

"Thanks for the help. I'll go to the Coast Guard. But you can't remember any other detail that might help me? Anything?"

He picked up the gasket and placed it on the engine block, then hefted up the massive head and placed it over the gasket. Sonny's daddy was amazingly strong. He had also apparently reached the end of his hawser as far as my presence was concerned. He flung a set of engine bolts into his left hand and held a big Snap-On ratchet wrench in the other and glared at me.

"Mister, I'm a busy man. I've told you all I know about that gawdamn boat. If you want to talk to Sonny, come back on Tuesday. We're closed Mondays. Otherwise, please *git*. Know what a rottweiler is?"

"Uh huh."

"Good. Know what they can do when they're angry?"

"I've heard," I answered, and began to scan the place.

"Well we keep one out back. Name's Roscoe. Turn him loose in here at night to keep an eye on things, ya know? Well he likes to meet people, but usually it turns out they're not so tickled to meet *him*—"

I thanked the man and left. I didn't dawdle. I hadn't the slightest interest in meeting Roscoe, dog lover that I am. I got in the car and cast a final glance at Reliable Marine Service. I started up and did a circle on the pavement.

"Toodle-loo Roscoe," I whispered, and headed up toward the Coast Guard station at Nauset Beach. A gash and a torn seam weren't at all the same thing. I found that interesting.

When I got there the beach parking lot was jammed. I knew it was a tiny station; there was a chance they couldn't help me. I parked and fought my way through throngs of vacationers to the tiny office at the base of the lighthouse. There was a transmitter there and a young man in uniform behind a government-issue gray metal desk. The black plastic tag on his right shirtfront said McNab.

I identified myself as the person who had reported the stranded vessel. He retrieved the report instantly.

"Here it is. Shortly after you called we diverted one of our aircraft to the site. The pilot tried to raise the skipper on the distress frequency but there was no response. Nor was there any distress call, for that matter. We sent the plane back as the tide rose, but the vessel was gone. We're assuming the grounding was intentional."

"She limped into Wellfleet all right. Just barely, but she got there. I want to get in touch with the skipper. Can I look up the boat?"

"Sure. She'll either be registered with the Commonwealth of Massachusetts or another state or, if she's over five tons, she'll be in one of those big books there on the shelf. Do you know her name?"

We thumbed through *Merchant Vessels of the United States*, an enormous two-volume tome that listed every vessel in American waters engaged in commercial activity that was over five net tons. Penelope was a popular name for boats. I counted over sixty of them, arranged alphabetically by their owner's last name. There was no *Penelope* that listed Boston as her home port.

"Do you think she is over thirty-two feet? It's at that length, usually, that a vessel approaches five-ton capacity."

"Over. Positive. I put her length at forty or maybe a bit more."

"Hmmmm. Then she could be new, just documented. Or she could be a noncommercial vessel. You can have a hundred-footer and not have to document it if it's not used for commercial purposes."

"Like a yacht?"

"Exactly. And quite a few trawlers, or trawler-type vessels, are converted into pleasure boats."

The first *Penelope* listed was owned by Jack Babcock of Newport, Rhode Island. The second was owned by Jesse Bullock of Galveston, Texas. Probably a shrimper. And so it went. There were *Penelope*s that caught salmon and crab out of Seattle, *Penelope*s that hunted sailfish and marlin out of Key West, *Penelope*s that seined for smelt from Sheboygan, that shoved coal barges down the Illinois River, etc., etc.

There were seven *Penelope*s in New England, but none of them were from Bean Town. I copied down all the information listed after each name. This included the vessel's dimensions and tonnage, and her documentation number—which is not the one you sometimes see on the boat's bows. The documentation number is engraved or embossed into the vessel's main beam below decks.

"There's one other thing," said McNab, leafing through the book. "The boat could have listed her home port on the transom instead of her hailing port."

"What's the difference?"

"The hailing port is the one that should be listed under the vessel's name. It's the place where she berths, where her skipper lives . . . her *home*. The home port may not in fact be the vessel's true home—"

This enigma was sounding more and more as if it had been created by government bureaucracy.

"—but is the port office where the vessel has filed her

papers. This is technically not kosher, but some boats do it, particularly ones that tramp around the seaboard a lot."

"So you're suggesting that one of these other *Penelope*s could be the boat I saw?"

"It's possible. There are ten documentation offices in New England, and so ten possible home ports. But a boat can be documented in one port and show another on her transom."

"But wait a minute. Boston is a home port, right? So if a boat berthed in Boston and was also documented in Boston, then we'd see her listed in this book, right?"

"Uh, right."

"If a boat has been documented in Boston but berths in, say, Nahant, then she would still be listed here under Boston, right?"

"Uh, yeah. Even though her transom would say Nahant."

"I'm sorry, Mr. McNab, but this is getting murkier instead of clearer."

"OK tell you what," he said. He tapped a pencil, eraser side down, on his blotter officiously, he scowled profoundly, and cleared his throat a few times. I was waiting in the wings. Pretty soon now, he was going to explain it all.

"It's uh, confusing—" he ventured.

"Do you have the slightest idea what's going on about this?"

"No."

At least it was a straight answer.

"Let's try this: supposing a vessel is documented in one of the nine New England ports other than Boston, but spends a considerable amount of time in Boston, OK? Suppose she's documented in New Bedford but hangs out around Boston. Would she then list Boston on her transom? Is that what you were thinking?"

"Exactly, sir. Thank you."

"Fine. So my job now is to contact these New England skippers who own boats called *Penelope* and find out."

"What? Find out what?"

"Find out if they laid eyes on the kid who drowned in the harbor day before last. He was a friend of mine."

"Why do you think they would have seen him?"

"Because I sent him out to look at the *Penelope*, and I don't like myself much for having done so. I think I might have been indirectly responsible for his death."

"Wow. No wonder you feel so bad. Who wouldn't?"

Just exactly what I wanted to hear. It made my day.

I left the tiny office with the names of the seven local boats carrying the name Penelope. According to McNab we couldn't find the name because the boat was new, was a noncommercial boat, or there was a foul-up with the port listings. The third possibility seemed the least likely to me since none of the vessels listed matched the green trawler's dimensions. To me the most likely explanation was a new boat and an inexperienced skipper. That would also explain the damaged hull—no doubt caused by faulty navigation—and the grounding on Billingsgate.

And then I thought of poor Sarah Hart, alone now. I still had to go pay my respects. I wasn't relishing the task, and maybe that's one reason I wasn't paying attention as I headed back to the car.

It happened as I was leaving the path and entering the big parking lot at the top of the beach. Even now as I think about that instant I am wracked with pain. I was walking out between two cars (not the brightest thing to do, I'll admit) when a kid on a moped hit me. More specifically, he hit my wrist. He crushed my poor wrist between the tail fin of an aging Cadillac Eldorado and his handle bar, which was traveling at a nice clip.

I don't remember the instant of impact because I went into semiconsciousness during it or shortly afterward. I awoke to see some pendulous breasts in a scanty halter swaying over me. It probably would have been a great view under other circumstances. The spectators ohhhed and ahhhed at me. I rose into a sitting position and looked at my hand. The back was gashed open and bleeding; it looked like a slab of barbequed pork. That would heal in a few days without difficulty. It was when I tried to move the fingers that the pain got interesting. It was the deep-down, systemic pain—the kind you feel go up the very center of your arm into your brain—that told me it was serious. The damage was not of the muscles or ligaments. Bones were broken. Of this I was certain as I tried to close my hand. The Cadillac's tail fin was badly dented. Old Knucklebrain on the moped had dealt both me and the car a good one. Except the car couldn't feel it. I moaned and was helped to my feet. Soon thereafter I came face to face with my accidental assailant, who'd also been injured—in a regrettably minor fashion—as he tumbled to the parking lot concrete after maiming me. His name turned out to be Jeremy Knobbs. Now is it any wonder that a guy so cursed in nomenclature would run down innocent pedestrians in parking lots?

I was in frankly awful pain, but refused assistance, not out of stoicism, but because I wanted to get home to Mary fast. She is a registered nurse. I wanted Mary. I wanted to cuddle my head into that deep Calabrian bosom and get sympathy. I wanted her to kiss me and say it was going to be all right.

"It looks pretty bad, Charlie," she said after looking at the left mitt for about four seconds. "This hurt?"

I let out a scream like the charging bull elephant in the movie *Ivory Hunters*. Then I picked myself off the floor and wiped the thick rope of saliva from my mouth.

"Hurt, huh? You've broken at least one bone, maybe more. Let's get back to Concord, now. I'll pack the arm in ice; then put on a sling—"

Don't remember much about the ride back to Concord. Two hours after entering Emerson Hospital's emergency room, Dr. Bryce Henshaw, noted orthopedic surgeon whom I'd never heard of (but was on call that night), was troweling a thick coat of plaster over the left wrist, now immobilized by a metal brace and insensitized by a big jolt of procaine. Colleagues and associates who know us stopped by to offer condolences. Didn't seem to help. Went home. Big drink. Felt better.

Next morning I got a call from Jeremy Knobb's father. His name was Jeremy too. It figured. It wasn't a good way to begin the day. I was quick to realize that I could not ply my trade as oral surgeon with one arm in a cast, and stood to lose a lot of dough. I was not overly fond of Jeremy Knobbs after what he'd done to me. After arranging with the senior Knobbs to speak with various attorneys and insurance personnel, I rang off and sulked.

"Mary, I'm going down to the library and check out a book before I meet with Jeremy Knobbs. I want to do a little research so I'll know exactly how to handle this."

"That's a good idea. What's the name of the book?"

"Ancient Assyrian Tortures."

"Oh Charlie, get off it. It *was* an accident. Also, you weren't looking where you were going, you admitted that."

I rubbed my new cast and groaned. "If the kid had had any sense at all he wouldn't have been flying through that lot. It was an accident but it was his fault."

"You're not really going to get a book on tortures are you? Why are you going to the library, really?"

"I'm going to get some fiction. God knows I'll have plenty of time on my hands—er, my hand—now that I'm unemployed. And I was thinking of researching tortures, if for no other reason than to soothe my troubled spirit."

"Speaking of tortures, I once heard that crucifixion was the worst ever."

"I've considered crucifixion for young Jeremy Knobbs. But I rejected it."

"On religious grounds?"

"Nah. Too swift."

4

I PICKED UP THE PHONE.

I was in a better frame of mind. Slightly. My insurance, for which I pay a small fortune, would adequately cover lost revenues caused by the injury. Additionally, I was pleased to discover that the policy—especially designed for surgeons—also provided for a sizeable cash settlement for any incapacitating injury to the hands, regardless of prognosis of recovery. So I had eight weeks of paid vacation until my wrist mended—which *would* happen, I was assured—and enough cash to pay for the *Ella Hatton*, which we'd bought earlier in the spring.

I could grasp with my left hand slightly, despite the cast. Still, I was in pain and irritated at my forced idleness. Young Jeremy was fortunate indeed to have escaped my wrath.

I dialed the number given to me by directory assistance. It rang twice and a woman answered. I asked for Mr. Babcock.

"Mr. Babcock? Is this Mr. Jack Babcock of Newport?"

"Yeah it's me. Who's this?"

"Mr. Babcock, I'd like to buy your boat."

"Who *is* this?"

"Name is Adams, Charles Adams. Do you own a boat, sir?"

"Yes but she's not for sale. That is . . . uh . . . unless you'd like to talk about it, I guess."

Obviously business was booming for Babcock, as it was for almost all independent fishermen in New England. No doubt five grand down and a promissory note and I could become a skipper tomorrow, and Babcock could get another job with a brighter financial future, like dispensing detergent in the local Laundromat.

"Didn't I see your boat up in Wellfleet the other day?"

"Nope. Never been up there. I'm out of Newport."

"Oh. What's your vessel's name, may I ask?"

"She's the *Penelope*. Hate the name. Wife's idear—"

"Uh . . . I must have it confused with another—can you quickly describe the boat please? Then I'll leave you alone."

"Sure. Sixty-two feet, white with red gunnels. Built in Gulfport, Mississippi, six years ago. Twin Cummins diesels—"

"Oh sorry, you know I made a mistake. It must have been another *Penelope* I saw."

"She's a beaut, no foolin'. Besides the engines she's got loran and radar. Long-range VHF radio. Four berths. I could transfer the mortgage and—"

I called the other six in the course of the day. Four times I spoke with the wife since the owner was out fishing. The only two vessels that could possibly match the boat I saw in Wellfleet were far away; one in Bath, Maine, the other in Elizabethtown on Martha's Vineyard. I was impressed by the statistics I had copied from *Merchant Vessels* too; the descriptions offered by the skippers and their wives matched the figures in the book very closely.

Next I called the Massachusetts Boat Registry. It didn't take more than a few seconds to discover there was no boat of *Penelope*'s description registered in the state. There was a sailboat named *Penelope* out of Rockport. That was it.

So much for that.

Since it was late, I decided to check the USCG Regional HQ next morning. I went in person. Driving Mary's Audi with my cast was easy since there was no gearshift to contend with. I parked in the lot behind the Boston Garden, walked by North Station, through the Garden, and found myself on Causeway Street. It's a typical Boston street: dirty, noisy, crowded and charming. The Green Line trolley tracks run over it, just like the way the El tracks cover Wabash Street in Chicago. I heard the rattle of the trolley and the cooing of millions of pigeons. It seems you never see baby pigeons or pigeon nests, and you hardly ever come across a dead one either. They must spring up spontaneously from bread-crumbs or something and disappear into thin air when they kick the bucket.

I entered the big headquarters building. On the fourth floor I found Lieutenant Commander James Ruggles. To my sur-prise, he had *Penelope*'s documentation certificate in front of me in less than ten minutes. Well, it seemed to wrap up the little puzzle. I asked Ruggles if he could give me the owner's name and address so I could contact him. He stared at the paper.

"New vessel, *Penelope*, noncommercial vessel—"

"Noncommercial?"

"Yup. What it says. Built this year. Hailing port is Gloucester. Officially that's the port that should be on the vessel. *Penelope* is technically in violation."

Then that explained everything. It explained the ground-ing, as suggested by McNab at the Nauset station: new boat, new skipper. It explained even the rather bizarre behavior of the boat and her crew once inside the harbor. Finally, it ex-plained *Penelope*'s absence from *Merchant Vessels*.

"Who's the owner?"

Ruggles hesitated a second.

"Why do you want the name? I'm obliged to provide it, but mind if I ask?"

I quickly told him about Allan's death, and my desire to lay at least some of the guilt to rest. He listened keenly and with patience, then looked back to the papers on his blotter. He rubbed his chin with his fingertips.

"Wallace Kinchloe, of Boston, owns the *Penelope*. His address is Five Blossom Street. That's right up the street; you shouldn't have any trouble—"

He stopped in midsentence.

"What's the matter?"

"Nothing. The address is familiar though. Here's the phone number. If you want to try it there's a pay phone down the hall. Good luck. Come back and let me know what you've found out."

I called the number. A musical voice oozing forced cheerfulness answered. It was the Holiday Inn. Stunned, I asked for Wallace Kinchloe. He wasn't registered. Was he ever registered there? They wouldn't say? I returned to Ruggles's office.

"Guess what?" I asked him.

"I already know. It's the downtown Holiday Inn. I just remembered."

"He isn't there either. Is there anything else on the documentation? How about a post office box?"

"Nothing. Tell me the story again."

So I did. Lieutenant Commander Ruggles continued to stroke his chin thoughtfully.

"According to this, Wallace Kinchloe was born in Danbury, Connecticut, August 4, 1913. He resided in Cohasset until a little over two years ago. Now he is listing his address as temporary, which fits with the Holiday Inn. Under remarks are two words: *in transit*."

"In transit?"

"In transit. Not much to go on. Here's more though; the boatbuilder who built *Penelope* is required by law to fill out one of *these*."

He waved a small square of paper at me. It had a fancy engraved border, two signatures, and some sort of government seal. Very official.

"This is a Master Carpenter's Certificate, which states that such-and-such a vessel actually was constructed at such-and-such a time and that delivery of said vessel actually took place at a certain time by a certain party. OK?"

"Of course. Like a title to a car?"

"Uh, no. The title is the Documentation Certificate that we've already looked at. This certificate actually corresponds more closely to the *certificate of origin* of a car, telling who made it where."

"Gotcha."

"Thing is. Thing is this: sometimes people fake them."

"Why?"

"Well think about it awhile. Sometimes it's advantageous to make a boat vanish or appear. Suppose a fisherman's down on his luck, and how many aren't these days? He's got a boat that's losing money and can't keep up the payments. The boat is a dead duck. So he hauls it someplace where it can be altered, mostly in the superstructure—you know, cabins, wheelhouse, anything but the hull, which stays. Metal boats are better because they can be made to look new more easily . . ."

I had settled back into my chair like dandelion fluff on a doormat. I was all ears.

"He gets a boatbuilder to do the alteration. Fine. Then the big thing: he pays the boatbuilder to put his name to one of *these*—"

He waved the Master Carpenter's Certificate at me again.

"Now let's return to our fisherman friend who's broke. 'What's happened to your boat?' people ask. 'Sunk,' he says, and files a big fat insurance claim. How can anyone dispute him? We can't find a trace of it. A lot of claims say the boat was stolen, not sunk. But the net result is of course the same. What happens? Six weeks later a 'new' boat emerges from the boatyard, with a new name and documentation number. But of course it's really the old boat on which the fisherman has now collected his insurance coverage and paid off the mortgage, and given the builder a sizeable chunk too. The results: a free boat. No more debts."

"Ah hah! Very clever."

"Ah yes. But remember: just as the owner has defied the law, the boatbuilder who does the alteration and deliberately falsifies a carpenter's certificate has his head in the noose too. Maybe more so, because if caught in perjury—which this is—he cannot ply his trade any longer. He is in what fishermen call 'deep shit.' "

I walked over to the window and look down at the cars crawling along toward the North End. Behind them was Boston Harbor. In the far distance, through the bluish-gray haze,

I could see tiny specks of fishing boats returning. They each trailed a white-gray thread of wake.

"The *Penelope* was built in Gloucester by Murdock's boatyard, Daniel Murdock, owner. Here's his signature."

I looked at the small square of paper and copied down the name.

"All I want to do is talk with Kinchloe for a few seconds," I said. "It's so frustrating to be unable to reach him."

"He might be living aboard his boat. That could explain the in transit."

"I bet that's it. So how do I locate the boat?"

He shrugged his shoulders.

"Hang around the harbors. Talk to the harbormasters and other fishermen and boaters. I don't know. We can't help."

"I'm wondering if he has a post office box."

"They won't tell you; that's confidential. You may inquire about a company but not an individual."

"I've got a way to find out. My brother-in-law's a cop."

"Ahhh. Let me know if you uncover anything interesting, OK?"

"Sure will. And, Mr. Ruggles, thanks a lot."

"My job; don't mention it. Buzz me anytime you have a question."

I left the building and headed home. The more I pursued the green boat and her owner the stranger it appeared. Then I remembered I had photographs of her, and of somebody on board. The developed negatives were hanging in the dust-proof cabinet in my darkroom. When I arrived I took out the long strips of film, cut them into convenient lengths, and ran a contact sheet. I examined the tiny pictures, just slightly bigger than postage stamps, with a loupe. I had taken six shots of the boat as we had passed it. I selected two shots of the boat and enlarged them. One shot was a side view directly off her beam, the other a view of her stern off her starboard quarter.

There was another shot that looked interesting. It was of one of the crewmen, or perhaps of Kinchloe himself, that I had snapped with the telephoto lens. I enlarged this negative as much as possible so that his head almost filled the eight by ten-inch paper. The tiny speck on the celluloid was blown up perhaps fifty times its original size, which resulted in a portrait that was so grainy it was impressionistic. It was as if Georges Seurat had painted the portrait. Nevertheless, it sufficed. The man wore a faint dark beard, had thinning hair, a prominent and handsome nose, and two whitish specks that were interesting. One was a white line around his neck, directly under the Adam's apple. It was probably a choker necklace, made of puka shells. Somehow, it didn't seem to fit on a middle-aged man in New England, as out of place as a walrus in Death Valley.

The other speck was in the middle of his right ear. It was scarcely noticeable, but it was there. If the man were not deeply tanned, perhaps I would have missed it altogether. He wore a hearing aid.

I looked again at the neck. Thick neck. Prominent Adam's apple. The man was strong—heavily muscled and fit. A thick neck with heavy jowls means fat. It is often associated with heavy drinking. But thick necks with clean chins and bulging Adam's apples tell a different story: muscle in abundance; no fat.

This man, whoever he was, was a curious collection of contradictions. The thinning hair and hearing aid clearly told me he was middle-aged. Perhaps we were contemporaries at forty-seven—maybe he was a bit older. Still he wasn't ancient. Why would he be deaf? Then I thought of a logical reason: perhaps he was a diver. The hallmark of the scuba diver is broken eardrums.

The beard, "surfer" necklace, and extraordinary fitness all bespoke a man who's trying his damndest to look younger. I have a special sympathy for those people, being one myself. But the picture had a strange quality to it. The man resembled one of the yachting crowd; he certainly seemed out of place aboard a trawler. Then I remembered Ruggles telling me the boat was noncommercial. Yet she didn't even faintly resemble a pleasure craft.

I took the pictures into the living room and showed them to Mary, who was reading a book on Chinese porcelains.

"See what I mean? See that dark line inside the hull?"

"You mean this, the line that's slanting?"

"Yeah. That's left by oil slick and dirty bilge water. Look how high up it is. I'd say it's a wonder she made it into Wellfleet. She was close to going down, even with her pumps working."

"Is this the man we saw? He looks kind of neat. He looks like a pirate or something."

"He does at that. And he's elusive too. Your brother is going to help me, I hope."

Detective Lieutenant Joseph Brindelli wanted to know why. I explained, and he reluctantly agreed to see about the PO box. He called back ten minutes later with the news that Wallace Kinchloe did indeed have a post office box at the main Boston office.

"It's number twenty-three nineteen, but you can't get into it you know."

"Sure I know, I just want to drop him a line."

And I did, asking him if he had seen a scuba diver in the harbor when he had his boat repaired. I had the postcard in my hand and was just about to drop it in the mail when I reconsidered. According to official records *Penelope* was a new boat. Brand-new. And yet, thinking back on my photographs, I wouldn't have described the boat as new. It wasn't old and beat-up, true . . . but new would not be the first word that would pop into my head if I were asked to describe her. I followed a hunch and called Reliable Marine Service in Wellfleet. The raspy voice on the other end told me I had the old man on the line. I asked for Sonny and in ten seconds was speaking to him. His voice was deep and hollow, and I pictured him in my mind's eye as big and fat.

"Do you remember a green fishing boat you welded a patch onto earlier in the week?"

"Sure. Who you?"

"I'm a guy trying to find the owner. Listen: would you say, judging from what you saw of the boat, that she was new?"

"New? How new?"

"Brand-new."

"Naw! She's six to eight years old at least. Tell by the steel. Maybe older. Somebody's yanking your chain, buddy."

"Thank you. Bye."

"Mary," I said that evening as I poured her glass of wine, "there's something fishy about that fishing boat. And it doesn't make me any more eager to have to visit Sarah Hart."

To make matters worse, Mary got a phone call later in the evening and informed me that she had to fill in at the hospital for Irene Hamilton who'd called in sick. This meant I was to drive down to *The Breakers* alone and comfort Sarah. It was not a cheery prospect, and one would almost suspect that Mary was trying to get out of it were it not for the fact that she has seen more death and done more comforting and grief therapy than an army chaplain at Verdun.

So the next day found me trundling down to the Cape again in the Audi. Just before noon I cruised to a stop in front of the Hart house in Eastham. Sarah's car was there. Dammit. People face death, and think about it differently. I have a hard time with it. I didn't realize this fully until I left medical school and began to practice. I suppose I had always assumed that I was in medicine to conquer death, which is of course impossible. Ultimately every doctor must lose all his patients. It was this difficulty that eventually caused me to leave medicine and go into dentistry, and then—I suppose in retrospect—a sort of compromise in the middle: oral surgery. It was just about the time my third patient died that I began to seriously reconsider medicine as my life's work.

And it was after my third patient's death, as we drew up the sheet and I felt the poisonous stares of his parents, that I knew I was going to leave. The boy was Peter Brindelli, aged eight. My nephew.

I walked up to Sarah's door and rang the bell.

Grief is its own anesthetic. Thank God for that at least. Allan Hart's mother, like so many grief-crazed parents I had seen, was in that state between shock and total surrender to the paralysis of grief. As such, her behavior was surreal, as if she were marking time before the axe was to fall. I remember clasping her elbow, the slip and slickness of the black silk blouse alive in my hand. She gazed up politely into my face. But her eyes had no life. Those pretty Irish eyes (and she *had* to be Irish; the black hair, cream skin, and light blue eyes confirmed it) stared at me, looking right past me.

"It's so thoughtful of you to have come," she lilted. "It's so comforting when—"

But then she bit her lip quickly, to stop it from shaking. Bit it till the blood came, and rushed over to the window, looking out. She stood there blinking and wincing for a while. Then I saw her hands move quickly, flash down into the window panes, and I ran to her. I grabbed her wrists hard, but not before she'd done the windows—not to mention her hands—a lot of damage.

Mary pulled up to the cottage at quarter to five, having finished her shift at three. She still wore her uniform. She found me out on the deck gazing off over the ocean. In my right paw was a gin and tonic big enough to float the *Queen Mary*.

"Hi, Charlie!"

"Mary, I have just had one of the most harrowing days in recent memory. I'm trying to put it back into the box and nail the top down so it'll quit leaping out at me."

I told her about my grim session with Sarah Hart. How I'd washed her bloody hands and wrists in hot soapy water and she hadn't even flinched. Not even when I smeared the cuts with tincture of iodine. How I had confided in her about my guilt feelings, and explained exactly what happened in the harbor. How she'd listened passively as I told her, as if there was too much grief for doubt or hate to enter her mind.

"She finally let it go after I was there about twenty minutes," I told Mary. "It was like a seizure. She screamed and clung to me, digging her nails in. She rolled her eyes and seemed to talk in tongues."

"I've seen it many, many times, Charlie. I can never get used to it. It kills people you know. The grief and depression can kill, sending people rushing after those who've died. And she's a widow too."

"She told me Allan was a very good diver. There's no reason to think he'd get into trouble, especially in a harbor."

"Does she have any relatives?"

"Yes. She's flying to Pasadena day after tomorrow to visit her sister for a week or two."

"Thank heaven for that at least."

I grabbed a hiking staff and walked out onto the flats, following the ebbing tide. It can be an unsettling feeling going out there with nothing with you. It's hard to explain. It's being too alone. I feel much better with other people, or just an object like a cane or staff to take with me. Far out there I looked back toward shore. Squinting, I could just barely see the tiny gray square speck of *The Breakers* that jutted up over the low horizon. Squinting still more, I could see a very faint motion above it. The American flag. Then I pictured myself on the deck of the grounded trawler with 7 x 50 marine binoculars a mile and a half farther out, on Billingsgate. I could see plenty of *The Breakers* then. Plenty. Especially if the owner happened to be prancing around on deck waving a gaudy beach umbrella trying to get my attention. I could see him just fine. Had they seen me? Did they remember me? Did it matter? There were a lot of unanswered questions, and I didn't like any of them. I walked around awhile, then went back to the beach at a slow jog. I took a sauna with Mary and then a cold shower. During all these maneuvers it was a constant hassle trying to keep my cast dry. We changed into beachy things and ambled out onto the deck and watched the tide move out, slow puddles of water-sheen beginning to leave the lower pockets of the flats. Distant gulls cried, a faint plaintive *eeeyonk, eyonk, yonk-yonk-yonk*. The groaner buoy bleeped. The dune grass hissed, gray-green as it bent to the wind. It would have been a lovely evening under ordinary circumstances.

"Charlie, the water's ready. Time to put them in."

She had stopped at the lobster pool and bought two gigantic specimens for dinner, no doubt to cheer me up. But it didn't.

The thought of the two big crustaceans scurrying and crawling their way into oblivion in the scalding water did not appeal to me at all. As one who worked on people's teeth and mouths I was acutely aware of pain. If death must be done, then best to do it quickly, cleanly, with the proper equipment. I fetched an ice pick from the back entry and then took the lobsters from the refrigerator. I grabbed them by their middles; they flung their arms out and backward in a futile attempt to take my hands off. Their big claws were immobilized by the pegs and thick rubber bands, and I was glad.

I inserted the steel point quickly and forcefully down between each animal's head and thorax. It made a noise like a stapler. They didn't say or do a damn thing; when I picked them up their bodies dangled like latex. I dropped the limp corpses into the boiling water and put the butter on to melt.

The dinner helped some; we sat outside and watched the sun go down. It hit bottom just when the bottle of chablis did.

The next morning at eleven they buried Allan Hart. The funeral was bad enough, but to watch Jack and five other young men carry the casket down the church aisle and out of the hearse to the grave was unbearable. It was that first shovelful of dirt that got me, and his mother. She wept openly, I silently, with little convulsive shuddders and throat squeals.

My fault . . . *my fault* . . .

We had Sarah and the rest over to the cottage afterward. Extremely glum. Boy was I glad when it was over. Then I sat and stared out across the water for the rest of the day. Life is boring and death is terrifying. And here we are dangling on spider silk, caught right in the middle.

The next day Mary went to a local art fair. When she returned we sat at the kitchen table eating two small chef salads. She had brought a copy of the *Globe* with her that somebody had left behind at the fair. She flipped through it absently, and I saw a picture flash by that I wanted to retrieve. I found it. It was a picture of a boat. White and low-slung with a small cabin, it was a lobster boat. I read the story. The boat, out of Marblehead, had disappeared almost two weeks ago. It did not look good for the skipper, a certain Andrew D'Corzo.

The article had set me to thinking. I had planned to make contact with Daniel Murdock, the boatbuilder who had signed the carpenter's certificate, as soon as I returned to Concord. But I remembered what Lieutenant Ruggles had told me in his office about vessels appearing and disappearing. Perhaps I should look for a boat that had recently disappeared and would roughly fit the dimensions of *Penelope*. If indeed the boat I saw wasn't new, then she had to have a previous life. What better way to discover it than to check on boats recently lost?

"How's the wrist?" asked Mary.

"Still hurts. And I can't drive golf balls. I can't beat you at tennis. I can't swim. I can't practice my trade except to remove stitches from previous extractions."

"What makes you so sure you'd beat me at tennis? And anyway it's your left wrist."

"How could I serve?"

"Oh. That brat. Did you ever decide on an appropriate torture, by the way?"

"Yes, I have in mind a dual program for the lad: the Agony of the Thousand Cuts to be followed by Impalement. Well?"

She nodded approvingly as she popped the last forkful into her mouth.

I got the number of Murdock's boatyard in Gloucester and called all day without an answer. Then I called the Boston office of the Coast Guard. At the Department of Marine Safety, they informed me that the USCG kept a case log—a file—on all recently missing boats, regardless of size or purpose. They had various investigative procedures to track them down too, like phoning likely harbors and boatyards. If the errant skipper left a float plan, or indicated even vaguely his plans of destination, the Coast Guard cutters would traverse the probable routes, looking for the vessel or wreckage of same. After a "reasonable time," the files were closed, with the vessel and crew presumed lost. I asked what a reasonable time was, and was told it varied. If a vessel disappeared during a violent gale, the reasonable time was not as long as under other conditions. This seemed to make sense.

"Where can I get a list of vessels lost during the last month or two?"

"From where, sir?"

"From the entire New England region, but especially from the Cape and the Islands northward to, say, Portsmouth."

"We have that information here. It's available to the public."

I thanked him and hung up. Mary was in the hallway in front of the mirror trying on a new straw hat. She canted it at various angles and spun on her toe.

"Honey, I'm going to put my unexpected vacation to use. I'm going to locate the *Penelope*."

"That's good. How?"

"Tomorrow I'm going up to Boston and look through some files. Then I'm going to track down some boatbuilders and reporters."

"You could work on the gutters and repair the broken window in the garage."

"Can't. Are you forgetting the wrist?"

I was at the outskirts of the city in a little over an hour, and shortly thereafter was pulling Mary's car into the lot behind the Boston Garden. I turned left on Causeway Street and went right past the regional Coast Guard headquarters to the smaller building next door that housed the Boston station. There I was shown the files that contained the case logs. I began to scan them, starting with cases that occurred in May. Some of these were already marked for abandonment; the CG was assuming the boat lost, the crew dead. Two of these were draggers that disappeared in heavy weather over Georges Bank. I went through all the files. As might be suspected, the recent cases were more numerous. Presumably these would be whittled down as people gave up hope and as boats were found. I imagined they found quite a few of them tucked away in small coves and in big marinas, the owner with his case of whiskey and his girlfriend explaining lamely that geez, they just seemed to forget about the time . . .

One case caught my eye immediately. It stuck out like Ayer's Rock. It was a boat named *Windhover* that disappeared—or rather failed to report back—June 25. She was out of Gloucester, and her dimensions matched those of *Penelope* to a T. *Windhover* disappears end of June in calm weather (so the report said). *Penelope* appears, having been allegedly built in same port, in Wellfleet two months later.

The *Windhover* was a noncommercial vessel engaged for the purpose of "archeological salvage" (this phrase directly from the report). I remembered now Ruggles's comment as shown on the *Penelope*'s documentation certificate, that she was also noncommercial. Most of all, her home port stuck out: Gloucester.

Penelope had allegedly just been built by Mr. Daniel Murdock of Gloucester. But Sonny Pappas, who'd repaired her, said she wasn't new. I felt little bells tinkling in the back of the gray matter.

The *Windhover*'s owner was a man named Walter Kincaid, of Manchester-by-the-Sea, a posh town just south of Gloucester. I left the Coast Guard and started up toward Beacon Hill with the name ringing in my head. Walter Kincaid. Walter Kincaid. Where had I heard that? I was standing on the corner opposite the Saltonstall Building on Cambridge Street when it came to me: Wallace Kinchloe. Wallace Kinchloe was the owner of the *Penelope*. Walter Kincaid—Wallace Kinchloe.

I trudged up the hill. The chimes at the Park Street Church boomed ten o'clock. I had a fifteen minute walk to Copley Square and the Boston Public Library. I crossed over Beacon Hill, just skirting the State House and dodging piles of dog shit that littered the old cobblestone sidewalks. On the average day in Boston you will smell four things, this being one of them. The other three odors are Italian cooking, garbage, and the Bay if the wind is right. I crossed the Boston Common, and made my way through clots of winos, dopers, religious fanatics, street jugglers, street musicians, thugs, pushers, and street crazies, to Boylston Street, where I turned right and headed up to Copley Square.

Once inside the library I made my way to the periodical room and scanned a series of microfilms of the *Boston Globe*.

I asked for the last week in June and the first week in July.
It wasn't long before I found the account of the missing boat.
This is what I read:

Windhover Still Missing

GLOUCESTER—The research vessel *Windhover*, owned and operated by Walter Kincaid of Manchester, is still reported as missing
by the Coast Guard. The *Windhover* set out from Gloucester June
25, and has not been heard from or seen since. Mr. Kincaid, a
retired businessman who founded the Wheel-Lock Corporation of
Melrose, used the vessel for exploring various archaeological expeditions along the New England coast.

According to his wife, Laura, Kincaid was headed to Provincetown as a first stop in an expedition that would take the *Windhover*
down the outer Cape coast to the islands.

The disappearance of the boat is all the more baffling to the Coast
Guard because of the mild weather recently, and accompanying
calm seas.

But what was really interesting was the photograph that
went along with the article. This was what I had been seeking. The *Windhover* looked familiar. Of course this wasn't
surprising considering that she was a converted commercial
fishing boat. Draggers, trawlers, and lobster boats look a lot
alike. So in fact, do pleasure boats. Yet there was a certain
lilt of the gunwale line, a rise and sheer of her stem particularly, that struck a familiar chord. I shunted the photograph
around in the microfilm viewer machine with the knobs on
its sides. I read the credit on the photo's bottom: Globe Photo
by Peter Scimone.

OK, I'd call him and get a print. I returned the microfilm
and on the way back down Boylston Street stopped at the
Boylston Street Union for a run and a sauna bath. I ran five
miles around the gym floor; there is no track at the Boston
YMCU. There is no pool there either. In fact there isn't
anything except an old four-story stone building that's loaded
with old musty locker rooms, an ancient gymnasium, and a
healthy population of cockroaches. The lobby, if such I may
call it, looks like the Greyhound bus station in Indianapolis
in 1936. And that's doing it a favor.

Well then—you might well ask—what does the YMCU *have*? What it has or rather what it *is*, is a microcosmic slice of that place called Boston, thinly shaved, stained, and mounted in a slide. If you want to see Boston, don't go to Newbury Street. Newbury Street could be anywhere. The North End is good; it could only be in Boston, or New York, but it's all Italian. Likewise the city of South Boston (or Southie, not to be confused with the South End of Boston) is all Irish. Moreover these ethnic enclaves leave out groups like the blacks, Chinese, and Spanish-speaking Bostonians. But everybody's at the Union. Everybody. Guys named McNally and Ferreggio. Washington and Pekkalla, Chang, Papadopoulos, Garcia, Frentz, Jainaitis, Hudachko, and . . . and *Adams*.

Just about every third guy who goes to the Union checks a piece at the front desk: .38 police specials, .22 autos, I've even seen a few .357 magnums and .45s too. They're cops, detectives, and prosecutors. We don't got no violence or trouble at the YMCU. Nope. Because the place is crawling with fuzz. And to help them out are the body builders, muscle freaks, and karate/Aikido addicts who can eat Buicks for lunch and break cement with their pinky fingers.

I have two friends at the YMCU. One is Liatis Roantis, the Lithuanian exmercenary who teaches martial arts. He spent some years with the French Foreign Legion and some with the U.S. Special Forces, where he taught guys how to kill people with their earlobes. Somebody once asked me to describe him. I said that if you took every Charles Bronson movie ever made and took all the characters that Bronson ever played and melted them down in a test tube, the result would be Liatis Roantis. I had taken four courses from him: beginning and intermediate judo and karate. Boy is he good. To mess with him in any way—especially after he's had about seven beers—invites death or severe permanent injury. He is a pit bulldog in human shape.

The other guy is Tommy Desmond, the immensely handsome Irishman from the D Street section of Southie. He can hit the speed bag and the heavy bag like a pro. The only thing he can't fight off is women. I yelled out a greeting to him as I ran around the gym. He was busy with the heavy bag.

"Oh my Jesus! Doc, how ya been?"

Whap! The big bag jumped up and swung near the ceiling. Tommy circled it with a look of detachment in his icy blue eyes, a sheen of sweat beginning to glow on his big shoulders.

Nobody can hit the bag like Tommy. He stands there gazing at it, his blue eyes darting back and forth as the heavy bag swings on its big chains. Then, almost lazily, languidly, he begins the crouch, the sideways lean . . . the bag is swaying and spinning slowly. Tommy's crouch deepens, the lean lengthens, the arm begins to snake around slowly! *WHAP!*

The bag is gone.

I had given him money once for a "charity" called NO-RAID. Supposedly it was to help the poor widows and orphans of Ulster. In reality it was to supply money to buy arms for the Provisional Wing of the IRA. After I found this out I gave no more money to Tommy. It was less because of my political stance on the issue than my hatred for violence. I think he understood; we were still friends.

I finished the run, took a sauna and a shower, and walked out by the wrestling mat. I saw two big bearded black men with shaved heads in white karate suits sternly circling each other. They rocked and parried on their toes, trying for a chance to take each other's heads off with their feet.

When I left the Boylston Street Union, I hoofed it over to the Cafe Marliave. I ordered an antipasto deluxe, a small spaghetti Bolognese, and a split of Bardolino. I hardly ever eat lunch, so when I do it, I do it right. I pumped coins into a phone and called the *Globe*. After a lot of hee-hawing on the other end, and spending half my life's savings in small coins, I was informed that Peter Scimone was really a stringer who lived up in Gloucester. I got his number and called him. I said I'd lay three crisp tens in his hands for a series of eight by ten glossies of the *Windhover* he photographed a month ago. He said for three crisp tens he'd begin running the prints instantly, and they'd be ready for me when I arrived.

Scimone lived down near the water in East Gloucester,

just on the borderline of the artists' colony called Rocky Neck. It was a shack, but nicely kept up and decorated with many potted plants hung from macrame holders. Peter emerged from his darkroom with four prints of the *Windhover*. I glanced at them and was instantly on edge, and excited. Even at first blush the missing *Windhover* and the phantom *Penelope* were very similar.

Scimone had done the job quickly on a moment's notice for the local Gloucester paper, and the print was a year old when the *Globe* bought it. He didn't remember much about any of it. A gray-haired man sat on the deck of the boat with two other men. On the dock behind the boat was an attractive young lady with long blond hair. Scimone knew nothing about her, had not seen her before or since. I paid him and left with the prints.

On my way back through town a name, crudely painted with a big brush on a mailbox—caught my eye. The name was *Murdock*, and the house was near the water. I pulled over and walked to the mailbox. If it was Daniel Murdock, and he couldn't construct a boat any better than he could write his name on his mailbox, I wouldn't want to be out in a millpond on one of his vessels.

I knocked at the door which, like the house, wasn't in very good repair. I waited. The gulls cried and cars whispered by behind me on the road. A curtain fluttered in a window above me. A voice called out asking me what I wanted.

I said merely that I wished to speak to the owner, Mr. Dan Murdock.

"I've got a boat that needs work on it. Where can I reach him?"

"Who wants to know?"

"Doesn't he do repair work?"

"Who wants to know? He ain't heah."

"Where can I find him?"

"Try the Schooner Race or the Harbor Café. He'll do it . . . if he's not too drunk. He owe you money?"

"No. I just want to talk with him briefly."

The window slammed shut and I walked toward the car.

But I stopped, and chanced to look back beyond the tiny frame house toward the harbor, whose slimy water, coated with prismatic and rainbowesque swirls of petro-chemicals, gave off a heavy aroma. A shack was back there, perched over the harbor like a stork over a lily pad. I began ambling down the gravel lane toward it. I was curious to see the spot of *Penelope*'s conception and delivery.

I heard the window slide up again with a *clunk*.

"He ain't heah! Mistah, go away!"

But stubborn soul that I am, I kept at it. When I was halfway to the shack, I heard the ring of a phone inside it. It rang once. That's all.

I stood in front of the doorway. The place was dark inside. I peered in through the windows. There was the looming dark shape of the bows of a big boat silhouetted by the shiny harbor water behind it. I tried the door. It wouldn't budge. But why only one ring? Had the caller hung up after only one ring? No. Murdock was in there, in amongst the tools, timbers, and old beer cans that lay strewn everywhere. I looked again through the windows of the dismal place, but nothing moved in the dark. I pounded on the door, then peeked again. Then left. The single ring was probably a warning signal sent by his wife. Lord knows how many people were anxious to make contact with Mr. Murdock. From his apparent drinking habits and the slovenly state of his operation, I guessed that he owed quite a lot of people money.

"Mrs. Murdock? Mrs. Mur*dock*!"

Curtain flutter. Window up again.

"Mistah, *look* he ain't—"

"I know. Listen, tell him a man wants very much to speak to him about the *Penelope*. Tell him I'll call again in a couple of days, OK?"

Window slam. No answer. I left for *The Breakers*. It had been a tiring day. As I drove back down to Eastham the vision of poor Sarah Hart stayed in my mind. I saw her in tears, pushing her fragile wrists through the broken glass of her window.

* * *

As soon as I arrived I sat at the leather-topped desk in the study corner of the living room and switched on the brass student lamp. I laid out the photos that Scimone had given me, and next to them the eight by tens of the pictures I had taken of the *Penelope* during her brief sojourn in Wellfleet. I studied the photographs for twenty minutes. At first it was obvious they were the same boat. Then for a while I saw how it was clearly impossible that they could be. Then I saw it *was* possible. The common dimensions were one factor, but I knew that the forty-foot—or thereabouts—length is one of the most common for bay trawlers. But the bows did flare out in exactly the same way. The sweep of the gunwale lines were congruent. These things, I knew, could not be altered. But what of the things that could be altered?

The superstructures of the two vessels were very different: the *Windhover* had a lot of cabin space, the cabin extending far forward and leaving only enough foredeck for a crewman to stand and heave a line; the *Penelope*, typical of commercial fishing boats, had a small wheelhouse with a lot of foredeck. The *Windhover*, however, preserved her work-boat appearance by retaining the tiny round portholes (invariably the mark of an older vessel) on her topsides just under the foredeck, whereas *Penelope* had instead the more modern rectangular single ports located roughly in the same place. In fact, I mused as I studied the pictures, *exactly* in the same place. Squinting my eyes slightly and glancing quickly from Scimone's photo of *Windhover* to my own pix of *Penelope*, I saw that the ports, which are very uncommon on small fishing craft, were located congruently on the two boats, except *Penelope* had one longish porthole instead of two round ones close together. And how difficult would it have been to cut out the intervening metal between the two ports with a power hacksaw to make one big one on each side?

"Do you want beer?"

"No."

"Do you want coffee?"

"No."

"Tea?"

"No."

"Me?"

"No."

"Hey what the hell *is* this—"

I felt a sharp kick in my calf.

"Come 'ere, Mary. Look at this."

5

OVERSLEPT THE NEXT MORNING; WAS UP LATE PLAYING chess with Jack, who told me Tony suspected he'd caught the clap. I told Mary, and Jack shot me a look as if we had betrayed his brother. Mary took it in passively. After confronting kidney failure, cardiac arrest, and terminal cancer every working day, gonorrhea was a minor affliction. Her face remained impassive, and beautiful. Dark olive skin, wide-set eyes, arched cheekbones, and mountains of black hair, still no gray at forty-three. Her nose and profile look as if they've been taken off a Roman statue. She cleared her throat.

"Have him call us and describe his symptoms to me or Dad, and then he should have a culture taken at the nearest clinic. Tell your brother he should be more choosy about whom he sleeps with—God knows he's handsome enough to be picky. And tell him to wear a condom too, that way we won't have to worry about pregnancy as well. Clear?"

There was a husky grunt in response from Jack, who said he had no idea she knew so much about it.

"About 'it'? Look, buster, I'm a nurse; I've been married twenty-five years with two sons. Don't tell me about 'it.' "

I suggested we call Tony and extend our sympathy and understanding. We did, and he seemed relieved.

"Thanks, Mom and Dad. And don't worry; it'll never happen again."

"Of course not," said Mary, "and if they give you medication, don't skip any pills; take them all."

Mary decided she'd go over to say good-bye to Sarah Hart, who was leaving for Pasadena. Just after she left I dialed the police station and spoke with Lieutenant Disbrow briefly. He said they were treating Allan Hart's death as accidental. Did I have anything to add or suggest? I said not at the present, but that I was looking for the trawler *Penelope*, and if Disbrow or any of the department saw her, could they let me know?

"Mr. Adams, we cannot do this unless you file a complaint or give us sufficient justification—"

"I understand. OK, forget it."

I called Bill Larson at the shack and told him to keep an eye out. If *Penelope* reappeared, he was to call me at *The Breakers* or up in Concord, *pronto*. This he agreed to. I showed Jack the photographs and told him to do the same if she surfaced in Woods Hole. Then I tried Murdock's boatyard again. The woman answered, her voice slurred and heavy. When I mentioned the word *Penelope* the line went dead.

There was no other avenue to follow. Obviously the only way I was going to make contact with Murdock was to skulk about and sneak up behind him and *grab* him. I just might do that . . .

Meanwhile I had another idea. It was perhaps foolish, but it was something, and the weather looked lousy again. I might as well drive up to Boston.

"Did you tell me you needed a new sportcoat?" I asked Jack.

"Uh huh."

"Come up to Boston with me. We'll leave a note for Mom. I'll take you to Louis's; they've got Harris tweed coats on sale."

"You wanna go *now*?"

"Yes. The sale ends soon. Besides that, I want to go to

Post Office Square. I want to peek inside a post office box. Let's get moving.''

We spun out of the gravel drive as it started to drizzle. I uncorked the vacuum bottle and poured coffee for both of us. When we got into the city we parked in the underground below the Boston Common. At Louis's Jack bought a steel-gray jacket flecked with blue and black. Having been thus bribed he was sent on two errands for me while I walked over to the post office. One errand was to buy some pipe tobacco at Ehrlich's. The other was to visit the Kirstein Business Library just around the corner and find out all he could about Walter Kincaid's Wheel-Lock Corporation.

Nothing in downtown Boston is far away; you can walk across all of it in twenty minutes. In less than ten I was inside the post office, my eyes scanning the ranks of postal boxes. Gee, there were lots and lots of them. Finally, I located 2319, and enjoyed the first piece of good luck I'd had. It was a lower box, barely three feet from the floor. I dropped to one knee and peeked inside. Past the gilded decals of big numbers I could see several envelopes. The one on top was dark navy blue with a white border. The name on the label said Wallace Kinchloe. Well, he wasn't lying about the PO box anyway. The return address on the envelope was interesting though: Queen's Beach Condominiums, Charlotte Amalie, St. Thomas. I took out pad and pen and wrote it down.

There were several other envelopes under this one, including what appeared to be a magazine wrapped in brown paper near the bottom. A *New Yorker*? No, not quite the same. Then I noticed that the second envelope from the top, the one directly beneath the blue one, had its upper edge peeking out. All I could read was the top line of the return address: A.J. Liebnitz and Sons, Ltd. Where it came from I couldn't tell. But I could tell this: the envelope was certainly classy looking. The paper was the thick parchment type with lots of little fibers in it, sort of like the kind in U.S. dollar bills. Also, the name A.J. Liebnitz was embossed as well as printed. It was obviously not your standard junk mail, the kind telling you that Finast has weiners on sale for 79¢ a pack. I wrote down the name A.J. Liebnitz and replaced pad and pen.

Finally, I took note of the date on the postmark on the letter from the Virgin Islands. August 12. Almost a month ago. Wherever Wallace Kinchloe was, he hadn't visited his mail box in quite some time. And the letter on top was the most recent one too. How long had the ones on the bottom of the heap been lying there?

At three o'clock exactly I met Jack at Brookstone's, as arranged. We looked at the fine woodworking and gardening tools from England and Germany, and I bought a big hurricane lamp with a walnut base and big crystal chimney for the porch at the cottage. Mary would love it. Less than two hours later I was sitting in the sauna bath turning over the events and discoveries of the past week. One think kept rising uppermost in my thoughts: whether Allan's death was accidental or not, it was beginning to look more and more suspicious. This only increased my desire to find *Penelope* and her captain. And that boat was proving to be, at each turn of the path, more and more elusive and mysterious.

Later in the week I kept my promise to Mary. After doing two hours of paperwork in the office I walked two doors down the corridor and entered Moe Abramson's office.

Soon I was reclining in a two-thousand-dollar belting leather Eames chair, watching the thirty-gallon aquarium. Two cardinal tetras chased each other from territory to territory. Small iridescent schools of neon tetras and zebra dianos winked about under the fluorescent light. A Mozart concerto hummed and danced in the background. Moe's office was plush indeed. Sitting there, one would never guess that he resided in an ancient Airstream motor home in Walden Breezes Trailer Park. In short, most patients assume that psychiatrist Morris Abramson is sane. In fact he's a nut. He gives almost every penny he makes to one charitable organization or another. He keeps trying to save the world. The last guy who did that got nailed up to two pieces of wood.

He glared up at me.

"So you're feeling better?"

"Much," I answered, noticing a slimy, eellike creature emerge from under a conch shell and slither along the sand on the bottom of the tank. "What the hell is *that*?"

He smiled at the creature. It had no eyes and feathery whiskers around its sucking mouth.

"That's Ruth, my loach."

"Well, Ruth's got a bad case of the uglies—"

"Look, Doc, it relaxes the patients. Gets their minds off themselves just a bit. They find they're so busy staring at the tank they open up more—tell me things they wouldn't ordinarily."

"You should keep a vomit bag taped to the side of the glass for people who have the misfortune to look at that thing too long. It's worse looking than a sand worm."

The slender, bearded man advanced a pawn on the board that sat on the desk made of solid teak with brushed chrome trim.

"Your move, Doc. So you're happier. Ah, you feel better about your job."

"Wrong. As you can see by the damaged arm I'm not currently practicing. Maybe that's why I feel better about it. I've been spending my time tracking down a boat and a man. Both are elusive. Of course it's probably nothing except my overactive imagination and sense of guilt."

Moe sat up straight in his chair and arched his eyebrows at me behind his wire-rims. He stroked the beard.

"But I'll tell you one thing Moe: *it's not boring*."

"So tell me . . ."

"How much will it cost?"

"Plenty."

"Who are you giving it to?"

"The Hadley School for the Blind and the Kidney Foundation."

"Who do you know who's blind?"

"Do I have to personally know someone who's blind to help? *Someone's* got to do it. Why not me?"

"OK," I said, and cleared my throat to begin. Ruth sliggered over to the edge of the tank and smushed her prehistoric snout up against the glass nearest me as if she, too, couldn't wait to hear.

"Cute isn't she? Kind of grows on you, like a wart," said Moe. "So begin already; I haven't got all day!"

6

MARY'S BROTHER, JOE BRINDELLI—DETECTIVE LIEUTEN-
ant Joe Brindelli—appeared at the Concord domicile
promptly at nine-thirty, two days later. He joined us for after-
breakfast coffee.

"Well? Anything?"

"I checked on Walter Kincaid, his wife Laura Armstrong
Kincaid, and the Kincaid Foundation."

"What foundation?"

"The Kincaid Foundation is a small one that was founded
to finance the exploration of various marine archeological
sites for the purpose of recovering quote 'maritime relics of
historical and artistic significance for the museums of New
England' unquote."

"Sounds like a front to finance his private yacht, the *Windhover*."

"Maybe. Certainly he used the foundation and its tax-free
money to finance his trips. And certainly again, we can assume that each and every time he stepped aboard the converted trawler it wasn't all for business. But I did hear from
more than one source that he contributed heavily to many of
the local museums, most especially the Peabody Museum in
Salem and the whaling museum in New Bedford."

"What were these marine relics?"

"You know—parts of old sailing ships, pottery shards, old whiskey bottles, coins, cutlasses, cannons—"

"And he gave it all to the museums?"

"No way of telling that is there? I wouldn't be surprised if he kept a few of the better pieces for his own private collection."

"Jack did a little research on the Wheel-Lock Corporation. They make some kind of rotary lock that is partly mechanical and partly electronic. These are very top-quality, high-ticket items and are mostly used to guard important things like banks, armories, research facilities, and so on. Kincaid patented the basic mechanism of the first lock back in 'fifty-seven."

Joe sipped his coffee, listening. Then he added.

"Kincaid's a New England boy, or was. MIT grad, born in Woburn sixty-two years ago. Hitch in the navy during the war. Married Laura Armstrong in the early forties. No children. Good credit rating—as you might expect—no dirt. Clean. The wife is from a rich family in England, though she was raised here. The Armstrongs immigrated here when she was a kid. Apparently they owned some kind of tile or ceramic factory over there and her mother sold it out after the father died. She's also clean as a whistle. I tell you, Doc, if it's dirt you're after concerning the Kincaids, there doesn't seem to be much of it. If there is—or was—any bad business with them it's an affair of the heart not of the wallet."

I sat and thought a bit.

"Did you get the number?"

"Uh huh, but only because I'm a cop. I don't want you climbing all over her and—"

"No. Don't worry. I'm just wondering how best to approach this thing—"

"I'll give you the number if you promise me you'll explain clearly and quickly to her what's on your mind, and not keep bugging her if she declines to meet you."

"Done. Thanks. Oh, and there's another name for you to check out."

* * *

"Mrs. Kincaid?"

"Who is this? How did you get my number?"

I explained the situation and told her I thought there might be a faint possibility that her husband was not dead.

There was a stony silence at the other end.

"Mrs. Kincaid?"

"I heard you. Now what is this? My husband. My *late* husband, has been missing now for almost two months. It's been hard enough as it is without people claiming they can find him."

"Yes I know. I'm sorry. It's just that I think there's a remote possibility that your husband's boat, the *Windhover*, is still around in a different guise."

Long silence.

"Mrs. Kincaid? Mrs. Ki—"

"What did you say your name was?"

"I am Dr. Charles Adams."

"And you're a doctor?"

"Yes."

"And how did you happen—look, maybe you could come out—just for a few minutes."

I received instructions from her on how to reach the place and departed.

It took me almost an hour to find it. It was on a semiprivate road called Rudderman's Lane and was surrounded by a high whitewashed wall. The house and grounds had the aura of formal French elegance: gravel drive with large turnaround that led to the double garage attached to the house, which had high, steeply sloping slate roofs over tall fan windows. The walls were cut stone with quions and timbers where applicable. Norman French—half a million dollars, perhaps more. Old Man Kincaid had done all right with his lock company, that was for sure.

I got out and walked across the gravel. My footsteps seemed to intrude on the silence as if this were more noise than the place had had in years . . . maybe decades. You can count on a direct correlation between the wealth of a neighborhood and the degree of silence it has. Silence and privacy. If the big wrought iron gates were shut and padlocked, nobody on the outside would ever hope to have the faintest idea of what went on inside number 11 Rudderman's Lane.

I pushed the button at the front door—I had to hunt for it amongst all the ivy—and heard a distant peal of chimes with the same timbre and resonance as the ones at Westminster Abbey. Nothing for a while, then I heard the electronic *pop pop* of an intercom, and noticed the small speaker cleverly hiding in the leaves.

Pop! "Who is it please?" *Pop!*

The voice, a woman's, sounded as it if were coming from inside an oil drum.

"It's Dr. Adams, here to speak with Mrs. Kincaid," I said.

Pop! "I'm around in back on the terrace; come on around through the yard." *Pop!*

I trudged around, walking on a creeping bent lawn, no doubt fastidiously kept up by a dozen or so Latin immigrants. I passed rose gardens, bronze statuettes, a fountain, a small Haiku garden with an enchanting teahouse. Besides money, the Kincaids had taste. The only thing that marred an otherwise flawless lawn was the ugly scar of dirt and newly sprouted grass at the side of the house where a septic tank had been repaired.

"Dr. Adams?"

I saw an attractive woman, late forties I would guess, rise off a redwood lounger and stroll toward me over the flagstones. The terrace was surrounded by a tightly trimmed hedge, and I entered through a trellis-topped gap in it to shake her hand. She was silver-haired, dressed in slacks and cotton-canvas blouse, with a nautical type rope belt and navy blue Topsiders. Rich causal. She'd been doing some gardening, she told me, and I could see the trowels and flats laid out on the side of the terrace.

"You have a lovely house here, Mrs. Kincaid. I see you have the same problem here we do in Concord. A new leaching field?"

She looked over in the direction of the recent excavation.

"No. Here in Manchester we have sewerage systems. Walter—my husband—had that big oil tank put in early in the summer. It's huge. I think it holds 5000 gallons or something. He always knew how to get the most for his money. Also, you may call me Laura, Doctor. You seem to be quite a gentleman compared to the police and reporters I've been shunning these past few weeks. I'm going in to get some iced tea, do you want some?''

She came back with the tea and we sat down. She was a good looking woman, fit and trim with a pretty face that was kept moisturized and tight by beauty treatments and preparations available to women with money. Then, as she turned her head away from me to set her drink down, I saw the tiny pale-pink dot under her jaw. I saw it only because she tilted her head up and around, and because her deep tan made the minute scar all the more visible. Mostly, I saw it because I make my living with jaws and faces, and what's inside them. Face lift. Jaw tuck. Nice job. Probably eight to ten grand worth of a master surgeon's time.

She turned to me and ran her palms down her thighs, stretching out her arms idly. Underneath her cordiality was a regal coolness, an air of impatience and condescension that I found annoying. However, I tried to see the situation from her perspective, and immediately I understood.

"Now Doctor, you say that you may be of some help in locating my husband . . . what exactly do you mean by that? I mean, it's pretty well assumed that Walter is dead.''

"First of all, Mrs. Kincaid—uh, Laura—you should understand that my thoughts are pure conjecture. This could very well be a fool's errand; you can discount all of what I'm going to say. The only reason I'm at all curious is because of the death of a young man, which I feel partially responsible for.''

She squirmed slightly on the lounge and squinted at me.

"Okay. A week ago I saw a boat grounded on Billingsgate Shoal, just off my cottage in North Eastham. It was a green trawler named *Penelope*, which stopped briefly in Wellfleet Harbor after the tide rose, and has not been seen since. Now what is odd is the fact that the boat I saw was quite similar to your husband's boat, the *Windhover*. Moreover, there is little previous history of the boat I saw . . . the *Penelope*.

She grabbed her glass, and I could see her hand was shaking. It was also covered with age spots. I placed her age closer to fifty-five.

"What are you trying to say, and what are you implying?"

"I don't *know*, that's the point I guess. What does it all mean?"

She let out a slow sigh and looked at the sky with a resigned expression.

"Doctor Adams, I don't know what you're trying to do to me, but this past month has been hard enough—"

"I'm sorry—"

"—without your raising false hopes about Walter's survival. Let me tell you quickly what happened. Then, when I've explained it, I trust that will be the end of the matter, OK?"

I nodded.

"My husband has been interested in marine archaeology for some time . . . say, the past eight years or so. He retired early from daily work at Kincaid Industries, although he was still chairman of the board and chief executive officer of Wheel-Lock. The daily tending of the business is in the hands of the current president. Anyway, he spent more and more time searching for marine relics along the New England coast. He bought an old coastal trawler and had it completely refitted with all kinds of electronic metal detecting equipment. Since he gave most of what he found to museums and the National Trust for Historic Preservation, he was able to finance the entire operation through a nonprofit foundation designed especially for this pastime. The foundation, and the searches, were entirely legitimate, of *that* you may be sure."

She slapped her hands down on her knees to emphasize the point. I nodded again, and sipped the tea.

"Almost seven weeks ago he left Gloucester Harbor on an expedition. He said he was going to take *Windhover* to Provincetown for a few days, then on around the outer shore, stopping at Chatham before going on to Nantucket and the Vineyard. He called in every three or four nights, either by telephone if he were in port, or by the ship-to-shore radio. When ten days went by with no word, I knew something was wrong and called the Coast Guard. They searched all over the Cape and the Islands for over three weeks. Nothing.''

''I'm sorry. What do you think happened?''

She shrugged her shoulders.

''The only thing I can think of is that the *Windhover* struck a ledge somewhere. Walter spent most of his time around old wrecks, or places where wrecks might be. These were almost always reefs or ledges—places where a boat can get into trouble. I don't think they got lost . . . that'd be impossible with all the loran, radar, and whatnot on board. I think the *Windhover* went down, either by hitting a ledge or another boat.''

''And you don't think it's possible that your husband, or anyone else for that matter, would deliberately disguise the boat as another in order to disappear, for whatever reason?''

Her jaw had set firm, her eyes bugged out a bit at me. She blinked rapidly and turned her head away.

''No. I think the idea is absurd.''

''Thank you. I guess I'll drop the whole idea then. By the way, who usually went on these expeditions with your husband?''

There was a momentary pause as she looked at her hands, then her nails. She was thinking of something.

She looked annoyed; she grabbed her glass and bit at it impatiently.

''I might as well tell you, Dr. Adams, since you'll find out anyway if you're curious enough—after all, it's hardly a secret—''

''I don't really want to pry.''

''Oh of *course* you don't, dear—'' She gave me a cute smile that cut clear through me. Underneath the patina of super-rich suburban housewife, Mrs. Walter Kincaid was tough as nails.

''Jennifer might have been along too. I'm not positively sure, but I'd bet on it.''

''Really? I didn't bring the *Globe*'s account with me and haven't laid eyes on it in several days, but I don't recall a woman's name mentioned.''

''*Girl's* name, dear—she was no woman, just a girl. No,

you're right. You won't come across an official listing of her name anywhere, Dr. Adams, because even her mother and father—wherever they are—have no idea of her whereabouts. But as I said, it's certainly no secret that she was Walter's girlfriend.''

''I see. Uhhh. Well . . . and you think she would have been aboard *Windhover* when she left Gloucester?''

Laura Kincaid stared steadily at me, as if passing final judgment on the matter. Then she spoke.

''That's interesting. Because I think the chances are pretty good that she *wasn't*. The *Globe*'s people are pretty thorough. They pump their sources pretty dry—leave no stone unturned, especially in a dramatic story like this one. I don't think she was aboard when the *Windhover* left Gloucester. I imagine only Walter was aboard. But she could have joined him somewhere else. Provincetown, Boston, even Rockport or Ipswich Bay. Walter believed in keeping up appearances. He wanted the appearance of propriety if not the real thing. Excuse me—''

She was interrupted by a beeping sound, of the electronic variety, which emanated from a small box on her cocktail table. A tiny red light was flashing in sync with the beeps. I had noticed the small contraption earlier, but had assumed it was a transistor radio. She turned quickly in the chair and clicked it off.

''Wait. I think it's the maid. Can you wait here? I'll check—''

And she hurried into the house. As soon as she disappeared inside I walked over and peered down at the contraption. It was as big as a small cigar box, and had a speaker-microphone screen and a button bar that said ''press to talk'' underneath it. No doubt this was how she had burbled at me upon my arrival. Under the sensor light that had been blinking I saw the words *door open*. There was also another light, a big red one the size of a quarter. Under it were the words *emergency: system breached*. Finally, there were two small yellow indicator lights labeled *front door* and *back door*. These were no doubt set off by the doorbell. Someone had opened the front door however, evidently without ringing. I returned to my chair and waited. The handy gadget was cordless and could be taken anywhere in or about the house. It was an intercom system and burglar alarm all in one. It made sense for a family like the Kincaids. In a trifle, she was back in her chair, explaining that the maid had stopped by to collect a coat she left behind.

"Now where were we?"

"Discussing whether or not the girl was aboard the *Windhover*."

"Ah yes, sweet Jennifer. Actually, maybe she *is* sweet; I never met her. They were always off galavanting over the waves together in search of buried treasure."

"Buried treasure?"

"Certainly. Or didn't you know, Doctor? Why that's the *real* reason for the *Windhover*. Walter wanted to strike it rich—by uncovering lost pirate gold. Of course it was probably an escapist dream . . . a hobby more than anything, but nevertheless that's what lay behind it all: buried treasure."

"How did he ever expect to find any treasure around New England?"

"Oh there's lots of it. *Tons* of it—so I'm told."

"Really? I thought it was all buried down in the Caribbean—"

"Oh no. Take a walk inside with me and I'll show you Walter's study. On the way I'll tell you how he got bitten by the gold bug."

We strolled up the flagstones to the back door. The kitchen was what you'd expect: huge, with work island in middle. Ceiling racks dripping with copper pans. Microwave ovens, floor-to-ceiling refrigerator-freezers, walk-in cold storage— the works. The glimpse I was allowed of the house set me reeling. I wasn't offered a tour because Laura was accustomed to her wealth and no longer impressed by it, and assumed others wouldn't be. One can always tell older money by the fact that those who have it wear it graciously, even casually, like an old cashmere sportcoat. We went upstairs and wended our way to the end of the house where a separate wing sprouted from it like an oversized limb. We opened double doors and stepped down into the two-room suite. I realized then we were above the double garage, in the old live-in maid's quarters.

"I assume that your maid doesn't live in, but shows up several times a week?"

"What? Oh, yes. Walter took over this set of rooms for his private retreat. During the past eight years, he seldom left it except to eat and work. He even slept here; the next room has a bed and bath."

The room was paneled in dark walnut, with beams on the ceiling. A magnificent burled oak desk dominated the center of the room, which was lined with built-in bookcases. Every man's dream of the perfect study. What struck me immediately, though, was the nautical air of the place. Ship models in glass cases topped the bookcases. Prints of clipper ships lined the walls. I noticed one that was in my study as well: Montague Dawson's picture of *Thermopolae Leaving Foochow*. There were charts of Cape Ann, charts of the Cape and the Islands, charts of Boston Harbor. I noticed the photographs too. Most of them showed a gray-haired gentleman aboard a boat. Sometimes at the wheel, sometimes hunched over a chart. One showed him in a wetsuit, hair dripping over his forehead, triumphantly holding up a gold coin.

Laura stopped before this last picture.

"That's Walter—that *was* Walter—as you may have guessed. That picture was taken in nineteen seventy-one when he made his first find."

"What is it, a doubloon?"

She bent forward, squinting at the picture closely.

"That or a piece of eight, or *something* . . . anyway, he found a small cache of them off P-town in 'seventy-one, and from that time on thought about almost nothing else. Except Jennifer and the other beach girls."

"I take it, Laura, from the tone of your voice and what you've said, that you and Walter weren't particularly close during the last ten years or so."

"That's putting it mildly, Doctor. I'm being open about it because you'd discover it anyway if you asked enough people."

She ambled over to the leather easy chair with an air of resignation and flopped down into it.

"We weren't enemies you understand. We didn't fight. To fight takes emotion—stress and strain. When the emotion is gone, then there is only a void. A peaceful, blank *void*. He went his way and I went mine. He went treasure hunting on his boat and I played tennis. He had his friends and I have mine."

She looked up quickly into my eyes during this last remark. I could read between the lines, and let it pass. It was a clear blueprint, a perfect scenario down to the last detail, of what so often happens during a marriage in the late-middle years, especially when there's adequate money—or even more often when there's too much money; a growing apart. No fights, no divorce. No separation or settlement. Just two roughly parallel lives lived out under the same roof, each with its own concerns, hobbies, and lovers.

"I see," I said finally. "And now that Walter is probably dead, will you keep this house?"

She gave me a shrewd grin.

"If that's your way of asking me the terms of Walter's will, it's a very clever one."

I gave a short laugh—a genuine one. That wasn't my intention; I was merely curious. But clearly Laura Kincaid had been questioned a good deal during the past weeks by reporters and police detectives. She was learning to spot the leading question immediately.

"Let me put it this way, Doctor Adams: Walter left me sitting pretty. He was incredibly successful you know; everything he touched turned to gold. I may keep the house; I may sell it. But whatever happens, life will sweep on as usual for me. This whole thing has left hardly a dent in my life, Doctor, one way or another. I was born rich, married a rich man who got richer, and I will die rich. We had no children. The man I married grew apart from me in recent years, and now appears to be dead. So that just makes it *official*, I guess, that's all. So here I am, same as always."

She slapped her hands down on her thighs, as if to say: *That's that.* She was crying silently. The lady who had everything had nothing. I had seen that so often among the rich. Laura Kincaid certainly wasn't alone, although that would hardly have been a comfort to her as she sat in the plush chair blinking away the tears.

"I'm sorry," I said, and patted her shoulder.

"Oh hell!" she cried, jumping up and wiping her eyes. "I'm not crying because I'm hurt or because I'm sad, I'm crying because it's so goddamn empty and *boring*."

"I know. Listen, you should get away. Take a trip somewhere. What's your favorite country?"

"Italy."

"Then go."

She sighed, and agreed that maybe I was right.

"Laura, I want to ask you one more question, please. If we for a second assume that your husband's death or disappearance was not accidental, can you tell me if there is *anyone* who'd want him dead?"

She thought for thirty or forty seconds—longer than I expected her to—before answering that she didn't think so.

As we were leaving the study, I noticed a photograph on the wall near the door. I had walked past it upon entering. It was an aerial view of an island. Next to it was a drawing of a cutaway view of what looked like a mine shaft. I squinted at the drawing. At various places along the shaft (which was vertical) were penciled-in remarks: "100 feet, stone tablet with inscription. 120 feet, oaken platform. 150 feet, rock layer," etc.

"What's this?"

"That is the great treasure at Oak Island, Nova Scotia."

"Oh yes, I've heard of it. Isn't the greatest treasure of all time buried there?"

"Yes, they think so. But so far, they can't get it out. Every year people die trying. Walter was convinced that the Cape held a similar treasure, and he eventually became obsessed with finding it. Why don't you join me for a drink on the porch, and I'll tell you about it."

I declined the drink but accepted the invitation.

We sat in the wide screened porch for twenty more minutes. I gazed out over the vast expanse of green. The interior was festooned with lush hanging plants. Laura Kincaid spoke a little more about her husband's obsession with golden pirate treasure.

"But he never really found it? The big haul?"

"Nope. He never did. But he sure enjoyed himself looking for it."

"And you say the *Windhover* was equipped with all kinds of electronic gear to help him locate it?"

"Oh God yes. Everything that a yachtsman could buy and install, he did. That boat could find her way in and out of a hurricane probably. That's the reason he selected an old trawler too; he claimed the hull was more seaworthy. And now let me ask *you* some questions."

"Fine."

"What happened to your hand?"

"A kid hit me with his moped and broke it. One of the reasons I have time on my hands is because of it. Should be OK in a few weeks though."

"Second question: why did you come here? What do you think happened to my husband?"

"Well. I don't know. For a while I suspected he was still alive. But after this visit I'm pretty convinced that your suspicion is true. A boat that strikes a ledge—especially at speed—goes down like brick. If that happened, he wouldn't have had time to call for help."

"You mentioned another boat you saw. What was its name?"

"*Penelope.*"

She sighed a slow, deliberate, and irritable sigh. "I don't know how many draggers there are on Cape Cod or in New England, but there must be quite a few. I'm sure some of them look alike. They all look alike to me. I think it's strange though, that you're so interested."

"A young man, a friend of the family's, was killed near the boat. I guess I'm a bit more than curious."

She stared at me, tightlipped, for several seconds. Then she lowered her head and grabbed her hands together.

"I don't feel well. I'm afraid there's nothing more I can tell you."

I thanked her and left. I went back out through the tall gates and over to the car.

Laura Kincaid certainly matched the background Joe had given me. Rich, well-bred, and frank, she had given me much more information about Kincaid and the *Windhover* than I'd had a right to expect. Her explanations laid to rest any doubts I'd had about the Kincaid family. If there was anything amiss with the boat *Penelope*, it had nothing to do with *Windhover*; their similarities were coincidental and, considering the basic design of the coastal bay trawler, not even noteworthy. And also, none of the men I had glimpsed aboard the green boat looked even remotely like the man in the study photographs. So much for that.

I started the engine and checked the side-view mirror. Then the rear-view. There was a car parked about a hundred feet behind me with a pair of big feet sticking out from underneath.

I purred down Rudderman's Lane and headed for home.

Mary was annoyed that I was late, and said she was getting a wee bit tired of my going around to these widows and comforting them. I mixed her a soothing bourbon and soda and we retired to the porch, where I told her the story of Oak Island that Laura had told me.

"What do you think's down there?" asked Mary.

"There are various theories. One: the Holy Grail is buried there. No doubt Billy Graham and Oral Roberts believe this. Two: the treasure of Charlemagne and the Frankish kings is buried there. Who knows? All I know is that New England was a pirate hideout. I never knew that before."

"Time to eat, Charlie. Flounder fillets with lobster sauce."

"Oh honey, you *should* have."

But during the meal I stopped eating twice.

"What's wrong?"

"This goddamn boat thing is like a boomerang. Every time I throw it away it comes back at me again. Take today for instance. Laura Kincaid's explanation for everything made so much sense I was convinced that following the Kincaid boat was senseless. But now two things are bugging me.

They're not big things mind you, but they're enough to keep the old curved stick winging back in my direction—''

"Well what things?"

"One: how many people on Old Stone Mill Road have you ever seen working under their cars on the street?"

She thought a minute.

"I've never seen anyone working on their cars here."

"Right. And there are two good reasons why. One: people who live on our road are rich enough to hire mechanics to work on their cars. Two: if by chance some car buff in this neighborhood did want to fiddle with his engine, where would he do it?"

"In his garage or the driveway."

"Exactly. And if this road is well-to-do, Rudderman's Lane is two or three times that. Yet today I saw a guy working on his car in the street there. Doesn't make sense. Like so many events and things of the past week, it just doesn't *fit*."

"What's the other thing?"

"Laura Kincaid's maid."

"Oh it's *Laura* now is it? My, my, Charlie, you do get acquainted with the women fast don't you?"

"C'mon. Anyway, the maid opened the door while we were in the back yard. That's a little strange I guess. But then Laura said she was retrieving a coat. A *coat*? It's late summer. Why would a maid leave an overcoat, much less want one, *now*?"

"Who knows? Eat your fish."

So I returned to the meal and had thrown away the damn worry stick again when the phone rang. It was Joe.

"You know that name you asked me to check on? Wallace Kinchloe?"

"Yeah."

"Uh, born in Danbury, Connecticut . . . lived in Cohasset?"

"Right. Ah, so you found him. Does he own a boat?"

"Uh, couldn't find that out . . ."

"Oh. Well where can I reach him then?"

"Can't."

"Well why not?"

"Because he's dead. He died in Boise, Idaho, a year ago."

"Oh," I said, and watched the damn stick turn and come back, flickering bigger and bigger.

7

NEXT DAY I WENT TO VISIT THE WHEEL-LOCK CORPORATION in Melrose. It was unseasonably cool so I went dressed with turtleneck, khaki pants, old Harris tweed herringbone sport-coat with leather patches on the elbows, an Irish tweed hat, and rough-out Wallabee shoes. I was smoking a Barling pipe. I was so goddamn literary I looked like I just walked off a dust jacket. I went in and told the receptionist I was starting a small biweekly rag in Concord, and for the first issue wanted to sink my teeth into a really "super" human interest story. As she went to fetch one of the senior secretaries, I looked around. Wheel-Lock had its own building, all done up nice in fieldstone, rough cast brick, and smoked glass. The building was small, and connected to the factory in back. The rough cast brick was a mixture of buff tan and cool gray. The carpeting was a rich chocolate brown with flecks of tan and gray. Abstract oil paintings in bright colors adorned the walls. The place had a rich but muted look. It was not gaudy or glittery, and I thought back to the Kincaid residence at 11 Rudderman's Lane. I had to admit the old boy had excellent taste. I found myself liking him—wishing somehow I could have met him.

On a low table was a pamphlet describing the Wheel-Lock Corporation and its products. On the wall was a copy of an old blueprint of the basic mechanism of the lock and the U.S.

Patent number. Inside the lock housing was a round wheel that resembled a cipher rotor. Somehow this device interacted with a bank of electrical circuitry, then reconnected with a fancy geared mechanism that drove a thick bolt of steel. In a glass display case were some recent models of the locks. They were considerably smaller, the result no doubt of solid-state circuitry. The locks were impressive, with thick case-hardened steel and brass and nickel fittings. I strolled around the lobby and saw photographs of various locks being installed. One was on a bank door in Kansas. Another was at some army base. There was a framed copy of the army government contract next to the picture. Though they obviously came in all shapes and sizes I gathered that the Wheel-Lock was basically a super version of the combination lock. It seemed a better mousetrap, and Walter Kincaid had reaped a fortune from it.

"Yes, may I help you?" said the prim fortyish lady with wide goggle glasses and a Diane Von Furstenberg dress. I explained my mission, and she seated us in the corner on a L-shaped couch with a massive cultured marble table. Above us was a gigantic Japanese lantern four feet in diameter, a sphere of paper and wire that was elegant in its simplicity.

"Now Mr. Adams, you're doing a story on Mr. Kincaid for *which* newspaper?"

"Uh, I know you'll think it's corny, but I've named it the *Colonial Gazette*, if you can believe it."

She looked at me quizzically. Obviously, I looked increasingly less and less literary to her.

"I . . . see . . ."

"Excuse me, may I have your name please? I'll mention you in the article."

"Mmmm. Mrs. Haskell. Doris Haskell. It doesn't matter if you mention me or not. Also, the papers have given very thorough coverage to Mr. Kincaid's—"

"Oh I know, Mrs. Haskell, but I don't want that stuff in the *Gazette*. The idea is to give a lot of *personal* background . . . you know, how he founded the company . . . perhaps some of the rough times early on . . . that sort of thing."

"Oh I can give you a pamphlet that will tell about Wheel-Lock's early days—"

"I'd appreciate it. But isn't there anything else you can tell me about? Something that's not written down anywhere? I mean you know as well as I do that the really *interesting* stuff—the personal, human interest stuff—is never 'official' information."

"If you are asking me to reveal some dirt or gossip about Mr. Kincaid, or some skeleton in his closet, you are out of luck on two counts, Mr. Adams. First of all, there is no information of this kind—at least that I know of, and I have worked here twelve years—Mr. Kincaid was a very upright man. Second, even if I knew of rumors about him I would, for obvious reasons, never divulge them."

"Oh no, I wouldn't expect you to. I'm not after that kind of scandal-sheet stuff. Tell me, is there anyone you know of who would want to kill Walter Kincaid?"

She was clearly taken back by the suggestion.

"What? I cannot imagine anyone who would be less a candidate for murder."

"So you knew him well?"

"As well as any of the older staff. You think he's been killed?"

"Not sure. Do you think he's alive?"

She sighed a bit and looked down at her hands.

"No I don't. Mr. Kincaid always kept in close touch with the office even though he was no longer directly involved with the day-to-day operations. He wouldn't have gone off for over a week without telling us. Something's happened to him—I'm sure of it—*but don't you quote me*! I'll deny ever having said it; the official corporate line is that we're not giving up hope."

"And you know of nobody who hated Walter Kincaid?"

"The only man—the only man who ever hated him is dead."

"And who was that?"

"He was Jim Schilling, a former vice president of Wheel-Lock. Mr. Kincaid promoted him up the executive ladder from a salesman. He had an incredible amount of energy and he was a terrific salesman. You know, good-looking . . . smooth. He was a real macho type too. Loved to hunt and fish. He was in terrific shape all the time. You know the kind.''

''Uh huh.''

''I think Jim Schilling was jogging ten years before the fad hit, you know?''

''Yeah. What happened between them then? They were good friends, right?''

''Oh yes. They were almost like brothers for years. They went fishing together lots at first. Then something—I don't know what it was—happened. Some think Mr. Kincaid began to fear Jim—you know, began to get the feeling that Jim was going to try to take over the company or something. They began to argue about different company policies, advertising campaigns—things like that. Jim started saying Mr. Kincaid was losing touch with the marketing end of the business—that he was too old. Mr. Kincaid found out about it and fired him. It was rumored around here that he regretted the decision almost as soon as he made it. But Mr. Kincaid was pretty stubborn, and wouldn't change his mind. Jim moved out to California right after that, and was killed the following year.''

''How was he killed?''

''They think he drowned.''

''They *think*?''

''Uh huh. You see it was on a hunting trip. Jim went to Alaska to hunt polar bears. No wait. It wasn't polar bears—another kind.''

''Alaskan brown bear?''

''Right! Hey how'd you know? Do you hunt?''

''Just birds occasionally. But I love to study wildlife. So Jim Schilling went to Alaska to hunt the brown bears. And then?''

''Well—let's see if I can remember, it was almost a year ago—they flew to a certain special place in Alaska in a small plane.''

''The Kenai Peninsula perhaps?''

''Hey, that's right again! How did you know?''

"Because the Kenai Peninsula is famous for big bears. The only place more famous is Kodiak Island. So who did he fly there with?"

"A pilot. A bush pilot—I guess that's the expression, right?"

"Yes. And the plane crashed?"

"Oh no. They landed all right and loaded up a boat with their gear, and went poking along the shoreline of that peninsula looking for bear. According to the story, Jim and the guide split up and Jim took the boat alone. They were going to meet at sundown or something, each one looking for bear that they could stalk—is that the right word, *stalk*?—the next day . . ."

"He was with the pilot? That's odd . . ."

"Huh? Oh I don't' think so, Mr. Adams. I think the pilot just dropped him off. I think the guide was an Eskimo or something. Anyway sundown came and went, and no Jim. The next day the guide went walking up the coast looking for him, and he found the boat, half sunk, washed up against a fallen tree in the water. No sign of Jim. He looked for the rest of the day—even built a smoke-signal fire and shot his gun and everything. Nothing."

"Hmmmmm. Too bad. Did he have a wife?"

"Yes. And two kids too."

"And they never found a trace?"

"Nothing. And of course even Mr. Kincaid said it would be unlikely that they would ever find the body. You know, with all the bears and wolves and things—"

"True. They'd make short work of any meat lying around."

"So that's the end of the only person I can think of who wasn't fond of Mr. Kincaid."

"Thank you very much, Mrs. Haskell. Oh, where did Mr. Schilling live in California, do you remember?"

"Yes I do. It wasn't that long ago. He lived in Newport Beach. When he lived here, he lived in Marblehead. He loved the water just like Mr. Kincaid. He was never far from it. I think he had a cabin cruiser there too, for deep-sea fishing."

"Ah yes. And he drowned. It's kind of ironic isn't it?"

She thought a minute, then answered that the more a man was on the water, perhaps the greater the chance, in the long run, of his drowning. I had to admit there was logic to what she said.

"Well, was there a storm or anything? Any signs of violence?" Something was beginning to tug at the back of my brain and I wasn't sure what it was . . .

"No—you mean up on the bear hunt?—no. They think he must have lost his balance and fallen overboard, then hit his head somehow. The shore's very rocky up there I've heard, you know, 'boulder strewn' like it is here."

"Was any of his gear found? His rifle?"

"You know, I don't remember."

"Sure. It was a while ago. Uh, when exactly was it—do you think you could pin it down a bit?"

She recollected that it was just before the holidays—between Thanksgiving and Christmastime 1978. Since it was now September 1979, that meant Jim Schilling had died about a year ago. I asked Ms. Haskell if she'd seen any newspaper account of Schilling's disappearance. She replied that she hadn't, that to her knowledge it wasn't even carried in New England papers. And of course since he had been forced out of Wheel-Lock any open talk and speculation about the incident was discouraged—if not absolutely verboten—by Walter Kincaid.

After another ten minutes of chitchat with Ms. Haskell, during which time I was presented with a brochure describing the facilities, products, and policies of the Wheel-Lock Corporation, I left.

After an hour's discussion, Mary and I figured out a way to sneak up on Mrs. Walter Kincaid.

"It's got to be a name she can't remember later and check up on," I said.

"How about people names—you know, like Smith and Jones?"

"That's good. That's the right track. Let's think up names that'll be impossible to remember."

In ten more minutes, we were ready. Mary dialed the number and I listened in on the extension phone.

Laura Kincaid picked up the phone after three rings. I felt just a tad sneaky doing this, especially after her gracious hospitality and frankness. But there was something gnawing at me I had to find out.

"Hello?"

"Hello, Mrs. Kincaid?"

"Yes. Who's this?"

"Just take a second, Mrs. Kincaid. Trelawney and Hoopes cleaners calling from Boston—you know the *uniform* people? Listen we've got your three maid's uniforms here and they've been ready for two weeks now and we're wondering when you can have them picked up or we can deliver them to your house but we've found nobody home so I don't know what—"

"*Who* is this?" Laura Kincaid finally managed to break in—but Mary, as planned, rattled right along without even slowing down.

"Er, hello? Yes, Mrs. Kincaid, the uniform people from Boston and we have your maid's *uniforms* here—"

"You're mistaken, I don't have a maid—"

"Beg pardon. Mrs. Kincaid? Well you must have gotten rid of her, right? Because we've got these *three uniforms*—you know the black rayon complete with *cap* just like you always ordered and we—"

"I'm *sorry*!" snapped Laura Kincaid irritably. "Now I told you I do not *have* a maid! I have *never* had one! Is that *clear*?"

"Sorry ma'am, you're not Mrs. Kincaid?"

"Yes, but I do *not*—"

"Mrs. Robert Kincaid, 309 Bullfinch—"

"No. No, you have the *wrong* Kincaid. Good-bye!"

And a quick ring off, almost a slam.

I went in and told Mary she was perfection. Of course Laura could always look up cleaners, or uniforms, in the Yellow Pages and see there was no Trelawney and Hoopes, but we'd hoped that the name would slip from her mind in the interim or, even more likely, she would assume it was a routine foul-up and pay it no further notice.

"So no maid, Mary. I thought as much. Then who—pray, tell me—was that person who opened the front door while Laura Kincaid and I were yakking on the terrace out back, hmmmm?"

"A good question, Charlie. It seems to me that the Kincaid household is fairly well secured. Intercoms and all. Exclusive area. It seems they value their property and privacy and go to great lengths to protect both. It certainly was not a casual stroller. I think she has a boyfriend."

"I agree. It's not a maid. It wouldn't be a lady friend. Why would she give the front door key to a friend? No, it's somebody she's intimate with. Someone she trusts even with the front door key. Yes, a boyfriend. But then why didn't she introduce him to me?"

"Because maybe it's none of your goddamn business."

I had to admit Mary had a point.

"From what you told me earlier, it doesn't seem that her marriage was that hot. Why not have a boyfriend? And now that her husband's dead, why not live with him?"

I nodded.

"But then why—since she was open with me about her so-so marriage—wouldn't she tell me about him?"

"Because maybe it's none of your goddamn business."

8

I SAT ON THE PORCH AND SMOKED AND THOUGHT. I HAD THE strange feeling that every line of questioning and research I undertook had a curious wrinkle in it—a strange bend in the stream that was totally unexpected and hard to explain. "Curiouser and curiouser," as the British are fond of saying. I considered doing a bit of further research on Mr. James Schilling. Something that Ms. Haskell told me was knocking around in the old gray matter and wouldn't leave . . .

I thought about it off and on for almost an hour, then decided to go ahead with it, even knowing that it might possibly upset poor Sarah Hart again, just as she might be starting to recover. But she was so perfectly situated in Pasadena. I called her for a chat to see which way the wind was blowing. If she seemed at all upset I wouldn't push it.

She was not upset so much as resigned and bitter—even vengeful. I told her what I wanted her to do and she instantly agreed.

"Doc, is this what you call a lead?"

"Probably not, Sarah. I just want to check it out is all. The best paper would be the *Los Angeles Times*. Schilling died sometime around November or December of 'seventy-eight. If you find anything, would you mind photocopying the article and mailing it to me? If the newspapers are on microfilm you'll have to get assistance from the librarian . . ."

She agreed and said she'd have it in the mail the next day.

Mary and I were due to return to *The Breakers* on Thursday evening. It was now past Labor Day, and the Cape would begin to settle down a bit. The traffic on Route 28 would only be terrible not horrendous. Late September/early October is far and away the best time on Cape Cod. The tourists are (mostly) gone, the water is still warm, the bluefish are beginning to liven up, and the colors of the foliage are beginning to change. So I couldn't wait.

But on Thursday morning I got a call at the office from my old friend Jim DeGroot, the semiretired real estate developer. He owns *Whimsea*, a thirty-foot Lyman cruiser that he keeps moored up in Gloucester. He was calling to inform me that the bluefish were rushing the season a bit; people were tying into them off Rockport and Halibut Point. The day before some lucky lass had snared *twelve* of them.

"Twelve?" I asked incredulously.

"Twelve. The paper said it was her first time fishing, ever."

"Ah. Beginner's luck. I have a patient at three, but it's only to remove stitches from a third molar extraction. I can get out of here before four, and meet you at the marina shortly after five."

Jim had also invited Tom Costello, a stockbroker friend of his I'd met several times before. The three of us sat up on the flying bridge as we left Cape Ann Marina northward up the Annisquam River and entered Ipswich Bay. *Whimsea* rocked and swayed beneath us in the big water, and her motion was exaggerated by our high perch. We sipped beer and took in the ocean. The tide was turning—coming in—which would bring the blues with it. The horizon was invisible in the haze, and boats of all sizes dotted the water. The air was cool, as it always is on the ocean even in midsummer, but as fall approaches, the cold intensifies, especially in the evening. As we rounded the tip of Cape Ann and began to head south, I hopped down and began to rig the big hooks with squid and mullet. We fished the Rockport breakwater for a while. No luck. Not even a hit. We crawled by trolling, watching lobstermen hauling up their traps. I thought again of the *Windhover* and, as I sat in the chair looking over the stern at the wake that churned and hissed behind us, told Tom about my visits to the Kincaid home and his corporation. He seemed interested. In between fiddling with his reel and tackle box, he asked me questions relating to Walter Kincaid.

"I'm kind of interested," he said, "because his company, Wheel-Lock, is about to go into receivership."

I was stunned. "*Why*," I asked, "when the company even supports a foundation? Besides, I have just been to the headquarters, and it *reeks* of affluence."

"Well it's a funny thing, Doc . . . sometimes the companies that appear to be doing best are actually on the skids. Now take Wheel-Lock. Five years ago, maybe six, it was doing very well. Privately owned. Nice profitability. A lot of Kincaid's business was with the government, supplying them with locks and security systems for military installations, arsenals, armories, bureau offices, and such. But then the contracts ran out—or at least diminished considerably as the Vietnam thing dwindled—and profits shrank. The foundation I know about, but hell, it's tiny. It's just a tax write-off, nothing more . . ."

"What's going to happen to Wheel-Lock now that the founder and owner is dead?"

As we talked, we reeled in the lines and switched to Rapala and Rebel plugs, put a strip of squid on the rear treble hooks and let them out again. We had Jim rev up a wee bit so the lipped plugs would wiggle and dance in the wake.

Tom Costello shrugged his shoulders and gave his Penn reel a few cranks. He sipped his beer and put it down.

"Dunno. I don't know of the arrangements he would have made in the event of his death. Surely he made *some* . . ."

"And you say the corporation is privately owned, or by a limited number of shareholders?"

"Right. I don't know how many but I can check. Anyway, rumor has it that when the board meets next they're going to file for bankruptcy unless some giant conglomerate will bail them out and take Wheel-Lock under its wings. But it's a little company. Only loose change, you understand? The only reason a bunch of us were talking about it is because of the story of Kincaid's death.''

"Tom, if Kincaid saw his company was going under, would feigning his death make sense?''

"Not usually, unless he had some hidden angle. The best thing to check would be corporate cash flow. Was any large sum drawn from company funds—for *any* stated purpose— within the last few months or so that looks suspicious? If so, your theory could hold some water. I think though that—*hey*! wait—oh shit, I thought—hey, there it is *again*!''

He flipped his rod backward over his head hard, reeled in fast and furiously as he lowered the tip again, then yanked back again, setting the hook. I saw his rod tip tremble.

DeGroot looked back and cut speed a tiny bit. When the fish headed in, he'd turn the boat slightly to follow it. But there wasn't much to do really but wait and watch Tom work the fish. The blue made three runs before Tom had it up alongside, and we gaffed it. Eleven pounds. A keeper, but nothing spectacular.

But ten minutes later Jim tied into one from the bridge, and I went up to man the wheel while he cranked it in. Nine pounds. We searched some more, and came up with nothing. Moving over to Halibut Point, Jim and I hooked two at once and Tom had to mind the helm. Then Tom came down and he and I tied into two more. They were running a little bigger, between twelve and fourteen pounds. As we hauled them in over the side they flip-flopped and slid all over the cockpit, trailing slime and thin bright streaks of blood. The blood is hell to clean up, and Jim, a true Dutchman, is fastidious. I grabbed the nearest blue and whapped him smartly on the top of the head with the billy. Nothing. He continued to flip and work his mean jaws at me. *Whap!* Nothing. *Whap!*

"Jesus Christ!''

"Hardheaded little devils aren't they?''

I whapped him twice more hard and he went limp. I plopped him in the well and went after the others. The blue-fish is shaped like a torpedo, black and silver with shades of blue. They say the blue can see well out of water, and go for you. I believe it. Their heads are pointy, with a lot of mouth that's long, but not wide like a bass's mouth. You see a *lot* of teeth. Their heads are solid bone and thick carapace. A few minutes later we had all the stunned monsters in the well. After a while, a few of them came to and commenced flipping around again. I killed them the same way I killed the lobsters, a quick thrust of knifeblade downward behind the head.

"You say look for suspicious cash flow in Wheel-Lock?" I asked Tom, returning to our earlier conversation. "I can't do that . . . but could you?"

"Not unless there was a special reason, like an investigation, or they wanted to let me. Wheel-Lock is a privately owned corporation. That stuff is private, and since they have no stockholders to account to, they can keep the information to themselves. The only people who can know it all—in a case like this—is the IRS."

"Have you ever heard of a firm called A.J. Liebnitz?"

Costello turned and looked at me, giving a low whistle. He thrummed the line through his fingers and thumb, feeling it play out.

"Uh huh. Was Kincaid involved with A.J. Liebnitz?"

"Don't know. Let's just say it's a guy who hasn't answered his mail in quite a while. Where's the company located and what does it do?"

"Adolph Jacob Liebnitz and Associates is located on Grand Cayman Island in the Caribbean. I think it's just south of Jamaica. Tax haven."

"I've seen the ads. It's a place where the very rich go to bury their funds."

"Yeah, and pay nothing. They can just sit around down there and sip zombies and piña coladas and collect interest. A.J. Liebnitz is a commodities broker. Precious commodities. I think he owns half the gold and silver in the free world."

"That's fairly interesting."

"Old A.J. is quite a guy. There was an article about him not long ago in one of the financial rags. Jewish refugee from the Nazis. Both parents wiped out. Brothers and sisters wiped out. Arrived in Lisbon without a cent. Now he's worth—who the hell knows?''

''And his firm deals mostly in precious metals?''

''I think now he's branching out more and more into gems and art treasures. If it's precious—sought after—A.J. has a hand in it. But he made his name in gold and silver, yes. His name crops up wherever they're traded: Geneva, Zurich, Brussels, Antwerp, London, New York, Paris. If the subject's gold, the name Liebnitz will surface before long. He knows all the big deals: who's buying and who's selling and where and when. At all the big deals and auctions one of his representatives is there. They've got branch offices in all the big money centers.''

''I'm wondering if I could write the head office for information about this guy . . .''

''Forget it. Liebnitz is as tight as a Swiss bank. Confidentiality of all clients' holdings is absolute.''

He turned the reel handle, watching the line make thin swirl marks in the ocean, and squinted in concentration.

''*Ab-so-lute*,'' he repeated with finality.

Disappointed, I gazed at the sea haze. Was there any way to pierce the shield of anonymity that surrounded Wallace Kinchloe?

''What if I were from a law enforcement agency?''

''No dice. Interpol, the FBI, and all the secret service organizations have been after Liebnitz and the Swiss banks for decades. They're tighter than clams. I'll tell you one thing though, whoever the guy is you have in mind, he's loaded: Liebnitz likes to brag privately that he only handles millionaires. His outfit is definitely not the minor leagues. Even to do business with him, you've got to be heavyweight.''

''What kind of minimum deal are you talking about?''

''I honestly don't know, Doc. But I know Liebnitz and clan pick and choose carefully. They have a minimum staff and want minimum overhead and bookkeeping. If you're not promising, they don't take you on.''

The line jerked and ran. I hauled and cranked. I was rewarded with what I was searching for: a ten-pound striped bass.

"You're dribbling at the mouth. You OK?"

I told him I was just salivating. A normal reaction to catching a big, plump striper. I was rewarded twice more with nice bass.

It was a perfect day. The sun sank low in the west, silhouetting the twin lighthouses of Gloucester. The tide was swelled to its fullest and *Whimsea* rolled and yawed lazily in the broad troughs. The exhaust noise wafted up to my ears in a faint and peaceful burble. To the east the sky was dark bluish purple—to the west, brilliant red-gold. We broke out the steaming chowder as Jim swung around for the trip back. We eased back, taking our time. We passed the twin breakwaters of Rockport, which are manmade piles of granite a mile offshore. They lay dim, huge, ghostlike in the gathering dark, like ruined hulks.

I sat on the bridge, downing chowder and beer and watching for lights and buoys as we entered the channel. My watch said quarter to nine.

"My cast stinks."

"What?"

"My cast and bandage. They're all full of fish slime. One of the biggest pains in the ass about this damn thing is I can't wash it. Hey, isn't Thursday night a good night for bar drinking? When I was in college we always used to go drinking Thursday nights."

Jim replied that to his knowledge the bars were usually pretty packed Thursdays, especially during the summer months.

"Instead of heading back with you guys I think I'll hoist a few in Gloucester tonight."

He looked at me in disbelief.

"I thought you hated bars."

"I do. But there's one here I want to pay a visit to. I'm told a certain boatbuilder hangs out there and I'd like to meet him."

"Well, you should stay out of all of 'em. They're for commercial fishermen and all pretty rough, so I'm told. They're not for the likes of us, Doc.''

"I was going to buy you guys dinner there. I just want to see a guy—"

"I'm not interested, Doc. Don't know about Tom. I'm going home. Listen: I want you to give me your fish too, in case you don't come back.''

I thought this was in poor taste, and so informed him. Tom declined also. We reached the harbor and made *Whimsea* fast and shipshape and parted company on the dock. I told Jim to please call Mary and have her proceed with dinner without me. I knew this wouldn't make me popular, but I had to speak with Danny Murdock. And according to his wife, the Schooner Race was his second home.

9

I CLIMBED ABOARD THE SCOUT, WHICH I HAD RELEARNED how to drive with my cast, dumped the thermos bottles in the back along with my fishing gear, and nudged my way out of the crowded marina parking lot. I headed into the center of New England's most famous fishing city, home of the indomitable fisherman, clad in his sou'wester, who stands watch over the harbor. He is cast in bronze, his hands on the ship's wheel, his eyes level and steadfast. He is probably looking directly into the teeth of a sixty-foot wave that is only seconds away from swallowing up his ship. On the statue's base are the words "Those That Go Down to the Sea in Ships." It is a memorial to all Gloucester fishermen lost at sea. It still happens, and every year the people still come to the harborside and throw wreaths into the water as the list of the dead is read. And then they sing beautiful hymns while the tide carries the wreaths out to sea.

The Schooner Race and the other maritime bars are located on Main Street across from Gloucester's inner harbor. This small body of water is always jammed full with trawlers and freighters. The big boats are stuck together like cars in a crowded lot. I pulled the car up across the street from the bar right over the water just behind some collapsed piers. It was dark as I got out. I smelled fish stink. It was lobster bait. Lobstermen take fish offal, let it ripen in old tubs until you can smell it a mile away, then put it in little plastic baggies. They tie these baggies inside the trap. Just before they dump the traps overboard they punch little holes all over the baggie to let out the stink and fish slime. That brings in the lobsters, which are bottom dwelling scavengers. Anyway, you show me a lobster port and I'll show you odors that will stay in your memory a long, long time. I glanced at the dirty harbor water that oozed eight feet below me. Thank God at least for the huge tides of the Northeast; they douched the filthy place twice a day. The rotting fish guts were getting to me; I couldn't wait to get inside.

I walked across the sandy parking lot that led up to the concrete walkway where I'd parked. I heard shouting down the street, and the rumble and blast of a big Harley chopper as it tore off and away. There was a knot of men standing around the entranceway of a small bar down there. It was the infamous House of Mitch. Compared to it the Schooner Race was your regular family pub.

I thought again of the bronze statue of the fisherman, and the men who still risked their lives in the small boats out in the North Atlantic. Some boats went out for one or two weeks at a time. The men got four or five hours' sleep a day. They lived on coffee, cigarettes, beer, and candy bars. When they got back, either flushed with success or bitter with failure, they got bombed. Sometimes a man could make five or six grand in one trip as his share of the take, after the skipper's expenses. But sometimes two weeks of hell resulted in nothing. And sometimes the boat didn't come back at all. I'd heard stories of boats going out in the winter and getting so loaded up with ice that they simply turned upside down and slid under. And there's not a damn thing you can do about the icing; you just can't chip it off fast enough.

I heard a juke inside as I approached the door. I entered. It was a pine-paneled place without windows. A big S-shaped bar snaked along the far side. Tables and booths lined the other walls.

I ordered a beer and sat in the corner. The place wasn't crowded although it was past nine. I looked around. Hell, the Race wasn't so bad. In fact it was downright charming.

The large mural photographs were stunning. They were pinup pictures of Gloucester's best-loved women. Then there were the rivals from the Maritimes too.

There was the *Gertrude L. Thebaud*, the queen of them all. She was close-hauled on a port tack, and well heeled over, her lee rail awash. The *Adventure* on a broad reach . . . and in the far distance the triangular shape of the second-place boat. Right over my head was a shot of the *Bluenose*, a boat from Nova Scotia notorious for dashing the hopes of the New England challengers. They lined the walls, these pictures of the Grand Banks schooners, the most graceful medium-sized sailing vessels ever built. They were built sleek because the first boats back to port could demand the highest prices for their catch.

I sipped and watched patrons dribble in. They looked young, which was Father Time's insidious way of tapping me lightly on the shoulder. I stared pensively down at the tiny stream of bubbles rising in my glass.

The jukebox was getting louder too. A song was playing that went: "You are *all* that I am . . . (bum ta bum *bum* bum) You know ya make me *feel* like a bran' ne*hew* man . . ."

It was a C&W number, by a guy named Clyde McFritter, or something similar.

The place was filling up faster and faster now; the boats were coming in. The girl behind the bar was kept solidly busy at the spigot, drawing mugs and pitchers of Schlitz dark. It seemed to me that most of the men were between twenty-five and thirty-five, and their clothes and general appearance were remarkably similar.

To begin with, most of them had beards or moustaches. They all wore jeans, topped with hooded sweatshirts, flannel plaids, or knit sweaters. Rubber boots. It might seem to most people that they were overdressed for late summer. But many of them had been over fifty miles out at sea—some perhaps as far as Georges Bank. And it's always chilly there.

They also wore either the knitted blue wool watch caps or the trucker's hats with long bills in front to protect them from the glare. The glare on the ocean is terrible, even on cloudy days. It can wear you out. The front of these caps bore the

logos of manufacturers of things very macho. Beer companies. Companies that made trucks and diesel engines, firearms and knives. I couldn't help wondering what would
happen if you went into the Schooner Race wearing a hat
that said Singer, or Hoover, or—God forbid—Mop 'n Glo?

Another standard item of the uniform was the folding
hunter knife carried in its compact belt sheath. When un-
folded with the blade locked open these are every bit as big
as the regular sheath knives. All the lads in the SR were
wearing them.

Bits of conversations floated past. Most concerned themselves with fishing. The names of the fish weren't attractive
ones like trout or salmon. Instead they had ugly names like
hake and cusk. I ask you, how'd you like to dive into a plate
of cusk? And if you've ever seen a cusk, you'd know why
they named it that . . .

It was past ten. I had better commence asking if I wanted
any results concerning the whereabouts of Dan Murdock,
erstwhile boatbuilder. Two fishermen came over to ask if they
could borrow a chair that was sitting vacant next to me at the
small table. I said sure and asked the nearest one—who was
wearing a bill cap with the words *Cummins Marine* above
the visor—if he knew where I could perhaps find a boatbuilder named Daniel Murdock.

The young man, whose name was Ted, lifted his head
toward the ceiling and chuckled. They were sitting on the
chairs backward, leaning their forearms over the seat backs
and sipping their shots and beers.

"Murdock? *Murdock*? Sure he could build ya boat, if he
ain't too bombed or strung out. What ya want him for?"

"I need some extensive repair work done on a boat I'm
thinking of buying. I've heard Murdock is good and—well—
pretty cheap too."

The men sat and swigged in silence for a few minutes as
if they hadn't heard me.

"Murdock . . . Dan Murdock . . ." the other man repeated. He said the name philosophically, as if it were a
special precept, syllogism, or school of metaphysical thought.

"Yes? Dan Murdock what?"

"Danny Murdock's a drunk, mister, that's what. I guess he was a pretty good builder but now he's a drunk. Spends a lotta time in here. Surprised we ain't seen him. Spends a lotta time drinking in here and hidin' from his old lady."

"Do you know where I can find him? If he comes in, can you guys point him out? I'll buy you a round."

"No need to, mister. He's right behind you, and fried to the gills."

"*Heah* ah is . . ." said a warbly voice in imitation of a black minstrel singer. He came shuffling over to us, sideways like a crab in a tide pool, working his feet like Buddy Ebsen. It was a poor imitation, mainly because he was gassed. He did a bad Cab Calloway. He did a frightful Bill "Bojangles" Robinson. He tripped and slid to his knees. I noticed he was wearing one work boot. Its mate had disappeared to God knows where.

He rose and fumbled with a pack of Camels. At least his taste in cigarettes was good. It had been twelve years since I smoked a cigarette. I still had dreams about Camels.

Murdock lighted the cigarette that jiggled in his mouth. But he put the flame halfway underneath it, not on the tip. It made for an interesting smoke. His missing work boot reappeared. The mystery of its absence was instantly resolved as it arrived, airborne, from the other end of the room. It flumped against his heavy mackinaw and dropped to the floor.

"Thanks!" yelled Dan Murdock as he picked up the boot and hopped around pulling it on. "Been looking for it . . ."

"Mr. Murdock? Am I addressing Mr. Daniel Murdock?"

"Hmmmm?"

"This guy wants some work done on his boat, right?"

The man speaking was Ted, who was jabbing a finger at Murdock, motioning for him to be seated. Murdock leaned over and swayed himself along to the nearest chair, grunting and exhaling smoke, and accusing the cigarette—which was not functioning the least bit properly—of having sexual intercourse with his mother. Or its mother. Or *any* mother. For a rolled piece of paper containing dried vegetable matter burning in the middle, it had an amazing sex life. Sitting down now and puffing and blowing, he finished pulling on his boot and fumbled with the laces.

"Well?" I asked.

"Well what. Who are you?"

His memory span was abbreviated.

"My boat. I'd like some work done on it."

He weaved in his seat squinting, trying to draw a bead on me. I thought I detected traces of faint recognition in the dull face. Had he seen me before?

"Wood or steel?"

"Steel."

"Commercial?"

I nodded.

"I don't do engines. Who sent you?"

He stared at me, as through a glass darkly, smashing out his Camel in the tin ashtray. He had brown hair and beard and a pleasant, youngish face. I would guess his age to be somewhere in the lower thirties. But already there were the telltale signs: the nose beginning to fill with tiny cracked purplish veins. The red eyes. The sagging eyefolds. It wouldn't be long before the booze would really start taking its toll on this young man. He fumbled again for his cigarette pack.

"What you want done?"

"I want the superstructure changed. More cabin space forward. You know, make a cruiser out of her. Also, I want a double hull."

"Hull? Double hull?"

"I want an extra hull portion added where it won't show— below the waterline. I want it accessible through a hidden hatch below decks . . ."

"How come?"

"I want a hidden cache for my cash."

He squinted at me, tilting his head. He was trying terribly hard to concentrate and remember what had been said in the previous two seconds.

"Your dough? Or somethin' else maybe?"

"What does it matter to you if the price is right?"

"Sure. What's her name? Where is she?"

I thought there was no point in playing games anymore. I leaned forward over the tiny table and glared at him.

"Her name is *Penelope*, Dan. And I don't know where she is. I want to find her. Badly. Where is she?"

He kept looking at me, squinting slightly through the gloom and smoke of the Schooner Race. His eyes came into focus, slowly at first, then quickly, totally. I peeled the label off the beer bottle and watched his face, and mind, coming back together through the booze and smoke. Like a silvery fish being drawn up through murky water, his consciousness became progressively sharper.

"Nah. Can't help you. What's your name?"

"Charles Adams. And I know your name because I saw it on a Master Carpenter's Certificate at the Coast Guard Registry. I want to know where *Penelope* is, Dan. You can help me a lot by telling me. If not I'll be mad. I am also supposing that if the authorities discover that maybe you really didn't build the *Penelope* after all, you'd be in hot water."

I suspected instantly I'd said more than I should have. Daniel Murdock slammed his bottle down on the table, got up, and swayed over to the bar for another. I watched him drink quickly from the bottle of beer then set it down. A shot glass appeared at his elbow. He tossed it off and returned to the beer. He turned and glanced at me, then turned back. His face showed hatred. But it showed something else even more. It showed fear.

The cards were on the table for Dan Murdock. The last hole card had been flipped over and he had the deuce of clubs. I sat thinking on what should happen next. Maybe the best thing was for me to skedaddle and let him ponder his ill fortune for a day or two, then phone him. Murdock was out of my vision now; a new group of men had just entered the Race. The bar was packed three deep, and the general noise level was still rising. It was almost impossible to hear Charlie Pride on the jukebox.

Four men came in. Two were old and heavy. One was tall, the other medium. All were dark, keen featured, and wide in the shoulders. They were not in good humor.

The young man named Ted leaned back and asked if I'd had any luck with Murdock. I replied some, and noticed Ted's expression change when he saw the four men.

"Here comes action," whispered Ted. "That's Joey Partmos and his brothers. They own the *Antonio*."

"So?"

"*So*? See the other bunch of guys down at the far end of the bar?"

"Yeah. So what?"

"OK. That's Mike DeCarlo and his bunch down there, owners of the *Caterina*. They were bragging earlier how they busted a school of haddock right out from under *Antonio*'s nose."

I asked if the *Antonio* could lay claim to said school of haddock, and was informed that though there was no law stating who had first option, there was a long tradition—an unwritten law—that the boat first "on" the school was by custom allowed to work it alone.

"But you see since the CB radio bug hit, everybody's always in touch with everybody else, and a guy who used to work for Joey, that now works for Mike, he knew the *Antonio*'s code words. That's how the *Caterina* busted the school—"

I was completely in the dark as to the busting of schools, CB-radio codes, and the like, but was informed thoroughly by Ted as we sat and watched the tension at the bar grow with each second. What Ted and his friend told me was this:

Like the truckers, fishermen use the CB radios to stay in constant touch with one another. Also like the truckers, they use code words and slang. The CBs are a big help to everyone, especially in rough weather, because a fully laden boat that pitchpoles or gets swamped goes down in seconds. The long-range VHF radios are useful for calling the Coast Guard on distress frequencies (which may *never* be used for idle chitchat), but the CB radios keep everyone in touch and allow nearby fishing boats and yachts to perform rescues the Coast Guard could never hope to accomplish. There just aren't enough USCG boats to do it all.

He was interrupted in his lecture by a waitress who flung

three bottles of beer down on our little table. She informed us that they were courtesy of the *Caterina*. The boys were celebrating their big haul.

From the talk that had filtered down to Ted earlier, she'd struck three big schools one after the other. But one of them, it was said, was claimed by the *Antonio*, and before either boat could work it properly, the school busted.

"You see Wayne Fletcher works for Mike DeCarlo now, but he used to work for Joey aboard the *Antonio*. He knew all the code words and things the Partmos family uses, so when they heard the *San Sebastian* calling *Antonio*, they knew where the school was, and *what* it was. Wayne says the two boats got there at the same time, but *Caterina* got what was left, not *Antonio*."

"Who owns *San Sebastian*? This is beginning to sound like one of Rossini's operas . . ."

"Tom Partmos, Joey's brother. The *San Sebastian* is out of Rockport. You see, the whole code idea started up over in P-town about eight years ago when everybody started buying the CB radios. Fishermen figured it was a good way to let certain friends or relatives know where the fish were without telling anyone else. The P-town fishing is almost all done by Portuguese families you know, and there's a lot of family loyalty. Some of these families have three, maybe four boats owned by brothers, uncles, or cousins. Well the beauty of the code is, you talk to your relatives on the CB and nobody else knows what the fuck's comin' off, right?

"You say: 'I'm standing in front of the five and dime eating popcorn,' and nobody understands, except your brother, who knows that means you're ten miles off five-fathom ledge and have found a nice school of haddock. Or you might hear your cousin call you and say he's at the bowling alley with a six-pack of Schlitz. An' you know that the bowling alley is really Grayson's Channel, and Schlitz means he's found mackerel—"

Fascinated, I listened to the explanation of the strange messages I'd been hearing aboard the *Ella Hatton* on the CB radio. These weird nonsense messages did have a meaning: telling "friendlies" where the action was.

But I was getting nowhere fast. Dan Murdock was not to be seen, though he might be lurking somewhere in the crowded bar. My watch said 10:45. If I left now, taking time only to visit the head, I would be home before midnight. That seemed to make sense. I wended my way through the crowd to the john. As I was coming back after washing up I saw him. He was emerging from a tiny nook that held a pay phone. It wasn't a booth, just a small bend in the big room where one could—in theory at least—talk with some privacy. He didn't see me as he went back to the bar.

I realized now that if I'd just left the Race a few seconds sooner, I'd have been home free. But the argument started before I even returned to my table. I walked past the bar, noticing that Dan Murdock was doing everything possible to make himself conspicuous there. Whom had he called? I was turning the possibilities over in my mind when I heard the first of the insults.

I'll tell you how to know when there's a fight about to start in a crowded bar: every conversation stops . . . but one. And that one grows louder and more heated until *it* stops, because one of the conversants is getting hit in the chops. As soon as I heard that one, rising, ominous dialogue, I knew something was brewing. Two men were shouting now in the silence of the Schooner Race. It was no surprise that it was Joey and Mike, rival captains of the *Antonio* and the *Caterina*. Perhaps the thing could have been amicably resolved if Mike had not mentioned Joey's sister. He not only mentioned her, but some specific parts of her anatomy as well, and the strenuous use she was giving them. According to Mike—who I think I could safely say was not a gentleman—Carlotta Partmos had been intimate with various and sundry lower forms of marine animal life, and also with other members of her family. However, she had curiously avoided anything in human form between these two extremes. I found this incongruous . . . And Joey Partmos found Mike's jaw with a left.

I was still stunned by Mike's remarks, but learned a few seconds later that Joey had begun the insults by mentioning the sexual misadventures of Mike's wife—especially her fondness for military bases. These comments were without foundation of course; they were meant to inflame the opposition. This they did.

It would have been ugly enough if the fight had been contained, but as so often happens at hockey games, the benches emptied, and the crews joined in. The ill feeling between the two boats had a long history—I learned later on—and now it was just boiling to the surface. The most amazing thing, though, was not the donneybrook but the detached, almost amused composure of the remaining patrons. Except for the dozen or so brave souls attempting to separate the combatants, the crowd remained passive, evidence that this sort of thing was not uncommon in the SR.

Whether I was too old or too highborn I couldn't tell, but I decided when the fight was only seconds old that the social climate of the Schooner Race had disintegrated to the point where I wished to depart posthaste. But this was made difficult by the enormous crunch of humanity that pressed against us as the crowd, in its eagerness to avoid the brawl, swayed back and forth in the long room, like water sloshing in a trough. I fought my way from the bar toward the door. Out of the corner of my eye I saw Danny Murdock. He was sitting in another booth. He stared after me as I went to the door. But I didn't make it.

Four feet from my goal, I was flung backward as a body crashed into me. I reached down and picked the man up, holding him under the arm. He was heavy and tired. Attempting to drag him over to a booth away from the action, I locked my arms around his chest and began to drag him back. This was a mistake, because just as I had clasped my hand around my plaster wrist another combatant charged us, butting him in the chest with his head, and then finishing off with a short choppy right to his neck. The man slumped in my arms. To all bystanders, it appeared as though I was not helping him, but setting him up for this abuse—much as the movie tough guys work in teams; one man to hold the victim, the other to work him over. The illusion did not stand me in good stead. Instantly, both the attacker and I were set upon.

They say you never see the knockout punch. Maybe so, but you surely may catch a glimpse of one that does a good deal of damage. This came winging my way, in the form of a hairy fist, from over the shoulders of the ranks nearest me. It landed on my left cheekbone, which is called the *zygomatic arch*. This bone is the part of the skull that wraps around the side of the middle face, protecting the sides of the eye sockets. It is easily broken. But even if not broken, trauma to it causes rapid subcutaneous extravasation of blood to the region. This is all to the good. But in a matter of hours the trapped blood begins to die and discolor, resulting in a pronounced bluish-black darkening that is called *ecchymosis*. In short, a black eye. As I jolted backward and began to slump down, I knew I was going to get a hell of a shiner. I crept forward, hunched over. Someone came in low, battering my rib cage on both sides with his fists. I didn't like it at all. In fact it aggravated me, and I wanted him on the floor. I first distracted his attention by ringing his chimes. I made a tight fist with my right hand with my thumb along the top of it. I hooked this pointy thing around and into my assailant's left ear as hard as I could. He didn't slow down fast enough, so I did it again. My hand came back wet and gooey. Caught his eye a bit. Gee, sorry about that, but quit hitting me in the ribs. He bent over and lifted his hands to grab for his injured head. I shook hands with him and yanked down hard and back on his right arm, placing my right foot out so he'd trip over it. The arm drag worked and he slid down at my right side, groaning and rolling around and grabbing at himself.

I was just beginning to shout my apologies when someone shot a forearm into the nape of my neck. I struck back, flinging my left arm around behind me blindly. My cast smacked something hard and hollow sounding, like a head. But it was too late; the neck chop had done me in. Suddenly the world seemed like I had two pairs of sunglasses on and my ears were plugged. I let the force of the blow take me forward; I stumbled on as far as possible to get out of the way. Friendly arms reached out to me. I felt myself half-dragged to a table. I faintly remember a couple of kids slapping me on the back. I remember seeing a cop, and several men being held by their friends and led out of the place. The world came back into focus as I was holding a glass to my lips and drinking. There was a faint clangor of bells. No, ice cubes against glass.

"Feel better?"

It was Ted, sitting next to me with several pals.

"That's a double of CC. That should help."

I finished it. It helped. Then a big mug of coffee appeared at my elbow, and I drained it. It was strong, but cut with plenty of cream and sugar. I felt a lot better, although pain was beginning to emerge in several places, most notably my sides, neck, and left cheek. I looked around the Schooner Race; all was calm. The rowdies had gone—or been taken away. The place was filled with peaceful folk. I noticed how bright pine-yellow the walls were—how stunning the mural photos appeared. My mind was collecting itself . . . the red Naugahyde seats seemed bright . . . the bottles seemed to shine with a new luster . . .

"Can you walk OK?"

"Yeah. Thanks. I'm going now."

And I did.

I left the Schooner Race and lugged my weary frame across the parking lot. I looked at my watch: 12:07. Mary would not like it. The song I had heard upon first entering the bar was going through my rattled brain: "You are *all* that I am (bum ta bum *bum* bum), You know ya make me *feel* like a bran' ne*hew* man . . ."

Well I'd be the hero though. DeGroot chickened out. But I went. I wasn't afraid, and I had the scars to prove it. De-Groot was a fraidy cat. DeGroot was also at home, snug in bed and undamaged. DeGroot was *smart*. I was a big dummy. I turned and looked at the bar for several minutes. Reason: as I left—finally—I noticed Danny Murdock slumped at the bar. I didn't want him following me. I wanted to make sure he stayed put.

Ten minutes and nobody emerged from the Race. I was half hidden in the far reaches of the parking area and could see without being seen. No, I was safe.

I found the Scout and fumbled for my keys. Over my shoulder the mucky harbor water shimmered white-gray in the moonlight. The air stank. My body ached. In the dark I produced the key ring, flipped through the bright jangling metal. From behind me came a faint sigh . . . a whisper of sole scuff . . . an indefinable cloth-wrinkle sound of stealth—

The lights went out.

10

WHEN YOU GET HIT ON THE HEAD REALLY HARD YOU CAN taste it in your brain. It is the taste of sour metal—of tarnished copper or bitter tin, of solder and rancid flux . . . and you taste it not with your tongue or mouth, but with your brain. And the place you taste it, just at that instant before unconsciousness or agonizing pain, is right in the center of your head. Above your throat. Behind your nose. Under the back of your eyes. When you taste it, you know you are in deep trouble.

Looking down into my hands to find the bright silver key, I had heard the faint rustle behind me. I was in the act of looking around when there came a sound like a super-tanker grating fast on a granite ledge—a million artillery pieces letting go at once. A tympani between my ears. Then a dropping feeling and a going away. And through it all, the metal taste I *felt* in the center of my head.

And then I felt nothing, saw nothing, thought nothing, until I came to. And coming to was most terrifying of all.

I awoke in a howling gale, a shrill symphony of mad whines and roars. Dim phosphorescent shapes glowed before me. It was dark and cold. The sound grew louder. Clicking and clacking not in my ears, but in my head—sounds I heard in the bridge of my nose. I was dying. I had to get out. . .

I was underwater.

Something from I-know-not-where told me a vital message as I regained consciousness in the depths of Gloucester Harbor. I did *not*, starved for air as I was, swim straight up. I swam at an angle, spurting precious bubbles of air as I went, until I saw a thick cylindrical shape pass by my right side. A piling, clustered thick with barnacles, mussels, and rockweed. Four feet below me I could barely see an orange starfish. Spent, I came up, popping and blowing, on the top of the scummy water. I still had not recalled why I had swum up behind the piling—what signal of self-preservation I had obeyed. Perhaps in my unconscious (or subconscious) state, a grim logic was working: someone had knocked me on the head and tipped me into the harbor. Ergo: that person was not the best one to come sputtering up to, flailing arms and water, screaming for help.

I clutched the piling, panting and blowing as softly as I could. Fortunately for me, a loud delivery truck came rattling along the street above, and so hid any noises I was making. Within half a minute the panting stopped. I clutched my numb fingers around the craggy shells that covered the piling, which was as thick as a telephone pole. I was glad the shells were there; they made it easier to hang on. I looked from under the pier back in the direction I had come, and saw a thin beam playing along the water. Flashlight. The beam came toward the pilings and I slid behind, out of sight. It played along each one with monstrous slowness and deliberation. It snaked around beneath the pier like the Serpent in the Garden. As it approached my timber, I sucked in the biggest breath I could manage and went under, holding onto the barnacles tight to keep from floating up again. The cold water helped my head—but the rest of me was shivering, the deep convulsive shiver that tells you there is not much time left.

I saw the water above me glow bright green-gray with streaks of silver—the shimmering of refracted light. But the light stayed there. It would not leave, and I was running out of air, and time. I knew if I surfaced, however quietly, Mr. X would spot me—see the ripples in the water and catch a glimpse of my yellow Windbreaker. Then what would hap-

pen? Whatever he had in mind, I was in no condition to put
up much of a struggle. The scrap in the Schooner Race
followed by the rap on the head followed by a ten-minute
dunking in the harbor was enough to take the tar out of
anybody—especially a guy pushing fifty. Would he bap me
on the head with a pole and watch me sink again? Did he
have a gun? Or was this person with the light some helpful
soul who had seen me pitched in, and wanted to help?

No. Certainly any helper or concerned passerby would
make a lot more noise—call for help, etc.—than the Quiet
One with the flashlight. Time was up; I had to move. I shoved
away from the piling and breast-stroked over to the next one.
Clutching it, I shoved off with all my strength—what little
there was left—and on to the next pole. This I latched on to,
surfaced and breathed. But I was careful, upon coming up,
to make myself breathe *in* a bit before exhaling. This insured
there would be no loud burst of expelled air. I breathed ag-
onizingly slowly and felt my heart pounding in my neck and
head. The beam of light was just moving away from the pole,
and swung lazily back and forth across the murky water. I
was under a narrow pier, and therefore was unable to look
up and see Mr. X. On the other hand, he was unable to see
me, which was beneficial. I spotted an old fifty-gallon oil
drum poking itself out of the water at an angle a few feet
away. I slid over to it and felt rock against my side. I lay,
halfway out of the water behind the old drum, and waited
until the light was switched off. Then came the sound of feet
from the top of the harbor wall. They died away into the
distance and I lifted my weary frame and stood up. I could
scarcely stay on my feet. My legs were numb, and I rubbed
and pounded them. I had the worst headache I could remember. I had begun to trudge along the bottom of the sea wall
when in the foot-deep water I heard footsteps again. They
sounded remarkably familiar—a heavy scuff. They died away.
I waited. Then they came back.

Jesus Christ. The guy was *pacing* the wall. Then there
could be no doubt. He wanted me dead. He was up there
killing time to make sure he was killing me. Then I remembered the faint sound I'd heard just before getting mugged.

It was a shoe scuff. Mr. X did not have a firm step. He dragged his feet when he walked. A slovenly habit, but then would you expect a bright, firm step from one who does murder by stealth?

There was another sound too that I heard at regular intervals: a nervous sniffing. A short sniff followed by a faint clearing of the throat. I decided then and there to keep those sounds fixed in my mind. If I ever got out of the harbor alive, I would find Mr. X.

And I would fix his wagon but good.

The pacing continued. Once it stopped for a while and I heard people walking past. They talked loudly and laughed a lot. Probably just closing up some of the local bars. Then the footfalls returned. Finally, I saw the light again, and snuggled down tight behind the oil drum as the beam swept over me and along the pilings. Then it played on the water for a few minutes, sometimes shining way out over the water. Then it went out, the footfalls faded for the last time, and I was alone under the pier.

I *hoped*.

After another half-hour's wait, I dragged and hopped myself along in the shallow water until I came to the next pier. There was a ramp leading right down to the water. Gloucester has huge tides, and these floating angular ramps rise and fall with the water, allowing people to get to their boats easily. I rolled onto the floating platform and ground my way up the ramp slowly and quietly. I couldn't feel my legs. At the top I slid into the shadow of a boatyard shack and waited. Nothing. Mr. X, convinced I was dead at the bottom of the harbor, had finally departed. Freezing, I lurched and staggered along the street. The Scout was parked where I'd left it. I didn't have the keys; they were either in the hands of Mr. X or else left on the pavement next to the car. In any case, I wanted to leave it exactly as it was. I fumbled in my pockets. No wallet, which didn't surprise me. My corpse, minus wallet, would inject the robbery motive. Also, it let Mr. X and his associates know exactly who the nosy fellow in the Schooner Race was. This did not set well with me at all. I hurried on, hoping that a brisk walk would warm me. It was warm out with no wind, which was lucky. Also lucky that I was wearing a wool sweater beneath my Windbreaker. Wool, of all materials, is the only one that is as warm wet as it is dry. My head and sides hurt terribly, but I would be all right.

Twenty minutes later I found a phone booth. I had deliberately slunk about to avoid police cars. I didn't want to be seen by *anyone*. A plan was beginning to form in my hurt head.

Slumped into the phone booth, I let the door remain open so the light wouldn't go on. I had change, and dialed our number preceded by 0—a collect call that was a bit frenzied, but brief and to the point:

1. Mary was to make extra-sure all doors, windows, etc. were bolted and the dogs inside, freely roaming throughout the first floor. Additionally, she was to keep my Browning 9-mm Auto at her bedside. At my insistence she'd learned how to use it.
2. She was to call Jim DeGroot and tell him to pick me up, in exactly the manner I would explain to her.

"I'll see you around three. Jim and I will sneak in the back way. Remember, no lights."

"Are you all right, Charlie?"

"Just dandy. Good-bye."

It would take DeGroot an hour to arrive, but I started on my way. I had a long walk.

I sat hunched, shivering, behind the short hedgerow that lined the edge of Brown's Boatyard Annex. It seemed forever before the red Olds wagon came cruising slowly along the street. In two seconds, I was in the front seat, telling Jim to turn on the heat full blast. I shivered until we were halfway home, then fell asleep. He woke me up behind our garage, and had to help me up the stairs to the kitchen door. I had stiffened up badly, and felt as if my body had been used as a plaything by a pack of mandrills. My cast was soft; I'd need a new one.

Mary pulled open the door even before we reached it and let us in. She hugged me and I groaned. She put her arms around my neck to kiss me and I groaned again. I told her to stop there. She turned on the stove light and busied herself with a boiling kettle. Soon each of us had a giant hot toddy cradled in our paws. I had shed the cold garments for flannel PJ's and a robe. Mary probed my skull first and pronounced it intact.

"The outside anyway. There's no telling about the inside."

"Let's look under the light . . . can you see, through my thinning hair, a bruise?"

"No. Whoever bopped you used something heavy and soft and your hair's not thinning."

"Yeah, like a leather bag full of buckshot. It's also called a blackjack."

Jim said it was madness not to call the police. Mary gripped the sides of her head with her hands, working her fingers in and out. She was about to cry. She was scared plenty.

"Jesus, Charlie, they wanted to kill you. They tried to *kill* you."

"Now listen," I said, exchanging the toddy mug for one with hot coffee, "everybody shut up and listen. Mr. X thinks he did me in. So be it. It's my guarantee of safety. Tomorrow the two of you are going back to Gloucester looking for me. You're going to ask around the Schooner Race . . . describe me to the owners and patrons. You're going to find the Scout and have the police tow it, or help you start it. Make a big deal about the fact I haven't shown up. The Gloucester police will do the rest. Sooner or later Dan Murdock and Company will get the word: I'm gone . . ."

"Who the hell is Dan Murdock?"

I told them, and Jim was all for making a beeline straight for him. But of course, I explained, their picking him out would refute my death, since how on earth would they have known about Murdock unless I told them?

Jim left surreptitiously ten minutes later. After dosing myself with aspirin, I went to bed.

It was 3:30 next afternoon when Jim dropped Mary off at the front door. She found me in the sunporch smoking a Cuesta Rey. I had slept till noon, waking only to see Mary off at ten.

"Well?"

"The entire town of Gloucester thinks you're dead . . . or probably dead."

"Excellent, my love. And surely certain interested parties now *know* I'm dead. They're only waiting for my bloated carcass to surface in the putrid water of Gloucester Harbor. And if the body is never found, so much the better—they'll think they're home free."

"Who are they and what are they doing?"

"That's what I'm going to find out. One thing there's no mistaking now, though, is that somebody really tried to kill me. To kill in a manner remarkably similar to the way in which Allan Hart died."

"Well—you're going to forget the whole thing, Charlie, *right now*. We've got, with luck, twenty-five good years left on this planet. I don't want to spend mine with a bloated corpse."

"Tell me what happened."

"Jim and I went to that bar. One of the bartenders remembered you—he said you were a good fighter for an old guy."

"Bless his heart."

"So we pretended to be really upset of course . . . and I think we did a good job of it. The whole place is worried, and people are asking around if anyone's seen you. Then we just happened to find the Scout. It was still where you said it would be. The keys were nowhere to be found, so the police helped us get a new key—don't ask me how. It'll work, they said, at least until I can have another made. Then we went to the station and I filled out a form and answered a whole bunch of questions about your appearance, habits, etc., and now they want me to send them a picture."

"Perfect."

"No it isn't, you dope. They're going to get in touch with Brian Hannon."

"Uh oh. Oh boy. I should have thought of that."

"Yes you should have. In fact I'm surprised Brian hasn't been over here yet. . ."

"He may have been. I heard the doorbell once, and the phone's rung on and off too. But according to Plan A, I haven't stirred."

"Well you'll have to talk with Brian. I think it's a crime, isn't it, to falsify a disappearance?"

"Hmmmm. I think you're right. It's certainly frowned on."

"And what are you going to tell him?"

"I'm not sure I'm going to tell him anything, and I'll tell you why: I have—really, truly, *officially*—nothing to go on but observations, hunches, and my near-death by murder."

"You've got to be kidding."

"No. While a lot of what I've found out *is* suspicious, there's no hard proof of any of it. Did Allan drown accidentally or not? Who knows for sure? Are the missing *Windhover* and the phantom boat *Penelope* one and the same? Maybe. Maybe not."

"Look, Charlie, somebody tried to *kill* you—"

I rubbed the bean with my cast. I was in truly great shape: broken wrist, black eye, cracked ribs, and a bruised brain bucket.

"I've been thinking that over too, Mary. Listen: just before I got mugged and dumped, I was in a bar fight. A nasty scuffle in which I figured prominently—not of my own choice—and in which several men were severely beaten and people were arrested. Don't you see how most cops would suspect that what happened forty minutes later was merely a continuation of the fight inside?"

"You mean somebody getting even with you?"

"Sure. I know I clipped somebody a good one on the side of his head with my cast. He must not be overly fond of me."

"Maybe he's the one who tried to kill you."

I considered this possibility, but later rejected it. The clientele of the Schooner Race was a rough slice of humanity, but I doubted if the patrons would stoop to murder from behind. Several people had been pretty beat up in the fight, but nobody was stabbed. Yet every person I saw there had a knife of some kind on his belt. No. Logic led me away from

that fork in the road. On the other hand, there was Danny
Murdock. Certainly he'd be interested in my demise. So
would the person who paid him to falsify the carpenter's
certificate. And he'd made a phone call just before the fight
broke out. Then afterward lounged about in front of the bar
where I'd be sure to see him. Another possible scenario began to emerge:

1. Danny Murdock is warned that somebody is inquiring
   around his boatyard about *Penelope*. The person who
   warns him is his wife.

2. Murdock, alarmed, gets in touch with *Penelope*'s
   owner, whoever he is.

3. Owner, also alarmed, instructs Murdock to keep mum,
   but to alert him if/when he ever sees or hears of me.

4. In the Schooner Race, after our initial encounter, Murdock phones the owner, who tells him to stay put in
   the bar so I'll stay there too, giving the owner, who
   could be the same nice fellow with the blackjack and
   the flashlight, time to arrive either in the bar or outside
   it, waiting for me to emerge.

5. Perhaps Murdock was to leave the Race, allowing me
   to follow behind, perhaps not. In any event, the fight
   caused me to remain in the joint long enough for Mr.
   X to arrive and arrange for my disposal. He must have
   known my description. But that wouldn't be hard:
   middle-aged man with salt and pepper hair, yellow
   jacket, thin, with left hand in cast. I would be easy to
   pick out, especially from a bunch of working fishermen, most of whom were young, Italian or Portuguese,
   or both.

The second scenario made a lot of sense, but it couldn't
be pinned down for sure. No, the police could—*would*—say
that the bopping on the head was either a robbery mugging

or a revenge action from the brawl in the Schooner Race. Certainly Danny Murdock, who did not follow me outside, had an airtight alibi.

"What about Chief Hannon, Charlie?"

"Let's wait for the Gloucester police to make their preliminary inquiries and spread the word of my disappearance far and wide. Then I'll see Brian and explain. Now I have taken out grouse and pheasant, which should be almost defrosted. I'm hoping a game dinner will speed my recovery, or at least improve my spirits. And speaking of them, how about a double Tanqueray with a dash of Boissiere on the rocks, with a curl of pungent lemon rind?"

"Oh Charlie, you've got a headache already."

"Yeah, but not for long," I said, making for the sideboard.

11

FOUR DAYS DRAGGED BY, DURING WHICH I SMOKED CIGARS, read, listened to Bach and Vivaldi, and healed. I had a new cast put on the wrist—not as big but still formidable. I began growing a beard. As I healed, I spent a good deal of time with six big NOAA charts spread out on the carpet at my feet. I puffed on my cigar and stared at them. Placed roughly together, they formed a jigsaw puzzle that became the cocked arm that is Cape Cod. It is shaped like a cocked arm, which joins the mainland at the shoulder. It is bent the way Arnold Schwarzenegger bends his to make his baseball-sized biceps pop. Only the arm is a skinny one. At the first end—the end of the Cape—is Provincetown. Wellfleet and Eastham are halfway down the inside of the forearm, on the bay side. At the elbow is the town of Chatham. Along the bicep side are the towns of the Brewsters, the Dennises, the Yarmouths, the Barnstables, and the Sandwiches. On the tricep side are Harwich Port, Dennis Port, and Hyannis. I studied the Cape, then I studied a big map that showed everything from Block Island Sound (the body of water to the north of Long Island) to Cape Ann, where Gloucester was. What was going on? What lay between Gloucester and Wellfleet, if anything? I puffed and studied, studied and puffed. If I were Sherlock Holmes, or had his talents, no doubt the problem would become clearer. But that wasn't happening to Yours Truly; the problem was getting murkier and more confusing. But I kept at it . . . glancing over the charts and harbor approached trying to get a hold on . . . on *something*.

I also knew I had to explain myself to our police chief, Brian Hannon. To explain to him why I wasn't really dead. I knew this had to be done before it became town gossip. He scolded me for twenty minutes. Then he notified the Gloucester police about the attempt on my life, and requested that my continued presence be kept confidential for my own personal safety. This they solemnly agreed to do, which pleased me. In addition, Brian promised a close watch on the house, mostly at night.

Meantime, if the house was being watched—which we and the police both doubted—I never left it or showed my face around Concord Center. We called Jack and Tony and explained the situation, urging caution and discretion. I added that I might be needing their assistance in a week or so.

I got one unexpected call. Mary answered the phone, as arranged, then handed it to me. It was Tom Costello.

"Pahdon me for calling, Doc; I didn't know you'd been killed. Listen: I checked with Jim and he said it was all right to talk to you if I kept my mouth shut."

"If you will greatly exaggerate the rumors of my death you may call me anytime. What gives, thou mighty sage of the ticker tape and prophet of the Big Board?"

"What gives is that my friend Jerry Klonski at Kidder is in touch with some of Wheel-Lock's potential buyers. They have examined the books and there's no suspicious cash flow, no irregularities of any kind about the place. Just thought you'd like to know."

"I do like to know. Thanks."

"And also, if you've got any more theories about the late Walter Kincaid, my advice is forget 'em. They almost got you killed."

"Thanks for the tip."

"My pleasure, Doc. Stockbrokers are in the advice business. I guess I can't help it. Let me know when you get sprung from Purgatory."

He hung up.

Then a bombshell arrived from California—sent whizzing in our direction by Sarah Hart, who was drawing her visit at her sister's to a close. It was a manilla envelope, and inside was the following piece from the *Los Angeles Times*:

Los Angeles Man Missing, Feared Dead

SPENARD, ALASKA—Nov. 10, 1978. Mr. James Schilling, a Los Angeles area businessman and sportsman, was reported missing Tuesday evening from his hunting camp on the Kenai Peninsula near Ninilchik. Schilling's guide, an Aleut Indian named Joshua Teal, told his supervisor at AL-AK Airways that his client failed to return to camp after setting off along the coast in a small motorboat to look for brown bear. Teal reported he found the boat awash in a small bay after a brief search. Schilling's rifle and some personal gear were found in the water. There was no sign of the hunter. Though it is possible that Schilling could have been attacked and dragged off by an angry bear, Teal said he thought it unlikely since the rifle had not been fired and there was no sign of violence.

Mr. Schilling was employed by the Plee-Zing Food Corporation of Costa Mesa as a regional manager. He resided in Newport Beach and leaves a wife, Barbara, and two daughters.

The story sounded reasonable enough. It is not usually printed in public reports because it is thought to be embarrassing or in poor taste, but the primary cause of sportsmen falling overboard from boats and drowning is urination. Almost all the recovered victims are found to have their flies open. The incidence is steep during the summertime fishing season when men go out not only to see how many fish they can catch, but how many beers they can drink. No, were it not for one thing I could easily envision Jim Schilling—with four or five beers or a thermos of coffee inside him—leaning over the gunwale relieving himself, perhaps while under way. Then the boat yaws or hits a sudden chop or swell and *bingo*, it's overboard into the icy Alaskan waters. And if you happen to hit your noggin on the way down—something I was now an expert on—the chances of your coming up again are about fifty-fifty. But it was the "other thing" that as much as told me the story was fabricated. It was the photo of James Schilling that accompanied the article. It wasn't a good reproduction because Sarah had photocopied it. But it was good enough. I called Mary into the sunporch.

"Look here, Toots. What do you think?"

She stared for four or five seconds before it hit her.

"Charlie, it's him. *It's him.*"

"Yep. It sure is. The beard helps, but it doesn't hide enough."

"Well what's he doing *here*?"

She was referring of course to our mysterious piratelike friend whom I had managed to photograph a few weeks previously aboard the phantom vessel *Penelope* in Wellfleet Harbor. The man was James Schilling, presumed dead. The man who hated Walter Kincaid. I decided that a good thing to do would be to have a lengthy and frank discussion with Mary's brother, Detective Lieutenant Joseph Brindelli. And I was in the process of thinking of calling Joe and moving toward the phone when it rang. Mary answered it and handed it to me.

"How are you, dead man? How would you like to come over tonight and have too much to drink?" asked Jim De-Groot.

We replied in the affirmative, with deep suspicions that the invitation was offered chiefly because of my skill—which I wear modestly—in preparing fillets of striped bass. Still a semi-recluse, I managed to slip into Mary's Audi and scoot down low in the seat. In a few days I would abandon all attempts at remaining invisible. Things in Gloucester would swing into their petty pace by then. But for the nonce, I was incognito.

"Ohhhhh, poor baaaaa-by," cooed Janice DeGroot as she planted a big one on my cheek and cocked a learned eye at mine. "That's the biggest shiner I've seen in years, Doc. Does it hurt?"

"Only when I laugh. I was informed by your spouse over the wires that we have been invited to abuse alcohol. Let's get down to it."

I found Jim in back lighting the grill. The fillets were all set: slabs of milky white flesh the color of quartz that would cook up to look like boiled egg whiles and would flake off in luscious chunks by merely pointing a fork at them. We greased up big squares of heavy aluminum foil and placed a fillet on each. Then we covered them with thin-sliced lemons and lots of butter. We covered this with paprika, thin-sliced scallions, and some Old Bay seasoning, then folded up the edges of the foil. Just before sealing the packets, we poured a generous jigger of chablis over the whole thing and added a sprinkling of finely-cut fresh chives. After ten minutes over the coals the packets sent forth a merry bubbling sound, and I poked several holes in each with a toothpick and watched the tiny jets of steam rise from them. The aroma was made more delicious by the two ounces of ice-cold gin that was wending its way through my interior, cutting a wide swath of destruction. I could have eaten a horse, and said so.

"Then how come you only weigh—what is it you weigh, Doc?"

"One hundred seventy-four."

"Well how come?" asked Janice.

"I'll tell you how come," said Mary. "Because he eats only what and when he likes. He has a light breakfast and skips lunch, when he runs. He pigs it up at dinner. But that's only once a day."

"All work should be put behind you by dinnertime," I said. "There should be nothing but pleasant things from six o'clock on. Music on the stereo . . . the chatter of friends . . . laughter of children . . . evening twitter of birds, et cetera. A cocktail or glass of wine . . . an easy chair . . . the aroma of cooking food. In short, this experience, *now*. What the hell's wrong with *you*?"

Mary was wiping away a tear. She was thinking of Mr. X, and the photograph of Jim Schilling. She didn't like any of it. We talked all during dinner about what was going on, what it all meant. It broke my rule of nothing but pleasant things after six, but there was no escaping it. Jim and I agreed on how easy it would be for Schilling to falsify his death, especially in a remote region of Alaska. If he were willing to part with a $300 rifle—which he was—the ruse would gain instant credibility. He could have either bribed the guide or arranged another escape route. Both Jim and I strongly suspected the latter strategy, since a bribed guide is generally a poor liar, whereas a duped guide is an earnest witness. It would have been simple for Schilling to arrange a clandestine meeting with a pilot a few miles from the swamped boat. Three hours' trudge would take them far enough away from the camp so the guide would never hear the small, single-engined pontoon plane. . .

But why?

We agreed the most logical explanation was that he wished to return to Massachusetts to seek revenge on his former employer. But if this were true, hadn't he taken a long time to act? What was he engaged in during the past year? It was all curiouser and curiouser, but unfortunately no clearer.

"Go to the police, Charlie," Jim said.

"No."

"Yes dammit!" screamed Mary. She was crying, and hadn't eaten.

"Ok," I said.

I wrote a letter to Chief Hannon summarizing the events of the past two weeks. It was no masterpiece but it would serve well enough to lay out what had been happening, both in my mind and the real world. I sent a copy to Joe too. Either Chief Hannon would be impressed, or he would think I was crazy.

12

"KNOW WHAT YOUR PROBLEM IS?" SAID THE CHIEF AS HE put my letter down on his desk and peered at me over his glasses. "You're crazy."

"I was hoping you weren't going to say that."

"What am I *supposed* to say for Christ's sake? You see a boat that looks like another and they both disappear. You ask around and discover that a certain man's private life and his business aren't all they were cracked up to be—as if that's a rarity. You get in a bar fight up in Gloucester—which, by the way, you are too old to be doing—and later get hit on the head and tossed in the drink. A hundred miles away, I might add, and two weeks *after*, you presumably saw *Windhover's* reincarnation down on the Cape. Now Doc. What am I supposed to say?"

I felt like a naughty kid in the principal's office. I stared idly out Brian's window and watched a gray squirrel hop along a giant oak limb, fluffing its tail and chattering. The word was getting around fast; even the squirrels knew I was crazy. A blue jay shrieked, and the squirrel chattered and flipped its tail in little quick jerks.

Brian Hannon picked up the phone and summoned an aide. He told the aide to run down some background information on James Schilling and Daniel Murdock.

130

"You did it. Why did you, if I'm imagining the whole thing?"

"I don't want you to suppose anything from it. Remember this: you still haven't a thing concrete to go on. It's one pipe dream strung to another, all the way along. But I can get the information, and will, if there is any to be got. I can do it without pangs of conscience because doing so will indirectly protect you, which is what I'm paid to do. We'll get back to you in a few days. You can be reached at home?"

"No. We're taking off for the Cape tomorrow early. I'll be spending two days or so getting *Ella Hatton* ready."

"Who's she?"

"My boat."

"Oh I see. Getting her ready to take her out of the water?"

"No. Getting her ready for a cruise around Cape Cod Bay. I don't want anyone except you and the family, and Jim De-Groot, to know where I am or how long I'll be gone. If you need me, call Mary and leave a message."

"And what do you intend to do on this cruise?"

"I'm going to find the boat: *Penelope, Windhover* . . . Whatever the hell her name is, I'm going to find her if I have to pick up Cape Cod by Provincetown and Buzzards Bay and turn it upside down and *shake* it."

"That's a dumb idea."

"I didn't expect you'd think it was a great idea. Mary is not too wild about it either."

I rose to go, but he detained me. He opened a small metal filing case behind him and drew out my card. It was my application to own and carry a handgun. These are very difficult to get in Massachusetts. If you are caught toting a handgun and are not so licensed, you are sentenced to a year in the can. No ifs, ands, or buts. Chief Brian Hannon, after some debate, had granted me the Permit to Carry two years ago when I took up target shooting. He examined some slips of paper behind the card.

"Hmmmm. Two additions since your original purchase. Ruger Bull-Barrel auto target pistol, caliber 22. Browning 9-millimeter auto. Tell me, Doc, you're not thinking of taking these along with you on your cruise are you? And if you do, do you really think you might need them?''

I paused at the doorway and turned.

"As Fats Waller used to say: 'one never knows, do one?' ''

"I still can't believe we went, Charlie," said Mary as she slid into the front seat. It was just before midnight and we were leaving the Surf Theater in Wocasset.

"How did you like them?"

"I can't believe they're legal. Honest to God I had no idea—"

"But how did you *like* them?"

"I think they're disgusting. I mean even the titles."

"I don't know, I thought the titles were rather clever, especially *A Hard Man Is Good to Find*."

"Hmmmm. What was the other one called?"

"*Genitals Prefer Blondes*."

"Well it was disgusting."

"Well then I'm sorry I took you."

"You didn't like them, did you?"

"I think a little dirt every now and then is nice. You sure you didn't like them even a little bit?"

She protested that she didn't. The movies exploited both men and women she said, and debased sex. And furthermore, if she'd any idea that they were that explicit and graphic she never would have consented to go in the first place. And she would never go again. I kept my mouth shut.

We had arrived back at *The Breakers* the day before. All through the drive we discussed—argued actually—the merits and disadvantages of my secret Bay cruise aboard the *Ella Hatton*. I was propounding the former, she the latter. I finally managed to convince her that I would be safe because I would remain inconspicuously in the background: in small bays and inlets, in snug harbors and along beaches.

We swung into the wide gravel drive, exited the car and started up the back steps. The surf was loud. Mary had been strangely silent during the ride back to the cottage, as if she were concentrating on something.

As soon as I shut the door behind us, she jumped me.

13

THE LIST GREW. THE PILES AND STOCKS OF SUPPLIES GREW consequently. These items were transported semisurreptitiously down to the *Hatton*'s slip in Wellfleet Harbor where, incidentally, there had been no sign whatsoever of *Penelope*. My beard was half grown and emerging iron gray. Dark glasses and a big floppy canvas hat helped further to keep my face hidden. With Jack helping out, I managed to secure the cargo aboard the *ella Hatton*. It was two weeks past Labor Day but the harbor was still full. The hard-core sailors didn't take their boats out until late October. A few diehards have been known to leave their boats in the water all winter, going on the assumption it won't freeze solid. If it does, the boat has had it, crushed between packs of moving ice like a grape in a wine press.

When we were finished, every cubby, hatch, and shelf in the *Hatton*'s interior was filled with canned hams, fresh corn and melons, cases of soda water and beer, wedges of cheese, cigars and pipe tobacco, and everything else needed for a couple of weeks afloat in comfort and style.

Ella Hatton's antique appearance comes mostly from her rig. The wide, low sails and the gaff rig . . . the bowsprit and the jibboom all bespeak an earlier age: the turn-of-the-century fishing and clamming industry on the Cape where these boats originated. Also the wheel, tiny portholes, wide rudder, and her soft, blocky lines have the plain, rugged look of a commercial craft rather than the sleek, faintly fragile appearance of the racing yachts.

She draws just two feet of water with her centerboard up, which means that she can be beached. Also, because of her flat bottom and wide shape, she sits perfectly upright when stranded on a tidal flat. This is important because in Cape Cod Bay stranding is a common, oftentimes intentional thing, and a boat that sits level is far more comfortable than one that lies on her side.

Jack and I finished stowing the gear after I had placed the two twenty-five-pound blocks of ice into the icebox beneath the cockpit seat. Then we closed the teak shutters, drew back the main hatch, and locked up tight with a big brass padlock. In the morning I would top up the fuel and water tanks and cast off.

"It seems to me we put about two tons of stuff aboard," said Jack as he stood up on the dock looking down at the catboat, "but she doesn't seem any lower in the water or anything."

"She's as wide as a pie pan. Maybe that's why."

We went back to *The Breakers* for dinner.

A driftwood fire was crackling away in the grate. I unrolled the charts on the low coffee table and we pored over them, roughly outlining my mission. Mary was to be settled in at the domicile in Concord with Joe, who was coming for an extended visit. He loved his Beacon Hill flat, but a sojourn in the countryside—particularly in fall—was an annual custom he looked forward to. From my point of view, considering certain recent events and possible future complications, I was glad an armed officer of the law would be staying with Mary. Tony had finished his summer job in New Hampshire and was up in Acadia National Park camping with friends. Jack would return to Concord with Mary in the morning; I didn't want him or any of my family at *The Breakers* without me.

I told them I would head west along the inside of the Cape first, nosing my way into the small harbors of Barnstable and Sandwich. From there I would either head north to Plymouth, or south through the Cape Cod Canal down into Buzzards Bay and the oceanside, although I doubted this. Whatever was happening—if anything—was happening in the Bay, or to the north.

Next morning after the breakfast dishes were cleaned and put away we shut *The Breakers* up tight, hiding all the valuables and locking it. Then Jack and I dragged the twelve-foot Swampscott dory up from the beach and put it on the roof rack of his Land Cruiser. We stowed the tiny British outboard engine in the back and headed for the harbor. I would tow the fiber glass dory behind the *Hatton*. It would enable me to come ashore from any anchorage and provide easy dockside access in any harbor I chose to enter. Besides these conveniences, it was unsinkable (the *Hatton*, with its lead ballast, was not) and would make a good lifeboat should the *Hatton* swamp in a heavy sea or dash herself to pieces on a ledge.

When everything was in order I kissed Mary good-bye and reminded her that I would call once a day without fail. She clung a bit too hard, too long. She was still worried.

Jack was to follow her to Concord and spend a few days there, tentatively to arrive in Plymouth on the third day to reconnoiter with me and the *Hatton*.

The two cars made tight turns in the harbor parking lot, then glided up to the main road, turned, and vanished.

I made ready and cast off.

When I was clear of the harbor, I cut the engine to a crawl and I began to watch my "telltales." These are strips of fuzzy orange yarn tied to my stays. They blow in the wind and indicate its direction. I wanted to be directly into the wind when I raised the main. I winched it up and the boom and gaff flapped spastically back and forth. The jib followed. The sails flip-flapped stupidly until I turned the *Hatton* downwind a bit, until the telltales were parallel to the leading edge of the sails as I hauled them tight. Then, a change came over *Ella Hatton*. The sails caught. The boat heeled slightly, and there was a sense of force, pressure, and *function*. I cut the diesel. In a few seconds our speed picked up because the slow-turning prop had feathered itself, thus decreasing

the resistance of the boat in the water. I trimmed the sails
still more and adjusted the *Hatton*'s course.

When a sailboat is properly trimmed in a fresh breeze—
when the wind direction, hull, and sails are all in perfect
symphony—she trembles. It is a stiffening tremble, as in a
woman reaching orgasm—a vibrancy of energy and force
that tells the experienced helmsman that the boat is perform-
ing optimally.

With the engine cut, there was only the sound of rushing
water and the creaking of the sheets and blocks. I sat holding
the wheel and kept *Ella Hatton* heading south. Both sheets
were fastened in jam cleats. These are cleats that hold the
lines by means of toothed cam gears, and can be released
immediately in a strong puff of wind. Jam cleats have made
solo sailing easier and safer. The *Hatton* bounced and dipped
along; I watched the green-blue water slide past, sending up
never-ending streams of bubbles and tiny whirlpools of silver
air and water. Farther back the brine swirled white-gray in
endless filigrees of foam. There was the hiss and chuckle of
moving water. The hiss I find a particularly pleasant sound,
the sound of effervescence, like soda water or champagne.

I slipped the loop of heavy line over the kingspoke of the
wheel and dove into the hatchway long enough to turn on the
radio. The dial was on the VHF channel 162.5—the weather
frequency. Amidst the buzzing, squelches, and droning came
the steady voice of the Weather Bureau.

". . . winds west, northwest five to eight knots, freshening to ten
to twelve knots by late afternoon . . . barometer thirty point two
and steady . . . seas one to three and rising . . . forecast fair and
windy tonight with partial cloud cover, visibility nine miles . . .
tomorrow windy and cool, with squalls likely in the evening. . ."

I listened on for the tide report, then ran forward again
and switched it off. For the nonce I had nothing to worry
about. The *Hatton* was booming along nicely, and I should
have no trouble reaching Dennis by five. I cracked open a
beer and kept my eyes on the buoys. Smalley Bar slid past
my starboard side. I looked up at Little Beach Hill on Great
Island where a pirate tavern had stood in the old days. Had

Walter Kincaid fulfilled his dream by discovering a horde of lost treasure? If so did he still have it, or did something grievous befall him? Whether he was alive or dead, Wallace Kinchloe was dead for sure. Someone else was then using his identity. That person appeared to be James Schilling.

I kept puzzling over this as I passed Jeremy Point. Lieutenant's Bar was ahead on my port bow. When I reached it, I would be at the foot of Billingsgate Island, where it had all started. A few minutes later I was there. There was no island to be seen though, because it was high tide. Billingsgate lay about three feet under, which meant I could wade over it. But I stayed clear; the *Hatton*'s centerboard was down, which meant she was drawing five and a half feet. I had read somewhere that Billingsgate wasn't always a sunken island. There was a village on it up until around 1845 when the inhabitants noticed it was sinking. The tides were creeping higher and higher and gales caused waves to sweep entirely over it— something that had never before happened. So they left. They took their houses with them too—just jacked them up, put them on rollers, and lugged them over to the mainland. And that was that.

Lieutenant's Point slid by on the port side. I glanced at the chart that was weighted down against the wind by three smooth beach rocks. I was leaving Wellfleet Channel, and headed the boat directly toward the ragged hulk of the target ship *James Longstreet*. The sky was clear cobalt blue, with puffy cottonball clouds that scudded across it like the Great White Fleet. These puffy round clouds are known as the "cumulus of fair weather," and they are associated with brisk, breezy days with high pressure and cool temperature. Nice days. But they also oftentimes precede violent weather, as the radio foretold for the next day. I took my marine glasses and scanned the shoreline. There was *The Breakers*, snug by herself on the blufftop. I peered again at the *Longstreet*. What was a ship named for a Confederate general doing in the New England waters? But then I remembered the planes from Otis Air Force Base had bombed it for years, so it seemed to make *some* sense . . . In twenty minutes I was within 1500 yards of the wreck, passing it on my way to Dennis. Two small boats were within the forbidden zone. They were in no danger of being shelled—the target hadn't been used in several years—but they were liable for a stiff fine if caught by the Coast Guard. The circle on the chart intrigued me, with its tiny half-sunken boat in its center, signifying a wreck. The words *Prohibited Area* were printed in bright blue letters on the chart. I swung the *Hatton*'s nose a bit more to the west, pointing her smack for the flashing bell buoy five miles ahead. Another five miles beyond this buoy would take me opposite the harbor of Barnstable. Two smaller harbors, Rock Harbor and Sesuit Harbor, I would skip; they are too small for anything *Penelope*'s size.

The wind held nicely at five to eight knots, more toward eight most of the afternoon. Shortly after four I was standing off Barnstable, my sails down, with my diesel turning slowly. I approached the place warily because Barnstable is infamous for muddy shoals and rocks. The harbor is long, windy, and narrow, and the channel continually shifts.

A short time later, I was officially in the harbor, but from glancing around, you'd never know it. Low sand dunes gave way to brownish-purple flats, ribbed and rippled from the ebbing tide. I crept my way cautiously forward, keeping one eye on the depth sounder. I cranked up the board. Drawing only two feet, I felt confident that getting all the way in to Blish Point where the marina was should be a piece of cake. It was.

I dropped anchor out in the far reaches of the harbor where I could enjoy privacy and anonymity. When *Ella Hatton* stranded herself in the falling tide I unlashed the ten-speed bike from its place on the cabin top and wheeled it ashore. I called in to Mary to say I was safe. Brian Hannon had not been in touch. No news. I asked the harbormaster, the tackle shop owner, and several of the pleasure boat set if they had laid eyes on *Penelope*. Got nos all around. I pedalled around the waterfront roads, inspecting each and every building on the water big enough to conceal her. Nothing. So much for Barnstable. While it was still low tide, I walked back out to the boat, cooked my supper, and turned in. I opened all the portholes to let the air in. The wind blew softly, bringing with it the faraway cries of gulls and the smell of mudflats and brine.

I awoke momentarily in the middle of the night, feeling *Ella Hatton* swinging around her cable, the moving water chuckling around her hull. . .

I left at next high water and was off to Sandwich, the small harbor town that marks the northern terminus of the Cape Cod Canal. Same story there: no *Penelope*. All during my time at sea I approached every trawler I saw. I was very careful if I saw an old basket hanging in the rigging because that's the sign that they have a net working. I slipped in close and hollered as we slid past each other. Had they seen a green trawler *Penelope* out of Boston? They all answered no. I kept the radio on all the time, hunting for gossip. The VHF crackled and droned and spit out a constant stream of routine information. The CB bands contained snatches of folksy conversation like:

Charlene to Joe and Mary: "Hey, Joey, you got any beer left? We're on a school here and we're dry and can't leave. Over."

Joe and Mary to Charlene: "I'm here. Got two cases left. Can we come over and help you get what's left if we give you one? I'm gone—"

I struck out all the way up the coast. The day was hot and sticky and I was under power part of the time. I didn't want to be late for my meeting with Jack up in Plymouth. Toward late afternoon it cooled a bit and the breeze freshened. I cut the engine and was making four knots on a broad reach with the board cranked halfway up. It got darker and darker, and the water had an oily roll to it. Bad weather coming.

I was standing off Plymouth when it got really dark, and scary. There was an electric feeling in the air of enormous pressure . . . of tremendous energy about to be released. The gulls were gone, either inland or in safe water, huddled in small rafts of bobbing birds. The wind got downright chilly. I dove below and got a Windbreaker, and scanned ahead for the four-second flash off Gurnet Point. It stood out clearly in the falling light. As I drew nearer, I would look for the giant

Miles Standish monument. But for now it was obscured by
the gathering clouds. A cold tickle of rain pelted me. The
wind stiffened still more; the telltales stood out straight from
the stays. *Ella Hatton*'s blunt, wide nose was heaved up again
and again, only to crash down with wide falls of powder-
white foam shooting outward before me. But it was mostly
a following sea that pushed from behind on her broad transom, giving us a hundred miniature sleigh rides on the crest
of breaking waves. This kind of water lifts the whole boat in
the euphoric way. Then there is the rush of speed on the
wave's peak and at this instant, a giddy rooster-dance of
wobbly falling, a shuddering uncertainty of going into the
trough. . .

You are going fast then, and it feels great. But if the water
is big enough, and the troughs deep enough, you can bury
your bow and pitch-pole right into solid water. That does not
feel great. Or you can broach in the trough and yaw broadside
to all the water coming down on top of you.

The sea wasn't that high. Not yet. But it was doing its
damndest working on it. While there was still time I dropped
the main and gathered it into the wide cockpit as best I could.
Then I started the Westerbeke and revved it up pretty high
to give me a lot of headway.

I was doing seven knots. The dory was becoming a real
problem. In the following sea it had caught up with us. Twice
it shot forward on the curl of a breaker and almost rammed
us. Fortunately, it swung over to our port side and came
around beside the *Hatton*. I watched it warily. The last thing
I needed, sailing in dirty weather alone, was a guided missile
in dory form leaping toward my kidneys as I tried to navigate.

A sharp right at Duxbury Light led up a wide and shallow
channel called the Cowyard. This was a good anchorage according to my marine atlas. A right jog led up another channel to the town of North Plymouth, a rather industrial place
with a big commercial pier maintained by a cordage company.

At the light I headed to starboard, right smack for the
Miles Standish Monument on the top of Captain's Hill. I
flipped on the depth sounder as I crept into the Cowyard,

finally cutting the engine when it read six feet. The *Hatton*
oozed along in a stall, and I dropped the big bow anchor over
the side with its twenty-foot length of chain, followed by a
much longer length of mooring line. When the flukes bit into
the sand the line around the bitt squealed and groaned. Then
I drew the line in and made it fast. I threw out a smaller
anchor over the stern and did likewise with it. The boat faced
the channel flow, so currents wouldn't build up on her broad-
sides. Meanwhile the untended jib had been flipping and
flapping about, and I let it down and hauled it in. Though I
was shivering now, and soaked to the skin, I leaned over in
the pelting rain and unhooked it from the forestay and stuffed
it down the forehatch. It was growing darker and colder by
the second. Thunder rolled up from the south, and the faint
glimmerings of lightning flickered there. The rain was sin-
cere now, in earnest you might say, and sang down on the
deck like a swarm of locusts: a high wavering hiss. I longed
for dry clothes and the warmth of the cabin, but I had to raise
the anchor light and bring in the dory first. Then I rigged the
"gizmo," a big tarp that fits over the boom and fastens down
on each side of the cockpit. It resembles a big pup tent, and
provides shelter over a great portion of the boat.

After rigging this contraption I was so cold and miserable
I regretted the whole journey. I squished along the foredeck
in my soaking Topsiders and rechecked the anchor lines and
the anchor light. At the stern, I pulled in the dory's tow line
and made her fast at my back door. Then I dove under the
hatch and shed the wet clothes. I was shaking so much I
could hardly light the lamps, but managed four times to dip
the lighted kitchen match into the brass slot and see the wicks
come aglow. Then I placed the glass chimneys back on and
adjusted the flames. The four lamps lighted the small cabin
space with golden light. I knew the oil lamps would throw
off a fair amount of heat as well as save my batteries. But as
the wind picked up and the temperature dropped still more,
I knew the night would be raw indeed. I had snuggled into a
pair of jeans, an undershirt, and a chamois-cloth shirt. But I
was still cold, and so lighted the tiny coal-fired heater near
the galley sink. I placed the special coal briquettes in the

slotted grate over two pieces of well-twisted newspaper, to which I set fire. A few seconds after closing the small door on the firebox a powerful—though miniature—draft was created in the stack, thus igniting the coal as tobacco is set glowing in a briar pipe. Through the mica glass I could see the cozy flicker of the fire sweep across the coals like small waves . . . cascades of red and yellow: hot and hotter.

I hopped up and drew back the companionway. It was perfect hell outside. It was raining almost sideways, and though *Ella Hatton* rode remarkably level in the Cowyard anchorage, the water gnashed angrily at her hull. The anchor light was defiantly aflicker, though I doubt I would have braved the weather to attend to it if it weren't. I saw the tiny conical chimney top spouting its proud plume of smoke, like the Tin Woodman blowing smoke rings.

The wind howled and pelted rain. I dove back below and slid the hatch closed. For ventilation, I kept part of the companionway shutters open and the forward porthole ajar. There was a hiss and a demonic crack, and blue-white light came shooting in beams through the portholes. A terrific thunderclap followed, and the *thump thump thump* of steady strong water against the *Hatton*'s glass hull increased.

Although the thought of dinner haunted me, I decided to skip the meal altogether. True, I could have filled my tummy with all kinds of canned and cellophane-packed edibles and perhaps some cold glunk. But why? It would be a miserable experience. But a stiff Scotch did sound nice. I fetched a king-sized tumbler and poured a moderate-sized dollop. I up-ended the bottle of Johnny Walker Red in the glass and counted to seven.

I added soda, no ice since I was half frozen, and watched the mixture make little swirly lines and patterns in the glass . . . like heat waves going in circles. Yummy.

I lay back in the bunk on the starboard side. A porthole was directly to my right. Above and behind me to the left was the companionway. Wicked sounds scudded down through it. Sounds of mad water and storm. And then I became fully conscious of the building din in my ears: the crashing of the rain upon the cabin top and decks. It roared and pounded. It ran and whispered in mounting rivulets along the coaming and through the scuppers.

I snuggled into the down covers and sipped. Outside there was wrack and ruin all about me: gale-force winds, pelting rain, and angry tide. Two feet from me was cold water, dark with endless murky bottoms and slimy things. I was alone, floating in a howling gale. But inside, the gimballed lamps shone brightly, the coal stove sent forth its warm radiance.

The whiskey had tugged lovingly at my brain now, so it was a wee bit soft at the edges. It was like the filmy curl of a breaker—that leading edge of a breaking wave that foams and tumbles leaping onward, that fizzes outward slightly in delicious anticipation of the Great Going On.

I shook the tiny grate and closed the damper cover halfway. The coals, now diminished, glowed merrily. Temporarily braving the storm's ferocity, I opened the hatch shutters and stuck my head out under the gizmo canopy. The rain sound shifted from a drum roll to a rattlesnake hiss. The anchor light was fine. I plunged back down below, leaving the shutters open. It would get cold in the cabin now. I blew out the gimballed lights, tossed off the last of the scotch, and fell back on the pillow, listening. I was propelled down a roaring musical tunnel of sound and motion to sleep.

14

I AWOKE AT 6 A.M., HUNGRY AS A TIGER. I EMERGED FROM my rabbit hole and poked my head out under the gizmo and looked around. It was bad.

Now in most places in the world, an all-night rainstorm means that the morn will dawn bright, sparkly clear, with blue skies and sun. In most places, yes.

In New England, an all-night rain means that Mother Nature is getting warmed up. She's doing her sitting-up exercises for the *real* bad stuff. The violent storm had given way to a thin drizzle. These spells of Heavenly Displeasure may last for two or three days. The sky is overcast, and changes from dark to less dark. What remains constant is the near-invisible rain of tiny threads of water droplets which, over an extended period of time, make everything damp: all your clothes, your socks especially, your skin, your carpets and bedsheets, curtains, and your spirits.

I could hear the faint patter of the drizzle on the tarp that formed the gizmo. I was depressed. I wanted a big hot meal with lots and lots of coffee. I looked at the tiny alcohol stove in the cramped galley. I shook my head. The last thing I wanted to do in my hungry and depressed state was to sit kneeling down in front of a small stove—you have to kneel down in a catboat; there isn't enough up-and-down room to do anything else—and cook my breakfast. I'd have to pump up the stove and clean up everything afterward. No, I deserved better after what I'd been through the previous night. I deserved to sit in a booth and order heaps of everything. I returned to the cabin and got dressed. Almost as an afterthought, I took my dark glasses to help hide the black eye, which was hanging on like a summer cold. I peeked out from under the canvas again and wished it weren't so.

The tide had receded, leaving a lot of muddy, dusky banks of purple mud and slime. The water was quiet. Even in the drizzle it reflected the dank earth and dull brick buildings of North Plymouth. It didn't even look like water. It looked like used motor oil. I heard a creak like an old rusty hinge. Birds. Two gulls were gliding over the slick, as if afraid to land on it. They glided motionless, wings steady, about two feet off the water, rasping and churring. They wheeled and pumped air with their long wings, settling on what looked like a giant cowpie in the middle of the still shine. Even the birds were depressed.

"This is awful," I murmured. I sat down on one of the cockpit cushions, which I dredged up out of the lazaret. If you wanna see ugly, I'll show you ugly: North Plymouth in a slow morning drizzle at low tide. There was a tall smokestack across from me near Gray's Beach. It marked the commercial pier built by the Plymouth Cordage Company, which (I later discovered) used to make hempen ropes, twine, and that grisly stuff you see in lumber yards called *sisal*. Anyway, the Plymouth Cordage Company was doing about as well as the Acme Buggywhip Corporation, which was not very. The cordage company was in a state representative of many older New England industries: like a punk poker hand, it had folded.

I heard a low growl off to my left, and saw a dragger bravely making its way through the muck out into the main channel. A bit later came the high whine of an outboard, and a skiff darted out from Duxbury Harbor and made a neat lazy crescent around past me and followed the dragger. The wake came at me in dark troughs on the shiny water.

I got the marine glasses out of the bosun's box and glassed the pier. Nothing. I could see only one side of it. But there were four draggers tied up there . . . no restaurant. I was getting hungrier. The dock was dingy. It was a series of abandoned warehouses and old pilings.

Everything was still and putrid. The water didn't move; it sat. The still air hovered in thick dampness. The herring gulls sat in long lines on the mudflats. They were all fluffed up and pouty, and didn't say a thing. No shoreside sounds reached me . . . not a screech of brakes, a pile driver, or a jet plane. Nothing. I was seriously contemplating returning to the bunk with a book and a bottle when I spotted an American flag hung limp on a masthead at the end of a small pier near Gray's Beach. I grabbed the binoculars and was delighted to see a gilded sign with a lobster on it. Further inspection revealed a sign in the window that said OPEN. Faint shapes bustled about within. Soon I had the dory whining along on the slick straight toward the old stone dock. It was apparently an old quay that had been refurbished and graced with a small restaurant. The big commercial pier was off to my left, and as I proceeded toward breakfast I noticed that the boat dock curved around the other side of the big brick warehouse, and was full of all kinds of vessels. Several draggers were moored off the pier in the gray water. The boats sat immobile, lapping up the waves of my tiny wake that struck their big, blunt bows. I passed them and headed on to the old stone quay. Arriving there I took the dory around and moored it next to a slanting foot ramp that was, at low tide, about 45 degrees to the water.

As I was making fast, I looked at the *Hatton* riding far off in the mist. She slightly resembled a Gypsy caravan because of the big gizmo tent that covered her boom.

I trudged along the big pier, clad in a waterproof parka, thick woolen sweater, and my droopy canvas rain hat that just about covered my face. Despite the clouds and rain I wore my sunglasses to hide my black eye. My pants were getting slowly soaked. But I didn't care; the wind was warm, and I would linger over breakfast and coffee, and the *Globe*.

I followed a group of patrons into the place. The varnished pine door was warm and sticky. The inside smelled a bit too much of cooking oil. But it was crowded. At seven o'clock that had to be some kind of recommendation. There were big booths separated from one another by pine partitions that rose up a foot and a half above the heads of the seated customers.

I sank into one of the booths at the far end of the restaurant. Nearby was a window that looked out into the harbor and the grim silent shapes of the big draggers that swung in a line into the current of the incoming tide. Was one of them the boat that awakened me in the wee hours? A waitress appeared and poured me coffee. It was actually pretty good (and I'm fussy—if you haven't already guessed). I ordered two poached eggs on toast, hash browns, bacon, and a side plate of kippers with extra lemon. I removed my dripping canvas hat and placed it on the seat next to me.

I drank the coffee and gobbled the breakfast. I had been sitting for perhaps half an hour with the paper when a sound— or rather certain sounds in sequence—sent my blood cold.

I don't know when I became aware of it. It crept upon me gradually as I was reading the paper. Sometime in the middle of an article about Ted Kennedy, I replaced the canvas rain hat upon my head and drew it down on all sides. I slipped my damaged hand into the depths of my thick woolen sweater, replaced the big dark glasses, and turned into my booth to gaze out the window, hunched over.

And yet if anyone were to happen upon the scene and ask me *why*, I couldn't have answered. Perhaps it was that same message—sent coursing through my injured brain—that forced me to swim under the filthy waters of Gloucester Harbor rather than surface to be killed. Like a Canada goose gliding low over a duckblind, I veered warily. I sat hunched, invisible as I could make myself.

The sound I was hearing was the scuffing footstep of a heavy man pacing back and forth behind me. Underneath that sound I could hear, at intervals as regular as Old Faithful, the sniffing, snorfing, of a man nervously clearing his throat.

I listened for ten minutes. There was no mistake. The fearful hour in the cold water was indelibly burned into my memory. *I knew.*

Mr. X, the Quiet One, the lethal sneak who sandbagged people, was behind me.

The pine partition of the booth kept me out of view. In the momentary dizziness of my discovery it was curious how my mind had remained in a rather pedestrian state as I stared out the window, watching the big draggers in the gray drizzle. I felt a thump at my back, and almost jumped out of my skin. I do not consider myself the least bit cowardly (I suppose nobody does), but the thought of that expert sapper behind my line of vision upset me. It upset me a good deal.

The thump was someone sitting down in the booth directly behind me, throwing his weight back against the partition. Was it Mr. X? I wasn't about to turn around and ask. Had he seen me? Probably not. First of all, he certainly wasn't expecting Yours Truly, having assumed that green crabs and slimy things were now dining on my remains. Also, there was the nascent beard, the pulled down cap, and my general low profile. I listened.

If indeed the patron behind me was Mr. X, or one of his accomplices, it didn't come out in the talk, at least in the few words I was able to hear. There was a continual reference to *dawn*, which I later decided was *Shawn*, or *Sean*, but I wasn't sure. The partition kept thumping me in the kidneys, as if the occupant of the next booth was on edge, or excited. I stared out at the boats in the rain. I focused in especially on the one I thought bore a strong resemblance to *Penelope*. I stared hard. The more I stared, the more I realized it wasn't her. Just wasn't, from a thousand big and little clues.

Perhaps one of these boats was the one that thumped by me in the night . . . but *Penelope* was not among them.

"We ready?" came another voice from the booth behind me.

"Almost."

Then they talked some more, their words drowned out by the clatter of dishes and chatter of customers. I looked at my watch: 7:40. Jack was to meet me at 4 P.M. at Duxbury/Plymouth Harbor. If I failed to appear he was to call out the militia. Another thump hit me in the kidneys and I heard the booth patrons get up and walk away to the counter.

I didn't move. Half a minute later the door slammed, and I saw the two men walking past the window. The bigger one was limping, ever so slightly. It was more a slight roll than a limp. It was Mr. X. He was wearing a yellow slicker and a blue billed hat. He had a dark beard. His shoulders were wide. Very wide. The man next to him hobbled along quick and nervous, like a fox terrier. There was something vaguely familiar about his manner. Finally I recognized him as the man in the runabout who had streaked for shore in Wellfleet Harbor to seek the much-needed repair job for *Penelope*. I remembered too the same man hobbling with great agility on the sand flats a few hours previous. The men reached the end of the dock and began to descend a ramp to their boat, which obviously rode on the water out of sight. But at the top the big man turned and stared at something. Then I saw him in profile, and I knew I was looking at James Schilling, presumed dead. My heart skipped about three beats in a row—Schilling was momentarily frozen at the top of the ramp. What was he looking at?

Then I realized he was staring at the *Hatton*. He kept looking at her a goodly time. Then he swung around, slow and stately as a bull elk, and looked down at the water on the side of the pier opposite the ramp he was standing on. That's where I'd tied the dory. And then, he kept swinging around and fixed his level gaze in my direction, though I was certain he didn't see me.

I didn't like it. I was about to glide casually over to one of the phone booths and hunker down into it, back to the window, if he came inside again. It wasn't that I was terribly afraid he'd attempt something in a crowded restaurant. If so, assuming he carried no firearm or hidden machete, I would get in a few good licks myself. Lord knows I had reason to. Besides I was getting to be an expert at fighting lately. But I had to remain invisible from Schilling. If he knew I wasn't dead, he'd keep after me. More important, he'd realize his cover was blown, and lie low or disappear. Had he recognized the *Hatton*? I remembered again the glare he shot us when I took his picture as we left Wellfleet. No doubt he'd gazed after the departing catboat uneasily. Now he sees a catboat in Plymouth. No. I was worrying unnecessarily. Still I couldn't help wonder if he knew, or even thought, that the man in the Schooner Race was indeed the same fellow who snapped his picture in the harbor. Had he put my two identities together? I thought of the photograph on my driver's license.

Schilling spun on his heel and they stomped down the ramp and seconds later I saw their dinghy—I swore it was the same one I saw in Wellfleet—heading toward the cordage company's commercial pier. I stared down at the empty plates and wondered what to do next. Wearily, I rose from the booth and paid my bill.

Then I entered the phone booth and dialed Mary. I told her what had happened, down to the smallest detail. There was a longish silence on the other end. When Mary finally spoke, her voice was shaking. She told me to get home fast or she was going to call the police and make them fetch me.

"Goddammit Charlie! Goddamn you, how can you keep *doing* this to me—"

And so it went. On and on.

"Let me talk to Jack. Is he there?"

I got number-one son on the line and told him to meet me at Duxbury Harbor with the *Hatton*'s trailer at dusk. Duxbury is next door to Plymouth. This meant he had to go to Wellfleet first, then deadhead back with the empty trailer in tow. But time was of the essence. I had located my quarry, and had no desire to sail back to Wellfleet in a boat that could be recognized. It would be a simple matter for a big steel dragger like *Penelope* to cut me in two with her high bows. That meant the cruise was going to end a lot sooner than anticipated.

But perhaps finding James Schilling, Mr. X, in Plymouth was more than just simple good fortune. Perhaps studying the charts and thinking a lot had paid off. Perhaps I wasn't as dumb as everyone seemed to think. I had some other theories too.

"Call me on the CB when you arrive in Duxbury. I may not be inside the harbor when you get there, but I'll be within earshot. Use the name Ella Hatton, not our name; we may have eavesdroppers."

He agreed and I told Mary not to worry, then rang off.

As I emerged from the booth I felt resentful. Schilling was sharp and cautious. Of that there was no doubt. He had a keen eye and memory, and used them. The distant boat had alerted him immediately. I felt outfoxed, and the dunk in the harbor added to my anger. I had worked myself up to a pretty good rage by the time I was whining back to the mother ship. I clambered aboard *Ella Hatton* fuming. The son of a bitch! With a pipe clenched between my teeth, I had a think session of about ten minutes, then decided to approach the big pier and see what I could see.

By the time I had the engine started and the dory in tow, I had managed to convince myself that Schilling had not recognized the *Hatton*. I drew up the anchors and crept along at a snail's pace. I was crouched under the gizmo, working the wheel and gazing out ahead through the triangle opening of the canvas flap. The boat slid into shallow water, and finally drifted to a stop between Gray's Beach and the pier. I crept still closer after waiting there awhile, until I was barely eighty yards from the dock. It was topped by a long warehouse that extended the full length, much like the big fish pier in Boston Harbor. I saw four big semi-trailer trucks on the dockside between the boats and the warehouse. They were refrigerated trailers; their compressors were grinding away. A few tiny figures moved behind the maze of masts, cables, and white crescents of radar antennae. Along the shore, behind the big warehouse on top of the dock were several other big buildings of red brick. They looked deserted. There was a huge chimney projecting out of this industrial wasteland. It was the same one prominently marked on the chart of Plymouth Harbor. It was a perfect landmark— much easier to find than the squat lighthouse called Bug Light in the center of the harbor. I let go the anchor cable and slouched in the cockpit, glassing the pier with the binoculars. No *Penelope* present, so Schilling had ditched her. But just then one of the draggers began gliding away from the pier and, as she left, revealed a white boat that was a dead ringer for the one I'd been looking for. I glassed her carefully from stem to stern. It was her. No doubt about it. She was painted white, and looked brand spanking new. Other than a coat of paint, she wasn't changed except for some kind of superstructure far aft. It looked like a raised hatchway. This altered her appearance considerably, especially in profile. It would fool anyone who wasn't looking carefully, or was unaware of what to look for. How long had it taken the men to add it on? Three or four days was my guess. And another carpenter's certificate. I wondered what her new name was as I hauled out my camera and a 300-millimeter lens from the aluminum case. I read the name on her bow: *Rose*. I set up the camera on the tripod and snapped away at the snow-white boat at the pier. Nothing projected from beneath the gizmo canopy. I was—for all practical purposes—completely invisible underneath it in the gray drizzle. But of course *Ella Hatton* was plainly visible to those aboard. She was tauntingly visible. Were it not for the fact I was moored in about three feet of water, the *Rose* could chug right over and have a close look. Through the long lens I caught a flicker of motion in the boat's wheelhouse. I raised the binoculars and had a peek. I'll be darned if someone in the pilothouse wasn't looking at me too. No, wait. The person was holding something up to his mouth. He was talking into a microphone. I scurried down under the companionway and turned on the CB scanner. I got a good variety of jabbering. But one in particular made me stop the dial. It was underlaid with a lot of hissing and buzzing common to Citizen Band transmissions:

"mmmmmmmmmm—ssssttt! No so I'll stay put for a-*sssssst*! You can catch us back here at the usual time."

"OK general. You meeting the other party then? When can I expect—mmmmmmmm—or later tomorrow?"

"sssssst! Yeah tomorrow's fine. I gotta keep a date first though. Got swordfish and tuna this time, *fsssst.* "

"OK but don't forget me."

"mmmrrrrmmmm No problem—"

Then there was a bunch of static and buzzing, and nothing else. I moved the dial around. Most of the people were calling each other "good buddy" and saying when they'd be in, or to tell their wives and girlfriends that they'd be gone another day or two. I couldn't find anything else. I peeped out to see the person in the wheelhouse sweeping a pair of heavy lenses over the *Hatton*. What did it mean?

I had placed a stern anchor to make sure *Hatton*'s sternside didn't swing around so people on the white boat could read her name or port. I grabbed the glasses and stared back, but from inside the cabin about a foot behind the glass of the tiny porthole. I *knew* he couldn't see me . . . but I could see him. It was the big man. It was him. For half a minute I was tempted to drag the 30-06 from underneath the forward bunk and level it at his chest. *What was I saying?* Had this slimy crook made a sniper out of me? Nevertheless, I found myself breathing more heavily than usual, and my pulse was pounding. I hoped, really hoped, he'd come a-hunting my boat.

But he didn't. Apparently, he did not recognize the *Hatton*, or its occupant, or anything else. For several hours, until almost noontime, the three figures walked to and fro along the boat's decks and up and down her hatches. They came and went often from the new superstructure aft, which was obviously a hatchway. So it was real, not just a bunch of welded metal.

Not much was happening. Trucks continued to arrive and depart the old quay, and loiterers and cane-pole fishermen trudged wearily about the long dock, trying their luck in the slimy waters below. The big warehouse had wide doorways every forty feet or so. Some were open, some weren't. Occasionally men went through them wheeling carts full of stuff. I saw a lift truck gliding along between the semi-trucks. The long rows of buildings and loading docks behind the big warehouse were quiet.

Just before one o'clock a blue van pulled up on the quay and the two men jumped from the *Rose* and went over to talk to the driver. Schilling put his head into the window and nodded. I snapped away at the proceedings, but then grew bored.

I decided to move on. There were three additional piers in Plymouth. One was reserved for the *Mayflower II* and the gift shops. Another was the main fishing pier. Finally, the Plymouth Yacht Club had a small marina at the southern end of the big, wide harbor. I weighed anchors and motored the *Hatton* in a wide sweep around the commercial pier. As I rounded it to make for the main harbor, I knew that Schilling or his men could read *Hatton*'s name and hailing port on her transom, but it seemed they had lost interest in me.

Hatton snuggled nicely into an empty slip at the fishing dock. On both sides of me were trawlers whose high topsides rose up cavernously and hid me from view except from the dock above. I wheeled up the ten-speed and rode down the dock, out to Water Street and up to Main, which was Route 3A. At that intersection I thought of something. Should I be armed? No. I didn't even know how to tote the pistols around. Then too there was the weight problem. Even small-bore handguns are much heavier than you'd think. At night it would be a different story. For now, I'd rely on Schilling's innate cowardice to protect me. It didn't take me long at all to return to the cordage pier. There was a big white sign telling me the place was called Cordage Park. Under the big letters was a directory. Ocean Spray Cranberry Company had a big spread there (as they did everywhere in the area), along with a wire cable company, a soft drink manufacturer, two electronics firms, and a fishery.

Some of the big buildings had connecting catwalks that joined them several stories above the ground. Others had big boilers and stackpipes attached to them—machinery that by the look of it hadn't seen any action in decades. Some of the buildings were U-shaped and had giant courtyards. The straight brick walls rose up six stories high around these gloomy places, allowing little light to enter. Most of these courtyards terminated in a truck loading dock at the far wall. But the steel shutters were locked down tight. The yards were deserted and silent. Row after row of these swept by as I cruised along. Then I crossed over the railroad tracks. No doubt these were the old spur that had once serviced the Plymouth Cordage Company. Oil drums were everywhere.

Some were bright red, most rust-colored or dirty gray. They were stacked in rows; they were strewn about; they were tipped over; they were crushed and torn. Just beyond the tracks was a tall Cyclone fence topped with barbed wire. A big sliding gate that led out to the pier was drawn back on its rollers, open. I parked the bike and loitered briefly near the gate. The *Rose* lay back by the pier beyond two other draggers. She looked out of place though, truly a rose among the nettles. The big gate had a sign on it that said it was closed at 6 P.M. sharp, and all strangers and vehicles had to be off the quay by then. Period. I took in the whole cordage compound in a long sweeping glance. If one were up to something shady this spot certainly had its advantages. Old broken-down warehouses. A quiet section of a quiet town. A semiprivate pier. A locking gate and barbed wire.

The place was basically quiet . . . almost too still in fact. Yet trucks did rumble in and out. I took a final tour around the huge old warehouse buildings and then headed out the main drive toward the highway. Then I heard a truck coming behind me. As it swept past I realized it was the blue van that Schilling had poked his head into. I snapped it as it bounced down the road ahead of me. I saw an elbow sticking out of the passenger window, but nobody turned to look.

Back at the fish pier I called Brian Hannon and told him I had located the *Penelope*.

"I'm overjoyed, Doc. I really am. You have made my day."

I asked him if he could request that the *Rose* be boarded by the Coast Guard on suspicion?

"Suspicion of what?" asked Brian.

"Who knows? Smuggling's the best guess I can think of."

"Absolutely not."

I told him I understood. But I said it in a very clipped tone.

"Look," he finally said, "I have a friend at the Massport Authority. After this episode he'll no doubt be my former friend . . . but I could . . . I *could* relay your message. They *might* tell the Coast Guard . . . they might not. But let me tell you. If it's a wild-goose chase I'm going to be all over you like a cheap suit."

He hung up. I called my brother-in-law, Joe, and requested

the same. Finally I called my buddy Lieutenant Commander Ruggles and informed him what I found. Three requests. Hell, unless a hurricane blew in, the USCG would have to follow up. There was no excuse not to. Except of course one: that a private citizen had suspected something. That wasn't very strong. Well, I'd done the best I could, for the time being, at least.

Plymouth lay roughly equidistant from Gloucester and Wellfleet, if that meant anything. Also, it was pretty close to Boston—if that meant anything. There was only one person besides the crew of the *Penelope/Rose* who could clue me in: Danny Murdock. Even dead drunk, he could be eloquent. His sodden brain held the pertinent dope.

I eased the *Hatton* out of her borrowed slip and hummed back up Plymouth Harbor. I passed the cordage works and saw the *Rose* still hitched quayside, a white-dressed damsel amongst thugs. It was now late afternoon and things had ground to a total halt on the small pier. I glided on toward Duxbury Harbor. I drifted to a stop and let out anchor chain just inside the harbor, and clear enough of the breakwater so I could see the dock across the water. When *Rose* left I wanted to know it. I packed my pipe and dismantled the gizmo; the rain had lifted and—Lawd sakes amighty—there was the faint promise of sun. I sat on the cabin top and puffed and sipped a Budweiser, crinkling and uncrinkling my toes.

I thought of the scrambled CB conversation I'd heard. It could be interesting, *if* it had issued from the *Rose* and *if* there was any marine doubletalk intended in it of the kind Ted had described to me in the Schooner Race. Somebody was referred to as the *general*, and he had something, tuna *and* swordfish. Good for him. The other party didn't want to be forgotten. According to the general, he wouldn't be. That meant that in the future—probably the near future—the men of the *Rose* were going to do something.

Why did he call himself *general*? Either he was really a general—something I found myself discounting immediately—or else general was a code name. Why general? There was Miles Standish, standing up above the harbor. He was probably a general. That could be it. The only other general

I could think of in the area was the *General James Longstreet*, the half-sunk target ship.

There were a lot of loose ends. I had to see Danny Murdock, drunk or sober. That was for sure.

I lazed about in *Hatton*'s cockpit for the remainder of the afternoon, reading, sunning, and watching the commercial pier. It was quiet as a tomb over there. The water was still as glass in the faint sunlight. The draggers were mirrored motionless where they sat. I could hear flies droning fifty feet away. I dozed in the dying sun.

The crackle of the CB awakened me. It was number-one son—the guy who loved whales. It was almost six. He was two hours late. We met at the dock and I ferried him out to the catboat via the dory. We had a long discussion on what had transpired, and decided that we'd wait it out, in shifts if necessary, until *Rose* cut loose and split. Then we'd make one more attempt at her interception. After that there was nothing much more we could do except to trail *Ella Hatton* back to Concord for her winter's sleep. We sat and talked. Jack told me Tony was under medication for his dose, which was good to hear. He said Mary was not the slightest bit pleased at this quixotic streak that had manifested itself in me, and I understood—in part at least.

"Oh, yeah, I forgot one other thing. Did you write a letter to someplace in the Caribbean?"

He took a thin aerogramme out of his pocket and tilted it around, looking at the postmark affixed to the tissue paper.

"Uh . . . Queen's Beach Condominiums?"

"Gimme."

I tore the flimsy thing open, and read:

QUEEN'S BEACH CONDOMINIUMS
CHARLOTTE AMALIE, ST. THOMAS, U.S. VIRGIN ISLANDS
"WHERE PARADISE BEGINS"

September 18, 1979

Dear Dr. Adams:
    Thank you for your recent inquiry regarding your friend and our

client, Mr. Wallace Kinchloe. While it is the strict policy of this development, and all the developments of the Chadwick-Longchamp Group, to maintain the utmost confidentiality regarding all its tenants and clients, we do feel at this time obliged to reveal to you and any other interested parties our concern over the absence of Mr. Kinchloe, who indicated an arrival date here in Charlotte Amalie of September 1. Since it is now getting on toward October, we are justifiably concerned, especially given Mr. Kinchloe's extremely prompt communications in the past.

You may rest assured that should he arrive here, we will notify him immediately of your concern.

Until such time as we hear from Mr. Kinchloe, we shall of course maintain his suite of room as per the agreement. However, if there is no word from him whatsoever by the first of the year we reserve the right, under the terms of the contract, to offer the suite for rent or sale. We would regret doing this, of course, and still look forward to hearing from him.

Sincerely yours,

John C. Pepper

John C. Pepper
Manager

I pondered the epistle, blowing pipe smoke down onto the page and watching it billow out around the edges. "An arrival date of September 1." *Windhover* disappears in late June. Allow, say, three weeks for Murdock to alter the boat and fake the papers. She would then be ready for Walter Kincaid, presumed dead and now alias Wallace Kinchloe, to put out to sea around the first of August, maybe a bit later. Roughly a month, then, to make it from Cape Ann all the way down the Inland Waterway to the Miami area, then island hop a bit to Bimini, the Bahamas, and on over to the Virgins. He could do it, but he'd have to hump a bit. Still, if he really wanted to get away, he wouldn't dawdle; he'd *scoot*. For a forty-foot-plus power boat a month was plenty of time to make it. Perhaps even with a quick duck southward to visit Grand Cayman Island too.

Sure. Plenty of time. Only he didn't get the chance, because just before he set out . . . what?

* * *

At nine-thirty that evening the running lights on the *Rose* flipped on. I glassed the boat and could see the faint waver of heat above her stack. She was going out.

"She's taking off, Jack, and so am I."

I left in the dory for the town pier and there placed two calls: one to Joe and one to Brian, telling them that *Rose* was on the march.

I got back to the *Hatton* in time to see *Rose* slide away from the quay and glide along in the still water for the harbor mouth. I opened beers for myself and Jack and we sat in the cockpit under the stars—for the weather had finally cleared— and talked. It was pleasant there with the water sloshing around. We made a late dinner and took our time eating. I told him how the *Hatton* had handled herself, and what I'd seen. I told him about Mr. X—Jim Schilling—sitting behind me in the cafe. We debated the cryptic message over the CB—assuming of course it *was* the *Rose*.

"I don't know, Dad," said number-one son as he pulled up the wool blanket and blew out the hurricane light in the bow. "This whole thing is so . . . *iffy*."

"Son, you're so right."

15

"AND THE THING THAT MAKES IT REALLY HARD, DOC, THE thing that really pisses me off, is the *apology* given to me by Clive Higgins. He's the guy I told you was my friend at Massport. Like I predicted, he's now a former friend. But he was so goddamned apologetic on the phone for not being of more *service*. Christ, Doc, why in hell did I ever listen to you—"

Brian Hannon was being true to his word. He was all over me like a cheap suit. I was standing on his carpet examining the weave. I was getting sick of being called into the principal's office.

"And you know what? Did you know your brother-in-law was in here too? Eh? Well, the both of us had some mighty pretty words to say about *you*, Doc. Yes in*deed*."

He stomped around behind his desk and lighted another Lucky Strike. He fanned out the match and filled his half of the room with smoke. He kicked his desk and cussed.

"He hasn't told you? Well, Clive and Joe together got the Coast Guard up for it. Told them to be sure and intercept the dragger *Rose* on her return to Plymouth. Which they did. *Yes sir!* Sent a special boat just for the occasion."

I decided to break my silence.

"And I take it, Chief, that they did not find anything of interest aboard her?"

"Brilliant. Just brilliant. You are excused, Doctor."

I left, but returned to stick my head back in the door.

"The Guard screwed up, Brian. They should've boarded *Rose* on her *outward* passage."

"Excused!"

I went home and dialed Joe at state police headquarters.

"I didn't rat on you, Charlie, I just got mad, that's all. Brian and I went out on a limb for you and it didn't pay off. We have the authority—official or otherwise—to call out a lot of people as often as we like. But we've got reputations, too. Too many false leads don't do either of us any good."

"They should've nailed *Rose* outward bound, not returning."

"Now you tell us. You sure?"

"Well, she was clean coming in, right?"

"Oh, Christ, this isn't trial and error. You're saying now she's taking something *out*?"

"Just guessing."

"Well, look, Old Friend, please don't *guess* on my account, OK?"

"Can I take this warm reception by both you and Brian to mean that I can expect no more help from official channels?"

"In a nutshell."

"Joe, I want a couple more favors. Please. They're easy."

There was a weary sigh and an assent. I outlined the three favors I wanted.

"Thought you said a *couple*, that's two."

"Should have said *several*, that's three." They were:

1. For him to request the contents of post office box 2319 when it officially became an abandoned box, and to let me know what these contents were.

2. To track down the owner of the blue van I saw and photographed on the fish pier in North Plymouth, using the license plate visible in two of my photos.

3. To accompany me to Murdock's Boatyard in Gloucester, lending his official presence if nothing else, and

perhaps obtaining a search warrant if he felt it justified. In short, to help me find Danny and get him to talk.

He listened—in apparent disgust—while this list was read over the phone.

"The first two I can do easily. The third is kinda outside my jurisdiction—"

"No, it isn't, Joe. You know it isn't."

"Look: if I do the first two and work on the third, will you get off my back?"

"For a while at least."

"Done."

He hung up. But I didn't feel the least bit guilty. While he stayed with Mary during the *Hatton*'s Great Quest, he drank my bottle of Glenlivet. The bastard.

If it seems that I've skipped over Mary's reaction to my homecoming, it was intentional. The fact is that she was not in good humor about it. Women from southern Italy are many things: beautiful, full-breasted, sensual, good cooks, shrewd, and lovers of the hearth and home. But they are not subtle. Subtlety eludes them, much as modesty eludes the French. So my welcome home from Mary wasn't pleasant, and we were still avoiding one another. I went out back to the cabin, a small guesthouse made of logs where I go when I want to really be alone and think. Danny and Angel went with me. It was cool enough for a fire, and I built one in the small woodstove. The dogs flumped down in front of it as it ticked and crinkled with heat and sent the air above it dancing. I had a good long think and decided that it was best to forget the entire thing. Joe had told me the details of the Coast Guard boarding. They had intercepted *Rose* as she re-entered Plymouth Harbor at dawn. She was clean as a whistle: no illicit goods, no safety violations, and all her credentials were in order. The owner's name was Marlowe. Roger Marlowe, and he had the identification to prove it. The Master Carpenter's Certificate was new, claiming likewise for the boat. *End of case.* The USCG wouldn't come back in no matter what I unearthed.

I had asked Joe to get me a description of Roger Marlowe. He refused, saying he'd bugged his contacts enough.

Toward dinner there was a soft knock on the cabin door. It was Mary.

"Dinner's ready. I take it you've talked to Joe and Brian?"

"Yep."

"And they want you to drop this thing?"

"Yep. Drop it. Drop it like the proverbial overheated ground tuber."

"Well good then. We can be friends again, Charlie. I'm really glad you're going to forget about this thing. In a few weeks your wrist will be good as new and you'll be working on all the lost practice. You'll forget about the whole thing."

She squeezed my hand as we walked back toward the house. There was meat sizzling and it smelled mighty good.

I was going to drop it.

Yes indeed.

Yes sir!

No.

After dinner two questions gnawed at me like rats around a grain dryer. One: how did Schilling know I was seeking his boat? That question was easy to answer: because Danny Murdock called him up from the Schooner Race and warned him that I was snooping around and getting hot on the trail. But the antecedent to that question was this one: how had Schilling *known* to warn Danny about me beforehand? How was the link made between my early watching of the boat and Schilling's need to have me eliminated?

That appeared to be the interesting question.

16

Joe Brindelli and I had just arrived in Gloucester in Mary's Audi. It was a warm, sunny day; a perfect Indian summer weekend. We rolled to a stop in front of Murdock's Boatyard and exited. We tried the bell with no result. We were walking along the side of the worn-out house when a familiar face stuck out the window above us.

"Who you lookin' for?"

"Daniel Murdock. Can you help us?"

I pointed to Joe.

"This is Detective Lieutenant Brindelli of the State Police. We'd appreciate your help."

She looked down at us quizzically for about fifteen seconds. Then her eyes crinkled up and her mouth turned down sour. Saliva drooled down her chin and her eyes were all wet and shiny. She was bawling. She left the window in a hurry. A few seconds later she opened the back door and hobbled down the short wooden flight of steps and lurched over to us, drawing the frayed robe around her as she came. She was looking down at the leaf-strewn sidewalk, crying. She was drunk too. Joe grabbed her by the elbows and she collapsed into him, sobbing. As for me, I had seen enough miserable women in the past month to last a lifetime.

Joe sat her down on the stoop. She told us she hadn't seen her husband in three weeks. Sure, he'd been on benders before but he always came back, pale and shaking, a few days later.

"Have you gone to the police?"

She nodded, clenching the old robe up around her neck.

"Two, three times. But they know Danny. They think he just run off drunk. They say they'll look for him, that's all."

"You," she said to me, "you were here before a long time ago."

"Yes. I finally found your husband over at the Schooner Race but didn't have a chance to talk with him—"

"—too drunk?"

"No. He just didn't want to. Can you tell me the last time you saw Danny?"

"The police asked me that, too. It was on September eighth, a Thursday."

That was the same night I'd seen him, and been clobbered. We left Mrs. Murdock and walked back to the boatyard. The door was locked and Joe returned for the key. It was the same as when I'd seen it earlier through the window. Benches lined three of the walls and were strewn with ball-peen hammers, swages, pressure hoses, cutting torches, giant vises, and welding equipment. There were ratchet tools, air compressors, gas bottles (metal tanks, actually), power hacksaws, and a hundred assorted other implements. Interlaced between all of them were empty beer cans. Though he preferred Budweiser, he was obviously catholic in his tastes, for there was a representative of every brand I'd heard of and then some. The center of the building was taken up almost completely by the big metal hull of a boat that was nearing completion. Danny Murdock did build boats, and was pretty damn good at it too as far as I could see. The big hull was cradled in a massive wooden dolly mounted on railroad trucks. The trucks rolled on tracks that led down and out the big hangar doors to the harbor. The dolly and trucks were hauled up the track by a big electric winch.

We walked around past the hull and down the tracks. Where they slid out of sight underneath the metal hangar door the ground was damp with dirty water.

"What do you think?" asked Joe.

"I think Danny Murdock's dead. And I think he's probably sleeping at the bottom of the harbor. Or else they took him for a boat ride first and dumped him somewhere rather remote, like perhaps halfway between here and the Isles of Shoals."

"You don't think he skipped? Does he owe money?"

"He's probably up to his ass in debt, but I don't think he skipped. His disappearing the same day I was bonked on the head is too coincidental. I think that Jim Schilling and Company sensed his fear, his regret at becoming involved with them. It wouldn't take a guy like Schilling long to decide what to do with him."

We climbed up inside the hull and searched it. Nothing.

Next we went after the papers. This was difficult because they were scattered to hell and gone all over the workshop. But most of them were in two big drawers under the main workbench. Orders and invoices were scrawled on forms that were obviously purchased from dime stores. The writing wasn't very clear and there was no order to the many sheets and lists. We scrambled through the jungle of paper searching for a recurring name, a large job order . . . *anything*. There was only confusion and messy handwriting.

Having struck out, we returned to the hull in the center of the shop. We wondered where the owner was and when he'd show up to claim his near-finished dragger. Almost all small boatyard work is done on a custom basis, with the shipwright receiving a hefty down payment at the outset. Where was this boat's owner? We gave the place a last look around. Then I remembered Danny's wife saying she was at her sister's the night it all happened. I grabbed a big hammer and idly tapped it along the hull. Nothing. It bonged the same all along its length. Then Joe asked for the hammer and went back up the ladder. I followed and he was pointing to two squarish upright stacks that projected up on each side of the vessel just forward of her beam. They were made of folded steel plate, about two feet across and almost ten feet tall. They were braced to the sides of the hull and acted as frames to hold the cabin and bridge, which hadn't been added yet. They were about eight feet apart. Joe bumped them with the hammer. They both bonged. But I got down low just above the keel and did the same. The port pillar didn't bong, it thumped. We examined the tops of these channels. The starboard one was capped with a plate that fitted it exactly. The port one had the proper cap, but the worst looking weld job I'd ever seen. The bead was all glumpy, and had been run two or three times in spots. I even saw the remains of two old welding rods that had frozen to the steel and had to be chipped off with a cold chisel. No master craftsman had done *that*.

"What do you think?" asked Joe.

"You asked me that before. You're the cop. I'd say we'd be smart to open these."

"I'm with you—"

"OK. The owner of this place is not here, but we were admitted by his next-of-kin. So I'm going to get one of those heavy-duty drills and poke through."

"I'm still with you."

He watched while I hauled a big half-inch drill up the ladder, cradling it on my hip, and set to work. I had a good carbon bit working for me, but it still took almost ten minutes to penetrate the half-inch plate at the top of the port pillar. Cautiously, I sniffed at the hole.

"Well?" asked Joe anxiously.

"Naw. I just smell kerosene, or motor oil. Maybe it's some kind of rustproofing. Let met try the other one."

I did. It did not smell like motor oil. So much for the upper portions, now to try lower down. I got an extension cord and seated myself just over the keel, right in front of the starboard pillar. It was dark down there but it didn't matter. I finished the hole. Nothing. Then I turned and began at the port side. Even before the drill pushed through all the way dark fluid collected on the bit. When the hole was finished and I pulled the bit out, a stream of it snaked out at me. I jumped to my feet and called for a light, which Joe provided. I looked at the fluid. It looked like old motor oil. I collected some on my finger and sniffed. It smelled like old motor oil. I wasn't going to *taste* it. . .

"I think it's old motor oil," I said triumphantly.

Joe's voice boomed and echoed down to me: "Why would anyone do that?"

"Dunno," I said as I climbed up and out of the hull and over to the nearest bench. I grabbed the longest welding rod I could lay my hands on and returned to the bowels of the boat. The electrode went into the hole about three inches and stopped. I jabbed it in. It made no noise, just stopped. I wiggled it about, pushing. Something. Not hard like metal . . . something. In the starboard hole it went in easily until it fell in, plunking down out of sight.

I rose to leave the hull, but just before I started back up the ladderway my nostrils caught the faint, faint whiff of another odor. In my mind's eye I saw the bloated corpses of cattle and deer, swollen like balloons, legs up in the hot sun. I saw the clustering of filthy birds in a writhing, flapping heap with hooves and antlers sticking out the sides.

"Well?" asked Joe.

"Well maybe they didn't drop poor Danny into the drink near the Isles of Shoals after all. But I've got a way to find out. Let's turn the heat up and get out of here for a few hours."

We decided to go to lunch. Joe thought it would be nice to take Mrs. Murdock along. He had a heart of gold. We had a tough time talking her into it. I suppose in her state she felt rather ashamed of herself and her plight, and simply wanted to hang around the wreck of a house and think about her wreck of a husband and her wrecked life in general. But Joe succeeded in the end, and Mrs. Katherine Murdock got dolled up enough to join us in the car. She actually wasn't that bad looking, though a trifle lumpy and dumpy from the life she'd led over the past dozen years. She had probably been really pretty once.

We went to a place called the Captains Courageous that overlooks the harbor. Mrs. Murdock put away three Southern Comforts on the rocks and felt noticeably better. I ordered a cup of clam chowder and a Heineken. Joe shot the works with a fisherman's platter. Mrs. Murdock fought down a clam roll and coleslaw. She gagged a bit on the food, even with the three stiff drinks in her gut. My guess was that with all the booze and worry she was having a textbook case of anorexia and pyloric stenosis. This meant that the more she drank, the less she ate. And the less she ate, the more damage the liquor was doing to her. I had a feeling though that she was shortly going to encounter a major life change that would either break or save her.

It was a grim lunch. In keeping with my feelings about that meal, I dined lightly. I was glad I did because before it was over Mrs. Murdock announced she had to go to the ladies' room and came back reeking of hydrochloric acid. She couldn't keep down the clam roll after all; she had puked it up. Poor thing. Joe bought her another Southern Comfort and we went back to the boatyard. On the pretext of having forgotten something, Joe and I went back to the work building. We knew by the smell right away.

I took a trouble light and shined it down into the hold. I lowered it down by its cord and saw the flies swarming around the hole in the portside pillar. They were going in and out like honeybees at a hive.

"Oh, Jesus, Charlie. Oh my God."

"Yeah."

"Look, I'll take her away from here. I'll take her over to the station so she won't be here when they cut him out."

"Good idea. Have them send a crew over. There are cutting torches here but maybe they'll want to bring their own. But get her away first, that's a good idea."

He took her in the Audi and I waited at the boathouse. Outside. The aroma was getting thicker by the minute. The first thing I did was turn off the ceiling-mounted hot air blower when we came back and the building had dropped into the sixties. But there was no stopping the putrid odor now. The motor oil was a good idea. A stroke of genius. Covering the body with oil was like preserving it the way the ancient animals were preserved in the tar pits of La Brea. But with the oil gone and the warm air let in, the weeks of festering were very, very noticeable.

Joe told me later that she didn't say any more on the way to the station than she had at lunch, which was nothing. Her husband was gone and she didn't know why or how. When asked about the *Penelope*, she proclaimed no knowledge of it. She seemed to be telling the truth, but she also admitted that she had suspected for some time that Danny was engaged with illegal modifications and shady people.

I did not particularly want to witness the unearthing of the late D. Murdock, but my presence was requested by the officials, including my brother-in-law who was apparently going to get some important brownie points at headquarters. It didn't take them long to cut him out of there, thank God. Three men wearing nose masks went down into the hull. They spotlighted the area and turned on the gas, and I heard the sharp "pop" of the acetylene torch as it ignited, then a hiss as they adjusted the long silver flame with a touch of blue halo around it. That went through the plate steel quickly. The first thing I saw slide out of the bottom of the big portside pillar was a booted foot. I recognized the boot, even with the oil slime on it. Old Danny Murdock would never again do his sloppy, drunken soft-shoe imitation of Bojangles down at the Schooner Race. Those feet were forever stilled.

He oozed out of there like baker's dough. Like pink-gray Silly Putty. He was a formless puddle of stinking goop.

"Can I leave now?" I asked, and headed for the door and fresh air even before I got the answer.

We rode back to Concord in silence. Twice we stopped the car on the side of Route 128 and got out and walked around slowly, breathing deeply.

We had Joe stay for dinner. Gradually, as the day progressed, he talked more and more of food. Still, we didn't eat much. Mary was in a sense glad of the discovery of Murdock's body, since it meant once and for all that I *hadn't* been imagining all this maritime skullduggery, and that finally the authorities would pitch in and help out.

"You're not alone anymore on this thing, Charlie, you should be glad of that," she said.

"Yeah, and I can bet the first son of a bitch to show up will be Brian Hannon. You watch. Pass the wine please and fill the glasses. I want to propose a toast: To Mrs. Katherine Murdock—May her lot in life improve."

"Hear, hear," echoed Joe. "After all, it could hardly be worse."

"—and the best thing is, Doc, you're not alone on this thing anymore. Why we—"

"You're excused, Chief Hannon," I said into the phone.

"Now wait. After all, who provided—"

"Excused!"

"Now look, goddammit! I went out on a limb for you. I'm telling you the way it *is*. I went along with your hare-brained scheme to play down your survival. I helped you plan that lamebrained cruise of yours aboard the *Ginger Rogers*—"

"The *Ella Hatton*."

"Well, whatever. And I'm investigating the people whose names you gave me. I've got some stuff, for instance, on the girl who went cruising with Walter Kincaid."

Dammit, the son of a bitch had me there.

"What'd you find out?"

"It can wait."

"Look. Be here at nine."

"No, *you* look. You cannot order policemen around. You will be here at the time I say. Clear?"

"Naw. Forget it, Chief."

"What time was that again? You said your place?"

"Nine."

Chief Brian Hannon sat sipping on a Tab.

"The oil. I wonder how they thought of the oil?"

"Because," said Joe, "there were drums and drums of diesel fuel outside. After stuffing Murdock down the steel channel, they covered him with diesel fuel, then put the cap on and welded it tight. If we hadn't discovered him there he'd have remained for ages."

"Now what about Walter Kincaid's girlfriend?" I asked.

"That she never was. I've tapped every source I know, official and unofficial, and I can tell you for certain the girl Jennifer Small just *isn't*, at least around the North Shore. Whoever told you about her is mistaken."

I considered this tidbit carefully. It meant a lot.

"And what about our humane friend Jim Schilling?"

"Looked clean as a whistle except for one big thing that he'd managed to hide for a long, long time: dishonorable discharge. Assaulting a superior officer. Did time in the stockade. Court martial. DD."

"Thanks for the help, Brian. Now can you plunder P.O. Box 2319 for me? My brother-in-law has cold feet in that department."

"Look, Charlie, I have cold feet because it happens to be *illegal*. It's illegal until the P.O. officially declares it an abandoned box. At that time—and I've got an intercept notice in—the contents will fall into my lap. And maybe yours. *Maybe*, Charlie."

I grunted in disgust.

"It would seem to me it might be a good idea to keep a sharp eye out for the *Rose*, and Jim Schilling, along the coast of Cape Cod Bay," said Brian.

I let out a whistle of disbelief.

"You mean with the help of all your *former friends*? The ones who were so put out and embarrassed by your jackass friend Doc Adams?"

Chief Hannon spoke out of the corner of his mouth as he clamped his fangs around a newly lit Lucky. He flumped around awkwardly on the couch as he stuffed his matches back into his pocket.

"Now goddammit, Doc, I never said that. Not exactly anyway. What I *said* was—"

The evening dragged on with slashes and parries, advances and retreats, assertions and reversals. I was pretty bloody sick of it before long, and was glad when my two Great Buddies, the law officers, departed.

I had what I wanted for the moment. Joe had delivered the goods on Item # 2 on my list of requests: the identity and whereabouts of the owner of the blue van I photographed on the pier in North Plymouth.

He handed me the data earlier on in the evening, telling me to do nothing until I talked with him. Well, I'd talked to him all right, so now I could do something.

And I did.

The next morning I went to the office bright and early, and went over my bills and invoices. I scheduled in patients for the third week in October when I knew my hand would be fine. I answered overdue correspondence by talking for two hours into a tape machine. I wanted to get the office work behind me. I wanted to clear the decks.

I went to the Rod & Gun Club shooting range and pumped two boxes of twenty-two rounds through my Ruger Bull-Barrel, fast-firing every other clip.

After lunch I headed west on the Mass Pike in the Scout station wagon. With me were binoculars, my camera system, and the fact sheet describing the owner of the Ford Econoline van:

Rudolph Buzarski
121 Mt. Pleasant Drive
Belchertown, Mass.

Age: 54 Ht: 6 ft. 1 in.
Weight: 215 Hr: Brn
Eyes: Blue

Upon reading this poop sheet, I began to disbelieve that Rudolph Buzarski was a shady character. Poles are the most crime-free of all ethnic groups. They may whack you on the head in a football game. They may beat you at bowling and chortle over it. They may get stinko at a polka party and break their accordions. But as far as really nasty behavior goes, they are damn clean. They also have the nation's lowest unemployment rate, a distinction that's generations old. Western Massachusetts is an old-line Polish enclave, full of truck farmers, dairymen, small contractors, and the like. I sped along the Mass Pike wondering about old Rudolph. He could be an onion farmer. He could have two dozen head of fine Holstein that he'd call by name and lead into the barn each night and kiss goodnight—each one on her big wet salty nose. He could be a tobacco grower, since the Connecticut River Valley grows a lot of the prime wrapper leaf for the cigar industry. He could run a small trucking firm. But he wouldn't . . . *couldn't* be involved with Jim Schilling.

I purred into Belchertown and got gas, asking for the whereabouts of the Buzarski place. I was told that the Buzarski *farm* was a mile ahead and to the right.

See, he *was* a farmer.

I took the route indicated and came upon his spread, set off from the main highway by a mile.

The Buzarski place was a showpiece. Out front there was a fruit and vegetable stand fairly dripping with the produce grown on the flat, green land of the Connecticut River Valley. The alluvial flood plain that lines the river on both sides for miles is rich. The proof of it was before me as I ambled around the stand eyeing the squash, early pumpkins, late tomatoes, sugar-and-butter corn, Indian corn, apples. It was a cornucopia. Off behind the stand the kelly-green grass shot away level for hundreds of yards, then commenced to hump and dip a bit. Behind the far rises were the distant mountains of the Berkshire range. It sure was pretty. The farm was too big. How could I find out about the blue van, and its driver, without arousing suspicion? If it were a small place a quick glance around and perhaps two questions could settle it. But this place was the King Ranch compared to most of the truck farms. Two big white barns with silos stood far away off to the left. A score or so of Holsteins and Brown Swiss stood munching in the pasture. There was a goat here and there. Far off to the right were two low buildings with slatted walls. From their shape, and from the ripe aroma that wafted over from them now and then, I guessed them to be hog barns. Was there anything Rudolph Buzarski didn't raise?

I studied the roads. There was the one I was on, Mt. Pleasant Drive. But there were numerous side and access roads that crisscrossed the Buzarski place. After buying some corn I returned to the car and headed along the access road that ran into the farm. If stopped, I could merely say I had gotten lost.

The house was half a mile in. It was modest, a shingle-sided blocky structure with a big porch around two sides. Tire swings for the kids. A big willow tree and three oaks near the house. Small kitchen garden. A trellis of roses. A birdbath. Norman Rockwell could have painted the scene, perhaps adding Grandma and Grandpa sitting in their rockers on the veranda behind the gingerbread latticework of carved railings and cornices and spindle screens, looking out over the farm from the hilltop house, listening to the robins cluck on the lawn . . . perhaps smelling the kielbasa and sauerkraut from the kitchen.

I stopped the Scout and began swearing to myself.

Why had it taken me so long to realize what had happened?

Obviously, I'd been *duped* by my own brother-in-law. Perhaps he and Brian cooked the scheme up together. Perhaps even *Mary* had had a hand in it too! I had been sent off on a wild-goose chase to stay out of trouble. It was glaringly apparent that the only place safer than the Buzarski farm was the vault at Chase Manhattan.

I continued my rounds and drove on slowly past the farmhouse. Before long I turned and found myself on the road that led past the two low buildings. They *were* hog barns. There's no smell like it, believe me. Buzarski had all kinds of pigs. He had Hampshires, Berkshires, and Chester Whites. He had a few Poland-Chinas. There were fall piglets fastened onto the teats of huge brood sows who grunted and dragged them around the muck as if they weren't even theirs. The big old brood sows made snorting and grunting noises. A big hog, which can weigh over 700 pounds, makes a noise like a walrus burping in a septic tank.

I passed the hog pens and came to a slow curve in the road, which led to an old barn set in a gentle slope that led up to some thick woods. The barn looked abandoned. Was it part of another farm? I was past the barn and about to dismiss my entire trip when I saw the blue van. It was parked on the far side of the old farm building. Next to it was a motorcycle. It was a chopper, an old Harley Davidson Duo-Glide on a modified, or "chopped," frame. There was a fancy paint job on the tank and a lot of shiny chrome parts. The motorcycle and van looked strange parked near the old barn. As I drove past I looked in through one of the building's broken windows and saw nothing but hay bales. It was converted to hay storage, as are many old buildings on farms. I crept past and kept moving. In the rear-view mirror I saw two men emerge from the old barn. One jumped on the cycle and kicked it over; the other climbed up into the van. I couldn't really see what they looked like because of the mirror's vibration. I took the next right turn, planning to get back on the main road. The van and cycle followed me. Both were going fast. They passed me on the narrow dirt road, one on either side, and blocked it. I cruised up and lowered the window slowly.

The van's door flew open and a youngish bearded man swung out and ran up to me. His eyes were full of hate. Beating him to my car was a large German shepherd, who leapt up at me, popping his jaws. The man asked me what the fuck I was doing there, and why the fuck didn't I get the fuck out of there? I explained I wanted to see Mr. Buzarski. He asked me what the fuck I wanted with him. His vocabulary had a certain poetic intensity, although a bit limited. But he did ask me a fairly penetrating question. What *did* I want with Mr. Buzarski?

"I'm wondering if he could sell me a couple of goats," I managed quickly. "I was following this road to get a closer look at them and I guess I got lost. Are you Buzarski?"

The young man with the limited vocabulary (and by extension, I reasoned, limited brain) looked confused for a second, then softened. He seemed greatly relieved at my explanation.

"Naw, he's my father-in-law. Dint ya see him out front? Big guy with a crewcut?"

"Gee. I must really be dumb. Sure I saw him. I thought he just worked here—"

"Yeah. He does. Alla time. And he owns this place too. You better get the fuck out. *Private!*"

"I would appreciate it if your friend wouldn't do that."

The motorcyclist, the Wild One, was busy attacking the grill of the Scout with his feet. It was making a loud racket and wasn't doing the vehicle any good either. He was probably wearing the boots that the Sears catalog calls "Mechan-

ic's steel-shank Wellingtons," the kind commonly called
motorcycle boots. The punk was beefy, with weak eyes. He
was smoking a cigarette and chewing gum. Chewing gum is
tacky. Cigarettes are tacky. When you run into someone who
does both at once you have tackiness multiplied. Tackiness
squared. He kept it up, delighted. He didn't look me in the
eye though. The weak child's eyes played over the shiny grill
as he kicked it. His face was too young, his body too old. I
leaned on the horn. He hadn't counted on this trick, and the
noise sent him jumping backward. He looked mighty silly,
and his friend lost no time in telling him so.

The humiliation enraged him. Snorting like a bull he came
around to the right side door and yanked it open. He grabbed
me by the knee and yanked. I let him. He grabbed me by the
shoulder, too, and began to pull me from the Scout. I let
him, not saying a thing. Twice he looked up at my face. He
was growing hesitant in the milliseconds since he had flung
open my door. I didn't want that; I wanted him full of con-
fidence and raring to go. He would be easier that way. At
least that's what Liatis Roantis had told us.

So I began shouting. Telling the Wild One to lay off. As
he pulled me off the front seat I resisted hard the last few
seconds to let him really yank at me. I wanted him to build
up a good head of steam. Then I came out fast. As I passed
him I grabbed his right upper arm, spun into it close to his
chest so the top of my head was nestled into his armpit. Then
I dropped down, bending my knees. His beefy body's mo-
mentum was already carrying it over my head. But I helped.
I began to stand up again, and at the same time pulled down
hard on the upper arm. My shoulder was the fulcrum, and it
flipped the motorcyclist over and past me. He sailed on over
my head like Dumbo the Elephant.

He landed upside down on his upper back. I could hear
the whoosh of air as it was driven from his lungs. Instinc-
tively he rolled over onto his stomach, trying to recover. He
resembled a wide receiver who'd landed the wrong way after
leaping for the long bomb in the end zone. He grabbed at the
ground in front of him and drew his knees up underneath
him. But as he rose to his feet I was already there, and when

I saw his head bobbling up toward me, I chopped it hard with my left hand just behind his ear. The good doctor who had replaced my cast had fastened a steel shank to my wrist and covered same with lots of plaster. It was very heavy and hard; it worked well. I was better than Bruce Lee. He fell without a sound.

But before I had time to turn around, the first man was on me and drove me to the ground. I felt a great pressure on my foot, and realized that the German shepherd had it in his mouth. He was growling and shaking his head, his front paws down in front of him and his rear legs up, as if in play. His tail was wagging. He wasn't a very good attack dog, fortunately.

We rolled around snorting and cursing for a while. Out of the corner of my eye I could see Wild One's feet working as he lay on the ground. He was lying on his side and looked as if he were trying to pedal a bicycle. If he got up there'd be big trouble.

Suddenly it was over. My attacker was yanked off me like a reverse thunderbolt. I got up. I couldn't see who had hold of him. All I saw were two huge hands on his shoulders. The fingers were wide as bananas. The nails on the fingers were wide and flat, and surrounded by black lines of dirt. Then I saw the crewcut, and soon Rudolph Buzarski had shoved his big round red face into his son-in-law's and was giving him quite a going over. He shook the boy back and forth, then flung him into the side of the van. A girl rushed up to the big man, pleading.

"Oh, Dad, please! He won't do it again—"

"Damn right! Now git! I want you out of here!"

He was yelling at the young man leaning against the van, though, not the girl, whom I supposed to be Buzarski's daughter.

"Take my van, but git!" bellowed Buzarski. He walked over to me.

"You hurt?"

"Nope. But I think I hurt that fellow there."

Buzarski glared at the Wild One as he staggered to his feet and sheepishly made his way over to his chopper.

"Shit," he said. "That's three hundred dollars I owe you, mister."

"For what?"

"For beating the snot out of that . . . that . . . hell, I don't know *what* to call him."

I got back into the Scout, told Mr. Buzarski I was sorry I'd disturbed his farm. He thanked me over and over, and insisted I stop once again at the vegetable stand where he overwhelmed me with free produce.

"Do you own the blue van your, eh, what's his name?"

"Randy . . . Randy Newdecker. Piece of shit as far as I'm concerned. I've had no peace since he joined the family. Sorry. Didn't mean to spill out my troubles to you. What were you doing that far back in the farm anyway?"

"Looking for a goat to buy, but I think after what I've been through, I'll pass. Does Randy live on the premises?"

"Yep. In the back wing of our house. You should hear the arguments—but you asked if I own the van. Yes. But Randy drives it. I've kind of given it to them. Since he has no job, it's maybe a mistake. He's got free room and board and transportation. What else does he need?"

"Spending money?"

Buzarski rubbed his stubbled chin with a huge dirty paw.

"Funny. Never thought of that. I guess that's the one thing in the bum's favor. He never bugs me for spending money."

We were standing in the shade of the Buzarski fruit and vegetable stand. All around was evidence of this man's handiwork, determination, and—from what I could gather from what I'd seen in the past hour—the ability to work fifteen-hour days for decades on end. I liked him immensely.

"Can I trust you?" I asked.

It was a deliberately stupid comment. A teaser. I wanted to see what the big man would say. But he didn't say a thing for ten seconds. He just flung his level gaze on the horizon and worked his jaw a bit. Then he wiped his other paw across his mouth.

"Don't see why not."

"How well do you know your son-in-law?"

"You're a cop, aren't you?"

"Nope. I'm a doctor by trade, but I've been interested in where your son-in-law's been lately, riding in your blue van."

Rudolph Buzarski propped his booted foot up onto an apple crate and squinted at the cows in the far pasture. Then his big round face seemed to harden, and the corners of his eyes crinkled up.

"Don't wanta hear it," he said, "I just don't wanta. He's not a good catch, that's for goddamn sure. But. But he *is* the catch if you get what I mean. He's in the family and that's that. You get going, mister. I believe you came to help. Maybe. But now I want you to go. Maybe I want to keep thinking everything's OK as long as I can. It's all I got."

So I went. As I walked toward the Scout, I saw Buzarski with his head down. His hands were covering his face and rubbing at his eyes.

Boy, did I feel great. If there was a chance to volunteer for a scientific experiment to see how long a human being could live in peace with a gaboon viper in a phone booth, I'd have been first in line.

17

So I ROLLED THE SCOUT OUT OF THERE WITH RUDOLPH Buzarski's payload of fruits and vegetables thumping around in cardboard cartons in the back. The gourds and squashes and ears of corn bumped around and played a crude symphony of guilt and sadness. Well to hell with it. I swung around and hunted side roads. After forty-five minutes I found one I liked. It snaked around above the flatlands of the valley flood plain and wended its way up into the wooded hills that surrounded the farm. I bumped and grunted along this for another hour until I found a way that took the truck off to the side to a small clearing just big enough to hide it. I left it and fought my way through tangles of thickets until I was looking down at the farm buildings below.

The farm looked even neater and more efficient from above. The buildings were squared with one another, the furrows absolutely parallel. The roads and fences were laid out in anal-compulsive rectangles and right angles. The faint roar of a tractor—invisible from where I waited and watched—wafted up to me on the warm wind. The same with a cawing of a rooster. Then mostly silence and wind-hum. I saw the old farm building at the edge of the property where I'd had the scrape with Randy Newdecker and his leather-clad friend. The old building looked gray and dusty compared to the dairy barns. It looked saggy and hollow compared to the swine buildings. I crept down through the trees and thickets to the edge of the woods. I was up on a gentle slope perhaps seventy-five yards from the building. A shape moved and pranced at the doorway. It was the German shepherd dog, tied to a stake with about forty feet of chain to romp around on. Enough to romp around on so that he guarded the doorway quite well, thank you. I was skunked. I returned to the car and headed home. It was three-thirty in the afternoon. I could come back after supper and be ready with all I needed for a nighttime siege of the building.

Mary and I were civil to one another, but it ended there. She knew I wasn't leaving the "thing" alone, but had been out snooping. We sat through a decent dinner and chatted, but I knew she wasn't leveling with me. For that matter, I wasn't with her either. At half past nine I left Concord in the Audi. I thought it better not to take the Scout again . . . it had become almost a landmark at the Buzarski farm in the few short minutes I'd spent there earlier. With me I had:

1. A quartz-beam searchlight, hand-held, that plugged into the cigarette lighter socket.

2. My 7 x 50 binoculars, perfect for nighttime use.

3. The .22 calibre Ruger Bull-Barrel auto-loading target pistol, with two clips.

4. A small crowbar.

5. A flashlight.

6. My quart thermos full of hot coffee.

7. A pack of cellophane-wrapped beef chunks.

The beef was a tough cut, a cheapie the stores like to disguise with names like "Family Steak" and "Value Cut." It was what I wanted, though, a tough portion of the cow that could stand abuse and yet be irresistible. The red sticker on the package said: "Great for Cook Out!" The meat was cut into golfball-sized chunks for shish kabob.

It was almost midnight when I reached Belchertown, and quarter to one when I cruised to a stop up the side road where I'd parked earlier. The road was tricky and rutted, and I was glad I'd thought to bring the quartz-beam spotlight. I left the car with my satchel on my back and made my way down the slope again. I managed to squirm up closer than before in the darkness. I got to within twenty yards of the barn door, and hid in a tiny clump of bushes that grew out of a rock cluster. I swept the binoculars over the ground. Their ability to gather light was as important as their ability to magnify, and I saw the sprawled heap of the dog asleep right in front of the door. There would be no getting past him without raising a ruckus. I could just see the outline of the main house on the knoll a quarter of a mile away. There was no other dwelling nearby though; that was good. Just the hog barns with their ripe smell. I was thankful for this aroma; if the dog had any scenting talent it would be hindered by this thick odor, and keep me hidden. But if the dog were to eat the meat he had to be awake. On my way down the slope I had gathered half a dozen rocks, one of which I now threw at the dog. No response. I chucked two more at him before I wised up and flung one right at the old barn. It whunked into the wood solidly and the big dog was up in a second, barking and whirling around full of self-importance. I glassed the house with care during this show to see if any lights came on. It remained dark. Before the dog dozed off again I flung a hunk of meat at him. The dope couldn't smell it, probably because of the hog barns. I switched on my flashlight and let the circular beam fall near the animal. I wiggled it on the ground like a fishing lure, and the dog rose and went over to it. I teased him around with the beam for a minute or so. The dog didn't bark because there was no noise. Finally, he found the meat. I saw his head bob up and down with the convulsive, gobbling motion common to dogs. I threw him another chunk, and he heard it land. He found it instantly and snarfed it down. He was getting the idea. I threw another. Same thing. He remained standing now and his tail was doing a slow wag. I heard a soft whine.

I figured he weighed between seventy and eighty pounds, and judged the dosage accordingly. Earlier I had selected five particularly big and tasty-looking chunks of beef and had inserted into the center of each a capsule containing 200 milligrams of chloral hydrate. This drug, a sedative/hypnotic, when mixed with alcohol is called a Mickey Finn, or knockout drops. Used alone in sufficient quantities it puts people to sleep. I didn't want to kill Fido, just immobilize him for about three hours. I figured three of the chunks would make him non compos mentis, and four would slide him right under. Five might be dangerous to him, but I needed a spare. I threw him three loaded chunks, which he gobbled down. I waited twenty minutes. The dog sank to his belly, his head still up, looking. I threw a small rock at the barn. He jerked his head in the correct direction and gave a little *whuff*! But he didn't get up. He was gassed, that's why. I threw the fourth chunk. Ten minutes after ingestion, the dog's head was on his paws. After ten more minutes I threw another rock at the wall. Nothing. I approached close to the dog and threw a rock at him. It skipped and caught his hind leg. Nothing. Fido was in the land of nod. I kicked his tummy gently with my boot and heard a faint sigh, then went on past him toward the barn.

The door was closed but unlocked. This was understandable; if indeed the old barn held something other than hay bales a locked door would only call attention to it. It was clear then that Randy Newdecker was relying on the dog to keep the barn safe. The pistol was zipped inside my Windbreaker, since I owned no holster. I unzipped the jacket. The crowbar was thrust into my belt. The flashlight was cradled lightly in the cast of my left arm. I had left the satchel of meat and the thermos of coffee back at the clump of bushes. There was a mere hint of moonlight, just enough to guide me through the small door next to the big one. Once inside the barn I softly closed the door behind me and stood and waited. I breathed slowly through my open mouth, hearing the faint rustle of my canvas jacket with each breath. I was being *very* quiet. I damn near jumped out of my socks when I heard a loud flutter from above. Either a pigeon or a barn owl. I crept forward between the rows and stacks of hay bales. They were stacked like giant bricks, each two by two by four feet and weighing eighty pounds. I snaked my way through the walls of dried grass. I turned here and there. I didn't know where the hell I was. After crisscrossing the barn for twenty minutes, I sat on a bale and considered. There was nothing of interest on the ground floor, which left the loft and the stable floor below. The barn was a typical older one: built on a slope with a main door in the end and another big doorway in the middle on the underside of the slope which gave access to the stable floor underneath. But usually there was a trap door or ramp connecting the two lower levels. It took me another forty minutes of searching before I found it: a wall ladder over an elongated trap door. It was the rungs that tipped me off; I brushed by them as I felt my way along the wall and knew there was a ladder. With my light I found the handle of the trap door, a metal ring set in a recess. I switched off the light and raised the door slowly. Nothing. Black as pitch down there. I didn't really want to go . . . I flipped the light on quickly and looked down. There was no monster lurking there. I stuffed the flashlight into my hip pocket where I could reach it in an instant and started down. It was mighty hard gripping the rungs with my left hand but I managed. The old stalls were still there. Most of them were stacked high with hay, but some weren't. Curiously, it was lighter down there than up above because of the long narrow windows above the stalls. They were rectangles of faint bluish light, like frozen ghostly fish swimming around the edges of the barn. I crept out to the center aisle and could see the stalls, perhaps eight on a side, receding away into the darkness. I began with the nearest stall and worked my way along. My watch said two-thirty. Each stall was taking about five minutes. If I didn't get lucky I'd still be there at dawn. And how long would my friend Rover stay zonked? Probably another hour at the most.

In the fourth stall, in the middle of the barn's belly, behind and underneath a few bales and scattered mounds of hay, I found it. Or rather *them*. First I felt the rough crate wood, and could see the pale gleam of whitish wood in the faint light. I switched on my flashlight. At the instant I did so I heard a sound from the far end of the barn. I shined the light quickly in that direction but saw nothing. Probably a rat, coon, or skunk. I cut the light and waited in the dark ten minutes before going back to the crates. Then I swept the hay off the uppermost one, and turned the light back on. It had a double swirl symbol stenciled on it, and underneath the symbol, stenciled in black paint, the words:

MILITARY ARMAMENT CORPORATION
POWDER SPRINGS, GA. U.S.A.

Looking for a place to insert the crowbar, I noticed that someone had already pried the crate open; there was an indentation between the lid and side of the box where a big screwdriver had been inserted. I pried off the lid. Inside the box, which was the size of a small footlocker, were four weapons. They were strange looking, unlike any firearm I'd ever seen before. They were ugly, made of stamped dull metal. They looked like pistols, with big squarish bodies and little teeny barrels sticking out the ends. The grip projected downward from the middle of the pistol body instead of the back end. Also in the box were eight clips (two for each gun) and four big metal tubes about a foot long (longer than the gun bodies). I picked one of these up; it was heavy and solid. Then I saw the thread mount on the end of the tube that matched the one on the barrel extension on the gun body. I knew what it was then: a silencer. I picked up one of the bodies. Used to fine shotguns and pistols, I couldn't believe how cheaply made it looked. There was no machining whatsoever. It was a rude collection of stamped metal and spot welds. It looked as though you'd find it at the bottom of a Crackerjack box.

A knurled knob on the top of the body moved backward if I pulled hard on it. There was a big spring in there, but no external locking and safety lugs like those found on automatic pistols. But this didn't look like an automatic pistol. It was, I suspected, a machine-pistol, or submachine gun. And one with a silencer too.

Son of a bitch.

There were two of these crates. Underneath those were three more crates that were noticeably larger. I saw the familiar logo on the sides: the interfacing triskelion of Colt Industries. I knew that weapon: the Armalite M16, the standard assault rifle of the U.S. Army. Joe and his friends at the State Detective Bureau had told me enough about these to make it clear they were worth a fortune on the black market. And finally, wrapped in a canvas tarp alongside the wall were two bulky objects that were wound, mummy style, in rust-inhibiting paper. I unwrapped one of the bundles enough to peer at it. It was a medium-weight machine gun. The ribbed metal housing over the barrels looked oddly familiar but I didn't know why. I wrapped the big weapon up again and placed it back the way I found it. I re-covered the crates and scattered the hay back over them. Then, my light out and stuffed in my hip pocket, I went over to the ladder.

Two rungs up, a light shone behind me. I blinked my eyes twice to make it go away. Surely they were playing tricks on me. Surely I was dreaming.

But I wasn't. I felt cold against the back of my neck. It was steel, and pressed hard up underneath the big bone in my skull that lies right behind the ear. It was the barrel of a gun.

"Dawn't move," said a husky voice, *"dawwn't!"*

18

I DIDN'T. I STARED STRAIGHT AHEAD AT THE BOARDS OF the old barn wall. They were whitewashed, and I could see the faint dried strokes of the coarse brush that had put on the whitewash, probably about fifty years ago. I *didn't* move.

"Who are you?" I finally managed.

"Dawn't ask. I'd as soon put a bullet in yer brain now . . . and who might *you* be?"

He had a brogue so thick you could cut it with a cold chisel. The sound of County Mayo, or Clare, or whatever, coupled with the weapons I didn't like. And that's when I disobeyed instructions and moved. I moved like all get-out, too, and I'll tell you why: *Because I thought I was going to die right then.* I thought I was going to get blown away, and all that nicely applied old whitewash was soon to be besotted with glumps of reddish tissue: skin, bone, brain, and ocular fluid, as the strange visitor from County Kerry (or Wicklow, or Donegal, or whatever) blew my head apart so bits and pieces of it would fly out from homebase and affix themselves to the wall. That's why I jumped for it.

And that's why I think people with guns pointed at them try a lot of that "brave" stuff. They aren't brave; they're *scared*. They're trying to survive. They know they are a finger-pull away from death and it has a tendency to bother them. If I could get free and manage to knock him off balance for a second I could get the Bull-Barrel out from my pocket in a wink. And though I'd never harmed a living thing with it, I knew I could give a gentleman a third nostril at fifty feet. I was very, very good with that little small-bore target pistol. So I moved.

I flung myself backward off the ladder. From the way he held the pistol and the fact that I had climbed two rungs, I judged myself to be above the gunman by about two feet. As I left the ladder I rolled to my left, and chopped down and back with the cast with all I had. I felt the hand strike something semisolid and the light wavered and flickered crazily around for a second. When I hit the floor I rolled over to get up, my hand already working the pistol from the Windbreaker's pocket.

But that was as far as I got.

I felt a huge pressure on my upper chest, just below my Adam's apple. I smelled shoeleather. I felt an iron grip on my right wrist just above the hand. Jesus did it hurt. Then I felt the cold pressure of the pistol barrel, again, on my neck. Only this time it was jammed up under my jaw. The husky voice spoke. It was panting a bit, but pretty level and *very mean.*

"Now *look*," it said, "I'll not kill you if you do what's right. But if you dawn't, yer a dead mahn, heer?"

I nodded.

He grabbed the Ruger pistol and jammed his flashlight up under his right arm and held it shining down on me while he slid out the clip. He flicked the rounds out one by one but very fast. I heard a brief *ka-chunk* and knew he'd ejected the round in the chamber too. He frisked my other pocket and grabbed the spare clip, which he disarmed as quickly as the first. Then I was amazed as he handed me back gun and both clips. With a swirl of hands and cloth he dropped the rounds into his coat pocket. I heard them rattle as they fell, like a beanbag. I still couldn't see the face. The light beam was right in my eyes and he was behind it.

"Get up then."

I did. And I sat with my back against a hay bale as he asked me my name and business, and why I was where I was, doing what I was doing. I thought it best, since he had a Walther PPK pointed at my chest, to tell him. But I made it a point to stall a bit, to tell mostly of my life and job, and to say how I'd been hunting a certain boat—

"Ah yes. I saw you on the docks at Plymouth—"

This stunned me.

"Ah yes, I've had my eye on you, sir. Let me see your wallet. Be quick with it."

He examined it and flung it back. I saw the faint outlines of his profile as he sat and looked at me. He was thick and not very tall. He wore a hat. He breathed heavily. I yearned for a glance of the jaw or cheekbone in profile . . . something my physician's eye could latch on to for future identification. But no luck. This man was a pro. The way he'd gotten the drop on me while my hands were on the ladder (and not a sound to tip me off), the way he'd countered my moves against him and emptied my pistol, the way he held the light and gave instructions, they all spelled experience in a certain line of work that I was obviously still amateur at. And his sidearm. I didn't know that much about handguns, but from everything I'd gathered, the Walther PPK was the pro's piece. It was the mark of the experienced spy, saboteur, policeman— especially overseas.

"Hmmph! *Adams* . . . an English name. Oh well."

I squirmed on the hay bale.

"Now look heer, Doctor Adams, you mind what I say. You stay away from heer. You stay cleer of that dock in Plymouth. My friends and I won't like it if you interfeer. Are you taking careful notion now of what I'm sayin'?"

"Uh-huh."

"Now rise and go—and—"

He didn't finish his sentence. He lunged at me and grabbed me by the upper arm.

"Shhhhh! Hush I say," he said in a coarse whisper. "You stay put, or so help me Katie you'll pay! Did you leave the trap open?"

"I think so."

The stocky man, still in shadow, moved with incredible

speed. He flung the beam of his flashlight to the rear of the barn.

"Then hide there, yah. Quick now, or we're both for it!"

He doused the light as I went behind a big pile of bales and waited. In less than three seconds I could hear the whine of a heavy transmission. The squeak of brakes sounded above. I heard the soft thump of the trap door being shut, the almost metallic sound of heavy shoes on wooden rungs, and then the man was beside me again.

"Heer it, mahn?"

I nodded and said a low yeah.

"And we're trapped," I whispered.

"Naw! Keep close. And no funnies, heer?"

I followed his heavy breathing farther back to the end of the barn cellar. Then I remembered that it was from this part of the cellar that I'd heard the sound earlier as I was opening the gun crates. No doubt it was my captor, not the skunk or coon I had supposed. Almost instantly we were making our way through a small door and up a ramp of gravel to the outside. We left the vicinity of the barn and made our way halfway up the wooded slope that overlooked the building.

"They'll find my satchel in those bushes," I said, pointing. "They're sure to find it—"

"*Naw*, laddie. I've taken it up the slope. You see, you gave yourself away with the flashlight game with the dog, don't ya know . . . though you put him to sleep right nicely. Come on."

Within thirty feet of the car he handed me my satchel.

"Now go, Doctor Adams. Go back to Concord and stay there if your own personal safety means a damn to you . . . heer? If you get in my way again I promise you I'll not be so kind."

Then he was gone, moving with that amazing speed, silence, and agility that was so odd for a thick man. I looked back down at the barn. It was dark, but I could see faint sweeps and flashes of lights in the windows. The van near the big door breathed and purred at idle. Twice I heard anxious loud whispers and the knocking of wood and doors inside. I saw a shadowy figure kicking at the dog, who was whining softly. I heard the opening of the van's doors, and a soft slamming of them too. I dragged myself up the rest of the slope to my car—Christ I was tired!—and glassed the building once more. The lights winked out inside the old building, and the van's headlights went on, shooting narrow white cones of light out onto the dirt road. It moved away slowly, then gained more and more speed as it receded into the distance. I poured coffee and downed it, then went back to the car, backtracked my way down to the main road, then onto the Mass Pike and headed east for home. I was hoping to run across the van so I could follow it, but they'd probably taken another route and had too big a jump on me. I didn't know if they were loading more weapons into the building or taking the ones I had seen out. They had used the same door I had used initially and which I had seen them use earlier. This was puzzling because the guns were hidden in the stable floor, but then I realized that the small door through which we had escaped was ill suited for vehicles, and the big one was inaccessible because rain had made a huge gulley in the sloping gravel drive.

With the help of the thermos of coffee I made it home awake, and rolled up the drive. As I walked to the front door—I hadn't bothered with the garage—I thought I heard a sound at the side of the house. I waited three minutes in total silence. Nothing. My mind was beginning to play tricks on me. I needed sleep, and less cops and robbers.

The coffee had me going now; I walked to the back of the house past the small sign that said ATELIER and entered Mary's ceramic studio. I switched on the light. The place was festooned with hanging plants of all varieties, each one in a huge custom-thrown urn. I saw her recent work on the big table. They were modeled after Chinese pots from one of the dynasties, and were trapezoidal in cross-section with angular, though handsome, lids. Some were two feet across. It takes a huge amount of arm muscle to throw a pot that big. They were glazed with a textured drip finish. I stood in silent admiration in the room. I also resolved to forget about Jim Schilling, the boat, and even Allan Hart. I would tell Joe and anyone else who wanted to know all about the guns in the

Buzarski barn and the blue van. Then it was up to them. This thing had taken too heavy a toll on Mary, and on us.

I went upstairs and kissed her awake and loved her back to sleep. We both said we felt a lot better. I slept very soundly.

In fact I slept so soundly that Mary told me later it was her third scream from the bottom of the stairs that stirred me.

I met her on the landing. She leaned into me, wailing and moaning in her nightgown. I felt her nails dive into my right forearm.

"The *oven*! In the *oven, Charlie—my God!*"

Then she ran to the bathroom, sick.

In the kitchen I saw that the oven door atop the stove was ajar. It was at eye level. I crept forward and opened it with caution. The face of Angel stared back at me. Her eyes were still open, but dulled. Her hound face wore a quizzical expression. There was no anger in it, no snarl to the lips. There was no fear either. Just a confused look, as if asking fate why this had happened to her. A tiny pool had gathered beneath her severed neck. Not much. Her long velvet ears hung down between the wires of the baking rack on which her head rested.

"Oh, my poor Angel," I whispered to her.

19

BRIAN HANNON'S FACE CRINKLED UP IN DISGUST AS HE stared into the oven.

"And we're *selling* the stove, Charlie. *Right now!* You hear, *right now* we're selling it! Goddamn thing and—"

Mary was crying hard again and running her twisted fingers through her hair. It was not only the loss of the pet, the murder of our dog, that had her on the brink. It was the stealthy invasion of our home, while occupied: the cold, professional, wanton terrorism of it. If they thought they had us scared, they were indeed correct.

"My God that's awful, Doc. That's an awful thing. Please don't any of you touch anything for a while. Mary, it might be a good idea for you to get out of this house temporarily while my men work. Doc, we never found the body. They came in through the window. Jimmied it up clean as a whistle. They bypassed the alarm too. They're pros, Doc. They knew exactly what they were doing."

"And the noise I heard coming in the front was them leaving by the window. They saw my headlights and hurried out."

"Doc, I think their message is pretty clear."

I nodded.

"What they're saying is lay off or you'll be next."

"The dogs were all outside last night. They were together,

but neither Danny nor Flack barked. How did they get to Angel without the other two knowing? And how did they catch and kill her silently? And why did they bring her inside?"

"They did it all for the message. They've showed they're silent. So quiet that dogs don't wake up when they're near. They're quick. So quick they can snatch a dog in her sleep and destroy her without a peep. And finally, you can't keep them out. They can get to you whenever they want."

I let out a long sigh as I heard Mary trundling up the stairs.

"That's not encouraging."

"No. I'd be extremely wary if I were you, Doc. Whatever it is you've been poking around in, *forget it*. You and Joe have discovered a body up in Gloucester. Now you stay out of it. Let the Commonwealth handle it. I guarantee your house will be guarded twenty-four hours a day."

"And what will you be doing?"

"I am gonna stay with you. I'm gonna be harder to shake than athlete's foot. Count on it."

He spun around and went to his men. I went to a pay phone and called the boys and told them to leave their present dwellings at once, and go to earth elsewhere.

"Call Chief Hannon in two days and let him know your whereabouts. That's an order."

I saw Joe pull into the drive. I was never so glad to see him. The rest of the day was taken up with state and local police, the dismantling and hauling away of the stove (at Mary's irrational insistence, although I admitted to myself that I never wanted to set teeth around anything cooked in that oven again as long as I, too, lived), and the tramping around through our domicile by state and local lab teams, who admitted to a person (two of them were women) that the breakers-enterers-murderers were very clean. No stray prints were found. The burglar alarm system had been circumvented with surgical precision. I cornered Joe and Brian on the porch.

"Has either of you any comments about the mode of entry? Does it not strike you as interesting that this group appears to be adept at circumventing burglar alarms?"

They nodded at each other without hesistating.

"Well?"

"Well what? It's always interesting that the M.O. has a definite pattern. We're up against pros here, that's certain."

"Yes," I answered, "and pros good enough to crack an armory maybe?"

"Oh I've thought of that," said Brian.

"Of course. I thought of it right away," added Joe.

"Oh you did? But then neither of you apparently thought that the *Rose* could be running something out of the country— namely guns. Instead you thought I was off my nut. Since then we've uncovered a body, some tangible evidence of gun-running, and a direct threat to Yours Truly. The question is, how seriously are you guys taking this?"

"Very," they answered in unison. I was somewhat heartened, but not very. To me they still seemed a bit like Tweedledum and his big fat brother, *dee*.

Before he left Joe hugged Mary on the couch and comforted her.

"I want you at ten-ten Comm. Ave. Tomorrow at ten," he said as he left.

On Commonwealth Avenue, right at the Boston/Brookline line, is a large store called Eastern Mountain Sports, abbreviated EMS. It sells down parkas, snowshoes, camping gear, and mountain climbing apparatus. The shelves are lined with pitons, nylon lifelines, ice axes, and small hammers to drive the pitons and steel rings into cliff faces. All this so people can scale sheer cliffsides and dangle about underneath ledges and outcroppings like spiders.

The people who die doing this stuff deserve it. It is nature's way of weeding out the insane.

Hordes of people flock to this emporium. Most don't pay any attention to the big dun-colored building across the street. It's blocky and ugly, and is conspicuous in having a splendid array of aerials and antennae on its rooftops. This is the headquarters building of the Department of Public Safety for the Commonwealth of Massachusetts. One of the biggest divisions in the department is the State Police. Joe has an office in this big building. The day after we found Angel's severed head in the oven, I found myself on the third floor of this building seated at a table. Joe sat across from me. Next to me sat Sergeant Kevin O'Hearn. We were flipping through a big book filled with black and white photographs.

They were mugshots, but not of people. They were pictures of weapons: military small arms. I identified one picture and rapped at it with my fingernail.

"You sure?"

"Yep. Positive. I knew it looked familiar. It's the M-60."

"Now look in this section."

Kevin O'Hearn flipped through the pages. These were smaller automatic weapons, assault rifles and submachine guns. I stopped briefly at one called the Skorpion, a Czech machine pistol, then went on. I glanced for a few seconds at the Uzi, the fine Israeli machine pistol made under license in Holland. It is (so O'Hearn told me) the most widely used submachine gun today. The White House Guards tote them. Not it; the Uzi was too rounded. The gun I wanted looked as angular as a hunk of two-by-four. Then I saw it, complete with the big tubes.

"Here. This one."

"Sure?"

"As sure as I'm sitting here."

O'Hearn gave a low whistle at Joe, then excused himself, saying he had to make a phone call.

"I remember now I read where these are made: Powder Springs, Georgia. I could've saved you some time."

"We wanted a positive visual identification. Kevin thought it might be the Ingram as soon as I told him about your escapade out west. The government's been looking for these things for two months now. You've made quite a discovery."

"They're hot I assume?"

"You could fry eggs on 'em."

"Can I go now? Mary and I are looking at dogs today."

The first rule when you lose a dog, either to old age, accident, or murder, is to get another one quick. We had an appointment to look at the new German sporting breed, the drahthaar, after lunch.

"In a little bit. Major Downey would like to interview you first. He's on his way now."

"Does he work here or out in Amherst?"

"He's stationed at Fort Ord, California. He's a major in the United States Army, Ordinand."

"Oh."

The phone on Joe's desk rang, He grunted into it and hung up.

"Major Downey and O'Hearn are down in the range. Come on down with me and you can see for yourself what man hath wrought."

"What do you mean?"

"Downey has a real live Ingram with him. You can see what one of the things'll do."

The range was located in a subbasement, presumably to deaden the noise of target practice. I heard the hum of ventilating fans and could smell the bitter odor of cordite. As a sometime hunter I liked the smell, though I could see why Vietnam veterans would hate it. Another smell I like is the aroma of Hoppe's powder solvent, used for cleaning shotguns. We approached a door and I could hear the solid *blam* of firearms. The sound was two-in-one because the shot was followed a millisecond later by the impact sound of the slug thumping against the inclined steel wall of the range eighty feet away. Joe opened the door and went in.

There were eight stalls to the range. Troopers and plainclothesmen occupied about half of them. They wore ear protectors as they fired their sidearms at the big suspended paper targets at the far end of the range. The targets were life-sized silhouettes of the human being. Parts of the body were outlined in white lines, with various scores. I noticed you got a lot of points for the head and chest, a bit fewer for the stomach and abdomen, and hardly any for legs, knees, and such. It was a rather ominous spectacle for the uninitiated. Most of the men were standing, but sometimes they dropped to a crouch and fired their weapons held in both hands. When they did this they emptied the cylinder, pumping off six shots very quickly. One pistol sounded particularly loud, and I remarked on it.

"Three fifty-seven magnum. The slug can go through an engine block. But if you think that's loud, you oughta hear a forty-four magnum—"

"I have. One of the guys at the gun club has one. When he shows up at the range everybody else leaves."

We met Major Downey. He looked all business: crewcut, suntan, leathery skin, no fat, and a crisp khaki uniform with razor-sharp creases. He shook my hand firmly and we all talked briefly about what I had related to Joe. Then I was told that an army intelligence team had a surveillance on the Buzarski farm. With the team were state troopers. The major took me over to a bench, upon which sat an aluminum case that looked like a suitcase. In fact, it looked just like a Halbriton photographer's case. Downey flicked open the latches and opened the lid. Neatly cradled inside a nest of cut-foam plastic was one of the weird-looking square pistols. It was identical to those I had seen in the crate in Buzarski's barn. Alongside the gun was the long metal tube.

"That's it."

"Doctor Adams, ten crates of these weapons disappeared two months ago from the armory in Schenectady, New York. They were purchased by the army for special assignments, and were being stored in the armory prior to being shipped to Fort Ord. The M-60's have been disappearing from a number of storage facilities. Perhaps you know that three years ago some were taken from the armory at Danvers."

"I remember that. They later turned up in Northern Ireland, by way of Holland."

As the major nodded, my thoughts returned to my strange assailant in the barn, the one with the peat from County Donegal still on his boots. The Irish Connection. And yet he'd been hiding too. . .

"If you gentlemen will follow me, I will show you why the government is so anxious for the return of these missing pieces," said the major in an official tone as he plucked the pig-ugly little gun from its fancy case. He pushed in a small button above the back of the handgrip and drew out the metal stock, the end of which he braced against his shoulder. He shoved a clip up the handle, pulled back the knob on the gun's top surface, and requested that a fresh target be reeled out on the wire. By this time we were surrounded by the other policemen, who gazed at the contraption with curiosity and awe. When the target reached the far end of the range, having been cranked out there on a pulley like a clothesline, the major darted underneath the shooting bench, raised the machine pistol to his shoulder, and fired.

The ranged exploded in noise. I felt as if I were inside a boiler being riveted. The soldier had two of his left-hand fingers inside a small canvas strap that hung down from the barrel. He pulled down on this as he released the two bursts, but the small gun bucked up nevertheless, spewing .45-caliber slugs so fast it made one solid wall of noise. He swung his torso back and forth quickly during the bursts. The shredded target fell apart. He had cut it in two.

"Sombitch!" said a trooper.

"Jesus Christ Almighty," whistled another.

Downey released the clip; it clanked down on the floor at his feet.

"Empty," he said. "That's a major disadvantage of the Ingram. At eleven hundred a minute, the cyclic rate is so high that a thirty-round clip empties in under one and a half seconds. But now I'm going to demonstrate the Ingram's great advantage." He took the metal tube from the case and twisted it onto the barrel that projected from the body by only about two inches, threaded. He shoved a second clip into the piece, ducked under the bench as before, and pulled the trigger.

What emerged this time was one of the strangest noises I've ever heard. It was like the faint sound of a buffalo stampede or like sheet metal being ripped behind a thick felt curtain. And behind this noise was another: a thin whistle of almost electronic purity. It made almost no noise whatsoever. But yet the slugs still poured forth. We saw the target's top half sliced to ribbons. Also, we heard the only loud noise there was: that of thirty lead slugs, each as thick as the tip of my little finger, thunking into the metal wall. That sound was loud—as loud as two jackhammers. But the tiny weird gun, for all its kicking and bucking, was almost totally silent.

"Well *Gawdamn!*"

Downey wore a self-satisfied smile, pleased at having so impressed his audience. It was almost a smirk. I decided I didn't much care for the major.

"I'm sure most of you are aware of silencers, and how they reduce muzzle velocity almost to the point of uselessness. But this"—and he rapped the metal tube with his hand—"is designed so that it actually *increases* the energy of the fired rounds. Don't ask me how 'cause I don't know. But it does. So there you have it: a silent machine gun that can be carried under a coat."

"Unbelieveable," said O'Hearn. "Jesus, I hate to think what they'd mean in the wrong hands."

"Which, having been stolen, they are," replied Joe.

We made our way up to Joe's office. I plunked down into a chair and listened to my ears ringing. I told him I had no idea the funny-looking little pistol was so deadly. I thought it was just a cheap pistol . . . a junky version of the army .45 auto sidearm.

"Nope. The reason your description caused such a flurry is because every major police bureau in the country has had a circular from the army sitting on their desks for these last eight weeks. The Ingram machine pistols, departed from Schenectady, turn up in Western Massachusetts. They are heading east then, probably on their way to Ireland. And incidentally we have no idea who your midnight companion could be. Neither do the Boston Police."

"Is that surveillance team going to pick up the young brat—Buzarski's son-in-law?"

"Last we checked the barn was clean as a whistle, so we've got no cause. We're just all hanging back in the bush observing the place through heavy lenses. We're also going to go after the *Rose* again."

I leaned back in the chair with my hands clasped behind my head and stared at the ceiling. It was one of those horrendous affairs with fiber panels with tiny holes in them. I had a thought or two, but said nothing. So far Schilling had remained at least one hop ahead of me. The only way to turn the tables was to put myself in his place, to think the way he would think, do what he would do, and intercept him.

"Is Hannon putting a watch on your house?"

"Yep. And I'd like one put on *The Breakers* too. If it can't be done by public cops I'll hire some. I'm pretty sure he's found out by now that I have two homes. Of course the grim warning of Angel is clear: I back off or maybe one of my family is next."

"And are you going to back off?"

"Absolutely. Wouldn't you? You saw what happened to Danny Murdock. How'd you like your sister, Mary, to get the same?"

Joe shuddered.

"That's smart; let us handle it. I'm also going to request extra protection in Concord for you, and we'll keep an eye on the cottage too. Where you going?"

"I'm going for a run and a steam bath at the Y, then home. And listen: if you're anxious to ever have a chance to talk to the Newdecker brat, I'd do it mighty quick. When Jim Schilling has squeezed the utility out of people they have a nasty habit of vanishing in gruesome ways. I appreciate the help; come out tonight and we'll hunt up some Chinese. The buffet special is on in Lexington. I'll pay."

I left the building and drove over to the YMCU gym on Boylston Street. I glanced at the watch: 11:45. Tommy Desmond would be there. He never missed his noon workout. I parked the car in a sleazy lot just on the edge of the Combat Zone and gave the attendant five bucks.

I found Tommy working the speedbag. He circled around the tiny teardrop-shaped bag doing a slow foxtrot, pawing at it with his mitts in small circles like a kid imitating a choo-choo train. The bag bounced under the platform and spoke like a conga drum: *whack*ata-*whack*ata-*whack*ata-*whack*-ata, faster than the eye could follow.

I told him I wanted to buy him lunch and talk. He nodded.

An hour later we were in J. J. Foley's bar and grill, wrapping our faces around a couple of cheeseburgers and inhaling beer.

"Liatis is in trouble again, Doc. You heah?"

"No. Same thing again? Bar fight?"

He nodded.

"Punk started it. As usual."

"And Liatis finished it."

"Uh huh. Four seconds. Cops aren't sure the kid'll live though. It's serious this time. He could go to trial and everything. Even all his friends on the force can't save him."

"Jesus. Chest kick?"

"Naw. Throat punch."

"He's got to quit getting bombed in those sleazy bars, Tommy."

He nodded sagely and chewed.

Let me tell you: if you ever find yourself in one of Boston's sleazy bars in the Combat Zone and a short, stocky man with a drooping moustache and thick accent asks you what you think of the Patriots' chances, or who you're voting for, or *anything* . . . your best bet is to place your drink back on the bar, make hand signs as if you're deaf and dumb, and back out of there smiling and bowing. And take the next plane to Fresno.

When he asked me what it was I wanted to talk about I mentioned NORAID, the IRA, arms smuggling in general, and my strange nocturnal meeting in the Buzarski barn. Tommy's big blue eyes changed. They took on a steely coolness, rather like the Vaughan Lewis Glacier. They had a piercing, laserlike gleam of intense feeling that could cut through a bank vault door. Sensing his change in mood I made it emphatically clear that I didn't wish to pry into his personal life or activities, or those of his friends and acquaintances. I just wanted an idea if the man I had met was, in his estimation, and IRA Provo.

His replies were cool and clipped, though polite. No, he thought. The IRA was definitely more sophisticated than most people thought. What I had bumped into sounded to him like a half-assed outfit, though certainly a dangerous one. He advised me as a friend to heed the man's warnings.

"If he is IRA, he'll kill you next time, Doc. Count on it. If not, he still might. But I know for a fact that most of the guns used in the North are smuggled through New York and New Orleans now—even though the money come from here. Also, they're getting more and more of their stuff from other terrorist groups like the PLO. Hello, Joe!"

"Hi ya, Tommy. May God bless—"

His name was Joe Berry, and he wore thick horn-rimmed glasses and had snow-white hair capped with a snap brim hat. His nose was long and cherry red. Tommy bought him a beer and he sat down, listening to Tommy telling me about the British domination and exploitation of the Northern six counties.

"Fookin' Brits!" he piped.

The waitress had stopped by our booth an inordinate number of times.

Her name was Maureen—she told Tommy this. She was very pretty. She was pretty all over, as a matter of fact. She couldn't take her eyes off Tommy. She was looking at him the way a cat looks at tuna fish. She leaned over to collect our plates, staring at Tommy dead level and moving the damp rag around on the Formica as if she were working a Ouija board.

"Did you like it?"

"Excellent," I answered.

She didn't hear me; she was looking at Tommy.

Tommy's eyes were darting between her face and chest, face and chest. He wore a huge smile.

"But Tommy," I said, "the guy gave me back my gun. Tommy?"

". . . Oh from Cork, eh? Hey Joey, Maureen's from Cork. Oh yeah. Hey don't they make 'em pretty in Cork, eh?"

"And not only that, but the guns could be going somewhere else. Like maybe South Africa, or even Quebec. *Tommy?*"

"And you're staying in Wollaston now are you? Well, I live there too—oh yeah."

Several patrons were holding their empty bottles aloft. The barman was glaring impatiently at Maureen.

"Uh Tommy, just one more, uh. . ." I began.

To hell with it. I gave Joey the money to pay for the meal and began to slide out of the booth. He nodded and winked at me.

"Happens alla time to 'im. Like a fooking' broken record—"

"Uh huh. I know. See you, Joe."

"Same to you. Watch yerself!"

I left J.J. Foley's and retrieved the car. At home, Mary showed me one of the big Chinese pots.

"Angel's head's in there, Charlie. I want you to dig a deep hole in the garden and bury it."

She had worked days on the pot.

"You sure?"

"Uh huh. And I'll tell you something else. I'm never going to feel good until they're found. I could kill them myself."

"Forget it, honey. They'll be caught; there's enough people looking for them, now, including the United States Army. When I get back let's go buy a puppy."

We returned in late afternoon with a cardboard carton filled with strips of newspaper and a four-pound composition of sinew, wiry fur, big brown eyes, and needle teeth. Mary picked her up out of the box at least a dozen times on our way home.

"We've got troubles now, Charlie," she said, kissing the mutt on the side of her muzzle. She was smiling.

"Then let's name her that."

"What?"

"Troubles. You said, 'We've got troubles now.' So let's name her Troubles."

"Where have you guys been?" asked Joe. He was standing at the sideboard, having just made himself a generous gin and tonic.

"Gee why don't you just come right in and make yourself at home?" I asked.

"Thanks, I did already. That's why I was given a key. What the hell's *that*?"

So we spent the next half-hour with drinks and the doggie. She pranced around the kitchen, sliding on the Spanish tile. She looked into strange places and whined and yelped—scampered back. We let the other two in, and Danny and Flack took to her immediately. Joe and I sat watching the animals frolic. I looked up and saw Mary pause at the window. She was looking at the newly spaded patch of ground in the Japanese garden. It was right next to the bronze lotus flower, the Asian symbol of immortality.

"C'mon hon. Time to forget. It's all part of the Great Going On."

"Well what you call the Great Going On is sad . . . and scary."

"Yep. And unfair too. But we're stuck with it. Come on, let's go destroy our intestinal tracts."

On the way to the Yangtze River, Joe said he had some promising news.

"We've located the *Rose*, Charlie. And you'll never guess where she is."

"Probably not."

"C'mon, guess."

"Gloucester."

"Shit. How the hell did you know?"

"Lucky guess I guess."

"How did you know, Charlie?" asked Mary.

"Because it's the most unlikely place for a man of Schilling's cunning to leave her."

"Is there something you're not telling me?" asked Joe.

"Course not. Now look, here's a parking place."

Two hours later, after ingesting gobs and gobs of hot and sour soup, fried dumplings with hot sesame oil and white vinegar, moo-shu pork, Szechwan spicy beef, garlic shrimp, peppered broccoli, and so on, and having wreaked perhaps terminal damage on our alimentary canals (the top half of which we were now conscious of, and the bottom half of which would manifest itself during the next several days), we returned home.

And speaking of digestive systems, when we opened the kitchen door and saw our new friend, I again pondered that most ancient of nature's mysteries: how is it possible that a four-pound dog can produce—in an incredibly short time—eight pounds of excreta?

20

The *Rose* WAS SITTING OUT THERE IN GLOUCESTER HARBOR swinging lazily around her hawser like a pregnant duck. Joe had two men staked out watching her. They'd spoken to other crews as well. Nobody had seen hide nor hair of the men of the *Rose*. Nor had the harbormaster. This didn't surprise me. I considered that the *Rose* had been just a bit too easy to find, just a wee bit too conspicuous. I departed the harbor with Mary and we drove down through Manchester. We headed along Rudderman's Lane.

"No answer at all? How many times did you try?"

"Once. The operator said the phone had been disconnected. Either Laura Kincaid has changed numbers—getting another unlisted one—or else—hah! I was right. Look."

The Kincaid abode was for sale. The sign was in front, and the downstairs curtains were all drawn. We stopped and got out to look. Mary drooled over it.

"Gee Charlie, I wonder what they're asking for it."

"I figure half a million minimum. If you think it's nice outside, you should see the interior."

We walked around. If anyone asked what we were doing, we had a perfect excuse. The lawn was as trimmed as ever. New grass was beginning to sprout thickly over the ugly scar in the lawn where the oil tank had been put in. Mary said she wondered where Laura had gone. I was wondering the

208

same thing. Out of curiosity I rang the bell. Waited. Rang again. We heard the same distant pealing of Westminster chimes, but nothing else. Nobody home.

"Level with me, Charlie. What the hell's going on? I want to know. *Now.* I'm sick of all this screwing around. What the hell's going on in your mind?"

"A number of things. One: I don't think Laura Kincaid is as rich as she led me to believe. I don't know why I think that, I just do. Two: wherever Jim Schilling is, he's not going to come back to the *Rose* for a long time. The Coast Guard search, and the watch on the Buzarski place—when the pinch takes place—will all tell him that the *Rose* is poison. If he's going to run any more batches, it'll be by some other means."

"Oh wait. I forgot to tell you, but while you were on your little cruise, Joe and I looked over your notes and your spare chart of Billingsgate Sound. We came up with a pretty neat theory to explain how the boat happened to get grounded on the shoal in the first place."

When we were home she showed me. She took a pair of dividers and placed one point on Billingsgate where we'd first seen the stranded boat. She then extended the other leg toward Wellfleet Harbor.

"Now, Charlie, I remember you said that *Penelope* was lucky to make it into Wellfleet without sinking."

"Right. She barely scooted in."

"Now you also said, from looking at the pictures you took of her, that she'd been near sinking before."

"That line of oil slick could've happened either after her collision or after leaving Billingsgate Shoal. It probably happened after she struck."

"So she came close to sinking twice, in all probability. Assuming she got this far almost sinking, it's then reasonable to assume that she could have traveled about the same distance the first time, right?"

"Ah hah! Yes, *yes.* You're saying that the point where she struck is the same distance from Billingsgate as Wellfleet."

"Look."

She drew the far point of the dividers in a big circle on the chart. The point swept past the neck of Great Island, went out into the bay, swung back, and came to rest within the circular dotted line on the chart enclosing the zone marked *Prohibited Area*. And right smack in the middle of it was the symbol of a wreck and the words *target vessel, do not approach within 1000 yards*. It was a clever bit of reasoning. If correct, it meant that the *Penelope* (now the *Rose*) had struck on the wreck.

"Wouldn't it make sense, Charlie, to go to a place that's prohibited?"

"It sure would. Especially at night. If you had a rendezvous to keep, it'd be perfect, knowing no other vessel's going to come within a thousand yards of where you are."

A lot of small craft violate the warning during the day, especially fishermen because the wreck attracts fish and lobster. But at night it would be just about foolproof. And they could use the old wreck as a drop too; hide the stuff inside it and scoot, then the pickup could take place hours later.

"Sure. But supposing they had an accident during the rendezvous and struck part of the wreck, or the rocks around it. Then they would probably head for the nearest harbor."

"Uh huh. But if they were taking on water too fast they would know they could never make it, so they'd head for the nearest safe place, which happened to be Billingsgate."

We looked at the chart. Mary drew her fingernail along the easternmost edge of the shoal.

"They slid the boat up here in the falling tide," she said. "Then they worked on the hull or whatever in the dark."

"And I happened to see them. I bet they still had the guns aboard too. I think that's why Allan Hart died."

"Really, how come?"

"Well, they're sitting in the harbor waiting to get the hull fixed and who appears but a diver, poking around under their hull. Also, do you remember the diving cap Allan was wearing? Remember it was loaned to him, a U.S. Navy cap?"

"They saw it and panicked."

"Could have happened. They could have beaned him right there in the harbor thinking he was on to them."

"But why did they let the boat be hauled up into that place?"

"What choice did they have? They had to skedaddle and you can't do that with a boat that's going to sink. They had a quick patch job done and then split. We saw them leaving. I've never seen a boat more determined to make time than the *Penelope* was."

"So you think our theory is pretty good?" she asked.

"I think it's just dandy. I had considered the *Longstreet* before but never in a specific way. Your little explanation seems to put the cap on it. Also, they haven't shelled the wreck in two years, so even though it's officially prohibited, and no doubt treacherous, it's safe from bombs. Yeah—you and your brother are to be congratulated."

"You're pretty sure *Rose* is a decoy?"

"Yep. I bet you Schilling and his people are operating out of Plymouth. It's pretty far from Gloucester; it's near Boston and Southie, and it's big."

"Well we're going to drop this thing anyway, right?"

The phone rang; it was Brian Hannon.

"Just touching base, Doc. Remember, don't go anywhere far without letting me or my office know, huh? I've got people watching your house and loved ones. You try to go anywhere, I'm gonna follow you like B.O."

"You remind me a bit of B.O."

"That's not funny."

I thanked him and hung up.

"I wonder if Jim's put *Whimsea* up for the winter yet?"

"One more fishing trip?"

I nodded.

"My hand's almost as good as new. That means I'll be returning to work shortly. I'd like to enjoy thoroughly what little screw-off time is left to me. I think I'll give him a jingle."

But before I reached the phone, it sang out.

"This Doctor Adams?"

"Yes, who's this?"

"Now listen heer, Doctor. I'm tremenjous upset you set yer goons ta watchin' that barn, don't ya know? They're muckin' up me plans. Now you call 'em off or there'll be the devil to pay. You tell 'em. I was kind the first time but twawnt be again—"

The line went dead.

"Who was that?"

"Wrong number," I answered, and dialed Jim DeGroot.

"I am amenable to such an excursion, especially since you have volunteered to buy all the gas," said Jim languidly as he stretched his feet out on the rattan stool of his screen porch. We were sitting out in the fall sunshine, watching the colors beginning to turn, and exercising our livers. "But we'd better do it this weekend 'cause it's getting close to the end of the season. Think there'll be any stripers there?"

"Probably tautog. They're thick in that part of the Bay because they feed off the quahogs and scallops. Got teeth in 'em like a gravel crusher. But I also want to do some snooping around and I can't use my boat; they're already on to it. Uh, don't mention this last bit to Mary or Janice, OK?"

DeGroot rattled the cubes in his empty glass and pondered. He said he didn't want anyone shooting at us. I told him there was scarcely a chance of that; we'd be fishermen. So we struck the bargain. Next Thursday we'd head south to Plymouth, then over to Wellfleet and the Bay, then back to Plymouth. It would cost me a small fortune in gasoline, but I felt I had to take one more try.

Mary and Janice were none too pleased. But we emphasized it was a fishing trip, nothing else. I suggested that Mary stay at DeGroot's during my absence. This was arranged to everyone's satisfaction. My children had let me know their whereabouts, via Brian Hannon's office. Tony, his summer "job" ended, had taken up residence at the home of a girl he'd met at the resort. I phoned him there.

"Do her parents think it's OK?"

"Oh sure," he answered.

"May I speak with one of them please?"

"They're, uh, not here right now."

"Well when are they expected back?"

"Pretty soon. Look I have to—"

"Wait. When is pretty soon? Half an hour?"

"Next month actually."

"Next month? Where are they?"

"Sri Lanka."

A female voice cut in. It was young and delicious.

"Doctor Adams? Hi! I'm Jennie! Listen there's really nothing to worry about. You see my older brother and his girl are here too and—"

"I'm so glad. You can't imagine my relief. May I speak with my son alone for a second please?"

"Dad?"

"Look. I'll be brief and direct. Keep it in your pants until you've taken all the pills. Secondly, don't come near the house. You can reach Mother at the DeGroots'. Good-bye."

I called Jack at Woods Hole. He was staying in a dorm at the Biological Station with some friends. He asked if Jim and I were to visit *The Breakers*, and I told him it was unlikely and for him to stay clear of the place.

Thursday afternoon at one, we left.

Before heading for the Cape Ann Marina I checked Gloucester's main harbor. The *Rose* was still there, deserted. I called Joe at the Commonwealth Avenue headquarters.

"I take it nothing has happened regarding the *Rose*."

"Nope. But it will. You have any ideas?"

"No. You remember Jim DeGroot? Well, we're taking off for a few days aboard his boat. Why don't you jot down a few particulars, so in case we don't turn up you'll know where to look. But don't tell Brian Hannon I called you."

"He just called me. Wanted to know where you were. Said he was going to stick to you like Duco."

"Well tell him then; just don't let him bother me. Now take this down, and Mary's number too."

We purred out of the marina by the south route. Plymouth lay forty-five miles to the south, a straight shot. As we passed Marblehead I had an urge to zip into the harbor there. But why? If Schilling were active, we'd never recognize the boat he was using. The only hope was to see if by chance we couldn't run across his track in the two places I'd seen him before. In short, we had to forget Salem, Marblehead, Lynn, Swampscott, Boston, Winthrop, Scituate, Cohasset—all the harbors between Gloucester and Plymouth. And I knew the odds of laying eyes on him were remote indeed. If I were him I'd lay low as a hibernating woodchuck for a couple of months. But leaving the *Rose* in a place where the police were sure to look, that led me to the conclusion that Schilling wasn't ready to hang up his jersey yet. And there *had* been a load of firearms in the barn; it was probably moved the night my strange friend and I paid a visit there. Where was that shipment now? Probably on its way overseas on some freighter or fishing vessel. If it was the last shipment perhaps Schilling would reappear and claim the *Rose*. No, maybe not. That depended on how well he'd covered his tracks.

Jim sat in the cabin instead of up on the flying bridge. It was too cold now for that. He eased the twin throttle knobs forward and the *Whimsea* lifted herself up out of the water a bit and began to plane. We clipped right along. I stood in the cockpit and watched the wake fan out behind us. The white and turquoise water mixed with the bluish exhaust smoke and rolled away behind us. The engines rumbled and spat and gurgled under my feet.

"Whatcha thinkin'?"

I went forward and joined him at the helm. I squinted at a long brownish-red freighter in the distance.

"I'm thinking that James Schilling and I are going to meet face-to-face before very long," I answered. "We've scraped sides twice. I think the next meeting will be definitive."

"Just so I'm not involved in it. If you seek him out, you do so alone."

"Don't worry. The police and the Coast Guard know where we'll be going; I saw to that. All I want to do right now is slide around the southern end of the Bay and keep my eyes open."

We poured coffee and sat and chatted as he kept the boat headed straight on. We had the VHF on and tuned to channel 16, the distress frequency. Nothing interesting was happening. I switched a couple of times to the commercial bands used by cargo boats and fishermen, and got nothing but the usual technical lingo about course changes, gross weights, ETAs, cruise plans, and the like.

We kept the VHF on for a while. Behind the voices and the static was a constant drone that resembled an aircraft engine, or the rocket ships in the old Flash Gordon movies:

> "mmmmmmrrrrrrrrmmm—vessel taking water—rrrmmmm-mmm—*snap*! Yeah we have her sighted 'bout sixty meters off Spectacle Island *snap*!—mmmmmmmmmmmmrrrrr . . ."

And so on, and on. It got a bit monotonous. We switched to the more lively CB scanner.

> "*fffftttt*! . . . eeeoow! . . . *ffft*! . . . my port engine's down, come back . . ."
>
> "Jimmy? Hey Jimmy?"
>
> "*ffft*! Yeah . . . said my mother-lovin' port diesel's down. No go—over."
>
> "You check out that fuel pump? Come back—"
>
> "Don't think that's it—*fffft*!—Maybe it's the effin' injectors or else I gotta clogged—*fffft*!"
>
> "You gonna stay out, Jimmy?"
>
> "Look I'll limp home on the starboard engine. You comin' out or what, come back?"
>
> "Soon's I get some bread to top her up. I'm hockin' my old lady's socks right now to get fuel . . . where are you, come back?"
>
> "I got—*sszzzznapp*! mmmmmmmmmmm . . . you there? OK, heading due north with Little Gurney Light off my port quarter 'bout three miles—you know where those deep troughs start? Over—"
>
> "Yeah, gotcha, good buddy. But look, you get an RDF fix or loran fix and let me know exactly. You shouldn't be effin' around out there with one side down—"
>
> "Yeah. I got—*fffft*!—so when I call you back you'll have it. I'm gone."

Back to the VHF:

> "—Coast Guard Station in Boston with the latest weather—rmmmmmm—at two o'clock the temperature is fifty-six degrees and steady, winds south southwest four to six knots, gusting to nine . . . barometric pressure twenty-nine point seven and falling . . . seas two to five feet . . . visibility eight miles and closing. Light fog and drizzle—"

The number of vessels increased dramatically as we passed Boston about eight miles offshore. Especially predominant were larger vessels: freighters and tankers, large trawlers, and a few big yachts. We all intermingled and crossed paths at big distances and continued on our separate ways with remarkable ease. I glassed all the boats continually, especially the medium-length trawlers and smaller powerboats. If I were running guns and had abandoned my boat, I'd want a fast powerboat, like a sportfisherman. But peering through binoculars at the boats that dotted the sea was a bit futile.

Shortly after three-thirty we were entering the breakwater at Plymouth. We slid around in the big harbor for an hour while I glassed everything in sight from *Whimsea*'s cabin, looking for anything interesting or unusual. We went over to the smaller harbor of Duxbury with the same negative results. Then we cruised around the north side of the big bay across from North Plymouth. I showed Jim the Cowyard, Gray's Beach, and where I'd seen the *Rose*. We went in real close to the big cordage pier where the draggers were tied up. The boats floated on the still brown water. A man on the wharf came out of a warehouse underneath a big corrugated steel door. He was wheeling a dolly with steel wheels on it. The cart was piled high with cartons and the steel wheels made a racket on the concrete. That was all that was happening.

"Big deal," said Jim.

"Yeah I know."

Then we heard the faint clacking of a solenoid and another big steel door began rolling upward in the brick building. A lift truck whispered out, holding crates aloft on its pincers. A man in a yellow helmet was driving it. The crates said *Ocean Spray* on the sides.

"This is so exciting I can't stand it."

"Let's swing by close, then go into town and get some bait."

We crawled right up to the big pier and watched the few figures moving back and forth along it. We were close enough for me to glimpse a grisly relic strung up alongside the Cyclone fence that marked the terminus of the big dock. I hadn't noticed it on my previous visit. It was a codfish head, cut off

right behind the gills, suspended on the fence with a steve-
dore's hook. It was as big as a bushel basket. Flies swarmed
over it.

"Will you look at that. Must've been a five-footer," said
Jim.

"Why do you suppose they've done that with it?"

He shrugged and spun the wheel lazily in his big hands.
He eased the sticks forward and the engine whined.

"Dunno. Trophy maybe. Or else it's a warning to stay out
of the yards when the gate's shut."

It was a grim reminder, and I thought of Angel's face
staring at me from the oven rack. We picked up speed and
soon landed at the main marina, where I bought Jim an early
supper (apparently the entire trip, not just the fuel, was to be
courtesy of Yours Truly) and we fueled the *Whimsea*'s tanks
and bought an ample supply of quahogs. These would be
affixed to heavy hooks and dragged slowly (or simply rested)
on the mollusk beds around the *James Longstreet*, a tempting
treat for tautogs and other fish. While we waited for dusk I
prepared the bait, shucking it from the shells and cutting it
into convenient-sized nuggets. We sucked down some of the
St. Pauli Girl beer we'd brought along and listened to the
radio. I was hunkered down in the cockpit out of the breeze
so I removed my shirt, soaking up the last precious bit of
sun, even though it was thoroughly filtered by clouds. Jim
pored over the charts of Cape Cod Bay.

Dusk came, and we left Plymouth Harbor.

We rolled out past the big breakwater again. A line of
herring gulls stood on it, beaks to the breeze, most with one
foot tucked up in their tummy feathers. They said *skirl, skirl,
skirl* . . .

When we got to the *James Longstreet* the sun had been
down forty minutes. It was growing dark fast. The old wreck
looked more ominous than I'd ever seen it. Its bridge looked
like a giant hunk of brown Swiss cheese. The hull was partially collapsed in the middle, where a lot of the steel reinforcing rods were visible, entwined in the concrete hull. The
fly-boys from Otis were pretty good shots, I guessed. They'd
nailed the old Liberty Ship right in the belly. In fact the

midsection of the old hull was so full of holes and cave-ins that occasionally you could see clear through it to the dark bluish purple of the water on the other side. We crept in close; DeGroot had his eyes glued to the fathometer fastened above the helm. It was a black box with a dial in the center, marked in feet and meters. A blip showed on the dial at zero feet, which was where the sound signal was emitted from *Whimsea* via a metal sounder in her hull. Another blip was appearing on the dial opposite the sixteen-foot mark. *Whimsea* rolled and lurched forward; the wreck loomed bigger and bigger.

Suddenly the blip jumped back and forth, and settled up toward its mate at the zero end of the dial.

"Shit!" said Jim as he reversed and throttled up. But it was too late. There was a thump and a shudder, and then a slow heavy scraping sound. *Whimsea* stopped. It was falling tide; if we didn't get moving soon, we'd be there for the duration. Jim and I ran a flashlight all around the inside of the hull. Nothing. That was good at least. We had been going slow enough and reacted soon enough so that the boat was still in one piece.

"What was it?"

"Dunno. But it was dumb to come in here. Why the hell do I listen to you? I suppose this place is full of shoals and rocks that aren't marked. Maybe they're big hunks of the *James Longstreet*, who knows? Of course it's not supposed to matter because we're not supposed to *be* here. And if the CG has to haul us off, we're going to look mighty silly and get fined to boot."

He gunned the engine once more, making the needle on the tachometer approach the red line. There was a grinding shudder as the propwash worked the boat loose. We shot backward and Jim cut the twin engines back.

"I'm not going back in there. It's a labyrinth of obstacles around that hulk."

So I talked him into letting me use the life raft. We inflated it with the compressed air bottle and soon I was in it, bobbing and rowing along to the old Liberty Ship. I got there quickly; the little rubber boat flipped right along over the nasty stuff that projected up from the sandy bottom. It wasn't hard to figure out how the *Penelope* tore a gash in her steel skin. Up close, the topsides of the ship loomed over me like a three-story apartment building. I paddled along toward the series of big holes in her beam. I looked back at the *Whimsea*. Jim hadn't set the hook, but was purring along in a semi-stall two hundred yards off the *Longstreet*'s port quarter. The boat's shape was faint, and growing fainter in the darkness and light fog. I could see her running lights clearly, that was about all.

I reached out and touched the *Longstreet*. I felt the rough concrete with my hand, and grabbed a projecting steel reinforcing rod and pulled the rubber raft along to the first big hole. The seawater poured through this, and I glided into the bowels of the ship. It was like being in an old wrecked cathedral. The superstructure of the bridge towered above me, black and ragged against the dark purple sky. All the portholes were devoid of glass, which had no doubt been blown out long ago by the concussion of the bombs. It was like a giant corpse with all its eyes poked out. Generally, it wasn't inviting, and the cold and the dark, and the sound of sloshing water, did not improve it either.

I took the waterproof spotlight and swept it around. There were plenty of nooks and crannies to hide anything your heart desired inside the old hulk of the *Longstreet*. There were bent railings, blown-away doors, exposed corridors, old hatchways, smashed and twisted bulkheads, ventilating ducts, stanchions, wells, supporting members—it was a maze of pulverized concrete and twisted, rusty steel. I shined a flashbeam all around me. I saw nothing out of place though. No crates, plastic-wrapped bundles, or anything else that caught my eye. I heard two quick beeps. Jim was telling me he wanted to split. I rowed out through the big hole and started back to the *Whimsea*, which was now almost totally invisible. The chop had picked up, and the tiny raft pitched around uncomfortably. I heard another boat and saw a set of running lights sweep past out behind the *Whimsea*.

"See anything?" asked Jim as he helped me back aboard. I told him, and he told me another boat had been snaking around in the prohibited zone.

"Maybe they thought *Whimsea* was in trouble."

"They didn't say anything. Just cut around me in a wide circle and left. Blue hull, white topsides. About our size. Let's get on back while we can still see our hands in front of our faces."

We slid and rolled a bit all the way back to Plymouth in the following sea. We used the compass and RDF a lot because of the poor visibility. We passed the outer light at the end of the breakwater and turned to port when we approached Bug Light in the harbor's middle, then made our way slowly back toward the marina. During my visit to the target ship, Jim had caught a tautog, which we cleaned and wrapped in foil. We got a slip at the yacht club's pier; at this time of year there were plenty available. We had a nightcap and turned in. It was one-thirty in the morning. After ten minutes DeGroot was sawing logs. I lay in the upper bunk, my head inches from the wooden cabin top. I heard the very faint patter of light drizzle begin on the roof. I tossed and turned. I rolled on my side and looked down at Jim. He was sleeping like a baby, that big Dutch head immobile on the foam rubber pillow covered with a canvas print of code flags and buoys. Jim had a basic calmness and world view which allowed him to march through life with minimal distraction and regret. He had enough Nordic discipline and stubbornness to shrug aside doubt and reluctance. I admired this, perhaps because I was a bit the opposite. Though never lacking in self-confidence, I seemed to view the world as a series of booby traps, a labyrinthine obstacle course of surprises and gross injustices, complete with Minotaurs at strategic locations. *Whimsea* swayed and rocked ever so slightly; the faint patter of light rain increased. Hell, I should go to sleep in no time. *Should* . . .

I slid out of the rack, opened the rear doorway and climbed the three steps up to the cockpit deck. I stood there just outside the door under the overhang of the cabin roof. I felt, well, *wistful.*

I had been conked on the head and thrown in the drink, attacked twice, been gnawed on by a dog, had a pistol held to the nape of my neck, my hand broken, my wife mad at me, my dog killed, my kids perhaps in danger, two people killed, and all I had to show for it was standing out in a twenty-eight-foot motorboat in the rain. Somehow it lacked something.

"Somehow it lacks something," I murmured to myself.

I wanted *an answer*.

I went back into the cabin and pulled on a pair of blue jeans, a long-sleeved jersey, and a navy blue turtleneck sweater over that. I put on thick wool socks of navy blue and my Topsiders. I pulled a dark wool watch cap down over my head. My beard, now almost luxuriant, was mostly black. I liked the way it broke up my face and covered the light outline of my jaw.

I put my wallet in my hip pocket. If the police saw the Midnight Skulker slinking around the docks, they'd want to know who in hell he was, especially clad like a cat-burglar. The note I wrote said:

2 A.M. Went over to the cordage pier in N. Plymouth. Should be back by 4 A.M., if not, raise hell.
Doc.

I left this smack in the middle of my pillow, set the alarm for 4 A.M., and left. I was unarmed except for my folding hunter knife, which I had slipped into my jeans rather than wearing it on my belt in its leather pouch. My Bull-Barrel was at home. Anyway, I had the feeling it had brought me bad luck before. The only thing I carried was a flashlight, a black steel one that was waterproof, and pretty hefty. The pier was lighted with overhead lamps in steel reflectors spaced about thirty feet apart. I strolled along nonchalantly. If anyone asked, I was out for a midnight walk, which of course was true. Off to my right at the state pier I could see the *Mayflower II*, and at the pier's base the Doric stone mini-temple housing Plymouth Rock, a bathtub-sized boulder upon which John Winthrop, Miles Standish, and Company set foot when they landed in the New World—or so they say.

I ambled on and passed the shopping center with its clam joints, bait and tackle shops, and souvenir stands complete with carved wooden sea captains (hand-carved in the Phillippines), ships in bottles (made in Macao), Yankee scrimshaw (plastic, made in Taiwan), miniature whaling harpoons (Hecho en Mexico), and little brass ship's lamps (from India). It was very American.

I broke into a slow, determined jog when I hit Water Street. While a lone walker might be arrested at two in the morning, a solitary jogger is admired. In about fifteen minutes I was in North Plymouth, at the gateway to Cordage Park. I was stumped right away; the big outer gate was closed and chained. Four strands of barbed wire guarded its top, and ran along the top of the entire tall Cyclone fence that enclosed the park. But I noticed a small stream that cut beneath the road and made its way, encased in concrete banks, into the park. It obviously emptied into the harbor. Where the creek, road, and tall fence met was a bridge railing of metal pipe. But the fence ran along both sides of the concrete bank. Nevertheless I had a vague hunch that if I could work my way fifty yards or so down the creek the fence would be less formidable. I ducked under the bridge railing and saw the dark water sliding by. It gurgled around light-colored rocks, old logs, pieces of old wire fencing, and junk. No headlights approached on the road. I lowered myself gingerly down onto one of the rocks, and step-stoned my way the first twenty feet. Then a low, mucky ledge of slime formed at a slow bend, and I tested it, walked on it. It didn't smell so great but it held me up. I kept my eyes on the Cyclone fencing just above my head. I waded in shallow water that was cold and stinky the last forty feet until I saw the fence bow out. There was a four-foot gap in it at the top of the concrete river channel. I grabbed the top of this wall and drew myself up under the fence. The outer fence had been breached. But there remained the inner one, which had appeared to be pretty tight indeed when I saw it previously.

There were lights on here and there in the complex of buildings. The nearby buildings were newer than the others, small wooden things with sloping shingled roofs. They resembled houses. Behind them were several huge warehouse-type sheds, then the really big buildings on and near the wharf that comprised the old factory. The entire place was absolutely still and deserted. For all its size I would have been surprised if there were no night watchmen. I left the side of the fence and waited between two small spruce trees for a few minutes. My feet were turning to ice. Nothing happening. As Jim and I had seen, the wharf was hardly Grand Central Station during working hours. At night it was like the innermost chamber of Tutankhamen's tomb. I kept in the shadows and skirted the edge of the park where no lights shone. If someone had been watching me I would certainly be visible, but they'd have to be looking. I didn't think anyone was.

I crept up alongside a building and looked at the inner fence, the one that sealed off most of the big cordage factory and wharf from all the other parts of the park. The gate, open wide in the day, was slid shut on its roller track, wound with heavy chain and padlocked. This fence, too, was topped with barbed wire. The place resembled Concord Prison, except the wire was strung straight on slanted brackets instead of being wound in giant spirals, concertina fashion. I stood in the dark and shivered and looked at the big fence. It looked tight as a bloated tick. It ended against the wall of a smaller brick building at the far end of the factory, toward the south. I walked along this deserted stretch of fencing, around the small building, and saw that it was perched on a sea wall about twelve feet high. It was low tide and the flats extended along this wall and—believe it or not—led all the way back to the park on the seaside. So the way to penetrate these fences was to do so where they met the water. I climbed over the parapet, hung by the top of the wall with my good arm, and dropped a few feet to the soft sandy muck. I then walked around the seawall, under the low building, and up on the beach. I had simply walked around the fence. Of course it meant that at high tide I was trapped in the complex. But I still had a few hours to look around before the water came in.

From the narrow beach, littered with flotsam, it was a short walk up to the roadway that ran around the factory on the harbor side and connected with all the courtyards and delivery routes on the other side. There were no lights on this side, but the whole place was sparsely illuminated by the water and overcast sky, which cast a faint metallic glow onto the buildings. An enormous vertical black cylinder was fastened to this side of the factory wall, with many big pipes issuing from it. It looked like a boiler tank, and probably was. Some of the pipes ran along the wall at waist level. I thumped one with my knuckle. Heavy cast iron. They were for steam all right, or had been once upon a time. They snaked all over the complex from building to building. They climbed walls, traversed rooftops, over courtyards, went into, under, over, through buildings, sheds, and abutments.

I walked along this narrow roadway that fronted the harborside. The big building was to my left. It was about four hundred feet long. At its end I found myself on the main roadway that led from the wharf and its warehouse all the way through the old factory complex, through the rest of what was called Cordage Park, and out to the highway. I saw the fence I had just circumvented. I walked up to it and peered through at the rest of the huge buildings on the other side of it. The roadway went straight ahead, and I saw the familiar series of courtyards created by U-shaped wings of the big factory buildings that opened off to one side of the road. Each courtyard was surrounded on three sides by walls six stories high. Big black pipes and high voltage wires crisscrossed these courtyards overhead.

I planted my fanny on an old truck tire and thought for a minute. It sure didn't seem as if there was much going on. A sound reached me from several courtyards down the narrow service road. It was an engine grinding away. I supposed it to be some kind of generator or cooling compressor. It sounded just like a semi-trailer truck idling at a truck stop. I rose up and walked toward the wharf. The end of the fence came back again and snaked around its far side. I noticed a foul stench as I walked, and saw the dark object stuck on the Cyclone wire. I remembered the severed codfish head, and went up to it. It was the biggest fishhead I'd ever seen. The big eyes were gone, eaten out by maggots. All that remained were two holes as big as tennis balls in the leathery carapace

of the skull. The mouth was bucket-shaped, like a bass's.
The big hook came up through the lower jaw. The fish, when
alive, could have swallowed a bowling ball without knowing
it.

I walked out to the wharf on the service road, the one Jim
and I had seen the lift truck on, the same one that I'd spied
the blue van on. Behind me the road went into the factory
complex and the courtyards of the big buildings. I saw big
dark shapes on the water. Four of them. The draggers sat
stone still in the shallow water. There were no lights aboard
them, not even little sparks on the spars, or cabin lights.
Nothing. The wharf, too, was dark. I crept along the building, passing the big corrugated steel doors. There were small
swing doors in between each one. There was a fifth boat
behind the four big ones, a small cruiser. And I'd be damned
if she didn't have a blue hull, white topsides. I moved slower
now, keeping snugly against the warehouse wall on my right.
The light was faint on this side of the buildings, the north
side, and I knew I was invisible in the shadows in my dark
clothes. When I was abreast the little boat I looked down at
her for a long time. She was quiet and dark. It was too dark
to read her bow numbers and I didn't dare show a light, so I
sat and tried to remember things about her. I had been gazing
and thinking for a few minutes when I saw a flickering motion out of the side of my left eye. I looked down toward the
foot of the long dock and could see nothing; it was all dark.
Then, looking back at the boat, the flickering came back. In
dim light you can see much better out of the sides of your
eyes than dead ahead. This is because the area of your retina
where the image is focused is also the point on the retina
where the optic nerve enters. Consequently it is almost devoid of the light-sensitive rod and cone cells.

I shrank back against the wall and sidestepped slowly about
eight feet to my right, toward the end of the dock. There
were two stacks of fish bins there, stuck into one another like
cardboard hamburger baskets. They smelled mighty ripe but
I was glad; nobody in his right mind would get within six
feet of them. I snuggled right in between them, and then slid
down to my knees. I peered out down the dock again. Now

the flickering movement was close enough to be visible when I looked straight at it. Two of them, and they weren't midgets either.

They came up the wharf slowly, as quiet as alley cats. They, too, wore dark clothes. I drew out the folding hunter and opened the blade, locking it. It was mighty pathetic, but if they saw me and came at me, I was going to lash out at them with a couple of wide swipes, then run for the end of the dock and dive in. I was getting good at midnight harbor swims.

I shrank back as the two men approached. As they walked by one grabbed the other by the sleeve and pointed at the small blue cruiser. The other man looked at it awhile, then turned to the other and spoke in a barely audible whisper.

"Them?"

The other nodded.

"We'll go in the back then. I haven't the stomach for it—"

"The word's come down. *McGooey*."

"Come on—"

They crept on toward the very end of the wharf. I caught the faint whiff—very faint—of liquor. One man spoke with a real brogue, but it didn't sound like the man I'd met in the Buzarski barn. The other man sounded like an American. I peeped out at them as they paused beside the wall. I heard a metallic clack. It was either a doorlatch or the cocking of a pistol. The men were gone. I waited perhaps half a minute to make sure they weren't going to pop out again, then eased up into a standing position. Inching along the wall I kept eyes and ears alert. Nothing. I picked up the pace, heading toward the fence.

But just before I reached the end of the long wharf building, one of the small doors opened in front of me along the side of the warehouse wall. I slid up against the wall, trying my damndest to shrink right into it. A figure emerged from the doorway and began to walk past me. I knew he would have to see me. There was nowhere to go.

He turned just as he passed me.

"John?" he whispered.

"Shhhhh!"

"Listen . . . I jus—hey, *you're not John—*"

But by that time I had shoved a hand into his gut just below the center of the rib cage. Not a fist, a hand. A set of fingers straight as I could set them, rather like an ice spade. A fist won't carry the force in far enough to hurt; that's what Liatis Roantis told me anyway. It seemed to work. He bent his knees a bit and bowed down right in front of me. I switched the steel flashlight into my right paw and thunked him on the nape of the neck medium hard. I didn't want to hurt him—whoever he was—any more than was necessary to effect a quick exit. He tumbled down without a sound, let out a slow sigh and rolled just a wee bit, like a kid in a scary dream. He kept moving to and fro, as if aware, even in his semiconscious state, of the discomfort I'd put him in. I reckoned he would not emerge well disposed toward me.

I started back down toward the foot of the wharf again, fast and quiet. But the good cards just weren't turning up.

Just before I reached the same small door it opened again. I was so close I swung into the wall right next to the hinges. The door covered me as it opened all the way, and I saw the shadow of a big man emerge and walk right on past me. He went over toward the edge of the pier, dipped his head into cupped hands, and lighted a cigarette. I saw the fiery halo surround his head. He wore a trenchcoat and a tweed hat. "John's" friend was in a semi-doze not thirty feet from where he stood. He would thrash and groan, maybe yell, any second. The end of the wharf was another twenty yards. But there was no cover. I knew the man who'd come out for a smoke would discover his fallen comrade long before I could make it. By instinct I'd caught hold of the metal door before it swung all the way shut. It was pivoted on a hydraulic door closer. I twisted the doorknob quickly, forcefully back and forth in a millisecond. No go. As I supposed, it opened only from within without a key. If I wanted to hide, it was now or never. I really had no choice. I ducked around behind the closing door and followed its swinging path into the blackness of the huge building. After all, I told myself, if the doors opened from the inside, I could always get out again.

You jerk, an inner voice answered. You said that about

twenty minutes ago when you scaled the inner fence. And now look what a sweet pickle you've gotten yourself into.

I had to admit it wasn't very promising.

21

THE PLACE WAS HUGE AND JET BLACK. I GROPED FORWARD
for twenty or thirty feet. Although I had my flashlight in my
hand, I didn't dare use it. Once I felt something hard bump
up against my chest. A tall oxygen cylinder. Thank God I
hadn't knocked it over; the noise it would've made in that
big covered arena as it hit the cement floor would have rung
out like a cannon shot.

I continued to feel my way along. Gradually my eyes got
accustomed to the darkness, and I could see the faint giant
oblong ring of pale gray up above. The warehouse building
had a sectioned roof, and a ring of narrow vertical skylights
that circled the whole thing.

I heard a creak and a *whish* behind me. I turned and saw
a pale upright rectangle of light. The door was open; somebody was coming in. I dropped to a crouch and then a crawl,
trying to hold my left hand out to ward off obstacles. In three
seconds I had run smack into a big pillar, which I promptly
scrambled around. I was none too quick, either, for just then
a light shone. It was the man I had seen leave after I walloped
the Friend-of-John, who now held up his Zippo as a torch to
see and search.

I stayed hidden behind the concrete piling. The man
snapped the lighter shut and was gone. I listened, but could
hear nothing; he must have been wearing rubber-soled shoes.

Had he seen the fallen man? How could he not? And wasn't that why he'd held up the lighter?

I hastened toward the door. There was a tiny window in it, probably the kind made of thick glass with chicken wire inside it. Using my sense of direction—which is awful—I managed to sneak back toward it. The tiny rectangle of window light got clearer and clearer as I drew up to it. Only a few more feet to freedom; with the man inside I could now safely depart.

Except that the door was now locked from the *inside* too.

The cards weren't getting any better.

I sneaked back into the far interior of the big building again. Now what? I crouched behind a pillar—either the same one or a mate to it—and thought. I looked at my watch; it was just after 3 A.M. If I could remain hidden in the building long enough Jim would seek me out. But how long would that be? My note said I should be back an hour from now. Fine. But Jim might sleep through the alarm or shut if off unconsciously. I could have a six- or seven-hour wait. If they knew I was in the building, there was no hope.

How to get out?

Perhaps I should try the back door, the one used by the first two characters I'd seen on the pier. Christ, the pier was more active at night than during the day. They had walked on up to the far end and hadn't come back. Since the door I'd entered was at the land end of the building, the smartest thing to do was to poke along the length of the warehouse and look for any way out. Any way at all. And I must do it quietly, slowly.

It was three-fifteen when I heard the noises. The first one was the slow dripping sound of water into a pool.

Having nothing else to home in on, I headed toward the dropping water. And when I arrived, I first heard the distant voices. I crept closer, and the voices grew louder. They seemed to come from underneath me and I couldn't figure out why. A light beam swept quickly around over my head. I froze, crouched, and felt my pulse rocket up to about 160.

The beam played around the place for another few seconds, then flicked off. Watchman.

I tried to remember in my mind's eye what I had seen in the light's path. No doubt I would have seen, and remembered, more if I hadn't been trying to shrink into the floor. There were stacks of crates and pallets. I saw the brief silhouettes of two lift trucks. Barrels . . . I saw some old barrels. Home-made ladders of nailed two-by-fours.

I remembered something else, too. It was a thing of wire mesh, like a cage, toward the middle of the building, and big. I never saw it in the beam because . . . because . . . why?

Because whoever held the beam didn't shine it on the cage for the simple reason that he was standing *next* to the cage. So then what was the cage thing? I had seen only the indirect illumination of it; there was no way of knowing exactly what it was, or did.

I was moving all this time, perhaps out of sheer nervousness more than anything. Most of the time I crawled because it kept my balance intact, my center of gravity low, and my profile down. I groused through the old place like an elephant feeding on the veldt at midnight. I kept heading toward the *poit! poit!* of the drip. Hell, at least it was a direction, a straight line.

A glow reached up through the floor. Pale, faint yellow: the glow of tungsten light bulbs. I snaked behind a series of cardboard cartons set on pallets. I oozed toward the big square hole in the floor where the faint yellow light was coming from. Then I saw—as faint as faint can be—the big crinkled wire mesh screening. It was the cage I'd been wondering about. An elevator shaft. A big freight elevator. But who'd have guessed that this dockside warehouse had a lower level?

Probably nobody would guess it. And that's probably exactly why somebody chose the place to sneak around in at night. Then the goddamned flashlight came on again. I was close enough now to see who the sentinel was. It was the Marlboro Man—the guy who'd stepped outside for a smoke and locked me in this place. I wanted to bean him, and take his key. But he shined the light down on the floor and opened a door at the side of the big steel cage. Before it closed I could hear the sound of his feet descending steps. It was a stairway that apparently wound around the elevator shaft.

The pier had big granite block sides that rose up a good twelve feet above the harbor water at high tide, maybe a bit more. But the construction of the wharf, the big stone blocks and ancient appearance of the structure, would lead anyone looking at it to assume at once that it was solid clear through. But this wasn't the case. Smack dab in its center was another level, reached by heavy elevator and adjoining stairway. Even if this cellarlike cavity in the dock was twelve feet high, it would still be above water level.

But I wanted no part of it. I wanted clear of the whole thing. I wanted to beat it out to a pay phone, chunk a coin into the slot and raise Mary at DeGroot's and tell her to seek out brother Joe and Brian Hannon, the Coast Guard, the militia, and all the rest and surround the place and stop all this bad jazz.

So I commenced worming my way along the floor again, but a bit faster now that the watchman had descended the stairway, and oozed my way to the back of the building. There had to be an exit back there. *Had* to. I left the big square hole behind, with its soft yellow glow and wire mesh skin. It was dark as pitch again and I felt better. I don't know why all the horror movies and gothic novels keep the myth alive that darkness is frightening. Nothing's further from the truth. When you're on the run the dark is your best friend. It's a great place to hide from keen-eyed predators. That is why 90 percent of small defenseless mammals have become nocturnal.

I belly-crawled, crouched, tiptoed, and slunk my way to the far side of the big building until a hundred ineffable messages—probably long-dormant auditory and kinesthetic cave man signals—told me that the wall was not far ahead. I have thought since that it must have been echoes that warned me. For all its silence, a big warehouse must have a noise level of some sort, perhaps ten thousand minuscule waftings, drippings, flutterings, hissings, and the like that swarm about the big place, like a school of fry in a tank. They must then echo off walls, and present a different noise pattern to a person approaching the building's terminus. Or *something*. Hell, I don't know why, I just knew it.

Then I smelled it: the very faint whiff of alcohol. It was as subtle and sweet as baking bread, that ethereal odor of hospitality, of food and friendship.

I turned around quick and headed the other way.

I was beginning to feel like one of those trick cars you wind up that never goes off the table. Every time it senses the edge, it does a 180-degree turn.

I couldn't get out of the goddamn warehouse.

And then a strange sensation over took me. Maybe it was the lack of sleep or my nervous state in general. I imagined that the elevator shaft in the center of the building was the vortex of a whirlpool. Try as I might, the inward spiral was swooshing me along its square yellow maw. It had perhaps licked out at me as I brooded aboard the *Whimsea*, as fine and subtle as the mycelium of wood-pulp fungus, hair-thin and stretching many yards, invisible. Once in the factory compound it had licked out again, like a rainbow of promise or the dry creek bed, the arroyo followed by the thirsty prospector. Once inside the building it was stronger and stronger, until now it resembled the lead tentacle of a giant squid, wrapped around my torso and drawing me in toward the gnashing beak amidst the folds of slimy muscle.

I had decided, upon smelling the faint booze breath, not to meet Mutt and Jeff, the guys I first saw on the pier who spoke briefly in my hidden presence. They didn't sound that friendly to begin with, and the metallic clack I'd heard as they rounded the far corner of the pier didn't add to their collective image. The best thing for me to do was to snake all the way back again to the other end of the building. I would find a hidey-hole there, deep behind or underneath some crates or skids or barrels, and *wait*. Wait till some bodyguard opened the door again, allowing me to dash by him and out. Wait till dawn, and Jim called the fuzz. Wait till hell froze over, but *not* to—

A giant spider jumped on my face. It clung across the front

of my skull with menacing ferocity. It squeezed its inky legs down tight.

A hand.

Then two quick belly chops and a kidney punch and I was down and doing a slow roll. But before I could yell the least little thing the spider came back, jumped upon me again, and found my mouth. It snuggled down and made a nest there, tight. I couldn't speak. I couldn't even breathe.

There were two of them. I saw a light flicker between cupped hands. Flashlight again. Strong arms had pinned mine behind me. They helped me to my feet. I wasn't eager. Who was it? Probably the watchman by the cage. I had made a small sound and been ferreted out. I didn't think it was Mutt and Jeff. I smelled no booze, and also they were, as far as my crude and damaged reckoning could place them, still at the far terminus of the big brick barn.

A whisper said: "Walk forward slowly until I tell you to stop. Keep your hands up above your head where I can see them at all times. If you drop them or try to turn I'll kill you before you know what's happened. Nod your head to show you understand."

I did. I felt the cold pressure of a gun muzzle in my spine.

"Now walk forward slowly where I point with the light."

He pointed it at the doorway to the stairs, and I started walking. The pressure left my back but I didn't try anything. The episode in the barn had taught me how foolish that course of action was. The man—and it wasn't the same one who'd gotten the drop on me earlier—certainly held the pistol aimed square at me.

"Open it and start down."

I swung the door back and entered. On the fourth or fifth step down the door snapped shut behind us. Then it grew light. I could see the winding staircase I was descending. Lights were on. Apparently it was a strict policy to show no lights on the warehouse's ground floor.

We kept walking around and around, down and down. Who was down there? What monstrous hairy arthropoid clutched at the middle of the great web, waiting for me? Was it Sydney Greenstreet, complete with cigar and fez? Emperor Ming? The Rockettes?

I had a feeling it was none of the above.

"Keep going," the voice said.

22

WE WALKED UNDER THE REFLECTOR LIGHTS OF THE lower level. Here the huge concrete pillars were much heavier and more numerous, about twelve feet apart and arranged in grids to hold up the entire center portion of the warehouse above. There was only one row of lights on; the pillars and old spools and drums that cluttered the place disappeared gradually into the darkness on each side of us. The place was big. Not as big as the vast amphitheater above, but big nevertheless. Ahead of us was a metal-clad door hung with counterweights on pulleys. I sure didn't like the look of it.

"Stop," he whispered.

We waited. I expected to feel a tap on the back of my neck, then a blinding white flash. Then nothing, because I would be dead.

But nothing happened.

"Who's there?" he asked. His voice had an anxious tone, which surprised me.

"Who is that behind us?"

No answer. I then heard the click of his flashlight. It was probably as good a chance as I'd get, and I was just about to begin my spin and high kick when he told me to move on. There went my last chance. We stopped in front of the metal fire door.

"Knock on it. Hard."

I did.

"Who is it?" said a barely audible voice.

"Hartzos. I found a spy, John."

"Police?"

"Don't know. He knocked Micky cold out on the dock, then worked his way in."

"Where were you, Hartzos?"

"He must've come in when I was with Micky. I got to get back up quick. Want help with him?"

"No. Step back." I thought the voice was faintly familiar . . .

The heavy door slid open. It was almost dark beyond. A flashlight shone on our faces.

"Well?" asked Hartzos.

Still the man with the light was silent.

"John, do you want me to stay?"

"Uh uh," was the grunted reply. I heard the sound of fading footsteps behind me as Hartzos the watchman returned to his post. They certainly had the place sealed off effectively. Two tall fences with barbed wire, a series of deserted buildings, a lower level of an old wharf with solid rock walls, and a swarm of silent guards that prowled around in the pitch black.

The man grabbed me by my upper arm hard and I felt a gun in my ribs. He spun me fast around and up against the doorjamb as he flicked off the flashlight. I heard the big door slide shut and John and I were alone. I didn't like the feeling one bit. When I next heard his voice it was right in my ear:

"Well, well, Doctor Adams, you certainly dawnt seem to have such bleedin' keen luck mucking about in old buildings, eh?"

"You!"

"Shhhhhh! Now you listen good these next few seconds or we're both dead, hear?"

"I hear. But tell me who you are—"

"Shhhhh!" He jammed me in the rib cage hard with the gun. The voice commenced again, in a whisper almost delicate for all the menace it conveyed.

"Who I am's not important. Savin' your neck should be,

and your chances aren't good. If they find out we've met before we're both dead. You've never laid eyes on me.''

"Right. Never laid—"

"C'mon!"

He marched me through a narrow hall into the room beyond. I will never forget that room. As I entered it I was almost buoyant with hope that I'd run into my friend from the barn again. But one glance around the dismal chamber with the damp rock walls was enough to take the tar out of anybody. The room was perhaps twenty by thirty feet. The ceiling was low. It was full of junk: old cable spools, machinery, and crates and pallets. A doorway in the far wall led to another room or passageway that was dark. What dominated the room was a chute that projected at an angle from above. At the chute's end was a long narrow table of sheet metal with wooden sides to it. It was a dressing table for fish. Along the sides of this table were troughs, no doubt for the fish heads and offal that were discarded. These emptied into another chute directly above a large grating in the floor as big as a door. The steel grate that covered the black hole in the floor had an ominous look. It could have been the doorway to an oubliette. A sound came up through the grating. The sound of sloshing water. This room, originally used to store cable, had been converted into a processing room by the fishery. Now abandoned even in that role, it made a perfect place to hide in.

The big man sat with his back to me. He was listening to a VHF radio, his head bowed in concentration. A slender, lithe figure emerged from the far dark doorway and stopped and stared at us. John prodded with the gun and I sat down on a stack of pallets.

"Jim, look," said the figure.

Schilling turned around and scowled at us. The slim figure disappeared into the dark doorway and reappeared immediately with something long and dark. It approached us silently, and then became fully visible a few feet from us. The delicate hands pointed a Colt Commando assault rifle at me.

"Ah the charming Doctor Adams. You surprised to find me here?" asked Laura Kincaid.

"Not really," I answered. "I realized that you were the only person who could have told Schilling about my suspicions. I told nobody else. And I think it was your big friend here who opened the front door while we were talking out in the garden. I know you don't really have a maid."

"Yes, it was a clever game you played with me. I realized too late who it probably was on the phone, and that made us even more anxious to get rid of you."

"Ah, but we *didn't*," said Schilling as he shuffled up behind Laura Kincaid. "You were lucky. I hit you too lightly up in Gloucester. I knew it before you hit the water. You had turned a bit at just the right instant and the sap slid off the side of your head—"

"So you waited around to make sure."

"But it wasn't good enough. You're a wily one, Adams, but stupid. Even our warning of the dog wasn't enough I see."

I turned to Laura.

"I guess it's not too difficult to imagine what happened to your husband."

She looked away impatiently for a second, then faced me, frowning.

"I knew you were trouble as soon as you called me. I told Jim to put himself out underneath the car so he could get a good look at you as you left. You were stupid to hunt out Murdock."

"And he was obviously stupid to help you," I said. I looked at my watch. "There are several things you should know. One: the police and Coast Guard all know I'm here. They also know you're not hanging around the *Rose*. Even they can spot a decoy as obvious as that—"

Schilling and Laura exchanged a quick glance. It was fleeting, but enough to tell me they were a little bit afraid.

"Second: this whole place is going to come alive shortly after four o'clock. That's in less than half an hour."

Schilling lost control. With a deep, gutteral roar he leapt forward and pasted me one on the side of the jaw and sent me sprawling on the smooth concrete floor. It was damp and very cold. Apparently I'd messed up his plans enough so that he was mighty irritated.

"It won't work, Adams, your making up a cock and bull story to throw us off balance. *You're* the one who's in trouble now. A few things *you* should know. First, the security here's tight. It's a wonder you managed to get in at all but as we can see, you didn't get far. Second, there are four or five ways out of here, including that long tunnel behind us. If need be we'll leave that way and we've got some stuff back there that'll make anyone chasing us wish he'd never been born. We were just getting ready to make our last run; we got skunked earlier tonight but now we're ready and nobody's getting in our way. You're leaving here too, Adams, but by a different exit."

He spun around and went over to the big grate, which he snatched up from a deep squat, just like an Olympic weight-lifter. He staggered three steps with the huge metal screen and dropped it. It clanged down in a flurry of sparks. Schilling walked over to the pit and peered down.

"Put you right in here with all the old fish guts."

I felt a deep sickening dread under my ribs. My lower half seemed made of water and my mouth had a fuzzy, electric feeling. I felt on the verge of some kind of seizure. I was *very* scared. I had to talk, to keep them talking. I needed all the time I could buy. I glanced over at John, who held his Walther muzzle down. In a sense he represented my only hope, and I didn't even have the faintest idea who the hell he was.

"I wouldn't have . . . wouldn't have become at all interested if it weren't for the boy's death," I said.

"That was an accident," said the woman. "Jim saw the Navy insignia and panicked. The boy was on the far side of the boat and he took a swipe at him with a fish billy. He just . . . never came back up."

"Ah. So that settles it. That easy is it?"

She struck me across the face with the muzzle of the rifle. The flash arrester did a nice job of opening up the left side of my cheek.

"You shut up. *Shut up!*"

"So you know my name. How did you find out?" asked the big man. He was built like a fullback, and had obviously worked out heavily to increase the beef up around his chest and shoulders. But there was something missing, something weak about the eyes and mouth that turned my stomach.

"I took your picture in Wellfleet. I'm not the only one who knows you didn't die in Alaska. Assuming you get away tonight, you've still had it, pal. They've got your number."

"Who? *Names!*" screamed Laura. "Name some names, *quick!*"

I did. I named Ruggles, Brindelli, Hannon, O'Hearn, and two others. I mentioned the army chap who couldn't wait to get his hands on the people who stole the army's rifles—

It was then I realized I had blundered into something that could make me inadvertently reveal something about John. Out of the corner of my eye I could see him visibly shudder. I saw his heavy shoulders sag a bit, and knew he was almost as distraught as I was.

Jim Schilling sat on an old crate and rubbed his big jaw.

"He knows the whole thing, Laura. I want him out. Now."

"Won't do you any good. All of them know too."

"Then where the hell *are they?*" he screamed, and glared at me.

He had me there. I sure as hell wished I knew.

"Just tell me," I asked, "who are the guns for?"

"They're going to Ireland," said Laura.

"Then you *are* supplying the IRA—"

She smiled a smug grin and shook her well-groomed head back and forth.

"No. They're going to our people in the south, to give the Irish bastards a taste of their own medicine. The arms we sent from here will be used to kill the IRA murderers and terrorists. If things get rough—as they will, I'm sure—then they'll be used against the populace of the south. If they can do it to us, we can do it to them."

She smiled serenely. It looked totally incongruous that this middle-aged, stylish woman should be holding a military rifle. But hold it she did, and with evident familiarity too.

"I remember now, you're English—"

"My, my, you certainly have dug around, haven't you, Doctor? Yes, I'm British. But my home was Ulster, not England. My family owned a factory in Belfast, until it was bombed out by the thugs from the south. When my father wouldn't give in to them, they killed him and burnt the factory to the ground. We were ruined. We came here to start all over again. I was so desperate for money I married a man I couldn't stand, a tinkerer-genius who founded his own company. Living with him was pure hell. For years I looked for a way out."

She looked in Schilling's direction, then back at me.

I looked at both of them quickly, then back at Laura. Then I shot a quick glance at John, who slumped scowling in the far doorway as if unsure what to do.

"Does he know about how you killed Walter?" I asked.

They were both silent for a few seconds. Then Schilling came back. I thought he was going to hit me again, but he didn't. Bless his cowardly heart.

"You may not know this," he said to me, "but changing the *Windhover* into *Penelope* was entirely Walter's idea. He made arrangements with Murdock's Boatyard and had the bogus papers drawn up in the name of Wallace Kinchloe—"

"Yeah, I know. And so do the police. I assume you two got wind of the scheme just at its completion and stepped in to take delivery of the boat from Danny Murdock, right? The fact that the boat owner's wife was one of the parties claiming the vessel no doubt convinced Murdock that Kincaid hadn't been betrayed."

"You've got it, almost exactly. Laura overheard a snatch of phone conversation between Walter and Murdock one afternoon as she went to his study to ask him about some bills. Before she knocked on his study door she heard his voice on the phone. The four words that stuck in her memory were— Why don't you tell Adams what they were, Laura?"

"Keep your mouth *shut*," she replied.

"So you intercepted your husband's plan to disappear just at the right time. His own game plan insured your success."

"That's true," said the big man, "but you must keep in mind what a thorough son of a bitch Walter Kincaid really was . . . and what ungodly hell he put us, and all his employees, through."

I sensed I had one hole card left. I had to play it exactly right or I'd cash in my chips—involuntarily—and wind up as crab bait at the bottom of that big, dark hole.

"Laura, I'm going on a long shot here, but I'm assuming that Walter didn't exactly leave you sitting pretty. Did he leave you the house? Is that all?"

She looked at me for almost ten seconds, the hate in her eyes growing all the time.

"Not even that. Just the furniture. The company got the house. Can you believe it?"

"I can believe it, Laura. I can also believe your late husband was a pretty smart operator. Perhaps he sensed your hatred, your infidelity."

"Infidelity!"

She brought the butt of the rifle around sharply into my jaw. Had it been solid wood it would have done real damage. As it was, the nylon stock threw my head back and made the right side of my jaw ache. It wasn't that bad. I knew I was in for much worse.

"Listen to me now," I said. "I happen to know that your crackpot husband struck it rich, *big*. He finally found that treasure trove he'd devoted his life to. I intercepted mail to an elite commodities trader that proves it. I know where the treasure is. You don't. I don't know how much you're expecting to make off these hauls, Schilling, but I can promise you it won't even touch what the late Walter Kincaid has laid up in his secret hidey-hole."

"Oh bullshit," said Schilling.

"No. He was headed for the Bahamas. You knew that of course, didn't you?"

"No. How did you find that out?" he asked.

"Kincaid had a post office box in Boston under the name

Wallace Kinchloe—the same name he used for the *Penelope*'s papers. I got access to the box through the police. He had bought a condominium on St. Thomas for three hundred thousand, and had also arranged for the deposit of a large quantity of gold bullion—tax-free—on the island of Grand Cayman. Kincaid was not only going to lose himself, he was going in style.''

''And where's the gold now?''

I stayed quiet. Schilling looked over at John.

''Now Adams, see that fellow who escorted you in here? He's a former member of the Provisional Wing of the IRA. He betrayed them, and now has their death sentence on his head. He knows a good deal about interrogation, don't you, John?''

The stocky man with the blue watery eyes nodded quickly. His expression didn't change.

''He knows things like how to scrape your shinbone with a knife blade, and how to smash your knees and shoulders with a mechanic's hammer . . . don't you, John?''

I didn't like the sound of any of this. And I knew that once they had the information they needed I was done for. I looked at my watch again. It was ten to four. Pray to God DeGroot would awaken.

Laura Kincaid approached me. Her face and eyes showed absolutely no emotion.

''Where is it?'' she asked. Her tone was polite, clipped.

''No,'' I said, and that was all.

Then I felt my entire lower half go red with searing pain. Laura Kincaid drew her canvas-clad foot back again to deliver another full kick to my crotch, but I had crossed my legs. I bit through my tongue in the pain, and half rolled over. I watched the spit and blood run out of my mouth through clenched teeth. I think I was whining or screaming with my mouth shut. The yellow concrete floor rolled back and forth. I felt another kick in the small of my back, and my head sank down onto my arms.

''Where is it, you shit! Where *is* it?''

I felt another kick, and another . . . and another . . . and another.

Things went dark and swirly for a while, then I heard Schilling's voice right above my ear.

"I really think she'll kick you to death, you know, if you don't tell us."

"Get away, you oaf. Let me handle it—"

"Laura, *please*—"

The last thing I remembered before passing out again was that Big Jim Schilling didn't call the shots. Tiny, pert, trim Laura Kincaid had him by the short hairs. I didn't blame Walter Kincaid for trying to lose himself one little bit.

When I woke up they had propped me up against the crates. They commenced to get very nasty. What they did to me almost ruined what little faith I have in the human race. I can't talk much about it, even now, because it makes me want to get a job in a munitions factory. John shot a grim and determined glance at me now and then, but did nothing more. It was only after I finally admitted that the gold—a fortune in bullion—lay sealed in the *Rose*'s hull that they dragged me over to the edge of the pit. I was kneeling down in front of it. I couldn't see into the empty blackness, but I heard the sloshing of water, the gurgle of slime and cold wet.

"Poor Doctor Adams, and such a handsome devil too. Your wife's going to miss you—"

And it was at that point that the horror and indignity of the situation hit me with full force. Until then I was immersed in fear or pain, or both. But now, I heard the words with an indescribable mixture of hatred and outrage. Outrage is what would happen to Mary and the boys.

"Hold on. It's not wise, I think, to do this now."

It was John. He was standing next to me.

Then he began to move casually toward Laura. He moved in an awkward shuffle, but moved nonetheless. He had replaced the Walther in his coat. He approached Laura Kincaid, who had again picked up the Colt Armalite Commando. She cradled the short-version assault rifle in her arms rather clumsily now, tired from her exertion. Still there would be no arguing with the clip of high-velocity rounds she could send forth at the twitch of her finger.

"Nobody can hear it. I want him out."

John was moving toward her. He shambled, but moved with a certain ominous stealth and deliberation that she picked up.

"Hey, did you search him?" asked Schilling.

John hesitated half a second, then shook his head. It was the half-second wait that did him in. I think he remembered that I'd had a gun before, and if he answered no and they found one on me, it was all over for him.

"Forgot. I thought Hartzos searched him."

Schilling patted me down quickly and recovered the Buck folding hunter knife. It was long but trim; it was no wonder Hartzos hadn't seen a bulge in my hip pocket.

Laura Kincaid backed up two steps warily, eyeing John.

"Get back from him, Jim. Get back from both of them."

"But I've got the knife—"

"*Get back*! John's not the kind to forget to search somebody they've found upstairs. What about it? Better speak up."

"I have naw idea what you mean, mum—"

"Look. Jim and I have wondered about you for some time now. You disappear nights—"

"Just to go down the boozer, mum. Get a drop."

"Now look. This is the last haul; by noon we'll be out of the country. Either you'll be with the rest of us aboard the *Coquette*, or else you'll be joining the nosy doctor here, swinging around the bottom with a bad case of the crabs."

"Mrs. Kincaid, I dawn't—"

"Jim, get his gun, *Now*. You move an inch, John, and you're dead. Why didn't you search the doctor. *Why*?"

Schilling slid his huge arm into John's coat and retrieved the Walther with amazing quickness. There went our last hope.

"I told you. I thought Hartzos would have gone over him."

I saw her raise the rifle up and aim it at my head. I shut my eyes tight and winced, but looked out through the slits, blurry and dim. Surrealistic. I was in a bad, bad dream.

Laura Kincaid was smart all right. She suspected John the instant she realized he hadn't given me a third-degree search, and now she made John show his hand, because he jumped for her gun, caught it by the barrel as if it were a striking rattler, and flung it out of her hands. But the big man grabbed him, spun him around, and mashed him hard under the jaw with a very big hard hand. With methodical coolness she retrieved the weapon. Schilling raised his arm above John and clipped him on the neck. The double whammy dropped him hard, and he joined me at the brink of the pit.

"Laura, I repeat: the place is being watched. They know I'm here. Whatever you do, they'll find out. Use your head."

I hoped like nothing else in the world she believed me. She stood silent for perhaps ten seconds. It seemed like an hour. Then she kept the gun on us while she called Schilling back with her. They whispered together, keeping us well covered. I heard the phrase "*then* go back to the boat" more than once. Then I heard three words of dread. I knew that John heard them too because I saw the brief, fleeting look of terror cross his face, then a look of—disappointment. Not further terror, or extreme sadness, just disappointment. Chagrin, as if having lost a good poker hand.

The three words were: *Do it now.*

I stared down at the black hole in the floor where the water sloshed. I saw two brief streaks of silver light reflection in a faint ripple, then they vanished. That was my life in there: that will-o'-the-wisp flicker of light for maybe a fiftieth of a second, then black again. I heard Laura Kincaid walking back to us. Slow measured steps. I turned and looked at her. At her eyes. They were the eyes of a pit bulldog. She stopped right behind John, perhaps a yard away. Without a word, she raised up the rifle until the muzzle pointed right at the back of his head. John didn't even turn around. He knelt on the floor, looking ahead of himself and down. His lips were moving, and he had that same disappointed look on his face. But it was gradually replaced by a look of intense concentration, and then of profound love. I heard him say, in a whisper so delicate it was barely audible, "Now take care of yerself,

Billy. Take care of your mother—and may you be happy, too, for all the days of your life—*May God bless*—''

I turned to look at the water again before I heard the shot. I didn't want to see John die.

23

THE SHOT WAS LIKE A PNEUMATIC SPRING COMPRESSOR. IT was not the sound I was expecting. It went *ptou!* An obscene, single-syllable French word. I had my eyes closed by then, and heard a heavy slumping to the ground. I murmured a thought in my mind: *And May God bless. Oh Christ . . . May God bless.*

When I opened my eyes after no second shot was fired John was still kneeling. He was looking at the floor right beside him, dumbfounded. Laura Kincaid was on the floor. She was doing a horizontal waltz there. She was dying.

I couldn't figure out why. I saw a flicker of movement out of the corner of my eye. Schilling was gone, rushed out the small doorway that ended in darkness. He'd killed her, perhaps to take the loot for himself. I looked back at the woman on the cement floor four feet away. Part of her throat was missing. It was pale white: fish-belly white. The white that no healthy skin ever gets.

And then the paper-white rift under her jaw grew dark. It oozed bright red. The whiteness was from the shock of the slug as it passed through her flesh, driving all the blood far away from it. But the blood came back through the thousands of tiny blood vessels, and now poured forth faster and faster. There was no big spurting; no artery had been severed. But I soon heard a sound from her that will haunt me for the rest of my days. I'd heard it before, when I was a kid, on an Iowa farm. They had slit a hog's throat, and beat it with sticks to keep it running around the yard so its heart would pump all the blood out. And I heard screams coming through the blood. Underwater screams. Under*blood* screams.

Laura Kincaid, what was left of her, kicked and slapped herself around on the cement like a sea turtle at a Caribbean marketplace. She flapped and flipped, and made ugly noises. She was nowhere near dead and suffering terribly. The wound in her throat had cut her windpipe, and she was in enough pain so her jaw was clenched shut. She breathed through her wound, and screamed and cried through it too. A huge football-shaped mass of brownish-red froth rose up from it, bubbling like perked coffee.

It was so ill-fitting for the pretty slim lady I had met in the big elegant house. It was so—clumsy. So *embarrassing*. In a grotesque way it was as if she had just stumbled at a debutante ball, or thrown up on somebody's priceless Nahin rug.

"Oh pardon me," her soul seemed to be saying, *"I'm soooo sorry—you see, I cannot help it. I'm dying . . . and it hurts and there's nothing I can do."*

She swung her head, now pale gray-blue, back and forth and hard against the cement floor. Then she settled down and grabbed at herself all over with her hands, whimpering. She was doing a slow, sad sidestroke into eternity.

Then they came.

I didn't notice either of them until I smelled the faint sweet reek of whiskey.

The taller one stepped forth with his pistol. He aimed at the thrashing woman. Much as I hated her, I would be glad when he ended it.

His partner ran over to the small doorway where Jim Schilling had disappeared. He flung his head snakelike around the edge for a millisecond, then flung it back inside. I saw his arm flicker, and heard a tremendous crashing boom, then two more. The noise was so loud I could feel it in my chest. His right hand held a huge revolver in stainless steel. He held it deftly, cradled it casually as if it were a water pistol.

I didn't like these guys at *all*.

The man stayed put in the doorway, glancing back at the three and a half of us.

The big man nearest me wore a navy blue pea coat. His face was scary because it was a caricature of a face, one you might find on a totem pole. The brown ski mask was decorated in coarse, wide-weave patterns that bespoke Navaho, Aztec, Eskimo—the American aborigines in general. His partner's mask was pure dark wool, a balaclava helmet that covered the entire face except for an eye slit. He looked like a medieval executioner. In fact he was.

The big man breathed heavily, odoriferously, and stared down at the thrashing form. He heard the thick bubbling from the torn throat, the muted scrape of skin and flesh on rough cement.

"For God's sake, man," whispered John.

The big man glanced quickly at John, as if temporarily distracted, then turned his gaze back to the woman on the floor.

"Thank your stars we've saved you, O'Shaughnessey. Say a prayer of thanks and be done with it. You know who I am. If you interfere now I'll put you away, same's we put the coont here anyway."

He aimed the pistol at Laura Kincaid again and I thought he was going to end it.

But he didn't. He seemed to enjoy watching her.

"Brian McGooey," he said to her.

I don't think she heard him.

"Michael Tomlins," he said.

Nothing but more of the same.

"Patrick Cahill."

Nothing much at all now.

"Bernard Upshaw," said the other, "and *Eamon Donneley, Sheila Coone, Aden Berry—"*

PTOU!

The man fired, and Laura Kincaid's left kneecap exploded.

The men in ski masks leaned over her as she thrashed in the immense pain of it. A great dark wet stain spread in her crotch. Still, they did not put her away. The room and the world rocked by me. I saw John's face dimly in the background. It had a look of profound sorrow.

Laura Kincaid had but a few seconds; she kept up her pitiable, spastic, and partnerless dance until, with a grunt, the taller one pushed his foot into her twitching form and shoved it into the hole.

"And now," he said turning in my direction, "who in blazes might *you* be?"

24

"I ASKED YOU A QUESTION."

"Charles Adams, M.D. I've been hunting this woman, Laura Kincaid, because I think she and her associates killed a friend of mine."

"Hmmmph! Well yer not alone in *that* department, Doctor, we can tell you. The question is, shall we have to kill you?"

"No," said John.

"And why not, assuming of course a couple of brigands like ourselves should be listening to you, O'Shaughnessey?"

"He's not one of 'em, I'll swear it," replied John, rising to his feet.

The second thug moved back over to the doorway again. "Come on!" he whispered hoarsely. "There's two more upstairs we didn't get; let's go out this way."

"Did he have a gun?" the big man asked John.

"Not when he ran out, I don't think. But knowing him, he probably has one by this time, and you bloody well don't want to be on the receiving end of it either. It'll hit you, tear you in pieces before you hear it."

There was a faint stirring above us. I heard what sounded like a slamming of a door.

"That's probably Hartzos returning," I said.

"Naw. Hartzos is no longer among the living."

"We've got to move *now*," said Thug Number Two.

Almost as these words were spoken all of us heard the sound of feet on the metal stairway. From the noise, there was more than one person on them.

"Where does that tunnel lead?" the big man asked John.

"It's an old cartway back to the main factory building. It goes underneath ground level."

"Then that's for us. Is he in there waiting?"

"I would imagine he's as far away as possible by now, and still moving."

"Just so, you two will go first." He prodded the gun in our direction. "Move," he said.

O'Shaughnessey saw the Walther on the floor and started for it, but the big man saw him and kicked the pistol into the hole.

O'Shaughnessey and I went through the narrow doorway. It was black on the other side. I felt myself beginning to trip on something very hard raised up about two inches. A rail. Then another rail. Then a brick wall. It was a narrow-gauge railway . . . a miniature railroad in which carts ran, very reminiscent of the type used in old mines. O'Shaughnessey seemed to know his way about, and lost no time in turning to his left and moving quickly along between the rails. I followed. Had I any choice? Thug Number One had his silenced Luger pointed at my kidneys. If Schilling were indeed waiting for us, we'd go down first. It was just tough luck. Of course after what I'd been through I could scarcely gripe.

Still I found it excruciating to walk. Until the past few minutes the fear and shock had held the pain at bay. But now I HURT. I hurt very, very much. I had received two hard kicks to my Sport Section and scores to my belly and back. My right testicle was aflame. I had taken Laura Kincaid's belly kicks well because I had managed to tighten my stomach muscles just as the blows landed. But my back had no such protection. I would probably piss blood for a week or two if I were lucky and it was nothing more serious than a bruised kidney.

"Coont!" growled Thug Number One as he gazed back into the dreary chamber before joining us in the dark tunnel.

"Yah *coont* yah!"

"I entirely agree," I murmured, and felt the encouraging prod of the big man's Luger.

We walked quite fast, knowing that remnants of the Kincaid/Schilling staff were at our heels. I heard a grunt of pain in front of me, and a metallic *screaking*. O'Shaughnessey had bumped against an old cart. It was a low wooden platform used to haul spools of wire and cord, but had a metal handle like a supermarket cart running along the back side, and he had run into it, knocking his breath away. When Number One Thug caught up with it and saw—with his flashlight—that the front end of the carriage was piled with old spools, he directed us to push it along the rails. Thus, under this crude armor, we advanced, with the two of them—well protected from Schilling should he be lying in wait—bringing up the rear. But as I leaned into the load I saw movement behind me. Number Two Thug whirled around, his leather coat flaps swinging outward with the spin. A yellowish rectangle of light showed behind us where the doorway was being opened. A dark figure blocked out a large part of the rectangle. I turned my head still farther back, and could see he was flapping his arms up, as if directing a concerto. His elbows stuck out to the side. Funny looking. No it wasn't funny. He was aiming a pistol with both hands. I dropped to one knee and spun over until the wall stopped me.

"Down, everybody!" I said.

I saw two things at once: the orange-white burst of flame from the dark figure's chest, and the same figure flung backward against the open door as if hit by an express train. Some recoil his pistol must've had—

But *no*—

The figure slumped down like a dishrag, and my ears were splitting, bursting with pain. The retort from Number Two Thug's pistol thudded into my chest cavity like a funny heartbeat. It must have been a .44 magnum. In the closeness of the tunnel the noise was unbearable.

And was he a pistol shot.

Four years at the range with small-bore weapons and I thought I was pretty damn good. But this guy, whoever he was, was in another league entirely. I heard John's heavy breathing next to me. I leaned forward close as I dared and asked him the question *sotto voce*:

"Who *are* these guys?"

"Shhhhhh! IRA Provos. The best they've got, kiddo. They'll kill us in a wink if we give them any trouble. Now mind, do what I do—"

"Who are *you*?"

"I am Stephen O'Shaughnessey of the Garda Síochána, the Irish National Police. 'John' is a pseudonym."

"Uh, which Ireland? The south?"

There was a pregnant pause, during which I heard a very distinct sigh of disgust and a slight smacking of lips which told me that my question had not registered favorably with the law officer. I felt an iron grip on my upper arm, and the growly grunt of his voice extremely close to my head.

"There is only *one* Ireland, Doctor Adams. The *Repooblic of Ireland*. If you learn nothing else out of all this *shite*, let it be that. Yah *twit*!" He shoved me away, hard.

"Move! Move on with yah!" called a hoarse whisper, and we began again to push the cart. "No," said Number One Thug, it was too slow. "Leave it to slow the others down." We crept around it and jog-walked the rest of the way through the transport tunnel, the two thugs (and one, at least, a superb shot with a big-bore handgun) at our heels. We kept up the pace until I saw a faint rectangular square of very pale blackish gray. Two seconds later, we were emerging from the tunnel, and looking up a gradual incline of old granite cobblestone.

The two men stood directly behind us.

"Why don't you two lads go on up and see if it's safe?" demanded Number One. So we did. I had it in mind to spring like hell as soon as I reached the top. It was still too dark to see well. After all I'd been through, all I wanted was to run, find the fence (any fence), and *scale* the sombitch.

"Up yah go now! Goddamn me, I say!" said Number One Thug in a very persuasive tone. "I've got six rounds left and will kill the both of you. The only sound they'll be hearin' is an ounce of lead squirtin' through yer guts like a jet plane. Now *up!*''

We reached the top of the ramp and didn't get our heads taken off. Gee, tonight was my lucky night. I could see that it was darker to the sides than it was straight above me. We were in one of the big courtyards that opened off the main factory roadway. In a while the other two came up behind us, and we moved on. I assumed the Provos wanted out of Cordage Park as badly as I did, perhaps to slink back to their car and skedaddle. Plymouth was only minutes away from Southie, where an Irishman down on his luck could find a haven for as long as he needed it. And then there was Charlestown. Talk about rough. I believe I would rather parade around in Harlem on a Saturday night dressed in a Ku Klux Klan outfit than hang around some sections of Charlestown.

If they elected to hide there until this thing blew over nobody could pry them out. Not even the Marine Corps.

I was saying all this to myself in my mind to take it off the fact that any instant I could have a whole handful of lead slugs thrown in my direction. And there wasn't a damn thing I could do about it.

We had bunched together now in a tight square of four men. Stephen and I were in front, the two thugs right behind us. All hell broke loose when we reached the roadway. The first thing I heard was a popping behind me. I realized later that the sound must have been the big .45-caliber slugs tearing into the factory wall. It was more a cracking-pounding than a popping; it had a hard, staccato timbre to it. Just as I turned, I could see that the wall was smoking. Only it wasn't smoke. It was all the brick dust and powder that had been blown off the old wall and hung like a faint gray curtain in the half-light of first dawn.

The tight group exploded, flung away in different directions by the blast like a clump of tightly racked billiard balls on the break.

I found the ground and rolled over and over, keeping my arms straight down at my sides. There had been no sound except the slugs hitting the wall. Nothing. But on the next burst I heard it. It commenced with a low whistle of almost electronic purity, and with it a sound like sheet metal being ripped behind a thick felt curtain. And then the loud pounding drowned out the weird sound, and it was as if I were in the middle of a buffalo stampede.

I heard a long, drawn-out groan coming from across the roadway.

"Hssssst!" came a whisper. "Adams!"

"Over here. O'Shaughnessey?"

"Naw lad. It's him you hear. My friend's caught a couple too. Come over here . . . *now*!"

The whisper had the ring of authority. I had a feeling Thug Number One, the big guy in the Aztec ski mask, meant business.

"No. I can't. He'll kill me."

His reply was swift and direct. I heard the *whang* of a slug two feet above my head against an iron steam pipe I couldn't see.

"The next one will go through you. I don't have time to fook around, Adams."

I flung myself out from my little nest of safety and rolled along the ground to the opposite wall. I knew this was the safest way to do it. All Schilling would have a view of would be my clothes and my navy watch cap. And not rising higher than a foot above the ground, there would be no way he could detect a flicker of my silhouette. Rolling is also much quicker than belly crawling. When I hit the opposite wall I inched forward. Number One Thug was hunched behind a concrete abutment that sloped out from the wall, providing about two feet of immunity from those big bullets. He half-cradled a limp form in his left arm while he held his silenced Luger in the other.

"Check him."

I pushed my fingers into the man's neck under his jaw. I felt a faint and irregular bumping of the carotid artery.

"Well?" whispered the big man.

"Bad."

"Thought as much."

I pulled open his coat and drew up his sweater. There were

four mean entry holes, dark and very wet and as big as dimes, that snaked their way up and around his trunk spiral fashion. He had caught the brunt of the quick burst, with four of those miniature shot-puts hitting him within the space of a tenth of a second. I was amazed he was still alive, and knew he wouldn't be for long. The first hole was in the left side, near the spleen. Then he'd taken one in the lower chest, one definitely in the lungs, and the last one up near the right armpit. He gasped, and I thought I heard him say something but I couldn't understand it. Then Number One leaned over and put his hand on the side of his head, as one does to a child who cannot sleep, and said something very soft in the man's ear. It was Gaelic. I don't know what he said. The man whined a little, and I thought I heard a sob or perhaps it was just pure pain. The shock was wearing off now, the enormous energy—like getting hit by four defensive linemen at once— that had stunned him was ebbing. And so was his life. Then he shuddered and relaxed. He said, "Ahhhhhh . . ."

I put my hand back into his neck.

"He's gone now," I told the big man.

He turned for a second, made the sign of the cross over the man's head, and said something else in Gaelic.

"Take the medal from around his neck and give it to me. Hurry."

He dropped the small chain and medal into his coat pocket. Then he asked me if I could use a pistol and I answered yes.

"Go get your friend, Adams. He's only about eight feet away. I'll cover you."

I heard O'Shaughnessey groan again and knew that if I didn't manage to get him pulled back behind the concrete he'd be cut in two by the next burst. I crawled around the abutment and hunkered down low. I saw a dark form on the ground, which told me how much lighter it had gotten. I grabbed the fallen man by the arms and dragged him back behind the shelter faster than I thought possible. Fear of getting blown away makes you amazingly strong and quick. I saw then how badly hit he was; there was a dark wet trail sliding out behind him.

We propped him up against the wall. He was conscious,

but spilling lots of blood. Way too much blood too fast. That told me a blood vessel had been severed. Not an artery that would pump and squirt crimson, but a big saphenous vein.

He'd taken slugs from the beginning of the burst that had killed the other man, the burst that had raked across them both, sending each successive round higher as the tiny gun had bucked upward with recoil. O'Shaughnessey was hit square in the left thigh and had a deep crease along the small of his back. An inch farther inward would have taken away both his kidneys and his spine. The thigh hit was bad; the femur was broken clean in two with perhaps an inch missing. The main problem with a .45 is that it makes such a goddamn big hole.

They had taken away my knife, so I asked Thug Number One for his. With it I slit the pant leg and rigged a tourniquet with my shirt sleeve and an old piece of metal window frame I found after several minutes of feeling around in the dark.

It stopped the flow pretty well, although I was certain his blood pressure was down by this time too.

The big man worked in the dark, studying me. I heard metallic clacking and guessed he was reloading the big revolver. Then he made up his mind and handed me the .44 magnum belonging to his fallen comrade. It weighed slightly less than a washing machine.

"This will just about take yer hand off when ya fire it . . . and break yer wrist, too. Hold it with both hands, and tight."

I heard a brisk chatter, and ducked. But it wasn't the chatter of an automatic weapon; it was Stephen O'Shaughnessey's teeth. He was freezing to death.

"Now you hear me good, Doctor. I'm going to move around behind him, slow like. If we stay here we'll stay pinned down, don't yah know. You keep that cannon pointed right where the corner of that building is . . . you see it now? Give me ten minutes, then fire a few shots at it, hear? And listen, the both of you: any fookin' around and yer dead, quick as a wink, hear me?"

"Yes," I answered. O'Shaughnessey moved his head back and forth in pain and didn't answer.

"What time have you?"

"Four-thirty."

"At twenty of the hour I'll expect to hear the gunfire. Then I'll come on him like blazes—" He turned to go.

"And good-bye Stephen O'Shaughnessey. May you repair yourself. But, may we not meet again. Stay out of me fookin' business."

He was gone. And for a big man he moved with utter silence. He had removed the hood from the dead man before he left, presumably so the police wouldn't think of him as the terrorist murderer he was. I was shocked to see the face of a boy, perhaps only nineteen or twenty. Tony's age. He had pale skin but dark, bushy eyebrows. It was now light enough out to see that his eyes were open.

"Oh shite! Ohhhhhh," said Stephen O'Shaughnessey.

I realized that if help didn't come soon he'd probably die. Four-thirty. Was DeGroot awake? Had he seen the note? Couldn't count on it. I had to get out and make a phone call—flag down a car. *Anything*.

"Adams."

I went over to him.

"How bad is it?"

"What's bad is you've been losing blood by the quart. You've also got a broken leg but I'm not worried about that."

"Now listen," he gasped, "I bloody well can't move and you know it. If I take the gun and cover you, could you find yer way out?"

"Yes."

"Well go. It's better than us sitting here and me bleeding to death, tourniquet or no tour—ahhhhhh!"

He shivered with pain, but took the big .44, then aimed it square at my heart.

"Go, Doctor. These are *orders*. Head straight back and make a wide circle around the both of them—"

I pressed my back up against the wall and sidestepped along it. Ten yards. Twenty yards. Forty yards. I was home free. I began a slow quiet walk. At the next corner I would turn right and head for the old sea wall, then drop to the beach and wade the shallow water right up to the road. No problem with fighting even the outer fence this time. Then I heard it. A boat was coughing to life out on the pier. It was a smallish gasoline engine. A cruiser engine. It went into high revs right away and groaned into the distance, toward the mouth of the huge harbor. My watch said quarter to five. It was past the time Number One said he'd put the rush on Schilling. Had he been waiting for my shots, or had he taken the boat? My guess was the latter; he sensed the situation had gotten far enough out of control so that his capture was imminent. And now I worried even more about O'Shaughnessey's safety.

A big boom sounded behind me. It could only be the heavy .44 magnum. Almost immediately afterward I heard the hoof-beat sound of pounding slugs hitting brick. Then the deep boom of the pistol again. Then running feet and a scream. Unarmed, it would do me precious little good to hang around. I only hoped the scream was Schilling's, not O'Shaughnessey's. I ran fast now for the corner of the building. I heard a flight of bees off to the side of my head, and my legs almost turned to water from fear. Those were .45 slugs sliding by me, hunting me.

I rounded the corner full tilt. Once I reached the sea wall and swung over it I was probably safe.

But as I ran the next twenty yards it got darker up ahead, not lighter. Another twenty yards confirmed it, and I could hear the hollow echo of my feet against the walls. And then I saw the windows, six rows of them, looming up ahead of me. I had turned one corner too soon. The way to the beach and the sea wall lay one more building past where I had turned. I was in the last courtyard. Oh God, I thought. Why now? Why this way, after all I'd been through? Why *now*, when I'd been almost—

There is no panic as great as that which follows a sense of relief, no despair so acute as that which comes back after renewed hope. I ran to the end of the enclosed courtyard. I yanked at two windows. They were barred. I searched madly for a ramp, a door, a fire escape . . .

"Adams!"

I turned and looked at the dim figure standing on the roadway at the open end of the courtyard. It was still quite dark.

He was leaning a bit too much. He took two quick steps forward and bowed in my direction slightly, like a Japanese houseboy. He'd been nicked by O'Shaughnessey before he'd killed him. But even a nick from a .44 was serious. So God bless Stephen O'Shaughnessey. The late Stephen O'Shaughnessey. But a lot of good it would do me.

The man made two fast twists of his body, back and forth. A swarm of locusts sang above my head, and then came the terrible pounding and popping sound above me as pieces of old brick and mortar exploded out from the wall. They fell to the ground in clacks and tinkles, like old flowerpots, and fine dust sat in the air. But the gun was quiet.

He started walking into the courtyard. I heard a distinct, clean *clang* of metal hitting the ground and then saw him reach back with one hand into a hip pocket. New clip. Thirty more rounds. And at least one of them would finish me. He walked again and I could almost hear the scraping feet, the throat snuffle and sniff of Mr. X. He had failed once but not this time. He had a machine pistol and I didn't have a goddamn thing.

Including, most especially, a way out or a place to hide.

25

I DON'T KNOW WHAT MADE ME GO LOOKING IN THE FAR corner, except plain old bloody desperation. The same thing that makes a trapped rat hug the sides of buildings, or gutter pipes, or old cellarways.

In the very corner of the courtyard, behind a big dumpster bin and several discarded oil drums, was a fire ladder. Not a fire escape, an escape ladder. Vertical, with rungs and such. And it went all the way up the building: six stories high. It also had a barred metal casing around it—a cylindrical cage of steel strips to prevent people from falling off it backward.

It was a way out, but not a good one. Inside the ladder cage I would be a sitting duck. A duck at a shooting gallery. And Jim Schilling, besides being a good shot, had a gun that couldn't miss. The rooftop was a long climb away, and time was very scarce. But the ladder was truly invisible; it snaked up the side of the old building in the farthest, shadiest corner of the dank place, and the bottom rung didn't come closer than about nine feet from the ground. It was the ladder or nothing.

I grabbed an oil drum and placed it underneath the ladder. I set it down quietly. Tired as I was I knew that a quick start spelled all the difference. In less than three seconds I was on the drum, then in contact with the rung, then climbing. I think that after about five seconds I was past the second row of windows, and heading for the third story. *Please God . . . please give me one more minute—forty-five seconds—*

I almost stopped and fell back down the vertical cage when I heard the popping and grinding of the old wall coming apart. Silence. Then another short burst. Schilling was scouring out the far reaches of the old brick court, using the machine pistol as a water hose. He spat another burst, and I heard the deep timpani boom of metal. He'd hit the dumpster and some of the oil drums. With luck he'd also knocked over my stepping stone, the drum I'd placed underneath the ladder. But I climbed as fast as my cast let me. The ground, what was faintly visible of it, seemed a long way down.

"Adams!"

Fourth floor. I *thought*. Please God please . . . just twenty more seconds.

I climbed by feel; it allowed me to go faster. I was panting hard now but keeping my mouth wide open. I looked down. Oh Christ. Christ Almighty: *a light*.

There it was, a pale yellow pencil beam snaking around on the asphalt far below. I heard the sound of an oil drum kicked over, and then a curse.

"Adams! Adams, you're *dead*!"

I could see the rooftop now against the pale gray sky. I could see the big tiles that lined the top of the brickwork.

I looked down, the light was now snaking around the corner of the yard, right beneath me. Good God, don't point it up. *Don't point it up—*

Ten more feet. My body ached in every muscle. Eight feet. Seven. I think during the last three seconds of my climb my body slowed a wee bit, thinking the goal was reached.

And the next second I was flooded with light, just as I'd been in the old barn when climbing on another ladder. I didn't stop. I redoubled the effort and the pain. I thought I heard a grunt or bellow come from far, far below me. I had grabbed the smooth, slick tiling on top of the brickwork when the wall around me burst apart in a shattering roar. Bits of mortar and brick stung my face and eyes. I kicked my feet desperately, spastically, climbing up, like getting out of a swimming pool. As I fell over the tile I felt a monstrous kick on my heel, and then a deep burning.

I lay on the tar and gravel of the flat factory roof and breathed deeply for a few seconds, then crept to the edge. I could see without even leaning over that the light beam was shining up the ladderway. But at this height the beam was pretty faint. There wasn't much he could see from down there. I glanced around. If there was no way off the roof I would have to wait at the edge in hopes of jumping or hitting him as he neared the top. If he followed me, which I doubted.

On the other hand, if there was any safe way off the roof, I was eager to take it. The light was off now. I hobbled over about twelve feet to the left of the ladder and peeped over. I didn't want to show my head near it. Jesus, it was a long way down.

Nothing. No visible motion. No sound. I scooted back as fast as the pain would let me, and reached out and down and felt the metal sides of the ladder. I grabbed and held. If he was waiting below and saw my arm, he could take it off with a quick burst. But I risked it; I had to know if he was on the ladder. Nothing. No vibration whatsoever.

Then where was he?

That made me nervous. Very. Because I knew Schilling knew the place well. He had to. If there was another way to the roof, he probably knew about it. Was there another ladder, fire escape, ramp, elevator . . . anything that would allow him to reach a far edge or corner of the big wide roof and come at me from behind?

I kept my fist wrapped around the steel, and turned and swept my eyes around the flat expanse of gray gravel, growing ever lighter as dawn came. A very big roof indeed. To think there was only one approach to its summit was foolishness. There had to be another. Where?

If I left my spot to roam about, would Schilling then come up the ladder? If I stayed, would he come up another way? Was he in fact doing that very thing *right now*?

What if I went back *down* the ladder?

You've got to be kidding, Adams.

I decided on a test. I pawed the rooftop until I had a small handful of gravel. I held the tiny stones in the exact center of the round cage and let three or four of them fall. After what seemed an eternity, I heard the faint bong of the oil drum. Schilling wasn't on the ladder. This meant, if nothing else, that this approach was safe for at least the time it would take him to make the climb, which was about ninety seconds, maybe more, since he'd been clipped by a slug. I had to risk a brief walk around.

I tried to stand and fell down again. I grabbed at my heel. The rubber sole of the Topsider was blown away, but my heel was intact. The slug had hit me obliquely, but obviously caused some internal trauma. Perhaps a broken bone. Certainly a horrendous bruise. I hobbled about until something hit me square in the chest. I lowered my arm to chop at it. It was one of those iron steam pipes, snaking over the roof about four feet high set on concrete supports. I ducked under it, then quickly turned back. If that thing snaked down the side of the building, I was for sliding down it, even though it meant there was a big chance of losing my grip and splattering all over the asphalt six stories below.

But I was in bad, bad shape. Two gimpy arms (the steam pipe chop had just decommissioned the right one), a shot-up heel, busted nuts and guts, not to mention an extraordinary case of general fatigue.

But I needed *off* that bloody roof.

The pipe wound to the edge, and across a roadway to another roof. Shit. Twenty feet of horizontal, six-inch, cast-iron pipe almost eighty feet up.

But if I could get across it I'd be *safe*. I thought of straddling it, letting my legs hang down both sides while I pumped along the length of it with my arms.

My damaged groin winced at the thought.

And then I noticed something else. I saw some big shiny cables and glass insulators right down next to the pipe. High voltage. Sitting there on the steel I would be connected to a natural ground. One stray swipe with arm or leg and I was gone, fried like a squirrel careless enough to skip the wrong way on a utility pole. I didn't like the look of the high-voltage wires at all.

So I returned to the ladder. I thought I saw a flash of light in the center of the steel cage. I approached the edge cautiously and peered over. The light beam climbed up at me. I drew back my head. Seconds later I heard the mean buzz of bullets in front of me, not two feet from my head, right where my face had been seconds earlier. Unlike a high-velocity rifle bullet, the .45 slug is a snail amongst hares. The average commercial jetliner can fly faster than this speeding bullet. It kills because it weighs as much as a golf ball and is almost as big . . . It never breaks the sound barrier, and so does not produce the telltale crack, the sonic boom that warns the quarry that it is being shot at.

I grabbed the ladder top. It thrummed and trembled. The fish was on the line.

I had company.

There was no choice now. I had to either find another way down or risk the pipe and the electric wires. I swung my head over the side two feet to the left of the ladderway, then moved it slowly to the side of the cage, with only my eyes peeping over the edge. I could see a vague glimmering down there. Far, far away. I grabbed the ladder top again. The vibration didn't feel any stronger. Then I noticed a pattern to the vibrations, a regular heartbeat of motion through the vertical steel. It was fairly slow. Schilling was indeed wounded—otherwise a man with his strength and vigor could dash up the rungs as fast as or faster than I had done.

I scurried back to the roof edge where the big pipe dove over the side and straight out to the next building. I swung cautiously over the tile, grabbing the inside edge of the big slick slabs with the tenacity of Beowulf, and poked my feet down. I felt them touch the pipe. I then stood on it, and was almost ready to release my grip, when I felt the sickening loss of resistance from below as the pipe sagged. I clung, and drew my feet up in a fetal position, then hunch-crawled back over the tile like a wounded spider all balled up.

The clock was ticking. I could now hear the faint *fring fring fring* of scraping feet on the metal ladder. He had that Ingram slung over his shoulder, his flashlight ready too.

I remembered—in a tenth of a second at the longest—

scoffing at a fish trap in northern Minnesota when I was a kid. I couldn't believe all that seething protein behind the wooden slats in the river could be so dumb. Now I knew exactly how those poor fish felt. Like me, they'd made a mistake. They'd made a wrong turn. That's all it took.

I turned fast to go to the far side of the roof. I would try one last quick search for a way down before lying in wait at the ladder's top, ready to lunge at the murderer with my hands and teeth.

I bumped into the metal pipe again, and heard it groan. I wiggled it. It gave some. Then I ran along its length for perhaps sixty feet before I found what I wanted: a completely crumpled section of the old steam pipe. Three sections of pipe lay scattered on the gravel roof. I grabbed the nearest one and heaved it up. It was black iron, three feet long, and very heavy. One end of the six-inch pipe had a flange, with holes around it for bolts. I dug the fingers of my right hand into this handle and tugged it back to the ladder. The light was again playing along its upper terminus. Then it went off.

I hefted the pipe in both hands. I could scarcely lift it. I rested the smooth end of it on the shiny hard tile. As it rolled a bit it made a heavy grating sound, like sand in a mortar and pestle. I reached over and grabbed the ladder sides. There was a heavy vibration, and speeded up too. I chanced it; I looked over. I could see Schilling scurrying up the ladder to kill me. He wasn't looking up. I moved my head way over to the edge of the steel cage—the left side—so I could peer at him with my right eye. He glanced up once. I saw the white face outlined by the dark beard. The wispy-thread line of the puka shell necklace against the tanned neck.

I hated him.

He didn't see me apparently, even in the soft light of full dawn. His head lowered again as he resumed climbing. I saw now the dark line along his back, wide, cylindrical, like a black man's arm with the hand cut off. The Ingram.

I hooked my fingers around the flange of the pipe and slid it over off the tile. The weight of it pulled down hard on my arms and drew my chest down tight on the tile so it ached. My left wrist burned. I walked forward two steps on my knees—felt my kneecaps digging into the loose stones that covered the asphalt roof. Schilling was about three stories below me. All the lines of the metal ladder cage seemed to converge upon him, the small winking figure in the center of the vertical tunnel.

I peered through the section of iron pipe. It had a wide bore, like a stovepipe. Through it I could see very clearly. I moved the pipe to and fro, from side to side, by shifting my weary body and shoulders. Soon I looked straight down the bore—as if down a telescopic sight—and could see nothing but the climbing figure far below.

I couldn't do it. Much as I hated him, I could not get myself to drop the pipe on him.

Considering the great weight of the pipe, the sharp, spade-like edge of the male end of it, and most especially the long distance it would travel, at thirty-two feet per second squared, it was deadly as a bazooka shell. It would slice him in half, pulverize him.

But I *couldn't*.

It's pretty hard to go to school for over twelve years learning to make bodies whole again after illness and trauma, and then decide to dissect one instantly by way of gravity. But the dark side of me—of *Homo sapiens*—was working too. I wanted him dead, and I knew it. Admitted it. Mostly because it was fairly obvious by now that he wanted me dead. And he would *do it*. He'd more than proven that. I had to wait. I needed a sign . . . a signal . . .

Then he looked up. I peeped at him through the lowered pipe. He was too far away, the light too faint, to read his expression. But I thought I saw, in the growing light, his eyes widen. He stopped climbing, and his slow, startled stare gazed up in wonder, and the beginnings of fear. Was it the fear that Allan Hart had felt? That Walter Kincaid and Danny Murdock felt?

He was halfway up the ladder. The network of steel rods surrounding him was a little over two feet wide. There just wasn't any place the poor bastard could go. I saw a broad swirl of light-flicker, a Fourth of July whirligig of dancing light beam and flash, and then a distant dry clatter. He'd turned on the flashlight and dropped it. My fingers and wrists ached now with the holding of the big steam pipe. I saw a great flurry of motion below—saw Schilling's big form sway back and forth, one arm moving quickly, then the other.

Then I got my sign. I received the signal, loud and clear. I heard the cocking of the Ingram's bolt, and knew he was about to send a fatal burst of slugs up to take my head apart.

I had drawn up my arms six inches as I saw him squirm around, my fingers still curled around the one-inch flange of iron . . . When I heard him jerk back the bolt, I let my arms drop in perfect unison, letting my tired hands flow outward with the descent of the heavy pipe. Because I knew I had to release it smoothly, on a very straight path, or it might hang itself up and bind in the cage. It fell straight as an arrow, a finned bomb, a mortar shell down its own tube. The last vision I had of it was curious: I could still peer down its ever-diminishing bore. And even more curiously, in the milli-second before I drew my head back from fear of it's being blown off, I noticed that in that pipe bore, Jim Schilling's head and shoulders loomed larger and larger—geometrically—awfully fast.

I had drawn my head back and down, like a mortarman, and waited for the bullets to sing up toward me. They *spanged* off the steel cage and rocketed drunkenly off the old brick wall.

But they didn't catch me.

Jim Schilling screamed. It was fitting that he should see his own death coming, and scream in terror.

He shouted, *"No!"*

Only the scream was cut off in the middle. A dull clacking sound interrupted it, like a melon being opened with a swipe from a machete—the blunt edge down. It was the sound of his skull being cut in half.

Then silence.

I looked over the edge after half a minute of catching my breath. I saw a big black shiny thing askew in the ladder cage, tilted at a crazy angle, wedged into the iron bars. And then I made out a pair of twisted legs and knees intertwined in the ladder rungs. They were doubled up, almost pointing up at me. Schilling was underneath the pipe; he hadn't fallen down the cage to the ground. That meant I had to go down there and kick him loose in order to get past him to the ground.

I didn't relish it.

Yet the alternatives were clear: either attempt the crossing on the wilted pipe (something I wasn't even remotely considering) or else climb down the six stories on the *outside* of the cage. Again: *no way.* So like it or not, to return to earth I had to haul myself back down that barred steel tunnel, and somehow dislodge the corpse I had just created.

The corpse I had just created.

I had never killed a human being before in my life. No matter how vile, how evil and cruel Schilling had been, the thought struck home.

I climbed back down. It was scary. It was now light enough to make me realize how damn high the ladder was. But I kept my eyes stoically glued to the brick wall in front of me, watching the rows slide smoothly upward a foot in front of my face.

Then I felt the pipe with my foot. I looked down, and wished I hadn't. I wished instead I'd simply waited up on top of the roof for a reasonable period (like three years) until somebody came and took me off. Jim Schilling, that big and brawny bully, was doubled over, compressed against both sides of the cage by the force of the death blow. His knees pointed up, bottoms of feet resting on the ladder rungs and against the wall behind them. His body was bent, as if in Moslem prayer, except he was facing straight up, toward the Pole Star, rather than toward Mecca. His back was pressed tight against the far end of the cage. His head was facing the pipe that had terminated his nasty life. But his face, and the entire front portion of his head, was curious by its absence. The pipe's lid had caught him as he jerked back, plowing down through the skull at midpoint, removing the front half, face, and mandible. What stared at the jammed pipe was a superbly cross-sectioned head, revealing much of the brain stem, soft palate, throat cavity, and larynx.

I placed my instep underneath the pipe and drew it up

with all my remaining strength, which wasn't much. I worked the free end of the pipe around until I could once again grab the flange. Then I lifted it up and dropped it to the side of Schilling's body. It rattled around in the cage a bit on the way down, then thunked sideways into the asphalt of the courtyard.

There remained Schilling. Even in death, he would be a pain. I shall spare the gruesome and clinical anatomical details of removing him from his death perch. My feet, and 175 pounds, finally dislodged his corpse from its weird Yoga stance by thumping down on the blood-soaked shoulders until he straightened out enough to slide down the tunnel cage and thump onto the ground with a sound like a sack of wet laundry. I then reached the ground, took a quick look around, and promptly toted myself over to a dark corner of the courtyard where I proceeded to throw up.

Copiously and repeatedly.

26

AS SOON AS I COULD STAGGER UPRIGHT, I LURCHED AROUND the corner and stumbled toward O'Shaughnessey. I wanted to pay him my respects, especially since I was the indirect cause of his death. Every part of my body hurt. But the fun and games still weren't over.

I stumbled along until my foot thumped an oil drum. Up ahead of me I heard the metallic clacking of a big hammer being pulled back. God Almighty I was sick of that sound. I fell forward as the big pistol boomed. There was a long, drawn-out whine. The slug had ricocheted off a wall and was now heading over to Duxbury.

"For Christ's sake!" I shouted.

"My Jesus, is it *you*?"

"I thought you'd been killed—"

"*Hmmmph*. Not bloody likely. I was certain *you'd* been killed. I thought you were Murdock."

"No. I killed him with a bomb. How are you?"

"Fine," said the Irishman. Then he slid over into a heap on the ground, the revolver clattering after him.

I raised his legs, putting them up on a concrete ledge, then covered him with my sweater. He needed help, and fast. Then I heard the *bree-ow, bree-ow* of the first police wagon. I saw them stop at the outer gate just long enough for one of them to cut through the chain with a pair of giant cable cutters. In two seconds they'd skidded to a stop in front of me, their rack of blue and white lights swirling and winking. I saw a big pair of shiny black boots approaching me as I bent over the fallen man. They grated and crunched on the gravel that covered the asphalt. The trooper stared down at me, bewildered. He reached down and picked up the big gun that was lying seven feet in front of me. His partner, gun drawn, was moving in a fast crouch around to my side.

"Get an ambulance here fast," I said. "Do you have an oxygen bottle? If so, get it over here on the double."

They did.

I pointed to the remains of Thug Number Two, the kid who had been so deadly accurate with the pistol, that lay almost invisible in the dark shadows of the wall.

"There's another dead man up in the far courtyard. Seems he went and lost his head. There are at least two more dead people in the big building on the pier. One of them you won't find because she took a dip. Be careful of that building; there may be some nasty people still inside it, though I doubt it highly."

"What happened? Tell us everything," said the older officer. But I didn't have time because just then two more cruisers came in, followed by the ambulance. I helped place O'Shaughnessey on the litter. We got a plasma bottle over him right away. He kept puffing away at the oxygen mask. Still, when I put the cuff on him, his blood pressure wasn't even registering on the gauge. Poor O'Shaughnessey had kept himself going the past hour on adrenaline and Celtic pluck. He certainly had no blood left.

I was hunched over him in the ambulance as we headed for the hospital. As the big van wheeled and started its siren, I looked out the back and could see the police cutting through the inner fence, then barreling through the gate in their cruisers. The blue lights were winking, sweeping along the old dirty buildings.

In the emergency room they typed him as A Positive; I rolled up my sleeve and they pumped a pint of mine into him. Then he got two more bags, and they had a third ready. As soon as he was stabilized he would undergo surgery to close that blood vessel. Then they would set the leg. It would require a steel pin, they told me, because the X rays had shown a big hunk of femur gone. But I'd guessed as much earlier; that big .45 slug had walked away with it, and taken the vein too.

An internal specialist looked over my Sport Section and pronounced it reasonably intact, though I still fairly rang with pain down there. My ribs were taped (two were cracked) and they placed a special walking cast on my left heel for the time being. It would be several months—at least—before I could run again. I didn't like that. During all this time the Law had been waiting patiently, unobtrusively, in the background. I had almost forgotten the polite young officer until O'Shaughnessey dozed off and the nurse came in to give him a bath prior to the surgery. Then he oozed up into the foreground and requested I accompany him back to Cordage Park, the last place on earth I wanted to go.

We swerved into the complex and I wobbled out of the cruiser. The night's adventures, coupled with the missing pint of blood—now hopefully speeding the Irishman's recovery—had done me in. The police had finished photographing Thug Number Two, and now drew a coverlet over him. Poor kid.

"Any idea who he was, Doctor?"

"No. He was an American though. He talked like an American, not from across the water—"

"Thank you. Now if you could just come with us back here . . ."

Oh no. I had to go and view Schilling's remains again. They had the body covered for obvious reasons. Even the hardened law officers couldn't stand the sight of the Headless Horseman. But three of them were staring into the pipe, transfixed. I bent over. The first thing that caught my eye was a gleam of gold amidst the clots of red tissue. The gold was set on yellow-white. It was one of Schilling's molars, riding on the jawbone that was packed tight into the pipe with the rest of his head. And then I saw a bright white dot amongst the gristle and gore: Schilling's hearing aid.

It was as if the head had been *canned*. I found the notion

outrageously funny. And then I imagined shopping at the supermarket, throwing things into the cart: can of beans, cling peaches, asparagus, human head, corned beef hash—

A demonic, aching giggle was trying to surface. I knew if I started laughing perhaps I wouldn't stop for days and days.

Watch it! Watch it, Doc . . . you're letting this thing get to you . . . you're taking it way too seriously—

I grabbed at my sides and sat down. Faces peered into mine, asking me questions. I told them to leave me alone. They persisted. Then I heard a faint but familiar voice:

"Yeah I know this isn't my jurisdiction, but I *am* a law officer. Matter of fact I am Chief of Police, OK? And this is Detective Lieutenant Joseph Brindelli of the—huh, you know him? Well good because we're here to *stay*."

Brian Hannon, my brother-in-law in tow, stomped around the corner of the building and toward me. He was flicking his eyes everywhere, his trenchcoat flapping open in the wind of his walking. He stuffed a Lucky into his mouth and cranked fire to his Zippo, trailing clouds of pale blue smoke behind him. Joe ambled along in his wake, murmuring apologies and explanations to the local officers.

"We're gonna nail this thing *down*. Bell, Donnato, get moving. Each of you take a building. We're gonna swarm over this place like flies on dogshit."

I waved my arms and they caught sight of me. DeGroot, bless his heart, had called them after the alarm went off, only he'd waited thirty-five minutes first just to make sure I was overdue. I confided to Joe that I did not feel like answering questions and leading the fuzz all over Cordage Park, showing them exactly what happened, how, when, and why. But he told me I bloody well would have to, and to bear up nobly under it, and that he and his loudmouth friend—this was said in a whisper—would stand by me.

And so I told the whole thing, from the time I left the *Whimsea* in the dead of night until the first police cruiser arrived and spotted me hunched over O'Shaughnessey's prostrate form.

"And the other man," asked Brian, "the big man you say

is an IRA Provo. You have any idea where he might have gone?"

"Laura Kincaid mentioned a boat called the *Coquette*. It was to be their escape. You might alert the Coast Guard and tell them to be on the lookout for it. I have a hunch it's on the big side. I kind of hope the guy gets away, this time anyway. He saved my life."

We called Mary, and she wept. But she was glad to hear Schilling was put away for keeps. Then we got into Brian's car to head for home. I saw a cabin cruiser swing into the dock. DeGroot flung a line to a waiting cop and seconds later was jogging down the pier toward us. He rapped on the window and I rolled it down.

"I see you're OK, Doc. Anything happen?"

"Nah."

"For a minute I was worried. I was listening to the VHF a minute ago; there was an explosion not far from here. For a second I thought you—"

"Where?"

"Some boat ten miles offshore from here. Blew apart and sank."

"Was her name *Coquette*?"

"How'd you know?"

"I'll bet you that blue and white boat we saw last night had something to do with it. Did anyone report seeing it?"

He shrugged his shoulders and then asked what all the blankets were for.

"To cover the bodies, you dummy. Listen, thanks for calling for help. Can you make it back to Cape Ann alone? I gotta go home and rest. I've been puking and bleeding too much."

At home I hugged Mary hard and lowered most of myself into a warm bath. I sat there and soaked and poured a hot toddy into myself, telling her everything. She stared wide-eyed at me, shaking her head slowly, murmuring. Then I crawled into bed and passed out. I awoke in late afternoon.

The phone rang. It was the *Globe*. They wanted the story

on how I'd smashed the gunrunning ring. I told them to speak with Brian Hannon. That would keep them busy.

It rang again. It was a man with a husky voice and thick accent.

"Gottdamn good, Doc! You chop them up really good, eh!"

"Who the hell's this?"

"Roantis."

"Hi, Liatis."

"You chop them up real good. Nice."

"I heard you were in some kind of trouble. Tommy told me. You OK now?"

"Hmmm. I got to go to trial. Dat's all."

"How's the uh, guy you hit?"

There was an uncomfortable silence. I heard him sigh in a resigned way.

"Well, Doc. I gott some bad news I tink—"

"Oh God. You mean he's dead?"

"No. He *lived*."

"Now c'mon, Liatis—"

"No dat's the bad news. *He dint die.* I'm getting too old to fight I tink. But other real bad news, Doc. The boy was killed with you, he was Tommy's nephew."

I sat up in bed. I felt too weak to hold the phone.

"Liatis, don't kid me."

"Really, Doc. It was Tommy Desmond's li'l nephew. The cops they found out it was Larry Heeney."

"I didn't know Tommy even had a nephew."

"I dint either. But he was."

"Tommy's gonna kill me, Liatis. But honest, I didn't—"

"No Doc. He's proud of you. Dint you know where those guns were going?"

"Uh huh. They were going to Ireland, to be used against the Republic—"

"Yeah Doc. That's what Tommy told me. They been after this bunch for years now. And that man was with you, who was also shot?"

"Stephen O'Shaughnessey—"

"Yeah. He is with the Irish police I tink."

"Right. And who told you all this stuff, Liatis?"

"Ask Tommy Desmond. But I tink you did real good, Doc. Nice job the way you chop them up."

"Thanks, Liatis. You've made my day."

I lay back in bed and stared at the ceiling. I wondered what Tommy Desmond had to tell me. How much had he known all along about the IRA's operations in America, especially in Boston and Southie? But I didn't have long to consider it because the phone rang again. It was Brian Hannon, telling me the press was all over him and his staff, and could I get down there, too, because I was *in part* responsible for cracking the whole thing. *In part . . .*

"In part? Gee, Brian, I'm glad you saw fit to mention my name."

"Hey c'mon, haven't I always given you a fair shake?"

27

I FINALLY HAD MY BROTHER-IN-LAW RIGHT WHERE I WANTED him: in the rearmost booth of Frankie Caeserio's Happy Landings saloon in Marblehead, Mass. We were busy killing brain cells. When I estimated the Body Count was to my liking, I was going to make a suggestion to him. The proverbial "offer he couldn't refuse."

It was three-thirty, *peee emmm*. The few sailing boats left in Marblehead Harbor rode on the gray slick outside the picture window of the Happy Landings. A bevy of local housewives were drinking and laughing up front, at the stand-up bar. They all had tennis outfits on, having no doubt just come from lessons given at one of the indoor clubs. They wore little skirts that flipped up when they wiggled their hips, and showed their panties underneath. Joe and I liked this, and kept our eyes glued on the set of thirtyish women, some with tipped hair, who shook and strutted at the old-time men's bar. We waited—like buzzards on a limb—for a glimpse of the curve of buttocks, the smooth sweep of inner thigh, the bounce and jiggle of bosom.

Middle age is a terrible, terrible affliction. Thank God Senility, Decrepitude, and Death put a stop to it.

"Another drink, gentlemen?" asked the cocktail waitress, who had a pretty interesting outfit herself.

"Gee . . ." Joe began, "I really don't think—"

281

"Sure, why not? I'm buying. Two more of the same."

She grinned and took the two tall-stemmed glasses back with her. She switched away from us, wearing an exaggerated (and, I might add, extremely abbreviated) eighteenth-century maid's uniform. It was sexist and tacky and revealing. It was extremely popular. I saw she was wearing the shiny pantyhose that I like so much. The ones worn by barmaids and stewardesses on the less-well-known airlines. The ones that catch all the shiny highlights of the legs, and feel slick to the touch if you happen to brush across them. The ones Mary maintains are cheap and tawdry. Yep, they're my favorite.

Via several longish talks with O'Shaughnessey, I'd found out a lot about the Kincaid/Schilling outfit during the past week. Some of the interesting stuff confirmed early suspicions I'd had. For example, the Laura Kincaid/James Schilling affair. Perhaps it was Laura Kincaid's expensive face-lift operation and her desire—her fetish rather—to remain imperially slim that planted the initial seed of suspicion. Certainly it was remarkably parallel to Schilling's quest for physical perfection and eternal youth. Walter Kincaid had borne the affair for some time with an almost parental patience and aloofness. But finally his pride and possessiveness forced him to fire Schilling. The fact that his wife didn't file for divorce and follow her lover must have told Kincaid something, i.e., that she placed extreme value on her plush surroundings. To give up Walter Kincaid was to part with the fortune he'd made. So they lived together much as she had described when we first met, with her taking off for long—and not-so-secretive—weekends with Schilling while he spent his spare time aboard the *Windhover* searching for artifacts and treasure.

"So what made Schilling pull the disappearing act in Alaska?" asked Joe as he cradled his third whiskey sour, which had just been placed in front of him.

"Because he'd just made contact with an old army buddy of his who'd pulled the first of a series of armory heists. Schilling was attracted to breaking into armories for several reasons. One, it allowed him to hurt the army, which had given him a D.D. and hurt his chances for landing any decent job. The fact that Kincaid overlooked it, or didn't know about it, was perhaps the only reason he got as far at Wheel-Lock as he did. Two, one of Wheel-Lock's biggest contracts ever was obtained during the early Vietnam buildup. Wheel-Lock designed the complex locks and security devices for armories. Since Schilling knew the systems and the locks, he knew how to get around 'em.''

"And by disappearing he could be more mobile and invisible.''

"Yep. And leave his wife and be with Laura. I figured he came back to New England shortly after his 'death' on the Kenai Peninsula to make contact with arms buyers. Right away he uncovered two hungry sources with lots and lots of dough: The French Separatists in Quebec and the Irish Republican Army. According to O'Shaughnessey he'd even trucked with the Mob for a while, but found that too risky, or scary. Dealing with foreign buyers was cleaner, safer. But there was one thing he needed badly to do it right: a boat. He didn't have the money for one big enough to range as far as he wanted.''

"And that's when they decided to kill Kincaid?"

"Maybe they never planned to kill him. But in early summer two events occurred that forced the issue. One: Kincaid's company began a sharp decline, one that perhaps was irreversible. Two: Kincaid found the jackpot he was seeking.''

"Yeah bullshit.''

"Wait. Wait. I'm getting to that.''

"I want my two grand back, Doc.''

"And you'll get it, whether or not I sell the *Rose*. But anyway, Kincaid decided that by disappearing, he could rid himself of his wife, his failing company, and all the unpleasantness he'd endured for the past several years and skip to the Caribbean.''

"It's curious he had the same idea Schilling had,'' said Joe.

"Not when you consider the fact that they had the same needs and motives. With a miniature Fort Knox in bullion sealed into the *Windhover*'s hull—which was now reshaped and named *Penelope*—he was going to slide down the Big Trough, skip over to Grand Cayman and deposit the fortune, tax-free, then head on over to his prepurchased condominium on St. Thomas.''

"Then why the hell didn't we find the bullion, Doc? *Why?* Even though we cut up that hull until the *Rose* looks like a goddamn tea-strainer. *Why?*''

"I'm getting to that—''

"I want my two—''

"Shut up and listen. Laura and Schilling discovered Kincaid's plan to disappear. Since he'd done all the groundwork for them, wouldn't it be easy for them to help him along? And they'd have the boat they needed too.''

"So Laura Kincaid wasn't independently rich as she claimed.''

"Doesn't look that way. Though she thought she would stand to gain at least something by her husband's death. That's why they thought of putting the house up for sale. Thought it would net them about four hundred grand, and they wouldn't have to run guns anymore. Just as soon as Schilling made this last series of hauls, they'd be home free.''

"And never bothering to check the post office box, they were ignorant of the condominium and the treasure.''

"Knew nothing about it, and couldn't open the box anyway without the key.''

"So then where in hell—''

"But wait. Of course just about then they had the mishap at the *James Longstreet*, killed Allan Hart in a foolish and desperate panic, and from then on had me on their tail, poking my nose in and disrupting things. As soon as I explained my theory to Laura—who was an excellent actress by the way, surely she had untapped talent in that department—she was alarmed. She had Schilling stick himself under his car so he could get a good look at me as I left her place. There were two people who could blow their cover: Danny Murdock and Yours Truly.''

"You think Murdock helped kill Kincaid?''

"Nah. He probably didn't even know Kincaid was killed.

Probably Laura fed him some cock-and-bull story about taking over the arrangements for her husband. As far as Murdock the bombed boatbuilder goes the only illegal thing he knew about was falsifying a certificate. BUT, they told him: *listen*, if a guy named Adams, who looks like such and such—or anybody else—comes asking you questions about *Penelope*, you call us on the double and we'll bail you out.''

"Mmmm. Hmmm," said Joe taking a deep sip and leaning back, "so the night you approached him at the bar he did as instructed."

"Sure. And I figured later it probably took Schilling no more than fifteen or twenty minutes to arrive outside the bar and station himself there, waiting for me to emerge. What place is fifteen minutes from the Schooner Race?"

"The Kincaid residence."

"Uh huh. Which further strengthened the link between Laura and Schilling. No, I wasn't at all surprised to find her in that warehouse pointing an automatic rifle at my throat. Not the slightest."

"Now how did O'Shaughnessey get involved?"

"Because the Garda Síochána was tracking down the rash of assaults in the Republic perpetrated by the militant wing of the UFF, the Ulster Freedom Fighters. They're the Protestant counterpart to the IRA. A guy named Reggie Thompson is their leader. Reggie's a tough customer—former Special Air Service Commando. They've vowed to head south, and give the Irish a taste of their own terrorist medicine. They're already charged with about twenty murders. Claim to have a base somewhere in the Wicklow Hills . . . ."

"But I still don't see how—"

"How it links to America? Because Schilling switched sides. After dealing with the IRA for two months or so, he discovered another group who'd pay double for the same merchandise."

"Reggie Thompson and the UFF?"

"Yep. So he told the IRA he was fresh out of small arms—even those he'd promised to deliver some time ago. This was a big mistake."

''Cause the IRA found out he was supplying weapons to the enemy.''

''Exactly. Actually, O'Shaughnessey tells me it was Laura who made the initial contact with UFF's men. That's why the IRA was so anxious to put her away. It wasn't long before the Provos, and their stateside contacts in Boston and Southie, had discovered the double cross on the part of the arms suppliers and put the hit notice out on both of them. They were dead ducks from that time forth. It was O'Shaughnessey's job to infiltrate the ring with a faked identity, then lie in wait to make the big haul, getting everybody in the organization, including most especially the UFF contacts. How successful he ultimately was only time will tell. But the big guy who saved my life—''

''What was his name anyway?''

''O'Shaughnessey won't tell me, although he knows.''

''They that close, the Garda and the IRA?''

''Not close at all. Stephen says if I knew the man's name my life would be endangered. And I believe him. But as I was about to say, Thug Number One, the Big Man, made a mistake when he stole Schilling's cruiser and blew up the *Coquette*. There was nobody from UFF on board. The boat, as its French name implies, belonged to the other customers—''

''The militant French separatists?''

''Yeah. The Provo blew up a bunch of Quebec nationalists who were, O'Shaughnessey thinks, going to take Ms. Kincaid and Schilling up to the Maritimes.''

''While they left the *Rose* floating temptingly in Gloucester Harbor.''

''Yes, and tempting enough so I bought her at state auction.''

''With some of my money.''

''With some of your money. Which you will get back.''

''Who the hell'd buy that spaghetti strainer now?''

''I am going to have it repaired and sold, don't worry. The electronic gear, fittings, and engine alone are worth more than what she cost us.''

''And you still believe Kincaid hit the jackpot . . .''

"I'm convinced of it. The letter from A.J. Liebnitz which you have laid eyes on should convince you as well. You yourself saw the space along the *Rose*'s keel reserved for the treasure. Now if you're ready, I want you to phone the Essex Realty Company of Manchester, and ask for the key to the Kincaid domicile. Say it's an investigation and we're taking a crew in to get prints and the like. We want to go *alone*, with no salesperson."

He rose and swaggered toward the pay phones.

"Remember, Joe. Official police business. No salesperson—we want the *key only*."

"Whaddayuh think I yam . . . dummer somethin'?"

Gee, I hoped he wasn't too bombed to convince them . . .

28

At quarter to six, after the last visitor had left the Kincaid mansion, we were allowed to proceed there—alone—with the key. I jingled it in my hand, happy as a kid on Christmas morning, as we trudged up the curved walkway and then around the side yard, with its creeping bent lawn, marble statues, and Japanese garden. Under my arm I carried a Polaroid SX-70 camera.

"Christ Almighty, some spread."

"Now look over there."

"What? That patch of earth? A *buried* treasure? C'mon Doc, you've read too many *Argosy* magazines. He wouldn't bury it for Chrissake, use your—"

"Course he wouldn't. He buried an oil tank there. I know because I checked with the realtor earlier for records of any recent house improvements. I called the company that installed the tank. I know the tank was connected to the appropriate pipes too."

"Well then why—"

"*But*. I also checked a bit further. I even spoke with the man who operated the backhoe prior to the installation. The tank measured just under ten feet long. Pace the turned earth and you see it's about eighteen feet long. What else is down there?"

"Look. After losing two grand on that old fishing boat I am not about to get a shovel and start digging."

"We're not going to do any digging. When I first started really thinking about this, I was on the phone for an entire day calling various stores, supply houses, and rental agencies. Walter Kincaid, in his own name, rented an air impact hammer and a small compressor last April. He also rented a small cement mixer. The agency has the records. But the really interesting thing is this: he bought a septic tank."

"No shit."

"Ah, the very phrase I was seeking. That indeed is the interesting part: *no shit*. The town of Manchester has had sewers for almost fifty years. Ergo: no need for cesspools, septic tanks, so forth. So why the septic tank?"

We went inside. It was just dark. The expensive furniture was covered with white dropcloths.

"It was the backhoe man who tipped me off about the septic tank. It was dropped in the hole and covered before the oil tank even arrived. You know I had to phone almost twenty septic tank companies before I found the right one? Kincaid had paid for the thing in cash. The company is in Stoneham. He sure didn't want to leave any tracks. While the oil tank was public and official, with records to prove and document it, the septic tank was strictly on the QT."

We descended into the basement—which people in New England call the *cellah*—and I located the southwest corner of the building, then paced off eight steps. We were in the furnace room.

We paced around the place for fifteen minutes. *Zilch*.

"Yah know, Doc, you're the best bullshitter I've ever known."

"Now why on earth would you say that?"

"OK, here's Doc Adams, the hero who cracked the gunrunning ring. Fine. But then you get me to tap the post office box of what's-his-ass—"

"Wallace Kinchloe. Who of course was really Walter Kincaid."

"Fine. Anyway, we tap the box and what do we find? A letter from this plush bank in the Caribbean that indicates that old Kinchloe's got a fortune in gold he's about to deposit there."

"So?"

"So *then*, what you do is convince me to go in with you to buy the *Rose* at auction, with the hopes—*no, wait*, not the hopes, the *expectation*—the expectation, mind you, of cutting open the hull and having gold ingots pour out all over us."

"Let's try over here near this workbench."

"But where *are* the ingots? Where *are* those doubloons?"

"Get over here will you?"

"No dammit! To hell with it; I'm leaving."

"OK fine. Leave me the key."

"What are you doing?"

"We've checked the oil pipes; they're in the right places. There *is* a big oil tank out there, buried beyond this foundation wall. It *does* have feeder pipes to the smaller tank inside. So be it. But look farther down the wall."

He joined me as we slid aside the heavy workbench. Low on the basement wall was a metal flue door.

I opened the metal door and shined the flashlight inside. I fully expected to see a tunnel, with 'all that glitters' at its terminus. The bottom of the flue was filled with ashes. It was elbow deep in stupid ashes. The back of it was lined with brick.

"Well?"

I felt back at the brick that lined the flue pipe. It was genuine: raspy, rough, ceramic—any description you could name. It was going *nowhere*.

We went upstairs. I checked the portion of the living room that was exactly above the room in the basement we'd just left. Nothing. We looked under rugs, behind curtains, in window sills . . . nothing.

"Charlie, look," said Joe in a tired, placating tone, "your hunch just didn't turn out, that's all. If there was a fortune, and if Kinchloe or Kincaid—whatever the fuck his name was—hid it away, don't you think he'd do it in some

rented place where he could get at it quickly and safely—
at a moment's notice—away from his wife and her boyfriend, huh?''

I admitted to myself that his theory made sense. Unhappy
and disgusted with his home life, why would he bother to
hide his treasure trove here?

''Let's go,'' I said. I picked up flashlight, Polaroid
camera, and began to zombie myself toward the front
door.

We locked the mansion up carefully as we departed, then
got in the car and purred off.

But two blocks away, I found myself turning the car
around. It *had* to be there. Had to. If it were a stash of cash,
or even jewels, another hiding place might make more sense.
But not gold bullion. It was heavy and hard to carry around.
It needed a *home*.

''You crazy?''

''Let's give that furnace room forty good minutes, Joe,
then I'll throw in the towel.''

''Done,'' he said with a weary sigh.

We went over the room with the systematic precision
only a detective and a surgeon could muster. In considerably less time than forty minutes we found a bucket
with a shovel in it. The bucket had been concealed behind the boiler.

''I may be crazy, but these look like fireplace ashes to
me,'' said Joe, raking through them.

We opened the flue again. The ashes in the bottom matched
those in the bucket. I didn't know enough about flues to be
sure, but I would bet odds something fishy was happening
with the furnace flue. And come to think of it, the door to
the flue looked awfully big too. We examined the iron door,
its hinges and mountings . . . everything. It looked as old as
the house.

''Goddammit Joe, there is a septic tank buried alongside
that oil tank. What the hell's it there for?''

''If there's an entrance to it, maybe it's outside.''

''Maybe, but I doubt it. I've looked it over three times
carefully. And remember how close to the foundation it is.''

I stepped back and looked at the brick wall in front of me. The big oil pipe came in at exactly the right place. OK, that made sense. The flue, and the door, was in exactly the right place. There was a flue, and I could look up it to where it joined the chimney.

No good. I could not detect the signs of disturbed masonry anywhere. But this Kincaid was a clever old guy. He did everything in style. He spared no pains, or costs. I knew that by his house and his company headquarters. He was a sharpie, was old Kincaid. Perhaps he'd been laying treasure away for years and years, and finally decided to construct some secret vault before disappearing. And he would enter the place on the eve of his departure, and take the stuff aboard his refitted boat, seal it in down near the keel, and slide away to Queen's Beach, "Where Paradise Begins . . ."

"It's in there, Joey. I tell you it's *in* there. It's just very cleverly concealed."

Joe opened his pocket knife and began picking and pecking inside the flue.

"Hey hey *hey*, look at this, Charlie. This corner mortar is peeling off like rubber cement."

The jackknife blade scooped away the old mortar along both back seams of the brick flue. Then we realized that it wasn't mortar; it was simply caulking compound—probably applied with a gun and smoothed down with a fingertip— covered with wood ashes to make it appear old. Joe worked quickly. In less than a minute both seams were clear; the back wall of the brick flue was free of the side walls by an eighth of an inch. I rapped hard on the back wall, which was two feet across. It didn't sound hollow; it was *gen-u-wine* brick. Joe shoved at it, tried to slide it. No go. It was solid. Joe hunched down in front of the hole and took his chin in his hand.

"Sombitch Charlie. She doesn't wanna budge."

"There's gotta be a gizmo . . . a lever or—"

"Yeah I know what you mean. Let's get back to looking."

So we scoured the place again from top to bottom. Nothing. Yet we'd found some fake mortar; that was enough to keep us at it. So we trudged around the furnace and all its pipes; we examined the floor and all the walls. Clean as a whistle. We were just about to give up for a second time when Joe noticed the small hole in the masonry right behind the furnace. It was only as big in diameter as the base of my thumb. It was low in the wall, about two feet from the floor. It was just about invisible. But it was the only thing in the wall that wasn't perfect. I shined the flashlight beam into the hole. I had a lot of trouble peeking in because it was so small. About six inches inside a brass nut shined back at me. The curious thing was, it was three-sided. It was an equilateral triangle. I stepped back and looked at the hole again. Its outer edges were worn and rounded. It was whitewashed the same shade of white as the remainder of the foundation wall. Yet inside it was a shiny brass bolt head of strange configuration. I'll be damned, I thought.

The innocuous-looking hole in the wall was ten feet from the ash door.

"Naw, it couldn't be—" said Joe.

"Oh yes it could. Thing is, where the hell is the gizmo used to turn the nut? Perhaps old Walter carried it with him. If that's the case we'll never—"

"No! No he wouldn't. Don't you see? The head's triangular. How many triangular bolt-heads have you ever seen in your lifetime?"

"None."

"Right. So the gizmo, as you call it, has got to arouse suspicion. It's in fact more of a *key* than a lever since it's shaped uniquely. Doc, he wouldn't tote it around. He wouldn't want to lose it; he wouldn't want it seen."

"You're absolutely right. And he wouldn't hide it anywhere near the hole either, would he?"

"Nope."

"Then let's follow the example of Poe's *Purloined Letter*. Do you remember where the missing letter was hidden?"

"Can't say as I've ever read the story."

"It was hidden in the most inconspicuous place: with a bunch of other letters. So where do we look for this tool?"

Walter Kincaid's workshop was very big, as one would expect of a millionaire engineer. There were drill presses, lathes, joiners, jigsaws, a drafting board, tap and die sets—the works. We rummaged through a whole passel of exotic micrometers, gauges, metal rules, combination squares, and just about everything that places like Woodcrafters and Brookstone's sell. We looked through exotic hardwood tool chests lined with green felt that held tools from Sweden and Germany. We looked through drawers and racks of lowly screwdrivers and nailpullers.

Nothing.

And then Joe saw a rack of carefully labeled cigar boxes that lined a high shelf. One of these was labeled "Miscellaneous Bits."

He took this down. Of the twenty or so metal drills and bits inside, one had a curious head. It was a round terminus as thick as my thumb, with a triangular socket at its end. My pulse revved up like a jackhammer. The base of the bit was the standard four-sided tapered shank that fits into an old-fashioned crank brace. I grabbed the brace from its place on the pegboard, inserted the strange bit, and tightened the chuck. Then we made our way back to the furnace room.

I inserted the crank contraption into the hole. The socket thunked home perfectly.

"Does it?" asked Joe.

"Like the proverbial hand garment."

I turned the brace; it wouldn't budge. Then I reversed the crank, and heard a slow regular grinding deep in the wall. Joe ran over to the ash door and shined the flashlight in. I kept grinding away, like a storekeeper cranking in an awning.

"Son . . . of . . . a . . . *bitch*. It's moving!"

I joined him and peered inside. The brick back of the flue was half an inch to the right. A narrow fissure was now visible along the left side. Darkness, the darkness of space, lay beyond.

"Walter Kincaid, you genius you—"

"The guy was an engineer, yes?"

"Uh-huh, and it shows too. He was an expert at locks. I think he also realized that concealment and secrecy are far stronger security than the thickest bank-vault doors."

"Sure. If you don't know where the money is, how can you get it?"

Joe took a turn at the crank. I supposed it was a rack and pinion design, in which a geared-down wheel with teeth moved a straight piece of steel with matching teeth. There were probably ball bearings or smooth metal wheels to help move along the slab of genuine brick, which would weigh a few hundred pounds. It worked slick as a whistle, and showed the inventiveness and determination of Kincaid. No wonder the guy was loaded. He was smart, cagey, and worked like a dog. He had probably designed the setup, machined and fabricated most of it himself or at the Wheel-Lock factory, and installed it alone, perhaps in the space of three or four grueling days of long labor during one of Laura's rendezvous with Schilling.

As Joe turned the crank I watched the fissure widen. For every eight turns of the crank the slab opened another inch. The bricks had been mounted in a steel frame set on big steel dolly wheels. I shined the light through a circular concrete tunnel a yard long and saw the glint of gold eight feet away. Now I knew how Howard Carter must have felt when they broke the seals of the last chamber in Tutankhamen's tomb, and entering, he saw the gold sarcophagus still in place.

"Howdja like to retire, Joe?" I said laughing.

We spent only about twenty minutes in the small concrete cubicle fashioned from the shell of the septic tank. A description of the treasure trove wouldn't do it justice. The most spectacular part of it was twenty-two gold ingots. Kincaid had lined them up like miniature loaves of bread on a clean pine board. I hefted one of the li'l critters. It weighed ten kilograms, and felt like it. It was stamped with an embossed seal of the double eagle of Austria on the bottom. What was it worth?

"Dunno, Charlie. Let's see, gold's going for about seven

hundred dollars an ounce, that's, uh, over eleven thousand dollars a pound, and these things weigh twenty-two pounds each—''

"Each one's worth almost a quarter of a million dollars.''

"Doc, I feel dizzy.''

"Twenty-two ingots, that's well over five million in the gold bars alone.''

"Charlie, I feel really dizzy.''

We rummaged briefly throught the rest of it. There were polyethylene file card cases filled with old coins. There were various historic relics in a big wooden box. There were pieces of scrimshaw and pewter. But mainly, there was the gold. In bars and coins, it sat there and glimmered in the beam of our flashlight.

"How we gonna carry this out?'' he asked me.

"We can't. It's not ours.''

"C'mon Doc. Listen, if we each take two bars we c—''

"No I'm serious, Joe. You're a cop; you know the rules.''

"So? I'll quit being a cop. I'll retire, as you wisely suggested. Now listen, we'll just—''

"Now *you* listen, the last thing we want to do is screw this whole thing up by taking it illegally. By the laws of maritime salvage, this gold and treasure is the property of Walter Kincaid, deceased—or at least presumed deceased.''

"Right. And then, it would go to his next-of-kin, wife Laura—also deceased, and without relatives.''

"So—and I've checked this—the treasure belongs, again by law of salvage, to whoever *owns the house.*''

Joe was so dizzy he went topside for a breath of air while I tidied up the chamber and left it intact. We cranked the brickway shut behind us and reputtied the seams with caulking compound we found in the workshop. Then we covered the seams with wood ashes, making them look astoundingly like mortar, placed new ashes in the bottom of the flue, swept up clean, and departed. I had the funny-shaped bit with me.

"I wanna keep this key,'' I said.

I stumbled on the way out in the dark basement hallway. I limped all the way to the car. In my pocket were a dozen color prints of the treasure. I had taken them for a special reason.

29

WE FORMED A SYNDICATE FOR THE SOLE AND EXPRESS PURpose of purchasing the Kincaid residence and splitting the swag. Since the realtor was asking a cool four hundred grand, a fairly hefty down payment would be required. We—Joe and Mary and I—figured that five thousand earnest money plus a hundred grand down payment would seal it up for us. But we had to move fast. Besides the three of us were Jim and Janice DeGroot, Tom Costello, and, at my insistence, Morris Abramson. Jim balked a bit at this. Who the hell was Morris Abramson and what part did he play in finding the treasure? After all, he said, another member meant another cut of the action. But I insisted. To make our stand official, Mary suggested that if Jim didn't like the arrangement he could always pull out of the syndicate altogether.

Jim shut up right away.

Leave it to Mary to nail things down when they get a bit sticky. I figured that with Moe in on the deal some worthwhile cause would come out smelling like a rose. But when I called him he told me he had no spare money at all.

"Sorry Doc, I gave my last bit of discretionary income to the Sisters of St. Jude. They run a halfway house for runaway girls. Try me in a month or so."

"It'll be *too* late you dummy. You know you're the stupidest Jew I've ever known?"

"You know you're the pushiest gentile *I've* ever known? And if there's one thing gI cannot stand it's a pushy gentile—"

"Don't worry, Moe, you're in the syndicate."

Mary and I decided to cough up ten percent of our claim, which would be the lion's share, to Moe. It soothed our consciences—made us feel a little less like outright thieves.

We sat in our living room and passed around the pictures. Everybody drooled and licked their lips. Especially De-Groot. If he could ever love anything even a tenth as much as he loves money, it hasn't been invented or discovered yet. The members of the syndicate were to split the proceeds of the treasure sale in portions and shares according to their contributions. As Chief Treasure Finder I reserved the right to invest, and claim, fifty percent in the Adams family's name. The name of the syndicate was coined by Mary: *Golddiggers of 'seventy-nine.*

We all thought it was cute. But then we were going to be filthy rich; we would have thought a hammerhead shark was cute.

We decided that Jim DeGroot would be the buyer. My involvement, or even Joe's, would tip off everyone that the house had an unexpected attraction. Jim made his initial contact with the realtor and phoned us.

"Old man Kincaid made a codicil in his will before he arranged to disappear," he said. "As Laura told you, he left the house to the Wheel-Lock Corporation, not to her. I betcha she and Schilling were surprised, and not too pleased, about that development. The board of directors of Wheel-Lock has decided to offer the house for sale, as we know. However, they must meet and decide if the buyer is a good bet. Then they'll affix their OK to the buy and sell agreement."

"Sounds OK. Just hang in there and wave that cash around. We're waiting on pins and needles."

The only absent member of the syndicate was Moe. While he wished the operation luck and success, he told me over the phone that the thought of money bored him.

"It's what you can *do* with it that's exciting, Doc. If I make anything let me know and I'll tell you where to send the check."

But Jim DeGroot returned to the domicile in bad spirits, and asked for large quantity of same.

"I can't believe it," he said, cradling his big paw around the frigid glass.

"Well what?"

"I just can't goddamn believe it . . ."

"Well what?"

"The *Hare Krishna*."

"Yeah. The Hare Krishna *what*?"

"The goddamn, bald-headed, dip-shit *Hare Krishna* have bought the Kincaid place!"

"I can't believe it," we said in unison. "I just can't believe it."

And we couldn't.

"Know what they did? They put down two hundred thou in *cold cash*. A registered bank check from the Merchant's National. *Cold cash.*"

"Jesus. All those shopping center handouts. All those flowers at Logan Airport . . . all that drum beating and chanting on the Common."

"I can't believe it," wailed Mary and Janet.

"The board of directors of Wheel-Lock met this morning. They are going to sell the company to an Arab consortium—"

"The Decline of the West . . ." I intoned.

"—and they looked at the offers the realtor presented to them. Ours was fine . . . but the Hare Krishna's was a good deal better."

"I can't stand it," said Joe.

There was a glum silence. I told the would-be syndicate to follow me. We arrived in my small, book-lined study in a few moments' time. I turned on the double brass student lamp.

"Do not despair, friends," I began.

"Can I have another drink?" asked Joe.

". . . because as I look around me at the warm faces of friends and loved ones—"

"Are you going to the bar? Make mine a double, OK?"

"—I seem to see a new ray of hope."

"I'm gonna throw up."

"Mary, would you please remove that big green book from the shelf behind you?"

"Which one, Charlie?"

"*The Golden Bough*, of course."

She removed the tome.

"Now stick your hand in behind the space."

She drew out a weighty hunk of Au. I directed her to place it on my desk, where we could all gaze at it.

Joe was indignant.

"Dammit, Charlie, I *searched* you after you'd sealed the place up, remember? It was a joke at the time . . . actually, you suggested it. I *frisked* you. You were clean."

I fondled the little darling on my leather-topped desk. I patted it . . . massaged it.

"I wanted you to search me, to determine I was absolutely free of any illegal metal. What you didn't know, my friend, is that I pulled a little prestidigitation while you were upstairs."

"I'm told that can cause blindness," said Janice.

"What happened?" asked Mary.

"When Joe went upstairs, and out, to clear his dizzy head, I slipped one of the ingots out of the tunnel and placed it in the cellar hallway right near the wall. When Joe came back after I'd cranked the doorway shut, I insisted he search me to make sure the treasure was intact. But on the way back upstairs I accidentally-on-purpose stumbled, fell in the darkness, and slipped the piece of bullion into my coat. Limping on the way out helped disguise the fact that it is pretty damn heavy."

"Why, since you made such a big stink about being strictly legal?"

"Because I wanted to be legal. But just in case some unforeseen event, like a bunch of Hare Krishnas buying the place right out from under our noses, occurred, I would still have a piece of it."

"Are we going to split this up?" asked Joe, rubbing his hands.

"No. A big portion of the proceeds is going to Sarah Hart. We're all bitching and moaning because we're not millionaires. Don't forget there's a very nice lady with her only child killed."

Nobody said a word.

"And don't forget poor Katherine Murdock," said Joe softly.

"Uh huh. She's going to get a cut too, at least enough to help pay off Danny's debts. I'm sorry I can't do the same for the Heeney kid. I don't help killers."

"Don't we get anything?" demanded DeGroot.

"Yeah. I figure we all deserve to split the remainder, whatever it is."

But Tom Costello begged off, saying he'd done nothing to earn it.

"You lose any money by putting up your hunk?"

"Yeah some, but—"

"Whatever the loss was, we'll double it . . . fair enough everybody?"

They all agreed.

"The problem now is that Mary and I have prepared a victory banquet. To wit: roast rack of lamb, prawns in lemon and butter, Caesar salad, asparagus in hollandaise—"

"And so on. Would you care to stay?"

And so we feasted heartily. Then, during the very middle of the meal, we all started laughing uncontrollably.

"Those goddamn shave heads," giggled DeGroot, "sitting there in that mansion eating raw spinach and chanting all day long . . . dead set against materialism . . . strong vows of poverty . . . *poverty*! And right below them sits five million bucks!"

He laughed the laugh of a hero in a Jean-Paul Sartre book.

Tom Costello rose solemnly and raised his wineglass.

"We must all swear—on our *lives*—to keep mum. Sooner or later those orange-robed crazies will want to move . . . then we pounce and buy the place . . ."

"Hear, hear! Here's to the vow of silence, and honor among thieves!"

"Hear, hear!"

In the center of the table sat the golden ingot and the crank key. We were parting with neither.

After the guests all left, at 1 A.M., I cradled Mary on my lap. We were watching the remains of a late movie. I kissed her.

"How'd you like to slip into something more comfortable?" I asked. "Like a garter belt?"

30

I awoke and looked out the window. It was gray and cold out, and would probably rain soon. I heard the pneumatic *thump-thump* of a basketball being dribbled. Jack and Tony were shooting lay-ups in the turnaround.

"Is Tony clean yet?" I asked Mary, who'd just awakened.

"Don't ask me, I haven't tried him."

"What's for dinner?"

"Don't you ever let up about dinner, Charlie?"

"I just wanna know."

"Tuna Surprise."

"*Tuna Surprise?* That had better be a joke. And also, it's in extremely poor taste."

She flumped over and began to settle into sleep again. I stroked her a bit.

"Maaaaaa-ry—"

"Oh c'mon, Charlie, I jus' wanna . . . zzzzz. . . ."

I looked out at the two strapping lads playing ball. They thumped it against the asphalt driveway, leapt and parried, shot and blocked, spun and danced under the hoop.

I was happy.

I wanted to take the instant, the entire situation, and *freeze it*. I wanted to dip it in liquid nitrogen and put it in Plexiglas, and keep it on my mantel. Only I, and everyone else in the scene, would be *inside it*, frozen, and we'd never change.

The puppy jumped up at Tony, and he smacked her on the snoot, then petted her. She bowed down in a half-crouch and let out a shrill bark.

But of course you cannot. You cannot stop it. The Great Going On continues, stops for no one. And the Great Going On is what gives life all its terror and sadness, but also all its joy and beauty. It's what makes us enjoy and appreciate *now*.

Mary stirred and nestled into the crook of my arm.

It began to rain. The boys whooped and ran inside.

And then it poured.

Rick Boyer currently lives in Asheville, North Carolina.
BILLINGSGATE SHOAL

About the Author

Rick Boyer currently lives in Asheville, North Carolina. BILLINGSGATE SHOAL was the winner of the Edgar for Best Mystery Novel of the Year, 1982. The Doc Adams series continues with THE PENNY FERRY, THE DAISY DUCKS, MOSCOW METAL and THE WHALE'S FOOT-PRINTS.